Advance Pr

New York Times Bestselling Author

CHRISTINA LAUREN's
Beautiful
SECRET

"Like Brit hero Niall, *Beautiful Secret* is bloody freakin' hot."
—Joyce Lamb, *USA Today's Happy Ever After*

"Christina Lauren reads our minds and creates, yet again, a perfectly scrumptious main character in Niall that all the ladies will lust after. This addition to the Beautiful Bastard series will convince you that under any stiff-upper-lipped Brit is a man just waiting for you to bring out a beast in bed." **—That's Normal**

"*Beautiful Secret* is so fresh, so adorably awkward, and—*wow*—the heat is *explosive!*" **—Rock Stars of Romance**

"Christina Lauren's most swoon-worthy book yet! The only way this book could be hotter is if it was on fire. No one writes romance like Christina Lauren does—with humor, heart, and the sexiest scenes around."
—Kate Spencer

"Will we ever stop falling in love with Christina Lauren's fictional men? The answer to this is HECK NO."
—Fangirlish

"Writing duo Lauren have really hit their stride, blending erotic romance with a flirty, funny new adult voice. . . . Lauren continues to write simmering sexual tension like no other, and the creative sex scenes keep things interesting."
—Romantic Times

Praise for **CHRISTINA LAUREN**
and the Beautiful Bastard
and Wild Seasons series

"A sexy, sweet treasure of a story. I loved every word."
—**Sylvia Day, #1 bestselling author**
on *Sweet Filthy Boy*

"*Hot!* . . . if you like your hook-ups early and plentiful."
—EW.com on *Beautiful Stranger*

"A devilishly depraved cross between a hardcore porn and a very special episode of *The Office.* . . . For us fetish-friendly fiends to feast on!!"
—*PerezHilton* on *Beautiful Bastard*

"Lauren has mastered writing delectable heroes and strong-willed heroines to match, and the contrast between rough-edged Finn and polished Harlow makes for a passionate romance. Each character's relationship with their families gives the story depth, all while setting readers up for [the next] story."
—*RT Book Reviews* on *Dirty Rowdy Thing*

"The thing that I love the most about Christina Lauren and the duo's Beautiful books is that there is always humor in them. As well as hot steamy moments and some of the sweetest I love yous." —*Books She Reads*

"This book, like the others in this series, sucked me in right away, and I couldn't get enough."
—*The Autumn Review* on *Beautiful Player*

"The perfect blend of sex, sass and heart, *Beautiful Bastard* is a steamy battle of wills that will get your blood pumping!"

—**S. C. Stephens, author of** *Thoughtless*

"Both dirty and rowdy. . . . In a story that is easily devoured in one sitting, the details are sparse but spot-on . . . and witty dialogue carries the plot swiftly to a happy ending."

—*Kirkus Reviews* **on** *Dirty Rowdy Thing*

"I loved *Beautiful Bastard*, truly. . . . I wasn't sure how Christina Lauren planned on topping Bennett. . . . They did it. . . . Max is walking hotness."

—*Bookalicious* **on** *Beautiful Stranger*

"Smart, sexy, and satisfying, *Beautiful Bastard* is destined to become a romance classic."

—**Tara Sue Me, author of** *The Submissive*

"Christina Lauren's done it again! The perfect dose of romance that sexy comedy fans of the Beautiful Bastard series have come to expect and adore."

—*The Stir* **on** *Sweet Filthy Boy*

"*Beautiful Bastard* has heart, heat, and a healthy dose of snark. Romance readers who love a smart plot are in for an amazingly sexy treat!"

—**Myra McEntire, author of** *Hourglass*

"Christina Lauren are my go-to gals for when I'm in the mood for a laugh-out-loud, sizzling sexy romance."

—*Flirty and Dirty Book Blog*

BOOKS BY CHRISTINA LAUREN

Wild Seasons

Sweet Filthy Boy

Dirty Rowdy Thing

Dark Wild Night

Wicked Sexy Liar

The Beautiful Series

Beautiful Bastard

Beautiful Stranger

Beautiful Bitch

Beautiful Bombshell

Beautiful Player

Beautiful Beginning

Beautiful Beloved

Beautiful Secret

Beautiful
SECRET

CHRISTINA LAUREN

G

GALLERY BOOKS

NEW YORK • LONDON • TORONTO • SYDNEY • NEW DELHI

A Division of Simon & Schuster, Inc.
1230 Avenue of the Americas
New York, NY 10020

First Gallery Books trade paperback edition April 2015

GALLERY BOOKS and colophon are registered trademarks
of Simon & Schuster, Inc.

For information about special discounts for bulk purchases,
please contact Simon & Schuster Special Sales at
1-866-506-1949 or business@simonandschuster.com.

The Simon & Schuster Speakers Bureau can bring authors
to your live event. For more information or to book an
event contact the Simon & Schuster Speakers Bureau at
1-866-248-3049 or visit our website at www.simonspeakers.com.

Cover design by John Vairo Jr.
Photo of silenced man © SensorSpot/iStock

Manufactured in the United States of America

10 9 8 7 6 5 4 3 2 1

Library of Congress Cataloging-in-Publication Data is on file.

ISBN 978-1-5011-1779-4
ISBN 978-1-4767-7801-3 (ebook)

To Kresley:

The first line, and all that follows, is for you.

One

Ruby

"I'm not saying I bet his cock is massive, but I'm not *not* saying it, either."

"*Pippa*," I groaned, covering my face in horror. It was seven thirty on a Thursday morning, for God's sake. She could not possibly be drunk already.

I aimed an apologetic smile at the wide-eyed man standing across from us, and wondered if I could speed the elevator up with the power of my mind.

When I glared at her across the elevator, Pippa mouthed, "*What?*" and then held her index fingers up about a foot apart. She whispered, "Hung like a bloody *horse.*"

I was saved from having to apologize again when we stopped on the third floor and the doors opened.

"You realize we weren't alone in there, right?" I hissed, following her down the hall and around a corner, stopping at a set of wide doors with RICHARDSON-CORBETT engraved into the frosted glass.

She looked up from where she was digging through

her enormous purse, the bracelets on her right forearm clinking like wind chimes while she searched for keys. Her bag was huge and bright yellow and covered in glittering metal studs. Under the brash, fluorescent lights, her long red hair looked practically neon.

I was dark blond and carrying a beige crossbody; I felt like a vanilla wafer standing next to her.

"We weren't?"

"No! That guy from accounting was standing right across from you. I have to go up there later and, thanks to you, we'll share accidental, awkward eye contact while we remember you saying *cock*."

"I also said 'Hung like a bloody horse.'" She looked momentarily guilty before turning her attention back to her bag. "Guys in accounting need to loosen up, anyway." Then, motioning dramatically to the still-dark hallway in front of us, she said, "I assume we're acceptably alone for you?"

I gave Pippa a playful curtsey. "Please. Go ahead."

She nodded, brows drawn in concentration. "I mean, logically it's *got* to be huge."

"*Logically*," I repeated, biting back my grin. My heart was doing that flip-tumble thing it always did when we talked about Niall Stella. Speculating on the size of his penis might be my undoing.

With a victorious thrust of her arm into the air, Pippa brandished the keys to the offices before fitting the longest of the set into the lock. "Ruby, have you seen his fingers? His *feet*? Not to mention the fact that he's about eight feet tall."

"Six foot seven," I corrected under my breath. "But hand size doesn't necessarily mean anything." We closed the door behind us and flipped on the main office lights. "Lots of guys have big hands and aren't especially gifted in the Man Parts department."

I followed Pippa down the narrow hall to a roomful of desks in a smaller, far less opulent corner of the third floor. Though cramped, our little section of the office was at least cozy, which was lucky considering I spent more of my time there, working, than in the tiny flat I rented in South London.

Richardson-Corbett Consulting may have been one of the largest and most successful engineering firms in all of Europe, but it kept only a handful of interns on staff at a time. Soon after graduating from UC San Diego, I'd been thrilled beyond belief to snag one of the spots. The hours were long, and the money had immediately quashed my shoe habit, but the sacrifice was already starting to pay off: after completing the first ninety days of my internship, an actual metal nameplate had replaced the piece of masking tape with the name *Ruby Miller* scribbled across it, and I'd been moved from what was no more than a closet on the second floor, to one of the joint offices here on the third.

I'd breezed through high school and survived undergrad with only the occasional freak-out. But moving halfway across the world and rubbing elbows with some of the finest engineering minds in the UK? I'd never worked so hard for anything in my *life*. If I managed to finish this internship as well as I'd started it, a spot at Oxford in the graduate program of my dreams would be mine. Of course, *finishing it well* most likely involved not talking about executives' cocks in the elevator at work . . .

But Pippa was just getting started.

"I remember reading that it was wrist to the tip of the middle finger . . ." she added, and used her fingers to measure the length of her own hand, and then held them up to further illustrate her point. "If that's true, your dream man is packing."

I hummed, hanging my coat on the back of the door. "I guess."

Pippa dropped her bag to her chair and leveled me with a knowing look. "I love how you try and look all disinterested. Like you're not staring at his junk whenever it's within a ten-foot radius of you."

I tried to look indignant.

I tried to look horrified and come up with some sort of argument.

I had nothing. In the past six months, I'd logged so many covert glances in Niall Stella's direction that if anyone was a qualified expert in the topography of his crotch, it would be me.

I tucked my purse in the bottom drawer of my desk and pushed it closed with a resigned sigh. Apparently my covert glances hadn't been quite as covert as I thought. "Unfortunately, I'm pretty sure his junk hasn't ever, and won't ever, be that close to me."

"It won't if you never speak to him. I mean, look, as soon as I get the chance I'll snog that ginger in PR till he cries. You should at least *talk* to the man, Ruby."

But I was already shaking my head and she snapped me with the end of her scarf. "Consider it research for your Structural Integrity class. Tell him you need to test the tensile strength of his steel girder."

I groaned. "Great plan."

"Okay, then someone else. The blond chap in the mailroom. Always has his eye on you."

I made a face. "Not interested."

"Ethan in contracts, then. He's short, all right, but he's *fit*. And have you seen him do that tongue trick at the pub?"

"God, no." I sat down, slumping under the weight of her inspection. "Are we really having this conversation now? Can't we just pretend my enormous crush is not a thing?"

"Afraid not. You're not interested in any of the other lads, but won't make a play for Mr. Uptight, either." She sighed. "Don't get me wrong. Stella's fit as fuck, but he's a bit on the prim side, wouldn't you say?"

I ran a nail along the edge of my desk. "I sort of like that about him," I said. "He's steady."

"Stodgy," she countered.

"*Restrained*," I insisted. "It's like he's stepped right

out of an Austen novel. He's Mr. Darcy." I hoped that would help her understand.

"I don't get that. Mr. Darcy is short with Elizabeth to the point of rudeness. Why would you want someone who's so much work?"

"How is that more work?" I asked. "Darcy doesn't lavish her with false praise or compliments that mean nothing. When he says he loves her it's because he *does*."

Pippa plopped down into a chair and turned on her computer. "Maybe I like a flirt."

"But a flirt is that way with everyone," I argued. "Darcy is awkward and hard to read, but when you have his heart, it's yours."

"Sounds a lot like work to me."

I knew I'd always been a touch on the romantic side, but the idea of seeing the restrained hero unleashed in a way no one else did—uninhibited, hungry, seductive—made it hard for me to think about anything else when Niall Stella was within a four-foot radius.

The problem was I became genuinely stupid when he was around.

"How can I ever hope to have an actual conversation?" I asked her. I knew I would never actually act on it, but it felt good to finally talk about this with someone who knew him, someone other than London and Lola, who were half the world away. "You know, one where we both know we're *having* the conversation? During last week's meeting, Anthony asked me if I could present some data he'd had me organize from the Diamond Square project, and I was kicking *ass* until I looked up, and saw him standing behind Anthony. Do you know how hard I worked on that? *Weeks.* Then one look from Niall Stella and my concentration was shot."

For some reason I was unable to call him by only his given name. Niall Stella was a two-name honor, like Prince Harry or Jesus Christ.

"I stopped speaking midsentence," I continued. "When he's near me, either I blurt out ridiculous things, or I turn into a mute."

Pippa laughed before her eyes narrowed and she looked me up and down. She picked up the calendar and pretended to scrutinize it. "Funny thing, I just realized it's *Thursday*," she sang. "That explains why your hair looks particularly sexy, and you're wearing that minxy little skirt."

I ran my hand through my chin-length, choppy hair. "It looks like it does every day."

Pippa snorted. In truth, I'd spent way too long getting ready this morning, but I needed the confidence today.

Because just like she said, today was Thursday, my favorite day of the week.

On Thursdays I got to see him.

In most respects, Thursdays *shouldn't* have been anything to get excited about. That particular Thursday's to-do list included such mundane chores as watering the sad little ficus Lola insisted I smuggle the 5,400 miles separating San Diego from London, typing up a bid proposal and sending it out in the mail, and putting the recycling out on the curb. A life of glamour. But pinned to the top of my Outlook every Thursday was also Anthony Smith's engineering group meeting, where, for one hour every week, I had an unobstructed view of Niall Stella, Vice President, Director of Planning, and, Holy Hell, The Hottest Man Alive.

If only I could add him to my to-do list, too.

An hour of prime Niall Stella time was both a blessing and a curse, because I *was* interested in what was happening in our firm, and found most of the discussions that took place between the senior partners to be absolutely fascinating. I was twenty-three, not twelve. I had a degree in engineering and would be *their* boss one day if I had anything to say about it. That a single individual had the power to hijack my attention was beyond mortifying. I wasn't usually flighty or awkward and I *did* date. In fact, I'd dated more since moving to London than I had back home because, well, English Boys. Enough said.

But this particular English Boy was, unfortunately, beyond my reach. Almost literally: Niall Stella was over six and a half feet tall and effortlessly refined, with perfectly styled brown hair, soulful brown eyes, broad muscled shoulders, and a smile so gorgeous, on the rare occasion it made an appearance at work, it brought my train of thought to a screeching halt.

According to the office gossip, he had finished school practically as an infant and was some sort of legendary urban planning mastermind. I hadn't realized that was an Actual Thing until I started working in the engineering group at Richardson-Corbett and saw him advise on everything from Building Control guidelines to the chemical composition of concrete additives. He was the unofficial final word in London on all bridge, commercial, and transport structure blueprints. To my utter heartbreak, he even once left in the middle of a Thursday meeting to direct a construction team when a panicked city worker called because another firm had botched a foundation design and concrete had already been poured. Virtually nothing got built in London without Niall Stella's hand in it somewhere.

He took his tea milk first (no sugar), had an enormous office on the third floor—far from mine—clearly never had time for television, but was a Leeds United man through and through. And although he was raised in Leeds, he went to school at Cambridge, then Oxford, and now resided in London. Somewhere along the way Niall Stella had developed quite the posh accent.

Also: recently divorced. My heart could barely take it. Moving on.

Number of Times Niall Stella Had Glanced at Me

During Thursday Meetings? Twelve. Number of Conversations We'd Had? Four. Number of Either of These Events He Might Actually Remember? Zero. I'd been wrestling with my Niall Stella crush for six months, and I was pretty sure he still didn't know that I was an employee at the firm rather than a regular takeout delivery girl.

Surprisingly, because he was almost always one of the first to the office, the man in question wasn't here yet. I'd checked—*a few times*—craning my neck to see through the mass of bleary-eyed people filing in through the conference room door.

Our meeting room was lined with a wall of windows, each looking out onto the fairly busy street below. My morning walk to work had been relatively dry, but as it did most days here, rain had begun to drizzle from a sky heavy with clouds. It was the kind of rain that looked like a harmless haze, but I'd learned not to be fooled: three minutes outside and I'd be soaked through. Even if I'd grown up somewhere rainier than Southern California, I could never have been prepared for the way the London air, between October and April, felt almost saturated with water, heavy and damp. Like a rain cloud had wrapped itself around my body and seeped straight into my bones.

Spring had just begun in London, but the little courtyard across Southwark Street was still dismal and bare. I'd been told that in summer it was filled with pink chairs and small tables belonging to a restaurant near the back. Right now it was all concrete and mostly naked tree branches, damp brown leaves blown across the stark ground.

Around me, people continued to voice their displeasure with the weather as they opened up their laptops and finished their tea, and I blinked away from the window in time to see the last few stragglers rush in. Everyone wanted to be seated before Anthony Smith—my boss and the firm's director of engineering—made his way down from the sixth floor.

Anthony was . . . well, okay, he was a bit of a jackass. He ogled the interns, loved to hear himself speak, and said nothing that sounded sincere. Every Thursday morning he relished making an example of the last person to walk in, sharply commenting with a saccharine smile on their outfit or their hair so everyone in the room would have to watch in leaden silence as they found the last empty seat and sat down in shame.

The door squeaked as it opened. *Emma.*

Emma lingered, holding the door open for someone. *Gah. Karen.*

Voices sounded from outside the room, growing louder as they came in. *Victoria and John.*

And then, there he was.

"Showtime," Pippa muttered next to me.

I saw the top of Niall Stella's head as he stepped in just behind Anthony, and it was as if the air had been sucked from the room. People and chatter blurred around the edges and then it was just *him*, expression neutral as he seemed to instinctively take in who was there and who was missing, his shoulders wrapped in a dark suit, one hand tucked casually into the pocket of his dress pants.

The urgent, fiery feeling in my chest grew.

There was something about Niall Stella that made you want to watch him. Not because he was boisterous or loud, but because he wasn't. There was a quiet confidence about him, a way he carried himself that demanded attention and respect, and a feeling that while he wasn't talking, he was watching everything, noticing everyone.

Everyone except me.

Having come from a family of therapists that discussed *everything*, I'd never been the silent type. My brother, and even Lola probably, would start calling me a chatterbox when I really got going. So the fact that I of all people couldn't manage a single articulate thing when Niall Stella was within touching proximity made absolutely zero sense. What I felt for him was a distracting kind of infatuation.

He didn't even have to attend Thursday meetings; he just *did*, because he wanted to make sure there was "cross-departmental consensus" and so his planning division "could at least have a working engineering vocabulary" since it was Niall Stella's responsibility to coordinate engineering with public policy and his own planning division.

Not that I'd memorized everything he'd ever said at this meeting.

Today he wore a light blue shirt beneath a dark charcoal suit. His tie was a mesmerizing swirl of yellow and blue, and my eyes moved from the double Windsor knot at his neck to the smooth skin just above, the heavy curve of his Adam's apple, the sharp jaw. His normally impassive mouth was turned down in consternation, and when I made it up to his eyes . . . I registered with horror that he was watching me eye-fuck him like it was my job.

Oh, God.

I dropped my gaze to my laptop, the screen blurring out with the intensity of my stare. The flurry of telephones and printers from the outer office flowed in through the open door, seeming to reach a crescendo of chaos, and then someone closed the door, signaling the start of the meeting. And as if the room had been vacuum sealed, all noise came to an abrupt stop.

"Mr. Stella," Karen said in greeting.

I clicked on my mail folder, ears ringing as I strained to hear his reply. One breath in, one breath out. Another. I typed in my password. I willed my heart to slow down.

"Karen," he said finally in his perfect, quiet, deep voice, and a smile spread unconsciously across my face. Not just a smile, a *grin*, like I'd just been offered a giant slice of cake.

Dear God, I am in so deep.

Biting the inside of my cheek, I worked to straighten my expression. Judging from the way Pippa's elbow connected with my ribs, I was pretty sure I failed.

She leaned toward me. "Easy, girl," she whispered. "It was only two syllables."

The door opened and Sasha, another intern, slipped in with a wince. "Sorry I'm late," she whispered. A glance at the clock on my laptop told me she was actually perfectly punctual, but Anthony of course wouldn't let it slide.

"All right, Sasha," he said, watching her squeeze awkwardly between the long row of chairs and the wall as she made her way to the empty seat in the far corner. The room pulsed with silence. "Lovely jumper. Is it new? Blue is a great color on you." Sasha took her seat, her cheeks brilliant red. "Good morning, by the way," Anthony said with a wide smile.

I closed my eyes, taking a deep breath. He was *such* an asshole.

Finally, the meeting started in earnest. Anthony went down his list of questions for each of us, papers were passed around, and as I swiveled in my seat to hand the stack to the person on my right, I glanced up. And nearly swallowed my tongue.

Niall Stella was only two seats away from me.

From beneath my lashes I looked at him, the angle of his jaw—always clean-shaven, never even a hint of scruff—his thickly lashed eyes and perfect, dark brows, his impeccable shirt and tie. His hair looked so smooth in the dim light of the conference room. I actually frowned when I noted it would probably be soft, too—because *of course* it would be—and I wondered for the hundredth time what it would be like to run my hands through it, tug him down, and—

"Ruby? Did we hear back from Adams and Avery yet?" Anthony asked.

I straightened in my chair and blinked down to my laptop, having stayed up late with this file just last night.

"Not yet," I said, with barely a waver in my voice. "They have our plans, drafted and ready for signature. But I'll double back with them if I haven't got a call by the end of the day."

And okay, yeah, that was startlingly articulate considering how Niall Stella had turned his full attention to my face.

Pretty damn happy with myself, I typed up a quick reminder and propped my elbow on the table, tugging on a strand of hair as I scrolled through my calendar.

But something felt off. I sat in this chair for one hour every week, and I was almost certain that I'd never felt what I was feeling now. It was a pressure on the side of my face, the actual *physical weight* of someone's attention.

I twisted the hair around my finger and casually glanced at Pippa. Nope, nothing.

With what I assumed to be a subtle lean forward, I craned my neck farther, glancing to my right, and immediately froze.

He was still looking at me. Niall Stella was looking at me. *Really* looking. Light brown eyes met mine and held what could never be called a glance, but a full-on *look*.

His expression was curious, as if I were a new piece of furniture someone had just randomly placed in the room.

My heart took off, pulse pounding in my veins. Inside my chest, everything felt liquid and wild, and if someone had yelled *Fire!* I'd have gone down in flames, because there was absolutely no way I could control even a single thing happening to my body.

"Niall," Anthony said.

Niall Stella blinked before looking away from my face. "Yes?"

"Do you mind giving us the status from Planning on the Diamond Square proposal? I want my team to get you some specs by the end of the week but we don't know the dimension of their shared space . . ."

I zoned out as Anthony, predictably, phrased his question in a way that made it about seven times longer than it needed to be.

When his question drew to a close, Niall Stella shook his head. "The dimensions," he said, and began shuffling through a stack of papers in front of him. "I'm not altogether sure I've got them—"

"The dimensions were set to be finalized this morning," I answered for him, and explained that the permits would be delivered no later than tomorrow. "I asked Alexander to send a copy of the blueprints this afternoon."

The room went so silent I worried for a minute I had simply lost the ability to hear.

Except everyone was staring at me. *Oh my God, what had I done?*

I'd interrupted without thinking.

I'd answered a question clearly not meant for me.

I'd answered a question *he* definitely knew the answer to.

I felt my brows pull together. But then, why hadn't he answered?

I leaned forward and looked at him.

"Good," he said. Quiet. Deep. Perfect. Shifting in his chair, he met my eyes and gave me a flicker of a grateful smile. "Forward it along?"

My heart had completely left my body. "Of course."

He was still looking at me, clearly as confused as I was over what had just happened, but pleased in a mysteriously lingering way. I wasn't even sure what prompted me to speak up. One minute Niall Stella was looking at me, and the next he was fumbling as he tried to recollect data and answer a question I was sure he could have answered in his sleep.

It was almost as if his mind was elsewhere. It was something I'd never seen happen before.

"Now for the big news," Anthony said, glancing through a stack of papers before handing them off and getting to his feet. I looked up, jarred by the change in his tone. Anthony loved having the attention of the room, and from the sound of it, he was gearing up for something big.

"The New York subway system was built with the idea that one-hundred-year storms happen only every hundred years. Unfortunately, that is not reality. Disasters like Hurricane Sandy have proven that what was once planned for once every century, has happened every few years. The US is spending *billions*, with talk of raised entrances and floodgates, and given that we've worked extensively with the London Underground, they want our input, too. So I'll be gone for one month to attend an International Summit on Emergency Preparedness for public transport, air travel, and urban infrastructure."

"One *month*?" a senior engineer asked, echoing what we all had to be thinking. I wondered if anyone was also echoing my mental fist pump at the idea of an Anthony-free office for so long a stretch.

Anthony nodded in her direction. "There are three separate summits taking place. Not everyone who is invited is staying for the duration, but given that our firm specializes in both public transport and urban infrastructure, Richard decided that he'd like us there for the lot of it."

" 'Us?' " asked one of the executives from Niall Stella's department.

"Right," Anthony said, tilting his head to the left. "Niall will be accompanying me."

"You're *both* going away for a month?" I blurted, instantly wishing I could take my words back and shove them down my throat. I was an *intern*. One of Anthony's unspoken rules seemed to be that we didn't speak at this meeting unless asked a direct question. I could feel the weight of everyone's eyes on me again. Even worse? I could feel *his*, pressing on my skin, probing.

"Er, yes, Ruby," Anthony said, clearly a bit confused. He walked around his chair to stand beside me, hands tucked into the front pockets of his pants. "But no worries, I know you've got the Oxford Street project nearly wrapped up, and my being gone won't affect signing off on that in any way. If you need anything from me, you can always call."

"Oh," I said, feeling the heat slowly fade from my face. "That's good to know, thanks." Of course Anthony thought my burst of word vomit was because I was worried that *he* was leaving—you know, my *boss*?—and that perhaps his absence might somehow interfere with my work.

"Smooth," Pippa said, as her long oval nails clicked across her keyboard.

"Shut uuuup," I moaned, sinking lower in my chair.

I had no idea whether Niall Stella was still looking this way, and the twelve-year-old part of me wanted to drag Pippa into the ladies' room and have her replay the scene, moment by moment.

But I knew that would be a mistake. The first day he seemed to actually notice me and I blew it, acting like some kind of psycho. I couldn't take her telling me that he'd made *that* face in my direction, the one where he frowned and looked like someone had just spilled cream on his hand-tailored suit.

I'd rather we go back to him not knowing I was alive.

———

The end of the day found me at our long, shared desk, sorting through a stack of permits. My Diet Coke had grown warm, and I was counting down the minutes to a hot bath and a hotter book when my email chimed, signaling an incoming message.

"Finally," I sighed. I'd been waiting for a confirmation number all day, and now—maybe—I could go home.

Or maybe not.

Pippa yawned next to me and stretched her arms over her head. It was already dark out and the walk to the Tube would be cold and wet. "Can we go now?"

My shoulders dropped. "Actually, that was an email from Anthony," I told her, frowning at my screen. "He wants to see me in his office before I go and I can think of at least a hundred other things I'd rather do instead."

"What?" she said, leaning over to peer at my monitor. "What does he want?"

I shook my head. "No idea."

"Doesn't he have a watch? We were supposed to be gone twenty minutes ago."

I typed out a quick reply, letting him know I was on my way, and began shutting things down for the night. "Wait for me?" I asked Pippa.

Pausing mid-drawer slam, she gave me a sad little frown. "I've got to hustle, I'm sorry, Rubes. I waited as long as I could, but I've loads to do tonight."

I nodded, feeling somehow uneasy being left in the offices alone this late with Anthony.

The halls were empty as I stepped into the elevator and headed to the sixth floor.

"Ruby, Ruby, come in," he said, pausing where he'd been pulling a few things from around the room and arranging them in a box on his desk. *Had he been fired? Dare I hope?*

"Close the door and take a seat," he continued.

I felt a frown tug at the corner of my mouth. "But nobody's here," I said, leaving the door open.

"Why did your parents name you Ruby?" he asked, eyes making a slow circuit of my face.

My frown deepened. *What?* "Um . . . I'm not actually sure. I think they just liked the name." Anthony clung to several old business rules, one of which included keeping a crystal decanter of scotch on a table behind his desk. Had he been drinking?

"Did I ever tell you that my gran was named Ruby?"

I eyed the scotch, trying to remember how full it had been the last time I was in here.

Anthony walked around his desk and took a seat on the corner nearest me. His thigh pressed against the side of my arm and I shifted in my seat.

21

"No, sir. You didn't."

"No, no, don't call me 'sir,'" he said, waving a hand in protest. "It makes me feel like I could be your dad, remember? Call me Anthony."

"Okay. Sorry . . . Anthony . . ."

"I'm not your father, you know," he said leaning forward, and there was a pregnant pause. "Not nearly old enough."

I tried to be subtle about the full-body shudder that rolled through me. I'm fairly certain that were it possible, Anthony would literally ooze over the desk, to pool at my feet. And then he'd look up my skirt.

"But that's not why I called you in here." He straightened and pulled a file from a stack on his desk. "I called you in here because there's been a change in plans."

"Oh?"

"As it happens, something's come up and I'm not able to go to New York."

What did this have to do with me? Did he really think I'd been so worried about him being gone that he needed to personally update me?

I swallowed, trying to look interested. "You're not?"

"No," he said, smiling in a way I assumed was meant to look generous, indulgent even. "*You* are."

Two

Niall

I adjusted the phone so I could hold it between my ear and shoulder and tapped a stack of papers together, placing it neatly in front of me. "I see."

Static vibrated across the quiet line.

"You *see*?" Portia repeated in a voice that had grown tight and thin. "Are you even bloody listening?"

Had she always sounded so impatient with me?

Sadly, I think the answer to that was yes.

"Of course, I'm listening. You've told me you're stuck. But I don't see what I can do about it, Porsh."

"It's what we agreed, Niall. You agreed to let me keep the dog if *I* agreed to let you watch him when I went on holiday. I am going on holiday and need you to watch him. But if it's a *bother* . . ." Portia's voice trailed off but the echo sizzled across the phone line like acid dripped on metal.

"Under normal circumstances, taking Davey is no bother," I answered calmly. Always calm, always patient, even when we were discussing who should care for her pet while she went to Majorca for a week to recover from the stress of our divorce being finalized. "The issue is simply that I will be out of the *country*, love."

I swallowed back a curse, wincing.

Love.

After nearly sixteen years together, some habits died hard.

Her answering silence was weighted, dense. Two years ago, the quiet ticking across the telephone line would have had me in a panic. A year ago it would have made my stomach sour and tight.

Now, nine months after I'd moved out of the home we'd shared together, her angry silence simply made me weary.

I looked up, at the load of emails in my inbox, at the stacks of contracts on my desk, and then at the clock, which told me it was long past time to head home. Outside, the sky had gone dark. Once I returned home tonight I would need to start packing for New York and would barely make a dent in the work in front of me before then.

"Portia. I'm sorry. I really must go. I'm sorry about the dog but I can't make it work next week."

"Right," she sighed. "Get *stuffed.*"

I stared at my desk for several seconds after she'd hung up, feeling faintly sick, before setting my mobile down. I had only two breaths to recover before the door to my office flew open and Tony stepped in.

"Bad news, mate."

I looked up, lifting my brow in silent question.

"The wife's gone and started contractions."

My siblings had enough children for me to know that Tony's wife wasn't far enough along for this. "She's all right?"

He shrugged. "Sentenced to bed till the kid is here. Hence: I'm staying in London."

Relief spread through my blood. Tony was a decent colleague, but a business trip with him usually meant nightly visits to strip clubs, and it was honestly the last thing I wanted to do for a month in New York. "So I'll go it alone, then," I said, my tone already lighter than it had been only a moment ago.

Tony shook his head. "I'm sending Ruby."

It took a couple of ticks for me to place who he meant. Richardson-Corbett wasn't a large firm, but Tony hired as many pretty young interns as his budget allowed. There were a few on his team now and I could never quite keep them sorted. "She the brunette from Essex?"

His expression of disappointed envy was so pronounced it was nearly audible. "No. The delectable bit from California."

Oh. I knew which one he meant. The one who came to my rescue today when I'd experienced an uncharacteristic stumble.

Ironically, I'd been flustered over the sight of her. She was *lovely.*

Alas . . . "She's the one who seemed concerned you were leaving for a month?"

I could practically see Tony's head growing, and he smiled proudly. "That's right."

"Is it really necessary to send someone, though?" I asked. "Most of the meetings will be logistics anyway. Engineering was only going to advise."

"Aw, ya prat. I'm sure you can get her to go to the titty bars with you."

I groaned inwardly. "That isn't—"

"And besides," he interrupted, "she's fit as all fuck. You may not need a girly bar if you're getting a leg over on Ruby. All legs, good tits, bloody *fantastic* face."

"Tony," I said with steady calm, "I'm not going to 'get a leg over' on an intern."

"Maybe you should. If I wasn't tied down, I sure as fuck would pull that." He let the silence bounce around the room, and I tried to hide my disgust that he seemed more disappointed that he was unable to shag Ruby than worried that his wife had gone into labor early. "How long since you've been out?"

I blinked away from his challenging expression, looking down at my desk. I hadn't dated since the divorce and, except for the drunken grope I'd received at the pub a few weeks back, hadn't been close to a woman in what felt like forever.

"Right, so you're staying here," I deflected, "and Ruby is coming along to New York. Have you gone over the agenda with her?"

"I told her the agenda is you get there, hit the bars, get pissed, get a leg over."

I wiped a hand over my face, groaning. "Bloody hell."

He laughed, turning and walking to my door. "Of course I gave her the agenda. I'm just taking the piss. She's a good one, Niall. She may even impress the likes of you."

I was alone in the lift, heading out for the night, when Ruby stepped in just as the doors were closing. Our eyes met, I coughed harshly, her breath caught . . . and descending in the weighted silence became immediately dreadful.

The lift moved too slowly.

The quiet felt enormous.

We were going on a business trip together, and glancing at her now—young and energetic and, admittedly, unbelievably beautiful—I registered we would be required to chat and get on, and there were few things I was worse at than talking up women.

She opened her mouth to speak, and then stopped, falling back into silence. When she looked at me and I looked over, she blinked away. Just as the doors opened in the lobby, I gestured for her to lead us out, and instead of moving, she nearly shouted, "Looks like we're going away together!"

"Too right," I said, but my smile felt stiff.

Try, Niall. Try to get it out of robot mode for at least one conversation.

Nothing. My brain felt like a sieve, completely void of social pleasantries. And she still didn't exit the lift.

The moment needed to end. I was bloody awful at small

talk, and close up, she was even more attractive than I'd expected. Several inches shorter than I, but by no means short, Ruby was willowy and toned, with short, playfully mussed golden hair, sun-kissed cheeks . . . and a truly perfect mouth.

Ruby was rather exquisite. On some strange instinct, I held my breath.

She shrugged a little, smiling. "I'm from the States but I've never been to New York. I'm really excited."

"Ah. Well . . ." I searched for a good response, looking around the small space before eventually settling on "That's good."

I groaned inwardly. That was bad, even for me.

Her eyes were enormous, green and so clear I registered with one glance down at them that she was unlikely to be a very good liar: her entire world spilled out her through those eyes, and right now she was an anxious heap.

I was a VP at the firm. Of course she was nervous around me.

"Will we meet at the airport on Monday morning?" she asked, looking back up. Her tongue slipped out to wet her lips and I fixed my attention to the middle of her forehead.

"Yes, I believe so," I began and then stopped. Was I meant to arrange a car for the two of us? Dear God, if three minutes in a lift was this bad, I couldn't fathom how claustrophobic the forty-five-minute commute to Heathrow would feel. "Unless—"

"I don't—"

"You—"

"Oh, sorry," she said, cheeks bright. "I interrupted you. Go ahead."

I sighed. "Please, go ahead."

This was abysmal. I longed for her to move aside to simply let me pass. Or, for the ground to open up, swallow me whole.

"I can just meet you at the airport." She hitched her satchel higher over her shoulder, gesturing inexplicably behind her. "At the gate, I mean. It'll be really early, you don't need to—"

"I won't. That is, I *wouldn't*."

She blinked, understandably confused. I'd completely lost track of what we were even talking about. "Okay. Good. Of course, you . . . wouldn't."

I looked over her shoulder to the blessed freedom beyond and then back to her. "That'll be fine."

The door to the lift began to buzz in warning as I continued to hold it ajar, a shrill soundtrack to what had to be one of the most awkward encounters ever.

"So I'll see you Monday." Her voice wavered with nerves, and I felt a cold sweat prick at the back of my neck. "I'm really looking forward to it," she said.

"Right. Good."

With a little tilt of her head, and a final blush that exploded rather sweetly across her cheeks, she stepped off the lift.

Without really intending to, my eyes drifted to her backside as she went. It was round, high, perfectly shaped in her smooth, dark skirt. I could imagine the curve of it in my palm, could still smell the whiff of rose water she left in her wake.

I stepped out into the dark lobby and followed her toward the exit. Without effort, my mind drifted to thoughts of how her breasts would fill my hands, the feel of her mouth on me, my palms on her backside. I wasn't rubbish in bed, was I? And even though Portia had generally treated sex as a favor to me, she had never once failed to enjoy—

This unconscious flash of interest was quashed when Tony emerged from the stairwell, giving me a wink and a little wiggle of his brow, murmuring, "Shagfest," as Ruby rounded the corner. Left in its place was a sour twinge of shame for letting his earlier suggestion worm its way into my head.

———

Growing up with twelve people in the house, air travel simply didn't happen often, and when it did—the odd puddle jumper with a few kids to Ireland and once, when it was only me and Rebecca left at home, Mum and Dad took us to Rome to see the pope—it put the entire house in an uproar of preparation. We had regular Sunday clothes that weren't as posh as our Christmas mass kits, and even those were yards below our air travel outfits. It was a hard habit to break, even when dressing before the sun rose, but this history dictated why I found myself at Heathrow, wearing a suit at four thirty on Monday morning.

By contrast, Ruby sprinted in just at my panic point—when the flight was boarding—in a zip-front pink hoodie, black workout pants, and bright blue trainers. I saw the response to her pass through the crowd in a quiet ripple. I couldn't tell if Ruby noticed or not, but nearly every set of male eyes—and many female as well—followed her as she made her way toward our gate.

She looked casual but fresh, her cheeks flushed from her run and her full, pink lips parted as she caught her breath.

She stopped short when she found me in the crowd, her eyes going wide as saucers.

"Shit." She slapped a hand over her mouth. "I mean, *crap*," she mumbled from behind it. "Do we have a meeting right when we land?" She began searching through her phone. "I memorized the schedule and I could have sworn—"

I felt my brows pull together. "No . . . ?" She'd memorized our schedule?

"I . . . you look *really* dressed up for the plane. I feel like a hobo in comparison."

I wasn't sure whether I was meant to feel insulted or praised. "You don't look like a hobo."

She groaned, covering her face. "It's a long flight. I thought we were going to *sleep*."

I smiled politely, though the thought of sleeping next to her on a flight created an anxious, gnawing sensation in my gut. "I've a few work things to do before we arrive. Feel better dressed for the occasion, that's all."

I wasn't actually sure which one of us had misjudged, but looking at the attire on most of the boarding passengers around us, I was beginning to understand it was me.

With one last wary glance at my suit, she turned and made her way down the jetway to board and stowed her tote in the overhead above our seats. I made every effort to not look at her backside again . . . and failed.

Sweet Lord. It was unbelievable.

Oblivious, Ruby turned and I pulled my gaze up to her face just as she gestured to the two seats. "Do you want the aisle or window?" she asked.

"Either is fine."

I removed my suit coat and handed it to the flight attendant, watching as Ruby slid into the window seat and tucked away her iPad and book, keeping a small notebook with her.

Seated beside her, and even with the rest of the passengers still boarding, a heavy silence descended between us. *Christ.* Not only did we have six hours on the flight today, but then nearly four weeks in New York together for the summit.

Four weeks. I felt mildly ill.

I suppose I could ask her how she liked Richardson-Corbett or how long she'd lived in London. She wasn't under my charge, but working for Tony, I was sure her time there had been . . . eventful. I could ask her where she grew up—though I knew from Tony it was California. At least it might break the ice a little.

But then we would be required to keep talking, and that definitely didn't seem to be going well. Best to just leave it.

"Can I offer you a beverage before we lift off?" the flight attendant asked before setting a napkin down in front of me.

I deferred to Ruby, and she leaned closer to speak to the woman over the din of travelers boarding the plane. Her breast pressed to the arm of my shirt, and I felt my entire body go stiff, careful to not seem to lean into . . . *it*.

"I'll have some champagne," Ruby said.

The flight attendant smiled uncomfortably as she nodded—no doubt it wasn't something they generally poured before five in the morning—and turned to me.

"I . . ." I began, haltingly. Should I order champagne, too, so it wasn't odd for her to do it? Or should I set the example for professional decorum and order the grapefruit juice I'd planned for? "Well, I suppose if it's not too much trouble, I could also—"

Ruby held up a hand. "I'm totally kidding, by the way. Sorry. Joke bomb! I mean no! Not a bomb, I'd never joke about . . . that." She closed her eyes and groaned. "I'll just have some OJ."

I looked up, sharing a brief, confused expression with the flight attendant. "I'll take grapefruit juice, please."

With our orders noted, the flight attendant left and Ruby turned to me. Something about her face, the unguarded honesty in her eyes . . . it triggered a tender protectiveness in me I was wholly unaccustomed to.

She blinked away, moving to stare so hard at her tray I was afraid she would crack it through sheer intensity.

"All right?" I asked.

"Just—sorry about that. And yes. I—" She paused and then tried again. "I wasn't going to order champagne. Did you really think that?"

"Well." She *had* ordered it, even if only in jest. "No?" I hoped that was the right answer.

"And that whole bomb thing," she whispered, waving a hand in front of her as if to push the thought away. "I am such an idiot around you."

"Just me?"

She slumped and I realized how it had sounded.

"No. I . . . that is, I take issue with what you're saying: I've never seen you act like an idiot around me."

"The elevator?"

Smiling, I conceded this. "Well."

"And right now?"

This twisted something inside me. "Is there anything I can do?"

She blinked up to my face and gazed at me with a familiar sort of fondness.

And then she blinked, shaking her head once, and it was gone. "I'll be fine. Just nervous about a trip with the director of planning and *blah blah*."

Wanting to put her more at ease, I asked, "Where did you do your undergraduate work?"

She took a deep breath, and then turned to face me fully. "UC San Diego."

"Engineering?"

"Yes. With Emil Santorini."

I acknowledged this with a small lift of my brow. "He's tough."

She grinned. "He's *amazing*."

A sharp curl of interest spiked through me. "Only the brilliant ones come out feeling that way."

"Push through or break," she said, shrugging as she accepted her orange juice from the flight attendant with a bright smile. "That's what he said the first week in the lab. He wasn't wrong. Three of us started in there at the same time. I was the only one still there by Christmas our first year."

"Why are you in London?" I asked, though I suspected I already knew.

"Hoping to make it into the Civil program. I'm already in the engineering general but haven't heard from Margaret Sheffield yet whether I'm in her group."

"She doesn't decide until just before the term starts. Makes the students completely barking mad, if memory serves."

"We engineers like our calendars and spreadsheets and plans. Not the most patient bunch, I guess."

I smiled. "Like I said. Barking mad."

She pulled the corner of her lip into her mouth and smiled back. "You didn't study with her."

"Not officially, but she was more a mentor to me than my own mentor was."

"How long after you finished did Petersen retire?"

I felt my eyes widen. How much did she know about my old department? About me? "I suspect you already know the answer to that question."

She sipped her juice and apologized quietly after swallowing. "I knew you were his last student but I guess I was curious to hear how bad it was."

"It was abysmal," I admitted. "He was a drunk and more than that—a ruddy awful person. But that was nearly ten years ago. You were a child. How do you know all of this?"

She pursed her lips slightly and I felt my skin flush warm. *Christ.* She was so beautiful.

"One answer," she started with a small smile, "is that I learned about Maggie Sheffield's work when I was a sophomore and we toured the Stately building. I grew kind of obsessed with getting to study under her before she retired. When I asked Emil about her, he also shared some of the history of your old department." Shrugging, she said, "I heard a few stories about Petersen."

I tilted my head, wondering which ones still floated around.

"He threw a bottle at a student?" she asked.

Ah. The one story that would never die. "He did, but it wasn't me. The worst I ever got from him was a verbal berating . . . or ten."

Ruby nodded, looking relieved.

She'd said *one* answer was this. "And the other answer?" I asked.

She looked out the window for a few breaths before saying, "I joined R-C and found out you'd studied at Oxford, and wondered if you'd been in Maggie's program. You hadn't but . . . I learned a bit about you anyway."

There seemed to be an extra layer to what she was saying, and I thought for a beat I understood the look of fond familiarity she'd given me only a moment before. But then she turned back, wearing a sweetly devious grin. "You'd be amazed how much you can pick up just by paying attention."

"Enlighten me."

Sitting up in her seat, she said, "You came over from your position at the London Underground to start up an urban planning division. You went to Cambridge for undergraduate, Oxford for graduate school, and were the youngest executive in the history of the Tube." Ruby gave me a shy smile. "You nearly moved to New York to work for the Metropolitan Transportation Authority but turned the job down to come to R-C."

Lifting a brow, I murmured, "Impressive. What else do you know?"

She looked away, blushing further. "You grew up in Leeds. You were a star on the Cambridge football club while you were there."

Had she looked any of this up last night? Or had she known all of this about me before this trip? And which answer did I want to hear? I suspected I knew which would make this small thrill in my stomach grow more intense. "What else?"

Hesitating, she said, "You own a Ford Fiesta, which I find endlessly amusing given that you probably make more money than the queen and are known to be a staunch public transportation advocate, so you never use it. An aside? I have no idea how you would even fit in a Ford Fiesta. Also, you're recently divorced."

My jaw grew tight as any amusement regarding her research endeavors was quickly extinguished. "One would think that detail wouldn't be discussed at work, nor available by easy online search."

"I'm sorry," Ruby said, wincing, and I watched as she shrank a little more into her seat. "I forget not everyone was raised by two psychologists. We aren't all open books."

"I'm tempted to ask how you knew about my divorce, but I suppose the office chatter . . ."

"I think it was all wrapping up when I started so people were talking . . ." She straightened and looked at me with wide, apologetic eyes. "It's not an ongoing topic, I promise."

I could only imagine my dark mood at the time Ruby had joined the firm. By that point I was so put off by Portia's dramatics I'd have happily resided inside a pint. I decided to change the subject. "Do you have siblings, or was it you alone with the shrinks?"

"One brother," she said and then took a sip of her juice. "What about you?"

"What—you're telling me you don't already know?"

She laughed, but still looked a bit embarrassed. "If I took the time to find that out . . . that might have veered into stalker territory."

With a little wink, I murmured, *"Might* have."

She watched me expectantly and as the plane began to accelerate, I noted the way her hands gripped the armrests. She was shaking.

Waffling on to distract her seemed like a rather good idea. "I have nine siblings, actually," I told her.

She leaned in, jaw dropping. *"Nine?"*

I'd become so accustomed to this reaction that I barely blinked anymore. "Seven sisters and two brothers, with me the second youngest."

Her brow creased as she thought about this some more. "My house was so quiet and calm. I . . . I can't even imagine your childhood."

Laughing, I said, "Trust me, it's true. You can't."

"Eight older siblings," she said to herself. "I bet at times that felt like having eight parents."

"Sometimes," I admitted. "My oldest brother, Daniel, was the peacekeeper," I told her. "Really, he kept us in line. I think it helped that there were more girls than boys; as a general rule our lot was pretty well-behaved. The brother just older than me, Max, was usually the one pulling pranks, and he got away with it because he was charming. At least that's how he describes it. I was quiet, and studious. Rather boring, really."

She grew still for a moment, watching me, and then said, "Tell me more?"

I leaned my head back against the seat, inhaling deeply, calming. It had been *years* since I'd so casually spoken with a woman other than Portia, a sibling, or the wife of a friend. Her interest was genuine and gave me a sense of confidence I hadn't felt in a very long time.

"Most of our adventures were taken on together. Forming a brass band. Deciding to write a picture book. Once we painted the side of our house with finger paints."

"I honestly can't imagine you with paint on your hands."

I gave a dramatic shudder and smiled at her delighted laugh. There was something there, some relief in her eyes, just beneath the surface that made me feel quite tender toward her.

I prattled on, completely out of character, but she listened with rapt attention, asking questions about Max, about my sister Rebecca, about our parents. She asked about my life outside of work, and so when I said with a teasing grin that she already knew about the divorce, she asked how my ex-wife and I met. Surprisingly, it didn't feel strange to tell her how Portia and I met when we were ten, fell in love when we were fourteen, and kissed at sixteen.

I didn't admit that the magic began to die only three years later, on our wedding day.

"It must be weird to have been with someone for so long and then see it end," she said quietly, turning to look out the window. "I can't even imagine." Her fringe fell over one eye; a small diamond earring decorated the delicate lobe of her ear. When she looked back, she said, "I'm sorry people were talking about it in the office. It must feel like such an invasion of privacy."

I looked away, not replying. Every potential response I might give felt too honest.

It's not that weird, and maybe that's what is weirdest about it.

I've been lonely for a very long time. So why am I acutely aware of it only now?

I never imagined wanting to talk about this again, but here we are. You could ask more.

But when silence grew, it became awkward. With her attention focused out the window and her body easy and relaxed, however, I registered with relief that it was only awkward for me. The tension from the lift had dissipated, something in her had calmed.

I was surprised to find myself thinking how much I liked being near her.

Eventually, Ruby drifted off to sleep, slowly slanting toward me until her head rested on my shoulder. I turned, telling myself I was glancing out the window, but took the opportunity to inhale the light floral scent of her hair. Up close, her skin was perfect. Pale, with a tiny smattering of freckles across her nose, and a clear, beautiful complexion. Her lips were wet where she'd licked them, eyelashes dark against her cheeks.

In her hand, she held a small Richardson-Corbett notebook and pen. I eased it from her lax grip and—against my better judgment—was propelled by curiosity to open it to the first page of what appeared to be work notes. Our agenda, some resources for engineering firms and projects in the area, a list of people she would meet in New York, and some bulleted thoughts on how she could use this conference to build her thesis proposal for Margaret Sheffield. I could tell she'd meticulously written down everything Tony had passed along to her.

At the bottom, in her neat penmanship, she'd written

```
Agenda note # 1: Don't be an idiot around
Niall Stella. Don't stare, don't babble,
don't go mute. You can do this. He is human.
```

Only now did it occur to me that this journal could have been a diary of sorts, rather than a professional ledger. She'd been so anxious to go on a trip with a VP from the firm that she'd written herself up a pep talk.

Easing it back into her grip, I closed my eyes, tilting my head to her as I silently apologized for invading *her* privacy this time.

I dreamt of soft skin resting on my bare chest and kisses tasting of champagne.

Three

Ruby

I woke to the sound of the flight attendant over the loud-speaker telling us we would soon be making our descent into New York.

My eyes fluttered open, and I immediately winced. A stream of cold, dry air blew straight into my face and an engine seemed to roar in the background. I was awkwardly twisted in my seat, not to mention in desperate need of the restroom, but somehow . . .

I was so comfortable. Whoever I was next to was warm and firm and delicious-smelling, and—

I straightened with a jolt, disentangling from where I'd wrapped myself around Niall Stella's arm and—*oh, God*—did I have my leg hitched up over his *thigh*?

The elevator was bad enough, and now this? *Oh, God.* Had I kicked a puppy or something in a past life? Why was I being punished?

I carefully disentangled myself from his body and looked around, realizing I had no idea what time it was. The cabin was still dark, and I noted that most people around us were sleeping, their shades drawn to block out any light. Smoothing my hair, I tried to stretch out my stiff muscles. My neck would be fine, but this bathroom situation would really need to be resolved. Sooner rather than later.

I sat back, ran my sweaty hands over my thighs, and gave myself a moment to take everything in. Yesterday, Niall Stella didn't know I existed. Today, I'd practically flown to New York in his lap. In twenty-four hours I'd gone from Ruby Miller: Secret Admirer and Semi-Stalker, to Ruby Miller: International Traveling Mate.

Not to mention the fact that if I'd been asleep on him, parts of him had definitely been asleep on me. And well, that was going in my diary *tonight*.

He hadn't moved yet. Which was bad because of the bathroom situation, but awesome because when would I ever have this opportunity again? Aside from that one hour at work a week, I never really got the chance to look at him like this. In meetings we were always surrounded by people, or passing quickly in the hall. Once, I stood behind him in the buffet line at a company gala, but all that really afforded me was a good look at his ass in tuxedo pants. Not a complaint, by the way. Niall Stella played soccer and rowed with a men's club on the Thames every Saturday. His backside was in my Top Ten Favorite Niall Stella Body Parts (I was leaving spot one open for the time being).

But here, I was so close I could count his eyelashes if I wanted. And I sort of did.

Niall Stella wasn't *that* much older than me—only seven years—but he looked so young like this. His hair was the tiniest bit mussed near the back, the front falling down over his forehead, shiny and soft. His pale green shirt was rumpled ever so slightly, and there, on the shoulder, was a dark patch of fabric.

Where I'd drooled.

Oh, God.

I wiped at my face, cursing that he'd been so warm and snugglable that I'd fallen into a sleep heavy enough to drool on his fancy, four-thirty-in-the-morning suit. Help. I searched the area around us, finding nothing more than a crumpled napkin on my tray. Picking it up, I dabbed carefully, hoping maybe I could fix it all and he wouldn't even notice. No such luck. Not only didn't it work, but it jostled him enough that his eyes flashed open to find my face only inches from his.

I smiled. "Hi."

He blinked a few times before his eyes widened, his gaze moving to the piece of tissue in my hand, and over to his shoulder.

"Sorry about that," I muttered, following it up with a shaky, nervous laugh. "I'm a delicate napper."

He smiled and there was a tiny, devious flash of dimples. "These things happen."

I wanted to slap myself for the thought that came next, the urge to climb over and straddle his narrow, fit hips. Fucking hell, Ruby. Did you not read agenda note #1? *Don't be an idiot around Niall Stella.*

He stretched, oblivious to my meltdown. "I seem to have dozed off myself there, so . . . I apologize for that."

"Oh, God, no. Don't be sorry. You looked adora—" I started, then snapped my mouth shut. "We'll be landing soon, I'm just going to get changed."

Without waiting for him to move, I climbed out of my seat, straddling his lap in the process. He made to stand before realizing I was a woman on a mission of escape and if he stood his crotch would come into direct, awkward contact with mine, so he simply grabbed his armrests as if holding on for dear life. It meant my ass was directly in his face, but I suppose that was preferable to an unintentional dry hump.

Life Alert? We have a situation here.

I didn't look at him as I grabbed my carry-on from the overhead bin and moved as quickly as my legs would go to the nearest available bathroom.

Safely locked in the tiny room, I exhaled for what felt like the first time in minutes. Why was it so impossible for me to act like a normal human being around him?

"Get it together," I told my reflection, and roughly opened my bag. I had everything I needed in there; unfortunately, the idea of changing in an airplane restroom was far better than the mechanics of actually doing it.

I banged my head on the counter as I bent to push my pants down my hips. We hit a pocket of turbulence as I lifted my foot to slip on my skirt, and it nearly ended up in the toilet before I was knocked back into the door with a loud bang. It took me ten minutes to dress and fix my hair, and there was zero question that every single person in first class—and probably beyond—had looked toward the bathroom in concern at least once, wondering what the hell was going on in there. But with my head held high, I stepped out and took my seat.

The fact that Niall Stella was noticeably still did not ease my nerves.

He didn't look my way, instead keeping his eyes straight ahead, and murmured an "All right?" when I'd rebuckled my seat belt.

"Perfect," I lied. "Being trapped in a tiny space, I decided it was a good time to dance."

A tiny smile tugged at the corner of his lips before he bent down and laughed outright. "I did some of that myself while you were in there."

Something inside me melted, and it was all I could do to not turn, take his face in my hands, and make out with him like there was no tomorrow.

⌘

The plane landed ten minutes ahead of schedule. Passengers began to stand and pull their things from the overhead compartments, and I stood in front of Niall as

47

we waited to make our way down the aisle toward the exit.

I looked over my shoulder at him, wanting to make sure he was all set. But he didn't look down to meet my eyes. He was staring with determination at the ceiling of the plane.

Something was off.

For six months I'd worked in the same building as Niall Stella and he'd never really noticed me. This was different. This wasn't the oblivious avoidance I'd seen in the past, this was deliberate. He was fidgety and flustered and if it would have been acceptable to shove me out of the way and run to the taxi stand to flee the scene, I thought he might do it.

First class and coach were filing out the same door and I turned again, smiling at him as we waited for the people in front of us to move. "We're a little early, so our driver might not be here yet," I said.

His eyes darted down to mine and then quickly away.

"Right," he said.

Okaaaaay.

I turned on my heel and continued on down the row, when a woman near me reached out, tugging on my skirt.

"Girl code, girl code," she whispered, and I looked down at her, confused. "Your skirt is tucked into your underwear."

MY WHAT?

She leaned in and I felt the blood drain from my face.

"Though between you and me, I don't think the gentle-man behind you minds one little bit."

I reached behind me and felt nothing but skin, fran-tically pulling my skirt free from where it had been completely tucked up into itself,

exposing

   my

      entire

        ass.

Life Alert? It's me, Ruby, again.

I thanked her and stepped out onto the jetway, roll-ing my carry-on behind me and praying that the ground would open up and swallow me whole. Once we were just inside the terminal, I made a show of looking for some-thing in my purse so Niall Stella would walk in front of me and I wouldn't have to fight the urge to constantly smooth my skirt down over my backside.

He's seen your ass.

Why did you choose to wear a G-string?

He's seen your naked ass, Ruby.

We stood side by side as we waited for our luggage, and honestly I wasn't sure which of us was more mor-tified. There was absolutely no way that he didn't see. I knew he saw. And he knew I knew he saw.

I stared at the turnstile, waiting for my bag to appear, when I felt him lean closer.

He smelled like fresh soap and shaving cream, and when he whispered, his breath was minty. "Ruby? Sorry about the . . . I'm not very good at . . ." He paused and I turned to meet his eyes. We were so close. His brown eyes had flecks of green and yellow in them and I felt my heart claw its way up my throat when he glanced quickly down at my mouth. "I'm not very good at . . . women."

My humiliation was replaced with something warmer, and calmer, and infinitely sweeter.

———————

I'd been in large cities before—San Diego, San Francisco, Los Angeles, London—but I was pretty sure they were absolutely nothing like New York.

Everything was massive, taking up as little ground as necessary while towering overhead. The buildings crowded the sky, leaving only a strip of gray-blue directly above us. And it was *loud*. I'd never been somewhere with so much honking—not that anyone on the street seemed to notice. The air was a chorus of horns and shouts, and as we made our way from terminal four of JFK to our car, and from our car to the revolving doors of the Parker Meridien, I didn't see a single person who seemed bothered by the cacophony.

Niall followed an appropriate distance behind me as we made our way through the lobby—close enough that it was clear we were together, but not *together*—and we checked into our respective rooms. I was there as Niall's colleague, not his employee or assistant or . . . even his friend, really, and so I wasn't given any information about where his room was or, say, what size bed he had in there. I didn't even get a formal goodbye; when his phone rang, he did little more than offer me a small, polite wave and disappear down a quiet hallway.

No doubt I looked like someone had just walked off with my puppy, and so I jumped slightly when the bellman coughed next to me, clearly waiting to show me upstairs.

Once inside the elevator, the weight of the day hit me like a truck, and it occurred to me that I'd been up since three and caught only a small nap on Niall's shoulder. A screen embedded into the elevator wall played an old cartoon: Tom nailed Jerry over the head with a hammer, and as they chased each other around a wooden barrel, the elevator climbed to the tenth floor, and I felt my eyes grow heavier and heavier.

I followed the bellman down the hall and watched as he opened my door. In the center of the room was a platform bed big enough for at least four people, opposite a huge flat-screen television. There was a set of art deco chairs in one corner and a window that spanned the entire far wall with a long desk tucked just beneath it.

The bed really did look like something out of a dream—crisp sheets and fluffy pillows—and my body sagged with how much I wanted to collapse, face-first right into it. Unfortunately, I'd learned the hard way how much jet lag sucks, and no matter how much I wanted to, taking a nap was exactly what I *shouldn't* do.

Dammit.

It was the second time in the same day I'd bolted up-right from a dead sleep. Drooling.

The room around me was almost completely dark, and for a moment, I had no idea where I was. Then it hit me: New York. The hotel.

Niall Stella.

I remembered showering and changing into a robe, deciding to rest my eyes just long enough for room service to get here and, well. Here we were.

I stood, groaning at my stiff muscles while I wiped my face on the sleeve of my robe. Man, when I slept, I slept *hard*.

As my eyes adjusted, I pushed open the drapes and forced myself to find my phone. There were two texts from my mom wondering if I'd landed yet, and one from Lola checking in. Having been unplugged all day, I held my breath before checking my email.

Meeting tomorrow: *that needs a read*.

Thoughts from Tony: *that can wait until morning*.

Sale at Victoria's Secret: *oooh, I'll flag that one for later*.

Note from Niall's assistant—*wait, what?*

She'd attached our updated schedule for the following day, along with the time we'd meet in the lobby, and a few points he wanted her to pass along. There was also the number to his cell, "*should anything problematic arise*."

I stared at my screen.

I had Niall Stella's phone number.

Dare I use it? Since I'd most certainly slept through my food being delivered, I could text him and see if he wanted to grab a bite to eat. But that didn't really fall under the category of *problematic*, no matter how hungry I was. And if he hadn't told his assistant to ask me about dinner plans, then I had to assume that was because he'd make his and I'd make mine.

Only then did I realize I really *had* begun to imagine the next four weeks with Niall Stella and me *together* in the temporary New York office, or walking along Broadway, or passionately discussing work over meals at great, locals-recommended restaurants. I'd unconsciously imagined the way he would laugh at my new and witty inside jokes over a beer at the end of the day and how we would share knowing looks across the table at our flurry of upcoming meetings.

But the reality was that I was most likely going to be sitting in the back of a crowded room taking notes, then returning alone to this hotel room for a month's worth of room service meals.

I couldn't text him, and I definitely didn't want to call room service again tonight.

I checked my reflection in the mirror opposite the bathroom, and *yikes:* hair like a pile of hay, mascara smeared, pillow lines from temple to chin. I'd looked better after an all-nighter in college. Unless I wanted to spend time making myself at least minimally presentable, I'd have to settle for a vending machine dinner of chips and diet soda.

With a handful of dollar bills and a stack of change shoved into the pocket of my bathrobe, I opened the door slowly and peered out down the hallway. It was surprisingly shadowed and unfamiliar (hey, jet lag!): the walls were covered in a dark-patterned paper and each door was illuminated with a tiny neon plaque and doorbells.

I spied the sign for an ice machine in the distance and tiptoed out, letting the door fall closed behind me. The carpet was soft and thick against the soles of my feet, a subtle reminder that beneath the cotton of my robe I was completely naked. I tried, but couldn't hear the blurred shape of voices in a neighboring room, or even the hum of a television. It was too quiet, too still. The hallway stretched ominously dark in front of me. I took a few steps past my room, narrowing my eyes to prepare for the appearance of anything unexpected in the distance.

"Ruby?"

I let out a high-pitched squeal of surprise, flinching, and then squeezed my eyes closed as I recognized the voice, debating whether or not I should turn around. Maybe I could run away. Maybe I could pretend to be someone else and he would realize his mistake and go back down to wherever his room was.

No such luck.

"Ruby?" he asked again, a hint of disbelief in his voice.

Because normal people don't run down the hallway in fancy hotels barefoot and in their bathrobes. And oh look, judging by the breeze sweeping up the inside of my robe, the air conditioner just kicked on, too.

Nice touch, universe.

"Hi!" I said—too brightly, far too loud—and turned on my heel to face him.

Startled, Niall Stella took a step back, nearly stumbling into the open doorway, which, coincidentally, was right next to mine.

Sharing a wall . . . maybe even a bathroom wall . . . where he showered . . . naked.

Focus, Ruby!

I went for casual. "What are *you* up to? I was just grabbing something to eat myself . . ." I said, lazily swinging the tie of my robe around before realizing what I was doing. I dropped it like I'd been burned.

"Something to eat?" he repeated.

I placed a hand against the wall and leaned there. "Yep

Niall Stella looked around the hallway and then to me, eyes lingering on my robe. And maybe, just if my eyes were correct, my chest. Where my now gaping, possibly exposing some boob.

We seemed to reach this conclusion at t

His eyes snapped to my forehead a material in my hands. At this rate, N me fully naked by the end of the

"From the vending machine

up to tuck a strand of hair behind my ear, groaning when I remembered how I looked. "I was just going to grab some chips. I mean the American kind of chip."

He made a show of looking around. "Not sure a place like this will have Fritos," he said, a pop of color staining his cheeks and a hint of a smile tugging at the corner of his lips. "Energy bars, perhaps? Caviar, definitely. Good thing you're dressed for it."

He was *teasing* me.

My brother was my best friend, his friends were my friends, and *this* is what I was good at. Banter. The give-and-take of joking with the guys. I could do this and not be an idiot. And not think about how I wanted to bang him. Maybe. Except he was wearing the charcoal suit—my favorite—and a dark shirt with no tie. I'd never seen him without a tie and it required superhuman strength to keep my eyes on his face, and not on that tiny stretch of skin exposed at the top of his open collar.

He had chest hair and my fingertips tingled with the urge to touch it. Alas, he was still waiting for me to respond.

"You're lucky I even put this on," I told him. "I usually eat Fritos pantsless on the couch."

His eyebrow did a cute little amused twitch while the rest of his face remained impressively stoic. "In fact, I understand those are the instructions on the package. Sadly, same is not usually true of caviar."

Or energy bars," I added, and he laughed.

"Too right."

Shrugging, I looked back at the door to my room. "I guess I'll have another peek at the room service menu."

"I'm going to lay you down," he said, "and make you come."

My eyes going wide as saucers, I whipped my head back his way. "You . . . *what*?"

With a confused draw of his brow, he said very slowly, "I'm going to head on down; would you like to come?"

"Oh," I said, struggling to take a breath in, and let it out again. "You're going to dinner downstairs?"

"You said this is your first time?" he started, and both our eyes widened before he added in a breathless rush, "In New York. Your first time in New York."

"Um, yeah," I answered, and closed my robe more tightly near my neck.

"Maybe you . . ." Niall started to say, but paused, reaching up as if to straighten a tie that wasn't there. He dropped his hands again. "I'm meeting my brother. He and his wife live in the city, and I'm having dinner with him and a few business associates downstairs. Maybe you could join us."

His brother lived here? I tucked this bit of information away, along with how badly I wanted to go—certain I was going to hate myself for this later—and shook my head. There was no way I was going to intrude.

"I think I'll probably just—"

"You'd be doing me a favor if you joined me, actually,"

he cut in. "My brother Max is a bit of a handful." Niall paused again as if he'd reconsidered, before giving a small shake of his head and continuing, "You'd be a welcome distraction."

Because I'm Captain of Team Clueless and intent on painting each interaction between us with either nudity or a shade of awkward, I stood there, speechless, blinking for far longer than was socially appropriate.

"Of course, if you'd rather not—"

"No, no! Sorry, I . . . can you give me ten minutes to change and—" I motioned vaguely to the disaster atop my head.

"Ten minutes is all you need?" he asked skeptically.

God, he's teasing me again.

"Ten minutes," I confirmed with a smirk. "Twelve if you don't want my skirt in my underwear."

Niall barked out a laugh that seemed to surprise us both before regaining his composure. "All right then. I'll wait in the lobby. See you in *ten*."

※

No person in the history of forever has ever changed as quickly as I did.

The moment the elevator doors closed behind him, I was off. My robe gone, I yanked a blue jersey dress from my suitcase and sprinted to the bathroom. I ran a washcloth over my face and raced to find my toiletries. I moisturized, concealed, and powdered at the speed of light. A dab of product in my hair and I turned on the blow dryer, smoothing out the bedhead one section at a time. My flatiron heated up in seconds and after just a few passes I unplugged it, setting it aside. Teeth brushed, blush applied, mascara swiped, lip gloss smoothed, I threw on my dress with five minutes left to spare. Unfortunately I'd forgotten to put on underwear, so I used the remaining time to pull a pair from my suitcase, find a portable charger for my phone, and slip into a pair of sensible heels.

I reached for my bag, double-checked that the various parts of my dress were all where they belonged, and with a deep breath and a tiny prayer, walked to the elevator.

FOUR

Niall

I stood, staring at where she'd emerged from the lift, and fell utterly speechless. She'd changed in under ten minutes, but looked . . . stunning. In an instant, I was both thrilled to be near her and resentful that this complicated wrinkle—the presence of Ruby—invaded what could otherwise be a dry, rote, and *easy* business summit.

Swallowing, I motioned behind me to the entrance of Knave. "Shall we get a bite?"

"Yes, please," she said, and her enormous smile, her long silhouette slightly vibrating with excitement, pulled every remaining thought from my mind. "I could eat an entire cow right now. I hope they have a steak the size of your chest in there."

I felt my eyebrow lift in amusement.

She laughed as she dug through her clutch for something, mumbling to herself, "I swear I'm normally more intelligent than this."

I wanted to protest that Ruby was ebullient and refreshing. But I held my tongue; this time, her observation hadn't really seemed to bother her.

"My brother will be there," I reminded her. "And his friends. I hope this is okay. They're good people, just . . ."

"Guys?" she finished for me.

"In a manner of speaking, yes," I said with a smile.

"Oh, I can handle *guys*," she said, falling into step with me. I noted, perhaps not for the first time, that she had the ability to say things that might sound peckish had they come from my lips but sounded playful and lighthearted coming from hers.

"I imagine you can."

Turning to look up at me at the hostess stand, she said quietly, "Is that a compliment?"

Her eyes twinkled under the spots of overhead lights just inside the bar, and again, she seemed to know already that whether or not it was a compliment, it certainly wasn't an insult. The truth was, it had been praise. What I should have said was that she seemed able to handle almost anything.

"I wouldn't dream of insulting any of your skills."

"See?" She shook her head a little. With a teasing smile, she said, "I can't tell if you're messing with me. You're so dry. Maybe I should have you hold up a sign."

I hummed in response, giving her a wink before turning to the hostess. "We're meeting some people here." And as I spoke, just over her shoulder I spotted my brother and his friends. "Ah, there they are."

Without thinking, I took Ruby's elbow and led her to a table surrounded by low, velvet couches and plush ottomans. Her arm was warm and toned, but once I realized how close to flirtation this had come I released it. It was the way I would lead a date to a table, not a coworker.

Our approach was noted when we were still several tables away, and the men seated—Max, Will, Bennett, and George—stopped talking to watch us. Ruby was tall but slight in a sort of gangly way, but you wouldn't particularly dwell on it. Her posture was perfect, her chin always straight. She had the grace of a long-limbed woman just barely inside the door to adulthood.

Four pairs of eyes moved from Ruby's face down her svelte body to her feet and back up before turning to me with renewed brightness.

Bloody hell.

I knew without having to hear one word from his mouth what my wanker of a brother was thinking. I gave him a subtle shake of my head but his grin only expanded.

Everyone stood, greeting me and introducing themselves to Ruby in turn. Hands were grasped, names given, and pleasantries exchanged. A tangle of nerves clutched me. This no longer felt like a business dinner or even a social dinner with my mates. It felt somehow that Ruby was on display, that I was presenting her. That this was an *introduction*.

"I feel like I'm at a job interview," she said as she took her seat beside George on a red velvet sofa. "All these *suits*."

I swallowed, feeling my face heat in embarrassment and relief as I realized she hadn't shared my sense about the evening. We hadn't been flirting after all.

I was rubbish at reading cues.

"The danger of Midtown, I'm afraid," Bennett said with an easy smile, and waved down the waitress to come take our order.

"A gin and tonic, with as many limes as you can get in there," Ruby said, and then glanced briefly at the limited bar menu. "And the prosciutto sandwich, please."

A woman with a fondness for gin and tonics, my favorite evening cocktail? Christ almighty. Even Max caught my eye, brows raised as if to say, *Well, well, well.*

"I'll have the same," I said, handing the waitress the menu. "Though one lime is fine."

"So how do you all know each other?" Ruby asked Max.

"Well," he tilted his head toward me, "this one's my younger brother, of course."

Ruby smiled. "I heard there's quite a gaggle of you."

"That's right," Max said with a small laugh. "Ten of us." He pointed to the men at his side. "Bennett here I met in uni; Will I met when I moved to New York and we made the poor decision to open a business together—"

"Your wallet cries in regret daily," Will said, dryly.

"George here works with my wife, Sara," Max finished.

"I'm her Boy Friday," George clarified. "In charge of schedule, refilling the flasks in her desk, and hiding Page Six from her whenever she and Max get caught out and about."

With the five of us already acquainted, our attention justifiably fell to Ruby, though I suspect mine may have regardless. In the dim candlelight, and against the backdrop of mirrored walls, heavy velvet curtains, and the dramatic polished wooden décor, she seemed to nearly glow.

"How long have you lived in London?" Bennett asked. "You're clearly not British."

"San Diego native," she said and reached up to tuck a strand of her hair behind her ear.

Bennett's eyebrows rose. "My wife and I were married at the Hotel Del on Coronado."

"Gorgeous!" Ruby's smile could light this room in the dead of night. "I've been to a couple of weddings there and they were stunning." Ruby thanked the waitress when she set down her drink, and lifted it to take a sip. "I graduated last June and moved to London in September, so about six months," she said. "I'm in the internship program for one year at Richardson-Corbett, but I'm attending Oxford this fall for graduate school."

"Ah, another urban planner?" Max asked, glancing over at me.

"No," Ruby said, shaking her head a little. "Structural engineering."

My brother sighed in mock relief. "So then you'll agree with me that urban planning is the most boring profession ever created?"

Laughing, Ruby shook her head again. "I hate to disappoint you, but I was an urban planning–public policy minor."

Max groaned playfully. "I hope to eventually come back to Southern California in a superhero costume and completely revolutionize the mass transit system there, or the lack thereof."

I found myself leaning closer a little, to hear her better.

"Southern California is clogged with cars," she said in the continued silence. "Everyone travels between southern cities by car and train, but there isn't an easy way to navigate cities from within without driving. Los Angeles grew so fast and so wide without an integrated transportation system, so it will be about retrofitting an already complicated urban setting."

Looking to me, she said as an aside, "It's why I want to work with Maggie." Taking a drink then going back to the others, she explained, "Margaret Sheffield, the woman I hope to study under, helped design building infrastructure around established Tube stations and in tight urban spaces. She's kind of a genius."

Even Bennett joined the rest of us in regarding her with a mixture of curiosity and awe.

"Jesus Christ. How *old* are you, Ruby?" George exclaimed.

I was grateful to have George at the table. He was willing to ask all of the questions I wanted to, but never would.

She reached up, tucked her hair behind her ear again in a gesture I'd come to translate as her single, uncomfortable tell. "Twenty-three."

"You're practically a zygote," George said, groaning. "All that ambition and you're not even a quarter century old."

"Well, how old are *you*?" she asked, her sunshine grin taking over her entire face. "You don't look much older than me."

"I don't want to talk about it," George whined. "It's depressing. I'm practically approaching Viagra."

"He's *twenty seven*," Will answered, shoving George playfully.

"But seriously. Let's get to the important stuff," George said. "Do you have a boyfriend, adorable-twenty-three-year-old-Ruby?" My attention darted down and I stared intently at my drink. "And does he have an equally adorable gay friend?"

"I have a brother," she hedged, and then frowned apologetically. "*I* find him to be pretty adorable, but sadly, he's straight. I could have made a fortune charging my girlfriends for sleepovers in high school."

Bennett nodded and said, "I like your entrepreneurial spirit."

George leaned in, saying, "Don't think I didn't notice the way you sidestepped the boyfriend question. Do I need to play matchmaker while you're in New York?"

"I honestly don't think you want to go there." Ruby lifted her glass and perched her straw on her lips, meeting my eyes. "This one here can attest, only a half hour ago I looked like a streetwalking crackhead."

"On the contrary," I argued. "No one wears a hotel robe with more dignity."

She giggled and then coughed as she swallowed. "You're my favorite liar."

"I'm being sincere," I told her, putting my tumbler back

down on a cocktail napkin. "I was also impressed with the way you managed to get a hair pointed in each direction. Few can achieve that simply by napping in a hotel bed."

She shrugged, her smile nearly giddy over our verbal banter. "Many have tried to teach me the ways of sleek hairstyling. Many have failed."

I looked up to a table of grown men, watching us with rapt interest. I was definitely going to get the third degree from Max later.

"So, no boyfriend," George said, grinning wolfishly.

"Nope," she answered.

"And not interested in anyone in particular?"

Ruby's mouth opened and immediately snapped closed as her cheeks bloomed pink. And then she blinked around the table, narrowing her eyes. "You can't tell me you guys all get together for drinks and talk about relationships. Are we moving on to shoes next?"

Bennett tilted his head toward George. "It's this one. Get him in a bar and it's always like this."

"I've told you a hundred times, Ben-Ben," George drawled, "you're the boss in the day, I'm the boss after dark."

Bennett stared at him coolly, and I watched George struggle to not fidget under the pressure. "George," he said, finally, fighting a laugh, "you have never said that to me."

In a burst of relieved laughter, George said, "I know but it sounded so good. I'm just trying to impress Ruby."

"Ruby, you're going to steal George away from me," Will said, smiling.

"Not likely." George reached forward to tap Will's nose with each word: "She. Doesn't. Have. The. Right. Parts."

"Okay, then," Bennett said, lifting his drink and taking a long swallow. "Back to discussing body parts. All is normal."

———

A silence fell over the table as everyone turned to watch Ruby leave the bar and head upstairs to bed. She had been utterly charming throughout dinner, and the group had groaned in unison when she'd excused herself because of our early morning. I, too, had been quite sad to see her go.

"Well, well."

I looked up to see my brother's smug expression.

"Now that we're alone," Will began, "I think we can all agree to drop any pretense that we're not ruined for civilized conversation, yes?" Each of them nodded in agreement and beside me, his glass now refilled, Will raised his tumbler to take a small swallow of scotch. "I also think we can all agree Bennett will be an important consultant on this case."

Max snickered.

"The conference?" I asked, confused.

"It's an all-too-common predicament," Bennett added dryly. "Knockout intern. Boss in denial. I'll draft up a step-by-step plan of containment."

I blinked, swallowing thickly as I realized what they meant. "She's not *my* intern. I have absolutely no say in her career." I shook my head, frustrated because it was exactly the wrong thing to say. "I'm not . . . that is to say, she's not interested. Nor I."

All four men laughed.

"Niall," Will said, leaning his elbows on his knees. "She nearly dropped her drink in your lap when George asked if she was interested in anyone."

"Was going to say the same thing," Bennett said.

"And something tells me she'd be first to volunteer to clean it up," Will added.

"Well, maybe that's because she's interested in someone who works with us at R-C."

"Yeah. *You*." Max lifted his glass and finished the last of the amber liquid.

"Sincerely," I said, fighting a smile. "She's a fantastic girl, but she's certainly not a romantic option for me."

Tilting his head, Bennett asked, "What color are her eyes?"

Green, I didn't say. I shook my head as if I didn't know.

"What was she wearing?" Will asked.

A blue dress that hit just above her knee, I didn't say. *A delicate gold chain around her neck and a ring on her right ring finger that I had to resist asking her about until George bulldozed in and asked about a boyfriend.*

I rolled my eyes, and my brother laughed again, this time pointing his drink at me. "Blokes don't notice these things unless they're *interested*."

"Or George," Will added, and George reached over to grab the back of his neck and try to pull him in for a kiss.

"Well, it's apparent I needn't think on this any further," I said. "You've all decided for me."

"It's what we do," Will said, adjusting the skewed collar of his shirt as he settled back into his chair. "It's a sickness, we know."

"I thought we'd lost that muscle, honestly," George said.

"It's a relief to know we still have it in us. The ladies will be so proud." Max rapped his knuckles on the table as he made to stand. "Alas, I'd best be off. New routine: Sara gets the baby to sleep; I do the midnight bottle feeding."

"Finally taking a bottle from you then? Guess you smell like a woman, too," I said to Max, reminding him of the little dig he'd thrown my way on my last visit.

Max laughed and patted me on the back, and we all stood, a silent agreement in place that we were ready to call it a night. I watched my brother gather his things and say his goodbyes, feeling the same mix of pride and longing for what he was headed home to: a wife, a daughter. A proper home.

"Kiss the girls for me," I requested as he made his way out of the bar. He waved a hand, retreating, and then disappeared from view. The hotel bar felt completely deserted, silent in an immediate way now that the four men had left.

I wanted to put a better name to the longing I felt watching him go. It wasn't tinged with envy or bitterness over my own circumstances. It was that I'd realized, when visiting Max and Sara only weeks ago, that I *knew* what I wanted— stability, a wife, a family—but now I was so far behind. I'd never been great with change, and it was daunting to face the prospect of altering my expectations about life and my future post-divorce.

I hadn't realized until now how I'd put off even *thinking* about what life looked like from here on out and how to make it what I wanted. I'd simply hit pause. For seven months I'd neatly plowed ahead: diving into work, into footie and rowing on the weekend, the occasional evenings out with my mates, Archie and Ian.

But to get what I wanted, I'd need to put myself out there and meet someone.

And now, through the power of suggestion—from Tony, from Max and Will and Bennett, even George—or maybe simply from being in the presence of a hypnotically beautiful and sweet woman, my mind immediately wondered if Ruby *could* be the type of woman I'd date.

But I didn't want to move toward Ruby simply because others thought I should, or because I had a space to fill in my life. Of course I found her attractive and—in the private spaces of my mind—could easily imagine having a go.

Could I ever be in a relationship with passion and honesty, with a degree of loyalty I'd never felt from Portia? My loyalty had always been first to her, but hers had never wavered from her parents, leaving me a distant second. It hadn't struck me as off, but in hindsight I knew it meant we would never have been able to be true partners in our marriage.

In the past year or two I'd come to realize I'd been resigned to Portia as my lot simply because she carried so much of my history with hers. But, despite my hesitation and oft-noted reserve, I was raised in a house of passion, and children, and the most absurd sort of adventure. Though I wasn't the one to pull the trigger on spontaneity and wildness, I needed it around me in the passive way that we also need air, or warmth.

Ruby's mischievous face lingered in my thoughts as I took the lift to our floor.

It seemed as though she was placed in front of me at the perfect time. Not necessarily so I could approach her romantically, but so I could gain perspective on how many different types of women were out there—and that they weren't all like Portia.

The process of splitting up a shared life with Portia into two separate ones was an excruciating, gradual process. First, it was the flat: with almost no discussion, we'd decided it went to her. Next, it was the car: also hers. She kept the dog, the furniture, and a sizable portion of the savings. I let it all go, strikingly unburdened.

Portia was my first kiss, my first love, my first everything. Married at nineteen, I'd believed in staying married despite misery, unfashionable as that view might have been.

It was simply that, one day, our misery reached a point where I could see no point to it.

I couldn't see her being passionate with me ever again, and for myself as well our lovemaking had long since taken on a sort of mechanical, transactional flavor. There had been no mention of children in years and, to be fair, I was unable to imagine Portia ever loving her children the way my mother had loved us: with enthusiastic kisses planted to our bellies and constant physical reminders of motherly adoration. Now, months away from the divorce, I wondered how I'd ever imagined a life with her: clean, cold, everything in its place.

In the end, our divorce had started over something as innocuous as a rescheduled lunch. I'd received notice of a meeting that would run into the time we were meant to arrive at the restaurant midday. Portia often worked from home, but an hour of flexibility turned out to be too much to ask.

"Do you ever consider *my* day?" she asked. "Do you ever consider what I put aside to spend time with you?"

I thought back to the romantic holidays she'd canceled, and the anniversary dinners she had missed because she stayed late at a friend's flat and forgot or, once, extended her girls' holiday for another week simply because she was having too much fun to come home.

"I endeavor to," I told her.

"But you fail, Niall. And, honestly, I'm sick of it."

Being Portia, she needed to have the last word. And in that moment, with a sharp clarity I hadn't expected, I was fine with that as the last word. I simply wanted out.

"I understand, Portia. You can only do so much."

She'd startled slightly at the use of her given name; I'd only ever called her "Love," for years. "That's just it," she said wearily. "Niall. I'm swamped. I simply can't live my life and carry the weight of all this, as well."

All this, she said, meaning: us. Meaning: the burden of a loveless marriage.

She looked up at me, eyes moving across my face, down my neck, and to where my hands were comfortably resting in the pockets of my trousers.

I could never escape the feeling that, when she looked at me like that, she was comparing me to someone else. Someone more posh, less tall, more American, less patient with her.

After what felt like minutes of ticking silence, she spoke again.

"We aren't," she began with exquisite understatement, "very natural together anymore."

And that had been it.

Five

Ruby

When my alarm went off at six, it felt like I'd only just closed my eyes.

From beneath my pillow I could tell the room was still dark. Even so, I could hear the echo of horns from the city outside, the bustle of people up and out and already braving the chilly morning, on their way to work or school or whatever adulting they had to do.

I rolled to my side, doing the mental calculation of how many more times I could hit snooze and not be late, when I remembered exactly where I was . . .

Who I was with . . .

How much *fun* I'd had last night.

And whose bed was likely just on the other side of mine, separated by nothing more than an insignificant, paper-thin wall.

He could be in bed, right now. I closed my eyes and let myself imagine that, and suddenly getting ready for a day spent with him felt way more important than sleep.

I leapt out of the bed and raced toward the bathroom,

careful to avoid any and all mirrors along the way. Today would be my first day of the summit. My first day working alongside Niall Stella, learning and being a part of what he did, not just a moving piece in the periphery.

And after last night, I saw him so differently. He was still the man who preferred to remain at the perimeter, watching and taking note of what was said and *how*, but he'd also been this relaxed, funny *guy*, with a bunch of other guys, just enjoying a drink in a bar. He could unwind, be social, laugh at himself and others in his gentle way.

He'd teased me again—in front of his brother—his dark eyes shining with amusement and fondness. I felt my stomach swoop low, my heart trip in my chest as I remembered. Would he be like this the entire trip? And if he was, how would I manage to keep from falling at his feet, professing my love?

Gah.

I could name at least a hundred ways in which I could screw this up on a normal workday. But today? Tired *and* suffering the effects of jet lag? Who knew what could happen.

I could practically feel the heavy bags under my eyes, but even so, a jolt of adrenaline surged through my veins. My heart raced when I imagined us working so closely together today, both of us bent over a file on the table, our shoulders side by side and his soft hair falling down over his forehead.

This was going to be a train wreck for sure.

Food was the last thing on my mind, but I needed to bring my A-game today. I ordered room service and was thrilled to hear the little doorbell only minutes after I stepped from the shower.

The scent of breakfast wafted in from the hallway, and any thought of not being hungry flew right out the window. I raced to the door, stopping to double-check the modesty of my robe before I let the waiter in, because it was far too early to find the humor in any accidental wardrobe malfunctions.

I signed the bill and was just closing my door when Niall Stella walked down from the elevators.

Holy hell. He had been to the gym.

"Good morning, Ruby."

Stay cool, Ruby. You've got this. "Morning. You're up early." I said.

The Number of Times I'd Seen Niall Stella Sweaty: one.

I tried to covertly look him over, but subtlety was a wasted effort. I thought Niall Stella knew how to wear a suit, but he wore T-shirts like it was his life's calling. I wanted to pray at the altar of his dark, sincerely tight blue shirt. He wore it so unself-consciously. So unironically. Knowing him, he picked it out for some complicated aerodynamic reason. And holy lord did it do wonderful things to his chest.

His posture was straight, stomach flat, and chest defined and bulkier than I'd expected. He wore what looked like soccer shorts and his legs were just as muscular as I imagined. Seeing him like this, I was struck by his height all over again. I was on the tall side and I'd never been around a man who made me feel so tiny and feminine. This close to him, and with the clean scent of his sweat between us, I was starkly aware of my curves, my mouth, and how he towered over me by several inches. Without effort, everything about him was so dramatically masculine.

"Room service delivery of Fritos?" he teased, and motioned to my robe.

I looked down and laughed. "I was planning on wearing this for the rest of the month, hope that works for you." I tugged on the tie and watched as his eyes followed the movement.

Sweet Lord.

I wanted to reach out and drag him to me, using the neck of his shirt to pull him down on the bed. Or maybe I could wrap the sweaty hem of it around my wrist, use it for leverage while he fucked me from behind . . .

Oh.

I felt my cheeks grow warm.

He leaned a broad shoulder against the wall, facing me. "The dress you wore last night was rather lovely. Perhaps you could alternate days?"

I laughed. "I—"

Wait, what?

My eyes went wide as I processed what he'd said. His

cheeks were pink, too, but he held my gaze. *Don't get flustered, Ruby. Don't get flustered.*

"That's a good idea," I said, feeling an enormous grin invade my face. I pretended to smooth the skirt of the robe down my thighs. "This might be a bit drafty."

Nodding, he seemed to bite the inside of his cheek to keep from smiling. "I suspect it would be."

I pointed my thumb behind me. "So . . . I'll just go put on some actual clothes."

"All right. Let me shower and I'll meet you downstairs?" he asked as I turned to go back in my room.

Imaginary Secretary, please add Watching Niall Stella Shower to my bucket list. Move it to the top, if it's not too much trouble.

"Good plan."

He nodded once crisply. "I'll be fast."

"No," I said, too loud, too quickly. I closed my eyes, inhaling a calming breath. "Take your time."

He paused with his keycard inserted into the door next to mine and looked over his shoulder at me. The tiny smile told me he read every thought on my face before I had a chance to pull it into order.

"All right?" he asked quietly.

"I'm good. Just need coffee."

His eyes twinkled with some mysterious delight. As if he enjoyed my absolute, desperate torment. "Right, then. See you downstairs."

Game on, Mr. Darcy.

The elevator ride to the lobby was the longest of my life. I counted down each floor on the screen near the top, my nerves twisting tighter the farther down I went. Niall would be waiting for me and then we'd walk to the temporary office together. Just us. No distractions. Alone. No big deal.

Except that it was a *huge* deal. This was the start of one of my most exciting professional experiences, and also a day full of the person I was fairly sure was the Most Amazing Man on the Planet.

I smoothed my dress, straightened the collar on my jacket, and double-checked everything: purse, laptop, cell phone, ass and underwear covered. Despite my nerves, I was still tired. My laptop case felt heavier than normal and seemed to weigh down my right shoulder, the combination of fatigue and jitters leaving me feeling slightly speedy.

I checked my reflection again in the gleaming doors, suddenly questioning my outfit. It would be cold out but likely too warm in the office, where the heat would be turned up to compensate for the March chill. I'd chosen knee-length boots with a reasonable heel; they would double as both comfortable to walk in, and warm enough should our day find us venturing out into the city and down into one of the many subway stations we'd be monitoring. I had every file and report I would need printed out. I was ready.

And yet, still terrified.

I reached the lobby and looked around for Niall, but I didn't have to look long. He was behind me, back near the registration desk, and *help me Jesus* because paired with the overcoat he had slung over his arm, his suit was straight-up business porn.

"Holy shit, you wear a suit well."

I'd thought those words a hundred times over the last few months. Thousands. I'd said them under my breath as I'd passed him in the halls and it was possible I'd had more than one X-rated fantasy that started out with those exact words. But never, not in any of them did he swallow, look down the length of my body, and reply with "I suspect you wear everything well."

And then immediately look like he wanted to shove the words back into his mouth and die.

Pardon?

When I was little I had an Etch A Sketch. I spent hours staring at that red frame and flat gray board, pulling it out to doodle whenever my bus was late or while entertaining myself on a drive home. Most people drew pictures or played games, but I was obsessed with drawing my name and perfecting the art of getting each letter down without seeing the line where they connected.

My mom would tell me to draw something else, that I would burn the image of those letters into the screen if I continued to do the same thing, over and over. And she was right. Eventually, no matter how many times I shook the board, hoping to clear the image, a ghost of the letters still showed on the screen.

I knew this would be the exact same thing, but it would be branded on my brain for the rest of time.

I suspect you wear everything well.

Had Niall Stella really said that? Was I having a stroke? Would I ever think of any other sentence for the rest of my life?

When I came to my senses, I realized he was already off and nearly gone. I quickened my steps and followed him out the hotel's revolving door and left, down Fifty-Sixth Street.

I suspect you wear everything well.

"—all right?" he said, and I blinked.

"I'm sorry, what?" I asked, rushing to keep up with his long strides. Seriously, walking beside him was like galloping next to a giraffe.

"I asked if my assistant Jo had sent everything along? Whether everything had come across all right? Normally I wouldn't send you things, as you're not working for me here, but thought it might be best if we were both on the same page."

"Oh, yes. Yes," I said, nodding. "Emails arrived yesterday as soon as we'd landed. She's very . . . efficient."

Niall Stella blinked over to me with his obscenely long lashes. "She is."

"How long has she worked for you?" I asked, my voice sounding a bit distracted, even to my own ears. I'd never been with him out in broad daylight like this, and I was feeling flustered with just how good-looking he was: his skin was gorgeous, clear and smooth and absolutely flawless. It was obvious he took his time shaving, and everything was perfect, right down to his sideburns. I wondered if he measured them with a ruler.

He considered this. "Four years, this twelfth of September."

"Wow. That's . . . specific."

He smiled, looking back to his phone.

I suspect you wear everything well.

The morning air was cool on my face, and I closed my eyes, grateful for the touch of biting wind this morning. It helped clear my head as we covered the first block, and turned right onto Avenue of the Americas.

Only now did it occur to me that this was my first morning in New York City. London felt like a city, yes, and it was huge. But I always had the sense that I was standing in a place that had been there for centuries, that the trees and buildings and even the walkways I strolled on looked much like they had since they were put in. New York clearly had its older buildings, but many things were modern and new, steel and glass that stretched to the sky. It seemed to be in a constant cycle of rebirth. Scaffolding lined much of the sidewalks and we simply walked under it, or followed signs that led us around.

I tried to use this time to go over what might be waiting for us today: setting up meetings with the local officials, getting the complete schedule of all the different speakers, and compiling a list of which stations were most in need of repairs.

But I couldn't focus, and each time the sound of traffic dulled and my thoughts finally started to string together, Niall would walk around someone and brush my shoulder. Maybe notice a loose board in a construction walkway, and touch my forearm while pointing it out in warning. We'd walked five minutes and if someone had asked what I'd been thinking about, I would have stuttered out some unintelligible nonsense and laughed awkwardly.

We reached the corner and waited for the signal to walk. Niall pocketed his phone and stood a respectable distance away from me, but close enough that the arm of his jacket brushed against mine when I hitched my bag higher on my shoulder. The morning was cold, and each one of his exhales sent a little puff of condensation out into the air in front of him. I had to force myself not to stare at his lips and the way his tongue peeked out to wet them.

When the light changed, the crowd moved in front of us, and I felt the press of his palm on the small of my back, urging me forward.

His hand on my lower back . . . just inches away from my ass. And if he was going to touch my ass, it was basically the same as him touching me between my legs. So, yes, my brain reacted like Niall Stella was touching my clit and I nearly tripped and sprawled flat in the intersection.

We reached the sidewalk on the other side, and he seemed to make a conscious effort to slow his steps.

"You don't have to slow down," I told him. "I can keep up."

Niall Stella shook his head. "Sorry?" he asked, feigning innocence. So one: he was trying to be polite and not point out that my far shorter legs were struggling to keep up with his. And two: he was a terrible liar.

"You're like eight feet tall with legs that are twice as long as mine. Of course you'd walk faster than me. But I can keep up, I promise not to slow you down."

A hint of a blush warmed his cheeks and he smiled. "You were nearly falling down there for a moment," he teased, motioning behind us. My heart was racing, and it had nothing to do with sprinting down the streets of New York.

"I was trying to be smooth and pretend that didn't happen," I said, laughing. I was glad he kept his eyes forward, because my grin was so wide it was about to crack my face in half. "Forget the fancy shoes, next time I'll wear my Nikes."

"Those aren't bad," he said, nodding toward my boots. "Quite nice, really. I remember Portia would wear the highest heels, even when we'd travel. She'd—" He paused, glancing over to me as if just realizing I wouldn't know any of this. "Sorry. Won't bore you with the details of all that."

Whoa, what?

Even in profile, I could see the way his brows drew together in a frown. He clearly hadn't intended a stroll down memory lane, but I couldn't deny the secret, dark part of me that delighted in the slip. That he'd let himself get into that comfortable place where he'd let his walls down, for just a moment.

"Portia was your wife?" I asked, keeping my tone conversational, light. Definitely not showing that I was hanging on his every word. He'd mentioned her on the plane, but hadn't ever said her name.

We walked a few steps before he nodded, but didn't add any more. I'd only seen the ex–Mrs. Stella in passing, but hadn't known it was her until she was gone, and it was too late to scrutinize every detail. I'd heard stories, little bits here and there, but never much. There seemed to be some kind of unspoken rule about gossip in the office: a little is encouraged, but too many details would just be poor taste.

We passed a trio of beautiful bronze and verdigris green headless statues in front of a towering skyscraper, one set on one side of the building, and two on the other. "Those are supposed to represent Venus de Milo," I said, pointing them out. "They're called *Looking Toward the Avenue*."

He followed my gaze. "But they have no heads," he noted. "They aren't looking anywhere."

"I hadn't really thought of that," I said. "Lovely breasts, though."

Niall made a sound as if he was choking.

"What?" I asked, laughing at his expression. "They are! The city actually gets a lot of complaints about them."

"The breasts or lack of heads?" he asked.

"Maybe both?"

"How on earth do you know all this? You said you'd never been here before."

"My mom had this sort of romanticized fascination with New York. I could be your tour guide and bore you with lots of random stuff."

"That sounds like an amazing time," he said, but his tone was strange. Was he being sarcastic, or—

Oh my God.

I stopped dead in my tracks, and Niall Stella had to turn. "What is it?" he asked, looking on ahead, as if he could make out whatever had caught my eye. "Is everything all right?"

"Radio City Music Hall," I gasped, continuing on with quicker steps now.

"Iconic," he agreed with a hint of amused confusion in his voice, easily keeping up with me as I practically sprinted closer.

"They do a Christmas show here every year and my mom is going to die that I'm this close." My gloves made it nearly impossible to grasp on to anything as I fumbled in the pocket of my jacket in search of my phone. "Will you take a picture of me?"

You'd have thought I just asked him to draw me in the nude.

"I can't—" he said, and then shook his head, looking around us. "What I mean to say is, we can't just *stand* here."

"Why not?"

"Because it's . . ."

He didn't say "undignified" out loud, but his face was screaming it.

I looked around where we stood, at the scores of people doing that very same thing. "Nobody's paying any attention to us. We could probably make out on the sidewalk and people would just walk right by."

His eyes grew wide before he sighed and pulled out his phone. "I'll do it on mine and send to you. Your case is covered in hideous girly rhinestones." A tiny smile pulled at the corner of his mouth. "Look at me. I'm far too masculine for such a thing."

I'd had a taste of it last night, but I was still blindsided seeing it again: Niall Stella was polite, brilliant, refined, and contained, yes, but Niall Stella was capable of being a *guy*, and he was a *total* flirt.

I knew I was pushing my luck, but damn, he looked so

cute standing there, a sea of tourists rushing by while he opened the camera app. He might have been protesting but the expression on his face when he snapped the first picture made him look a little . . . charmed?

"Right," he said, and turned the phone to show me. "Quite lovely."

"Okay now, you come here." He crossed toward me and I took his phone, examining the photo. "Let's get one together," I said, holding his phone out in front of us.

"Wha—" he started to say, but thought better of it. "Your arms aren't long enough."

"Are you kidding me? My selfie game is strong. Just . . . bend your knees a little, this is like my head and your deltoids, which—don't get me wrong—isn't a bad thing, but—"

"I can't believe I'm doing this," he said, snatching the phone from my hand.

"I promise I won't tell Max you took a selfie on Sixth Avenue," I whispered, and he turned his head, eyes meeting mine.

He was only inches from my face. We were practically married right then.

He held my gaze for a fraction of a second before he cleared his throat. "I'm holding you to that."

It took a few tries to get the right angle, and for the last one, he wrapped an arm around my waist, and pulled me in tight.

And that was it. I mentally entered a "one" in the

Number of Times Niall Stella Put His Arm Around My Waist and Pulled Me Close column. I knew right then what it would feel like to celebrate Christmas and birthdays and a job promotion and have the best orgasm of my life all at the same time.

He looked at the photo and turned the screen so I could see. It was a good picture, fucking great actually. We were both smiling; the camera caught us mid-laugh as he'd tried to snap the photo with his gloves still on.

"What's your number?" he asked, looking down at his screen. I watched as his cheeks grew redder than they were already from the sharp, cold wind.

I recited it, watching as he typed. He hit SEND and smiled up at me: a little shy, a little playful, a little something else I wasn't sure I was ready to believe. In that moment, he didn't look anything like a vice president, an intimidating ultra-crush, or a man who finished school before he was twenty. He just looked like a beautiful guy, outside in the city with me.

In the pocket of my coat, my phone buzzed.

I tried not to think about the fact that he now had pictures of me, and of the two of us together, on his *phone*. I tried not to think about the fact that he now had my cell number. I tried not to think about how easy it had just been between us, when I stopped worrying about how to act around Niall Stella, and had just enjoyed this unguarded moment with Niall. Just Niall.

As he pocketed his phone and motioned for me to follow him to the crosswalk, I noted his enormous grin.

I tried not to think about how he looked pretty thrilled with all of this, too.

⌐══════⌐

Our temporary office was on an empty floor of a large commercial building. The entire suite had been rented as temporary office space for visiting consultants by the Metropolitan Transportation Authority. It's true, beggars can't be choosers, but honesty time: our office was the size of my hotel shower, and the heater was clearly cranked up to Sinner's Inferno. The window had been permanently painted shut, and we figured that out only after Niall struggled with it for a good five minutes. He definitely had my attention the entire time. His broad back demanded separate billing: Niall Stella and The Deltoids.

I suspect you wear everything well.

Too small an office meant Niall was mere feet from me all day, making it nearly impossible to concentrate on even the simplest task. And too hot meant that within an hour of arriving he'd removed his suit jacket and—after much visible consternation on his part—loosened his tie and unfastened the top button of his shirt. He'd also rolled his sleeves up his forearms. If I could, I probably would have ratcheted the thermostat up another ten degrees to get a peek at his bare chest. See also: why I should never be in charge.

I'd never seen his forearms before (a giddy check in the Number of Times I've Seen Niall Stella's Bare Forearms column), and, as expected, his skin was perfect: arms toned and wrists tapering into long, slender fingers. As covertly as possible, I watched the ticking of muscles when he typed, the way they flexed in sequence as he spun a pencil around his desk when he was thinking, the way the tendons in his hands tightened as he drummed his fingertips on the arm of the chair.

Niall Stella was a fidgeter.

We didn't talk much as we worked at our respective desks, sifting through boxes and setting things up. For lunch we stepped out, stopping at a vendor selling hot dogs from a stand on the corner. This took some persuasion on my part.

"You go to the one with the longest line," I explained, patiently waiting my turn. "Don't you ever watch the Food Network? See how there's a huge wait for this one and only two people in line for the one across the street? The short-line hot dogs are probably made out of feral cat."

He sighed, muttering something in his posh accent about how he'd probably be dead by the end of the day, and throwing a "You call these chips?" in there, too.

"How *does* your brother survive in a city with such meager offerings?" I teased.

"No idea."

"What are you doing?" I asked, stopping him as he went to put some fancy vomit-colored mustard across the bun. It had *seeds*, for God's sake.

He blinked at me, bottle held aloft over his hot dog like we weren't even speaking the same language.

"You can't put that on a street dog," I told him. "There are rules about these things."

"You enjoy your generic, artificially colored *mustard*," he said, and I could practically see the air quotes suspended above his head, "and I'll use mine." Our new marriage could already use some counseling.

I moaned a lot while eating my dog, just to prove a point: it was way better than his.

He closed his eyes in suppressed amusement, shaking his head at me.

"You know," I said after swallowing a giant bite, "if I didn't occasionally catch you smiling in that little secret way you have, I might assume you were either the most disciplined emotional being on the planet, a Replicant, or Botoxed."

"It's Botox." He took an enormous bite of his hot dog.

"I knew it," I said. "You can barely hide your vanity."

He choked-laughed, and reached to steal the napkin I had in my hand. "Too right."

We returned to the office, but with the phone lines not working yet and the heat (I may at one point have complained that I was melting), nothing was really getting done. Meetings started the next day, we'd unpacked a few boxes of files, but we both seemed distracted—for different reasons, I'm sure—and by two that afternoon, he was already packing his things up to go.

Niall had plans he needed to look at and phone calls to make, all of which he could take care of in the hotel.

We walked back in silence, on the opposite side of the street from Radio City, but I could have sworn I saw his lips twitch the tiniest bit as we passed.

⸻

The next morning, I woke before my alarm clock, anxious to start the day and—you know, because I'm pathetic—walk to work with a certain someone. But there on my phone, next to a text from my brother and three from Lola, was one from that Someone: Take a car and go on without me. I've a few things to do and will be there later.

The hope inside my chest crumbled like a dry cracker. I replied that I'd see him there and then walked the few blocks instead of taking a car, choosing a different route and taking a few photos for my mom along the way. When I reached the office it was still sweltering, and I sent a silent prayer of thanks for the short sleeves I'd worn and that I'd been smart enough to ditch my Spanx. It wasn't like there was anyone there I'd need to look marginally slimmer for, anyway.

It was boring as hell being there by myself, but the phones were working and I was finally able to get some work done, assure Tony that we were here and everything should be up and going soon, and meet a few of the other people sharing the offices with us. Niall showed up around noon, his arms full as he walked into the office.

He unloaded everything on his desk and chair, and I watched him with curious eyes.

"Morning," he said, hanging his coat on a hook near the door. "Or, afternoon, rather. Still hot as Hades in here, I see."

"I've called someone and they'll be here to fix it tomorrow, but you're lucky I kept my pants on."

"Debatable," he mumbled.

Or at least I thought he did.

"Pardon?"

He ignored this, putting a large shopping bag on his desk, and getting distracted by whatever he had inside. He wore his glasses, today. Good God. On anyone else, those particular frames—dark rims and a thin band of chrome slicing down the arms—would communicate a certain carefully crafted designer individuality. But I knew Niall Stella dressed impeccably because he bought the best and probably had a really picky, perfectionist tailor—not because he paid much attention to trends.

"A woman picked out your frames," I said, pointing to his face.

He looked up from his bag, setting a folder down on his desk and looking confused. "I'm sorry?"

"A saleswoman picked out those frames. You walked into the store, she descended in milliseconds because"—I glanced down his body in a gesture meant to communicate *I mean, obviously*—"and she insisted on finding just the right pair for you."

He studied me for several breaths and then lifted his gigantic, splendid Niall Stella hand to lower his glasses and asked, "What does *this* mean?" while repeating my gesture, his eyes on my body, his mouth suppressing a little smile.

"It means, 'a hot man in a suit walks into a store, and he doesn't have a wedding ring? Like a starter pistol to a greyhound.'"

"How do you know that when I bought these, I wasn't wearing a wedding ring?"

He was testing me. He was amused. Holy shit, Niall Stella was *still* being flirty today.

"You're suggesting my sleuth skills are subpar. That I don't know your timeline? I thought we established early on that my creeper dial goes up to eleven."

His eyebrow twitched in a tiny *Well?*

"You got those new glasses in November." He waited for the last piece of information. The one that made me sound completely insane. "Fine," I groaned. "You stopped wearing your ring in September."

He laughed, putting his glasses back on and returning to his digging in the bag.

"Do you think I'm weird?" I asked, voice weaker than I'd attempted.

He nudged his glasses down his nose again, letting his eyes move over my face before murmuring, "Yes, weird in the sense that you are unexpected and I am rarely surprised by people. I think you rather exquisite."

Exquisite? That was certainly an interesting adjective.

Before I had a chance to respond to this—and let's be fair, it probably would have taken me a decade—he stood up straighter, grinning. "I've brought you something. Reckoned it was almost lunch, so . . ." He pulled a white—albeit greasy—paper bag from his chair, and lifted a hot dog from inside. Covered in regular mustard.

"You lowered yourself to my classless mustard standards," I cooed, taking the dog happily.

"How could I deny you? You moaned through every bite yesterday."

Only then did it occur to me how that must have sounded. "I—"

"And until the repairman gets here . . ." He pulled a box from the bag to reveal a large desk fan.

"You bought a fan?"

"We wouldn't want you melting, now would we?"

And that was it. Finally bold enough, I stood and rounded the desk in front of him, and did what I'd wanted to do for six months: I straightened his tie. I took my time, using the opportunity to right the knot and smooth the silky material down his chest.

He sucked in a breath and I waited, worried that maybe I'd crossed a line, that perhaps I'd taken this small progress we'd made and ruined it by being too forward. The silence seemed to balloon between us, stretching, growing heavier with each tick of the clock.

"Thanks for lunch," I whispered.

"You're quite welcome." A tiny flicker of a smile, a flash of his dimple, and then his expression straightened and his eyes searched mine for a small eternity.

Finally—and while my pulse jackhammered in my throat—Niall took my hands, moving them up his body. I could feel his torso, the defined planes of his stomach beneath his dress shirt, and then his hard pectorals.

Now it was my turn to suck in a breath. The possibility of something happening between us had gone from an adorable little fantasy to a check mark in the Number of Times Niall Stella Ran My Hands Up His Chest column. What were we *doing*?

The faint scent of his cologne hung in the air, a hint of coffee and fresh paint from an office somewhere on the same floor. I leaned in slowly, my body on autopilot, my brain not even in control of the equipment anymore.

He leaned in, too: small, stuttering movements that made the space between us disappear. His nose brushed the edge of mine and I could see his eyelashes, feel his breath across my lips. I closed my eyes, not sure I could be this close to him and see these things and ever be the same again.

"Are you going to kiss me?" I asked, surprising myself as the words tumbled from my mouth.

His chest was pressed against mine, but he didn't do what I thought he would. He pulled away just enough to meet my eyes.

"I fear I wouldn't be able to stop," he whispered.

Life Alert? This is not a drill.

"Maybe I wouldn't want you to." His brows lifted but he didn't speak; instead he waited for me to continue. I wasn't sure I could, but eventually I managed, "I've thought about this exact moment, and what I would do or say."

He pulled back to better study my face. "You have?"

Closing my eyes, I admitted, "For months now."

This time his brows disappeared into his hairline and I barreled on: "I thought it would always just be a crush. I never really expected us to interact for any significant amount of time. But we're here and together a lot and this flirting is fun, but I'm about to completely lose my mind . . ." I looked up, meeting his wide eyes. My mouth had sprinted away from my brain, leaving it in the dust. I closed my eyes again, groaning. "And now I've made you uncomfortable."

When I looked at him again, I found him studying my

face, expression soft. "You haven't. Not at all. I'm just . . . unaccustomed."

"Unaccustomed to girls admitting they have crushes on you?" I attempted a lighthearted laugh but it came out really awkward, more bark than chuckle. "I have a hard time believing that."

"Well," he said, stepping back and shrugging a little apologetically, "it's true. As I mentioned, Portia is the only woman I ever . . . that is to say, there's been no one else." He ran a hand across the back of his neck. "Aside from the fact that this is a work meeting and we've only just met, there is *that* consideration. I feel a bit out of my depths here."

I gaped at him, at Niall Stella, the unexpected flirt with a body that screamed *I've-Had-All-of-the-Good-Sex-in-the-World*, who stood before me reminding me that he'd been with one woman his entire life. I knew he'd met Portia when he was young but it hadn't really sunk in until now that he'd only ever been with her. No high school manwhoring. No college years full of wild shagging. No early twenties with a different woman every night. Zero oats sowed.

I could practically feel my synapses reorganizing.

"So, you see," he said, smiling a little, "if you've any interest in me at all, you'll need to come into it knowing I'm driving quite blind."

And right then, when I expected him to hold his gaze to mine, to take my hand and squeeze it, or do any other

human thing to hold the moment, or at least acknowledge that a moment *occurred*, he blinked away, turned
to his desk, and began reading a report until I mumbled
something about needing to use the ladies' room, and
left.

SIX

Niall

Come meet us for a pint.

I'd only just returned to my room, my mind and gut in a twist, when the text from Max arrived. The only thing I wanted more than to fall face-first into my mattress was a pint.

In fact, what I wanted *most* was to be with Ruby.

How is it possible, I thought, *to have become infatuated in a matter of days? In a space of time that could still be easily measured in hours?*

There was a tiny part of me that seemed to be expanding, doubling inside my rib cage every day. This secret space, an unexplored romantic nucleus, told me the reason Ruby had burrowed so easily in my mind and under my skin was meaningful. And not because she was a rebound, or a distraction, but because she fit me. I wanted to trust this tumbling sensation I had near her not because the feeling was familiar, but because it *wasn't*.

And yet, when given the chance to explore things, I'd immediately closed up.

Best to bury my nose in a pint.

The blokes were down at Knave again, almost as if it was their regular haunt. I knew better; I knew my brother well enough to know he was going out of his way to keep an eye on me. That he could sense something was off in my mood.

He and the lads were seated around the same low table we'd inhabited the other evening, each halfway into a cocktail and snacking on the smattering of appetizers on the table. It was nearly eleven, and I hadn't eaten.

"Be a good chap and look to the side while I polish off the lot," I joked, sitting down next to Max and reaching for a small handful of mixed nuts.

He laughed. "Figured you'd be famished."

"What," Bennett asked, looking around as if searching, "no Ruby? I have to admit I'm a little disappointed."

"Ah . . ." I started, and then put an entire slice of bruschetta in my mouth to avoid answering.

"Think *she* might want a bite to eat?" Will asked.

Swallowing, I mumbled, "Frigging hell, you're all subtle. I'm sure she ordered in. And since we're on the subject of women: why are you lot constantly on me? I don't see your women around anywhere."

"Careful what you wish for," George said. "Chloe the Barbarian is meeting us here."

"Chloe the—I'm sorry, are you talking about Bennett's *wife*?" I asked, positive I must have misunderstood.

But Bennett waved me off. "Sara and Hanna are at

some sort of party. Chloe should be here shortly. And don't worry," he said. "They call each other much, much worse."

George shrugged and then leaned forward. "Chloe and I have a special bond. Namely being so terrible nobody else would want us." Bennett cleared his throat and George blinked over to him. "Except for him, and he's pretty rotten himself."

And as if she were summoned, one of the most beautiful women I'd ever seen walked into the bar. She wasn't tall, but she certainly carried herself as if she stood head and shoulders above everyone around her. Dark hair spilled half-way down her back and she wore a tight black dress and heels so high I feared for her ankles.

"Speak of the devil," Bennett said, and stood, watching with a proud smile as his wife walked toward him.

"Look away," Will said, just as Chloe reached us.

Confused, I glanced at each of the men before I blinked back up to Bennett and Chloe and had to quickly look away. To say that their embrace was passionate would be a gross understatement, and once again I felt the sting of my failed relationship, and the fact that I'd barely even pulled my head from the sand to join the world, let alone considered finding that for myself.

Will groaned. "Get a room, would you?"

Chloe kissed her husband once more before she turned her attention to us. "You're just jealous because your fian-cée is sitting with a bunch of women talking about books, instead of here, gazing adoringly at you."

"When you put it that way . . . yes, I am," Will said. "Why aren't you with them, again?"

Chloe ordered a drink from a passing waitress and took a seat at our table. "Because this is my only free night this week, and I intend to spend it banging my husband. Speaking of"—she looked at Bennett commandingly—"finish your drink."

Bennett lifted his glass. "Yes, ma'am."

"Gross," George said.

"George," Chloe said, greeting him with a smile.

"Dark Mistress," he replied.

"And you must be Niall?" she said, turning her attention to me.

"Yes," I said, and offered my hand. "Lovely to meet you."

Chloe returned my handshake with a firm grip. "You, too. Where's the girl?"

"Girl?" I asked, looking at each of them.

Chloe smiled, and I had to admit the effect was quite stunning—if somewhat frightening. I could only imagine the terror this woman could inflict on a poor soul when she put her mind to it.

"I assume she's talking about your Ruby," Max said.

"She is not *my* Ruby," I corrected.

"Sure she isn't," Chloe said. "That's what they all say."

As I was busy choking on a bite of truffled Tater Tot, the realization settled in. I'd nearly *kissed* her at *work*. "Right, you all settled this the other night."

"Course we did," George continued. "You're the only one who was confused. You turn into a robot around her—"

"To be fair, he's always a bit of a robot," Max cut in.

"Cheers, mate," I mumbled sarcastically. "Funny how I'm the only one here who seemed to be in the dark about it."

Chloe's drink had arrived, and she lifted the stemmed glass. "That's because men are idiots," she said over the rim. "I mean, don't get me wrong, women can be jackasses, too, and are every bit as capable of messing things up as men. But in my experience, when these things go wrong, it's usually the one with the penis who's fucked it up." She looked at me with her amused certainty for a moment before adding, "No offense."

"Well said," Max told her with a laugh.

They studied me for a few seconds longer before turning back to each other, picking up where they'd apparently left off when I joined them. All except for Chloe, who continued to eye me.

"You never said why you and the girls can't come to the Catskills this weekend," Bennett said to Max.

"Sara's remodeling the entire flat," Max said, running his palm over the top of his head. "Her designer is coming. I think walls are coming down and . . . *oi*."

"Max, you'd better get a handle on that," Bennett said in warning. "Do you remember when Chloe painted the apartment? A kid with a crayon would have done a better job."

"Watch it, Mills," she warned.

"Don't you start with that, *Ryan*," he said back. I was

completely confused. "The green kitchen? Even you have to admit how terrible that was."

"I will not. It was process of elimination; maybe I needed to try out a few before I knew what I really wanted," she said, smiling sweetly at him. It was pretty clear they weren't talking about paint colors.

George was already waving a finger at them both. "No, no, no, don't you bring your foreplay to this table."

"This remodeling with Sara is a very . . ." Max continued carefully, never one to criticize his wife. "A very *ongoing* situation."

"Delicate," Will added.

Laughing, my brother murmured, "A touch."

The waiter placed my pint on the table and asked if we needed anything more. I went ahead and ordered a second—best to be prepared, after all. The waiter looked at each of us and then, satisfied we were done, turned to leave.

Will leaned in as a strange hush overtook the table. "*George.* What about him? He's cute . . . right?"

"No!" George hissed. "That would be like fucking beef jerky."

"Good God," Bennett muttered, wiping his palm down his face. "No one is even talking about fucking. It's *one* party."

"Wait," Will said, shaking his head. "George, you're a *top*?"

Groaning, Max said, "For the love of God, William, stop talking."

I couldn't take it anymore. "What is happening here?"

George ignored all of us. "Seriously, he's pickled! He's so tan I bet it's reached his liver."

"I need someone to explain what is happening," I repeated.

"These two are idiots," Chloe told me. "George needs to find a date to an RMG party, Will here is suggesting he ask our waiter. Obviously George is suggesting he's not a suitable candidate."

"Sorry, 'RMG'?" I asked.

"Ryan Media Group," George said. "Bennett decided to throw a soirée, and here I am, dateless. These boys are trying to help. It's embarrassing to all of us. I'd really rather talk about what you're going to do about Ruby."

I knew we would circle back to this. In fact, part of me needed to talk about it . . . oddly. I'd barely needed to talk about my divorce, but this had me twisted in unfamiliar ways.

"I . . ." I stared down into my pint. "I don't actually know."

Silence fell over the table. Finally, I admitted, "She told me she has feelings for me. In fact," I said, looking up, "she's had them for quite some time."

"One look at her and I knew that," Bennett said.

"Same," George offered.

"Ditto," said Will.

Max was the last to chime in. "I don't really need to say anything, now do I?"

"We nearly kissed today in the office," I blurted, and for some reason every head whipped over to Bennett, who displayed his middle finger in a wide arc around the table. "Suffice to say it's all moving a bit fast for me. I've only, well, we've worked together for months but I've only *known* her a matter of days."

"So what *are* you going to do?" Chloe said.

"Well, I . . ." I started, and she continued to blink at me like I must be dense. "Like I said, I—"

"She told you she has feelings. You almost kissed. You said it's all moving a bit fast, so I'm guessing that's why you're here and she's not."

"Yes," I told her.

"So either you're interested, or you're not."

"It isn't that simple," I said. "We work together."

Chloe waved her hand. "None of that matters." When everyone gaped at her, she said, "What? It doesn't! Obviously I don't know all the details, but from what I hear, she's a pretty, smart girl, and eventually she'll be noticed by someone a lot smarter than you. Don't be an idiot."

I laughed, taking a sip of my drink. "Cheers."

"As usual, Chloe cuts right to the chase." My brother put a gentle hand on my arm. "Just call her. See if she wants to come down and join us?"

Nodding, I stood and walked over to a quiet area of the bar, dialing her mobile.

As it rang, it occurred to me that I'd never called her.

That we hadn't made plans for tonight.

That she might have made plans, and maybe Chloe was right and someone smarter *had* noticed.

"Hello?"

I startled, having somehow talked myself out of the possibility of her answering. Inside, I was an enormous knot.

"Hello?" A pause. "Mr. Stella?"

I shivered at the sound of her voice. "Ruby. Call me Niall, yeah?"

"Is everything okay?"

"Would you care to come down for a bite to eat?"

She hesitated on the other end, for what felt like an eternity.

"Unless you have a . . ." I paused, fumbling for words. "That is to say, an agent . . . of . . . pleasure in your room."

Oh dear God—what did I just say?

"An *agent of pleasure*?" she asked, and I could hear the restrained laughter in her voice, as well as the gentle slur of alcohol.

I groaned quietly. "I mean company. Or plans. Ruby, I don't mean to presume. I don't even know if you're—"

She cut me off with a quiet laugh. "It's almost midnight. I'm alone up here, I promise. But I just got out of the tub, I've had a cocktail or two, and ordered room service."

My brain tripped over the image of Ruby in the tub. Naked. Tipsy. Wet. Warm, soft skin. Muscles lax.

"Ah. Well, right."

Ruby paused again. "I mean, I suppose I could . . ." Her words fell away.

"No, Ruby, I don't mean to . . . I just wanted to make sure you'd eaten. It was a long day. And we . . ." I closed my eyes, murmuring, "We . . . rather, *I* fear you're out of sorts."

I could hear her breathing, so quick and shallow. I felt a tight pinch in my chest at the thought that she was anxious again, suffering in some way over me, or this. I knew I had the ability to do something for her . . . I simply didn't know how to start.

"I'm okay, I promise. Thank you."

We sat on the line for several long, wordless seconds. "Right, then. Good night, Ruby."

"Good night . . . Mr. Stella."

Returning to the table, I took my seat and lifted my second pint to my lips. I felt worse than I had before; I was bloody awful on the phone, which was saying something given that I was often awkward in person as well. When Max wordlessly asked whether Ruby would be joining us—with a small lift of his brow, an expectant expression—I shook my head. I wasn't sure whether I was relieved or gutted that she wasn't coming down. And then I settled on relieved, because I knew I wouldn't be able to keep from moving to her, wishing for her hand on my leg, wanting to meet her eyes and see that the same longing was still there, and I would be shite at simply asking for it.

Bloody hell.

Bennett and Chloe had left, chased off by George, who said he'd rather light himself on fire than watch the two of them make out. I ordered a gin and tonic, then another, contributing to the conversation before eventually becoming lost in my own jumbled thoughts. I went from tangled, to calm, to tipsy, finally convincing myself it was a good idea, at one in the bloody morning, to go upstairs and see her.

"Where you headed?" Max asked. "This is my one night a month out. No sodding way you're cutting out early."

"Meetings all day tomorrow, mate. G'night."

I ignored their catcalls and continued on to the elevator, to the tenth floor, to the door that led to her room.

My knuckles landed heavily on the wood; Jesus, even my knock sounded drunk.

After a few tense seconds, the door opened and Ruby stood before me in a tiny pink silk tank top and matching shorts that barely covered her—

Dear God.

She weaved slightly against the door. "Everything okay, Mr. Stella?"

I cleared my throat once, and then again. "Bloody hell. Do you always sleep in that?"

"Yes . . ." she said, and I could hear her smile when she added, "unless there is *an agent of pleasure* in here with me."

Finally I could tear my eyes from the sight of her breasts, bare beneath the camisole. "You love to tease me."

Her tongue slipped out, wetting her lips. "Yeah."

I stood at the doorway, feeling like I must be looking at her the way a man would look at a woman he desired if he hadn't had dinner, or sleep, or masturbated in days.

"Do you want to come in?" she asked. "I'll warn you. I've had a few cocktails. But I do have a few items left unclaimed in the minibar if you like Midori or Jägermeister."

"I shouldn't touch you," I blurted and immediately squeezed my eyes closed. "Sorry. I've been drinking as well, and . . ." Opening my eyes, I looked at her face. She was smiling, looking . . . *relieved*. "I don't know why I'm here. I couldn't stop thinking about what happened today, and how much I wanted to see you. But I really shouldn't touch you, Ruby."

I could see her pulse in her neck. I could tell that she was *trembling*.

"You *shouldn't*?" she asked. "Or you don't want to?"

Without answering and without really thinking about what I was doing, I stepped forward, moving into her room. She took a step back, letting the door close behind me. The thud reverberated in the quiet.

"Is it really true what you said earlier?" I asked. "You think about this? With me?"

She flushed, from her neck to her cheeks, but still managed to sound brave when she said, "Yeah."

She'd stopped moving but I hadn't. I kept drifting forward until I was barely an inch away from her. In fact, I could feel her breath on my neck. Could smell the sweetness of orange juice, the sharp tang of vodka on her lips.

113

This is stupid, Niall. Get the hell out of this room.

"What do you think about?" I asked.

"Having you in my hotel room." She smiled, looking at my lips. "As an agent of pleasure."

Laughing a little, I ran my hand down my face, admitting, "These past few days . . . I think about it, too. You've hijacked my brain."

"Is that bad?"

I looked down at her. She looked nervous but also confident; I was here in her room; she'd regained at least some of the power between us. "No, it's not a bad thing. I'm just not sure I know what to do with you." I had no idea why I said this, but it didn't seem to trip her up in the slightest.

"We'd figure it out together."

Meeting her eyes, I asked, "Would we?"

Ruby nodded, reaching out and putting her hand on my chest. "I understand you. I think you understand me, too."

I swallowed, at a loss for words.

"I'd tell you what I like," she whispered. "You'd tell me what you need."

She ran her hand down my chest, over my stomach, and then—just before she reached my belt—she let it fall away.

I should leave. I should go to my room and let us both sleep it off.

Looking up at me, she asked, "What *do* you need?"

"This," I said. "The odd certainty I feel when I'm this close to you. The way you look at me."

Her wide eyes searched mine. "A lot of women look at you this way."

"No, you're wrong. Maybe they look at me the way men look at you—where it's clear they want you, and are thinking of you sexually—but not the way you do, where it feels you can see beneath my skin." Pausing, I added, "Besides, I've never been one to want 'a lot of women.'"

Her smile was so radiant, I forgot whatever else I was going to say.

My heart was beating so hard in my chest that I felt unsteady. It seemed to mix potently with the alcohol, and yet I never wanted this feeling to end. I'd never experienced a rush like this. She was so close, smelling of rose water and the indescribable scent of a woman. She would fit so perfectly tucked into my chest, beneath my chin. Or riding me, with her legs around my waist, her chest slick with our sweat.

"Ruby, what are we doing?"

She tucked her hair behind her ear, laughing a little. "You're the one who came to my room. I think we're both a little drunk. You tell me."

"I . . . I'd like to explore this."

Her smile straightened into something more earnest. "Me, too."

"But maybe tonight isn't the night. I shouldn't touch you." *Maybe once I've said it a hundred times, I'll believe it.* "We've been drinking. I want to be sober if . . ."

She closed her eyes, and the disappointment was evident on her face. And then, a transformation occurred: Ruby opened her eyes, looked up at my face, and in an instant went from guarded to mischievously coy. She turned, walking into the room a few feet and picking up a slip from the bed. "But if you *did*, how would you touch me?" she asked, folding the garment neatly before placing it in an open drawer in front of her.

I barely had to consider the question before my answer burst forward: "Desperately." I took a step toward her.

"Roughly?"

"I—no," I spluttered, "I wouldn't ever—"

"I *like* thinking of you touching me roughly," she interrupted, calming me with a smile. Another piece of fabric lay on the bed—a tank top, I believe—and she reached for it, examining the hem before she set it in the drawer, too. "Of your big gentle hands shaking, needing to touch me, and you're so *impatient*."

"I would be," I admitted, and when she looked up at me, asking me with her eyes for more, I murmured, "I *am*." I could barely catch my breath; at my sides, my hands were shaking. "I try to be careful, but it's a wasted effort."

She pushed the dresser closed with her hip, and took a step toward me. "You pull off my clothes before we can even make it to the bed," she agreed, playing along as she lifted her hand, fingering the strap of her camisole, waiting for me to stop her.

I couldn't in a million years.

Sliding her hands down over her breasts and lower, to the hem of the garment, she began to lift it up, over her head . . . and off.

My heart stopped and when it started again, it was ten times too large, ten times too fast.

Ruby dropped the silk to the floor without looking away from my face.

Her chest was bared to me, lush curves, small, pink nipples, and perfect, pale skin. I swallowed, fighting the savage tempo of my pulse. I wanted to touch her, kiss her. I wanted to lie on top of her, move inside of her.

She took one step backward, and then turned, walking away from me and over to the bed.

"Ruby." I had no point to make. Her name was just an instinctive utterance. Nearly a plea.

"You touch my breasts like you know them." She turned back to face me, running her hands over the swells, pushing them together, roughly pinching the blush peaks. "You *suck* them. Like you're greedy."

Christ. "I *am* greedy."

"You love my breasts. You're filthy with them, sometimes."

I nearly choked. Never in my life had I played such a game. "I am?"

"You are. You rub yourself all over them."

I felt my skin flush, my body pulsing beneath my trousers at the intended meaning. "Myself . . . ?"

"Your cock."

My mouth watered, and I stared at her lips, imagining her kissing me there.

"But right now, you want me naked." It was a question, innocently buried in confidence.

She hooked her thumbs in her shorts, daring me again to stop her.

I nearly had to shove my fist into my mouth to keep from groaning aloud. The drink made me bold: "I do."

She slid her shorts down her hips, swaying seductively for me, easing the silk down her thighs. She wore no underwear beneath, and her naked form was smooth, soft. I'd never seen anything more beautiful in my life.

"You like looking at me," she said, but this one wasn't a question. No doubt my expression telegraphed my every thought to her.

Like how I wanted to climb over her, be as greedy and filthy with her body as she suggested.

Like how I wanted to do something as innocent as touch the slickness between her legs with my fingers.

Swallowing heavily, I told her, "You're the only thing I want to look at, darling."

Ruby lowered herself onto the bed, pushing her body to the middle of the mattress, and then lay back, letting her knees fall to the sides. "So . . . look."

Without shame, I stared between her spread legs. Blood pounded in my ears and I leaned against the armoire for support. "*Christ.*"

She ran her fingers up her legs, from her knees to her

thighs. And then, while I watched, she ran the fingers of one hand along the wet skin of her sex.

"You like to taste me, too," she whispered.

I could only swallow and nod. *Nothing in the world would pleasure me more.*

"But you tease me."

I looked up at her face upon hearing the pout in her voice, feeling my brows draw together. "I do?"

"Yes," she whined sweetly. "It's awful. You make me beg for your mouth on my clit."

Her . . . clit? I wiped a palm down my face, dizzy. All of this—all of it—was spinning so quickly out of control. "What . . . that is to say, *how* do I do that?"

Offering a tiny one-shouldered shrug, she said, "You kiss my thighs, and my lips just here." She circled her fingers between her legs. "You lick where I'm wet, too." Sliding her index finger lower, it soon glistened with her arousal. "See where I get wet?"

I nearly pitched forward onto the bed. My voice was barely audible: "And quite."

"But that's how you tease me. You never lick me here." She moved her fingers higher, circling her clitoris only once. "At least not until I'm nearly crying for it."

I took a step closer to the bed. "That seems a bit un-sporting of me."

Ruby giggled, tipsy, smiling up at me. "It does, doesn't it?"

With blood pounding through my veins, I began to feel the power I had over her body. *Simply look at her.* It was impossible to ignore how she was responding to this. "But it's only because I love the flush of your skin when you start to need it, darling."

Her lips parted, letting out a sharp exhale. "But I *do* need it."

"No . . . you still only *want* it," I corrected her. "And I rather like the taste of your thighs instead."

Her hips lifted from the bed, fingers obediently moving to her thighs.

My heart hammered against my sternum. I wanted so much to join her in this game. "Your breasts are perfect."

She moaned, closing her eyes.

"I always keep one hand on your breast while I kiss you here."

"You do," she agreed, sliding a hand up her torso, cupping her breast in her palm. "I love that. But your teasing makes me crazy. Please let me feel you."

"Just a glancing kiss, my darling."

With a relieved moan, Ruby grazed her fingers over her clitoris again, crying out.

"Let me slide my tongue into you."

Her eyes flew open and she watched my face as she eased her finger inside. I watched it disappear, in and out of her, before looking up at her face. She seemed almost on the verge of tears.

I was lost in the game, drugged by the sight of her. I wasn't myself. I wasn't anyone I knew. She made me this way. "Do I love your taste?"

With apparent effort, she said, "You know you do."

"It makes me wild, doesn't it? Makes me . . ."

"Hard," she finished for me.

I laughed, stepping so my knees touched the mattress, only a foot away from her. Bending, I placed a hand beside each of her hips, careful not to touch her. "I'm already painfully hard, darling. I was going to say it makes me *possessive*. Makes me want to fight any other man who's ever tasted you."

She let out a softly ragged breath. "You're hard?"

"Well, look for yourself."

Her eyes dropped to the zipper of my trousers, seeing the ridge pressing there.

"Let me see," she said, licking her lips.

I shook my head but ran my hand over the front of my zipper, letting her see the shape of me.

Christ. What is happening? What am I doing?

"Not tonight," I whispered.

She started to sit up, mortification slowly cooling her expression.

"Because I wouldn't be able to stop," I assured her quickly. "I'm barely hanging on, Ruby, please don't stop what you're doing."

"Is this okay?" she asked. Her cheeks pinked, sobering.

I nodded, not wanting her to break this moment. "It's more than okay. It's a bloody dream."

"I want to touch you," she said, barely audibly.

"You can't."

Her eyes moved to my face. "Ever?"

"Shh," I murmured, leaning back over her. "I'm kissing you between your legs; how can you think of anything else right now?"

With her eyes glued to mine, she began to stroke herself again, slowly, as if waiting for me to tell her exactly what to do.

"That's it. Let me suck on you, yes . . . just there. I want to hear you come."

Ruby arched off the bed, her fingers sliding in tiny, tight circles. "I . . . I . . ."

"So soon?" I whispered, fighting every urge I had to bend and suck at the skin at the hollow of her throat that was only beginning to glisten with sweat.

"I'm insane for you," she choked.

"You feel so good on my tongue," I murmured. "My senses are full of you."

The sight of her was unreal; easily the most erotic vision of my life. Her thighs were soft and toned, spread before me. I would only need to bend down and put my mouth on her to make this game a reality. I pressed my palm against my trousers, and moaned.

Her eyes flew open as she came, lips parted, voice tight and desperate.

I knew in that heartbeat I would never get the sound of her orgasm out of my head, the little gasping noises, the sharp cry.

Her entire chest flushed, nipples tight as she lazily

touched herself, smiling up at me. I was envious of her fingers, sliding around such luxuriant slickness.

"Let me touch you?" she whispered. "Please."

"You *are* touching me," I told her, leaning back over her again. "Your hand is stroking me."

A teasing smile played at her lips. "My *hand*? That seems a pretty sad gesture of reciprocation."

"Well." I shrugged. "It so happens your mouth is greedy for mine at the moment."

Understanding bloomed in her eyes. "Oh."

"You love to taste yourself on my tongue."

Her eyes flamed, lips parting in a sharp burst of air. "I do."

"I love to indulge you," I told her, and she nodded. "Besides, you love the weight of me in your hands."

Ruby's throat moved with the frenzy of her pulse. "I do," she said, breathless and wild. "And I could kiss your demanding mouth for days."

"You do sometimes."

"God, why aren't you *inside* me?"

I smiled at the sound of her sweet, gentle whine. "Because we haven't made love yet."

Her eyes went wide at this sudden reveal in our strange, surreal little game. "We haven't?"

I shook my head. "We're waiting."

She laughed, and the sound was so sweet I nearly bent to taste the echo of it on her lips. "We do everything else?"

I nodded. "Nearly."

Her eyes were still so wide, so genuinely hungry when she asked, "What are we waiting for?"

"To be sure."

And finally, I reached my thumb out, sliding it back and forth over the skin of her bare hip.

"Sure about me?" she whispered.

I stared at her sweet, full lips, the tiny anxious furrow to her brow before telling her, "Sure about *me*. Sure about all of it before I can't turn back anymore. I don't take any of this lightly."

"I know," she whispered. "I can wait."

Truth had settled in. And how odd, too, that it happened after the most erotic vision of my life. I felt unsteady, as if the past twenty minutes had been a dream.

It could have been awkward; we were coworkers and only last week she'd been a stranger to me. Now she was completely naked and had just masturbated while I spoke to her. It could have been the most terrifying moment of my life. But with the alcohol in our blood, and satisfaction loosening her body, it wasn't.

I grew brave enough to slide my palm over her hip, cupping it.

She reached down, covered my hand with hers. "How do we sleep together after we've done this?"

"With me curled around behind you," I said and then swallowed thickly. "You fit into me perfectly."

"But you never wake me for sex."

"I wake you to touch you again, because I'm insatiable

for you, but not yet for that." Did she understand? Or did it make me odd that, in this day and age, the idea of sex changed things? Meant something?

She closed her eyes, moving her hands to rest over her pounding heart. "Do you know how much I want to feel you?"

"I do know," I told her quietly.

"I hope you kiss me someday."

I swallowed, reality pressing back in. "So do I."

"Do you always kiss me good night when you leave?" she asked, returning to our game. Her eyes, so wide and vulnerable, warned me to be careful. They told me, maybe, that even Ruby herself didn't know how careful I needed to be with her heart.

"Always." But I wouldn't tonight. I couldn't, at least not on her mouth. Instead, I bent and pressed a single kiss to the skin just beside my hand, over the soft skin of her navel. Her hands ran briefly through my hair, sending a renewed pulse of heat through me.

As I stood, Ruby sat up. Watching as I grabbed my coat, she didn't bother to reach for her clothes.

"Is it going to be weird tomorrow?" she asked quietly, eyes sobering. "Have I ruined this already?"

It was all I could do to not go to her, kiss her senseless in reassurance. I didn't know what I needed in order to be able to take this final step.

"To the contrary."

She smiled a little, but I suspected she wanted what I wanted, which was for me to stay the night with her. Even not touching, it was better to be near her than anywhere else.

"Good night, Ruby, darling."

"Good night, Mr. Stella."

Her name was a constant, looping mantra in my thoughts, but not once had I heard her call me Niall.

Seven

Ruby

I opened my eyes to the sun beaming in the window, the phone ringing with my wake-up call, and an immediate dousing of cold, hard *Holy Hell what have I done?*

You know, just an average morning after I drunkenly masturbated in front of Niall Stella.

I rolled face-first into my pillow and groaned.

As the details returned—and oh, they did—I wasn't embarrassed exactly. I remembered the he-said-she-said. I remembered how hard he'd been, how breathless. I remembered how he stared so intently at my hand between my legs, completely unashamed to simply *look*. Seeing him there, hungry in that way, completely open in his desire . . . I'd been a woman *possessed*.

My fear was that, after a few hours alone to contemplate what we'd done, *he* would be mortified. If the suggestion of a kiss in the office yesterday turned him stiff and silent, what happened last night might make him crawl back into his shell and never emerge again.

How often had I fantasized about something happening between us? Countless times. And in every fantasy, I was brave enough to tell him what I wanted, and it unleashed something in him to know that I could be a safe place for him.

That I understood his reserve and would let him shed it when he needed to.

Then last night—suddenly—he *was* right there. And for once I wasn't mute, I wasn't a babbling mess.

He'd looked so gorgeous, eyelids heavy and cheeks warm with alcohol, the uptight and buttoned-up persona barely hanging by a thread. He'd worried he was being presumptuous, or that he was somehow taking advantage of me, but he was wrong.

I'd wanted to see that final thread unravel. See *him* unravel. I'd wanted it so much I could hardly breathe. My skin felt like it was on fire, so sensitive I might turn to ash with just a touch. He may have thought keeping his distance had been for his benefit, that we'd been drinking and he wanted to be in full control of his senses when we did more, but somehow, it had been exactly what I'd needed.

I bet he thought intimacy happened in ordered stages: admiring, flirting, consensus about feelings—but not too much discussion—permission to touch, kissing, hands up shirts, hands down pants, the I Love You, and then, finally, sex. I wondered if, in his mind, what we'd done— or hadn't done—last night still allowed him a certain amount of emotional distance.

How could he not know that it had been more intimate than any sex I'd ever had?

How could I show him?

I knew I needed to get up and get going, but I wasn't ready yet. My stomach was in knots and my muscles hummed with a tangle of nervous energy too big for my skin. I missed my friends and having someone to talk to. I missed shuffling out into the living room on Sunday morning and having coffee with the girls, huddled over steaming cups while we talked about our lives and work and school and men.

Tucking the blankets around me, I rolled over and reached for my phone. I was three hours ahead of California, but I reasoned that this was still far preferable to the UK time difference, where I was getting up just as everyone else was going to bed. I'd stayed up late countless nights so I could listen to London or Lola unload; it was their turn to do it for me. *I needed to talk to someone.*

Without another thought, I sent a group text. Most of Lola's late nights were spent working, so there was little chance of her answering. She was the sensible one, the driven-to-succeed-since-she-was-tiny one, and probably would have her phone set on *do not disturb* hours ago. Mia and Ansel rarely answered the phone after the sun went down, and Harlow, more often than not, was up on Vancouver Island newlywedding it up with Finn.

London, my best friend, was my best bet.

Anyone awake? I need help :(

My phone buzzed almost immediately.

You have a phone so you MUST know what time it is, came London's reply.

I know and I'm so sorry. But . . . something happened. I held my breath as I hit SEND.

Something or ~something~?

I'm not sure which something I'm supposed to use??

The phone vibrated with a call just a few seconds later, and I answered before the first ring had even finished.

"I assume this is somehow referring to Niall Stella."

I groaned. "Of course."

"So when I say *something*," London began, sounding tired and groggy. She worked as a bartender, and I wondered what time she'd actually got off this morning. She cleared her throat and if I hadn't been so thankful to hear her voice right then, I might have felt the tiniest bit guilty for waking her up. "What I mean is, something like you had coffee together? Or *something* like he's seen your vagina?"

I rolled onto my back, blinking up at the ceiling. "Uhhh," I started. That was disturbingly close to the mark. Could she hear it in my voice? Was there something in the way I sounded that screamed, *I bared my entire body to him last night, but yeah, he mostly stared at my vagina.*

"Oh my God, you little shit. You had sex with him?"

I brought my hand to my forehead. "Not exactly," I answered truthfully.

"Not exactly? Ruby, honey. You know that I love you, but I've been up late every night this week with work. I need some sleep, not a brain teaser."

"Okay," I started, trying to work out how exactly to explain what had happened. "Imagine having phone sex, but in person."

I could hear rustling in the background, the sound of London getting comfortable, or smothering herself with her own pillow. Honestly, it could be either. "You went from 'he doesn't know I'm alive' to masturbating in front of each other in less than a week?"

"Well . . . if we're going to get technical, it was just me doing the masturbating," I told her, imagining the face she must be making. "Also, I don't ever want you to say 'masturbating' again, starting now."

The rustling stopped. "Wait. Wait, wait, wait. Ruby Miller, are you telling me you put on a little show for your dream boy?"

"I guess? I mean, obviously?"

"You've been talking about him for the last, what? Five months? I assume you're thrilled with all of this masturbation."

"London, you just broke the oath."

"I said 'masturbation,' a different word. And why are you calling me at four thirty in the morning? Are you requesting a long-distance high-five or someone to hear you melt down in mortification?"

"Maybe both?" I groaned. *I* didn't even know how

I felt; how could I possibly expect someone else to help me? "I don't regret it, but I'm not sure where we stand right now. We're not *together*, we're colleagues. I'm actually not even sure we're friends. Plus, he was drunk and I was mostly drunk and this morning I can almost hear him freaking out across the wall."

"Freaking out as in *he's* regretting it?" she asked, and I thought I could hear her sit up.

"I don't know." I chewed on my lip, considering. "I hope not."

"But he's into you, too?"

"Yeah, I mean. Yeah. As much as he can be this quickly? He went through sort of a bad divorce and it's left him a little—"

"Ruby, I know this must have been your way of putting yourself out there, but what did you expect would happen?"

"Um . . ." I started, because to be truthful, I wasn't really thinking at *all* in that moment.

I sighed. Was I thinking that he would realize he'd loved me all along and sweep me off my feet? That he'd admit to looking for me all his life and there I was, willing to get myself off in front of him the entire time? Um, probably not.

"I'm not sure really," I said instead. "Maybe that it would be the first step."

London yawned and I heard the sound of blankets being rearranged, as she settled herself back in bed.

"That's a hell of a first step, but make it work. Go into the office today, face him like the kind of woman who masturbates—sorry, sorry—in front of the love of her life and doesn't regret a thing. You know I don't have a ton of faith in the male population, but if he's half the man you've described—because really, why else would you fall for him?—he'll be smart enough to catch on. Go get him, Gem."

Making last night the first step proved to be a bit more complicated than I'd hoped. It seemed Niall Stella was going to go out of his way to keep things exceedingly, frustratingly normal between us. He'd gone in early, and was packing up his laptop for a meeting when I arrived, head down and phone pressed to his ear. He acknowledged me with a small nod, a smile, and then he stepped out past me, into the hall for privacy.

In the handful of seconds it took me to walk around his chair and reach my own, I came up with at least twelve different ways to translate his small smile and semi-avoidance, each more insane than the last.

It was one thing to dissect everything he said in a meeting or to a colleague when there was zero chance it had anything to do with me, but this? There was no way he wasn't also thinking about what we did last night. *Everything* had a meaning today.

I heard him talking, still just outside our office door.

Was he waiting for me? He'd looked like he was packing up to leave; was he coming back in first?

"That doesn't make any sense," he said into the receiver, his posh accent the only thing keeping his words from sounding clipped or flat-out annoyed. "The timeline we were given for estimated completion was a full six months before the date you're giving me today. The alternative is unacceptable."

My ears perked at this; I'd never seen or heard him sound angry before.

He was silent while he listened to the person on the other end of the line, and I had the strangest sense of his eyes on me. I unwrapped my scarf, slipped out of my coat, and hung it on the hook behind the door. His attention pressed on my skin and I shook my head, careful to let my hair fall forward and hide the warmth I could feel blooming in my cheeks.

"Tony, I'm not leading the Diamond Square project to be a yes man, I'm leading it because I know what the bloody hell I'm talking about. Tell them that, or better yet, let me. I won't have any problem setting them straight," he said, followed by the distinct sound of his exasperated sigh.

Tony. *Gross.*

I grabbed my notebook and turned to join him. "Everything okay?"

He nodded, but shoved his phone into his pocket, not bothering to elaborate about the call. "Aside from a meeting with some of the MTA engineers this morning, I'd like to visit some of the stations, see for myself a few of the proposed floodgate sites." He gave me another polite smile.

Niall was back in his shell.

Nodding to the stairs, he asked, "Would you care to accompany me?"

———

The South Ferry station was one of the hardest hit by Hurricane Sandy. With a street-level entrance of only one hundred feet above sea level, the tunnel was flooded in minutes. The seawater destroyed practically everything in its path, damaging wiring and equipment and filling caverns deep enough for workers to swim through. This was why we were here, to think ahead of Mother Nature and design a system that would prevent catastrophic damage like this from happening again.

Traffic whizzed by as I followed Niall down into the newly reopened station, my eyes on his broad shoulders as he descended the stairs in front of me. He looked Serious Business today. His expression had remained neutral throughout our cab ride to the station, conversation kept to a minimum. He wore a dark suit and darker overcoat, his brown cashmere scarf continually escaping the lapels of his coat and trailing over his shoulder behind him. There was purpose when Niall Stella walked.

A handful of engineers was there to meet us, and Niall

introduced us both, taking the time to get each person's name, and listening attentively as they took us from one end of the tunnel to the other. It was dizzying to see him like this—so knowledgeable and completely in his element—while simultaneously remembering what he'd looked like last night. In six months I'd amassed a catalog of Niall Stella memories, and the few unguarded ones I'd made since coming to New York seemed to eclipse them all.

Niall called me over to stand next to him, and I watched as he crouched down, took measurements, and inspected one of the proposed entrances. My brain was a mess of focus and inattention: I wanted to absorb everything around me, but having him so close after last night turned me into a complete mental maniac. *Was he thinking about it? Was he pretending it didn't happen?*

A horrifying thought occurred to me: *Was it even possible he didn't remember?*

He called out numbers or various notes while he worked, but it was noisy, the sound of trains and people making it difficult to hear him. I had to stay close, so close that his shoulder would occasionally brush against the side of my leg.

I assumed it was accidental, and tried not to react as goose bumps spread along my skin. But by the second and third time, I began to wonder.

"Ruby," he asked me, looking up quickly. "Did you

make note that this was the last of the stations to re-open?"

I nodded. Of course I had. But given how important it seemed to him, I took down the information again anyway, my pen stopping, tip pressed into the paper as I felt his palm wrap around my calf. It lingered there for only a moment, fingers trailing slowly up toward my knee, gripping ever so slightly, before they were gone.

Every nerve in my body seemed to run on a circuit, beginning at where he'd touched me and stopping just between my legs. I swayed on my feet, my nipples tight and my breasts heavy as an ache moved up my thighs.

My heart twisted. He remembered; he just had to wrestle his way out of his own head.

The more time we spent near each other, the more he seemed to unwind around me and his wordless flirtation slowly built over the rest of the afternoon: his hand pressed to my lower back as we left the station, his fingers quickly brushing the hair off my forehead as we stood in line for coffee, and, once, his thumb sweeping across my lower lip, back and forth and back and forth as our subway train moved through a dark tunnel.

I couldn't breathe. Could barely remain upright.

When a seat opened up on the train and he urged me to sit down, he stepped close enough that his belt buckle was only inches from my face. In front of me was the long expanse of his torso, slim shirt tucked neatly into his pants. And, lower, the clear downward line of his cock against his thigh, already half hard.

Sweet Lord.

I reached up, hooking a finger through his belt loop as he gazed down at me, wordless and rapt.

When we rose from the station, he came up behind me as I stopped to get my bearings. His large hands curled around my hips and he pressed into me.

I *felt* him.

I mean, I felt *him*.

I lost my breath when his mouth came against my ear and he said simply, "We're headed to the left."

By the time we got back to the temporary offices I was ready to explode. I felt tight and swollen between my legs, the skin of my thighs slick and wet. My senses seemed to be dialed up to a ten, and even the most basic things—the lace of my bra brushing across my breasts—felt wanton.

But what I thought had to be leading up to something . . . didn't. Instead of closing the door to our empty office and touching me—I didn't care for one second that we were at work—he moved to his small desk and sorted through a few files while I stood there, hot and confused and speechless.

It was torture to feel this way. To be infatuated, to feel his interest grow but see him continually close back up after each tiny step of progress. I wanted to simply *ask* him, but worried that would close him up for good.

Beyond that, I *ached*. It was an entire afternoon of quiet, gentle foreplay and my body felt like a pitchfork struck against an iron beam. I was practically vibrating.

Our bathroom was private, thank God, and going into it I flipped the lock, taking what had to be my first real breath all day. I could still smell the faint scent of his cologne, as if it had somehow been burned into my senses. As I crossed the room to the small leather bench that sat just under the window, I let myself imagine how he would smell up close, with my nose pressed directly against his skin.

With that image in mind, I took a seat and slipped my panties down my legs as I imagined the warmth of that skin under my touch. My fingertips became his, and they skirted up my thigh and between my legs. If I listened closely, I could hear his voice as he spoke to someone on the phone. I pretended he was speaking only for me.

I was so sensitive, so wet, that the slightest touch, the graze of a fingertip over my clit had my hips rocking forward, wanting more. With my eyes closed, I listened to him talk, his accent curving the words into something that sent a current of awareness from my nipples to my pussy. I imagined him pushing those words into my neck; the rise and fall of his voice became the rhythm of him moving in and out of me. I imagined him just on the other side of the door, *knowing* that I was touching myself, and begging that he be the one to do it next time.

The very idea was enough to send me over the edge,

and I came against my own hand, my body arching into the touch.

Only then did I notice how quiet the outside office had grown, and that I might possibly have been too loud. I could hear the even tick of the watch on my wrist, the faint hum of traffic on the street below, but no more voices, no footsteps pacing through the office.

Once my legs were steady, I stood and righted my clothes, moving to the sink to freshen up.

Stepping out of the bathroom, I crept into the hall, nearly crashing into him on the way out.

"Sorry!" I gasped, attempting to catch a stack of files as they scattered across the floor. "Let me get those!" I exclaimed, definitely emphasizing my growing under-current of embarrassment.

Niall ignored me, and bent to gather the papers himself.

I tried to avoid meeting his gaze, certain what I'd just done had to be written in flashing, neon ink across my forehead.

I smoothed my skirt and tucked my bangs to the side before I looked up at him. He was studying me, head tilted.

"What?" I asked, feigning innocence.

"Are you all right?"

"Of course I am."

"You're flushed. Are you quite sure you're not feeling poorly? I can certainly manage by myself today if—"

"I'm fine," I said, shrugging out of his reach, feeling a small flash of irritation.

He followed me to my desk, watchful gaze nearly burning a hole through the back of my head.

"You haven't been . . . running up stairs?" he asked haltingly, as if he knew it wasn't quite right.

"No, I . . ." I considered lying, but knew he'd never buy that. "Jesus, you're like a dog with a bone. Can we change the subject, please?"

His eyes softened as they scanned my face, and then he inhaled sharply, glancing over my shoulder as if remembering where we were. "Come on then. Out with it."

"I was . . ." I started, wondering who I'd have to kill to get the ground to just open up and swallow me whole. Seriously, this playing field was starting to feel a little uneven. "I was just . . ."

"You were . . ." His brows drew together and his gaze flickered to my hand at my throat as he seemed to understand. "In the ladies' room? Just now?"

"Yes."

"At *work*?"

Ugh.

"I'm sorry . . . After last night and then today . . ."

"Wait," he said, swallowing thickly. "You were thinking of *me* in there?"

"Of course, I—" I began and then stopped, closing my eyes and taking a deep breath. How did he stay so quiet, so still? "You touch me, but then you turn aloof. The mixed signals make me feel crazy."

And now I felt crazy with a side of humiliation.

I almost jumped when I felt the gentle prod of his finger under my chin. "Did you come, my darling?"

Fire slid into my veins, and when I looked up at him, I saw the same burning in his.

I licked my lips, nodding.

"Tell me specifically what were you thinking about."

"Touching you," I said, my mouth suddenly dry. "Kissing you."

He nodded, eyes unfocused as he stared at my lips.

It was all the invitation I needed. I stood on my tiptoes, running my nose along the warm skin of his neck. He made a sound that was something between a whimper and a groan, and tried to put the smallest amount of space between us. Looking down at me, he seemed to struggle to work through a hundred different things. I could immediately tell he was torn. Maybe I was right, and post-divorce, he felt a little gun-shy. Maybe he was worried this was all moving too fast. Or maybe he simply wasn't comfortable doing things my way: sprinting headlong into what was sure to be mind-blowing sex and staying in bed until our return flight left for London.

In that moment, I felt like I'd take whatever I could get, even if that meant ten years of flirtation leading up to a single, careful kiss.

"Are you okay?" I asked quietly.

"I just wonder if we should . . ." He swallowed, wincing slightly.

"Ship me back to London and never speak to me again?"

He laughed but shook his head. "Please, no."

"Talk about what happened last night?"

He reached up, ran his thumb across my chin. "Yes."

Relief and anxiety threaded together in my chest. "My mom always said if you can't talk about it, you shouldn't be doing it."

His brow lifted at this, and he studied my face, lips curled up in the sweetest, hopeful smile. "Quiet dinner it is, then."

* * *

Niall met me at my hotel room door, dressed again in my favorite charcoal suit and tie. It was cut perfectly for his long, muscular frame and the gray brought out the yellow in his honey-brown eyes. Those eyes would be focused on me all night. Just me.

I might combust.

We took a cab to Perry St, an upscale restaurant housed in a high-rise glass building just off—you guessed it—Perry Street. It was elegant and chic, with floor-to-ceiling windows and minimal décor. Tables and earth-toned booths packed with diners filled the large dining room, and I was suddenly worried we wouldn't be able to get a table.

"Table for two," he told the hostess. "Reservation un-der the name Stella."

I tried to ignore the way my heart leapt at the idea of him making dinner reservations for the two of us.

We followed her to a small booth in the very corner of the room.

"Oh my God, this is gorgeous," I said, taking in the breathtaking view of the Hudson River. "How did you know about this place?"

"Max, of course," he said, taking his seat.

"Right. Max," I said, praying that didn't sound as breathless to his ears as it did to mine. He'd called his brother asking about dinner. If I couldn't feel his foot pressed up against mine under the table, I might have floated away. "Has he lived here long?"

He nodded, taking a sip of his water. "A few years."

"He seems *so* happy," I said. "They all do."

He smiled. "They are, it seems. Max and Sara just had a baby, you know?" I nodded, and he hesitated a moment before asking, "Would you like to see a picture?"

"I'd love to." *Love to* might be too small an exclama-tion, *dying to* might be a bit more accurate.

Niall retrieved his phone and flipped through his cam-era roll.

"There she is," he said, fondly, finger running along the edge of the screen. It was a picture of Niall holding a tiny bundle, a small hand reaching out from the blanket to grip his thumb. But it wasn't the beautiful baby that had my heart dropping into the depths of my stomach—though she was gorgeous—it was the look of adoration he wore as he looked down at her. The Niall in this photo was happy, practically blissed out. He was relaxed and smiling and absolutely in awe of the little girl.

"What's her name?" I asked, looking up to find him wearing the exact same expression now.

Dear God.

Ovulation in 3 . . . 2 . . . 1 . . .

"Annabel Dillon Stella. Beautiful little thing, in't she?"

My eyes widened at the softening of his accent. "Gorgeous. She looks a little like you, I think. Look at that nose."

If possible, his expression grew even happier. "Yeah?"

I nodded.

"The Stella nose, she's got, lookit that."

The server came by, asking if we'd like to order cocktails before dinner. We both laughed, and then our eyes met across the table. With the mention of drinks, the memory of last night was laid bare between us.

I held my breath.

"Maybe a bottle of wine?" Niall suggested quietly, glancing to me for agreement before he quickly studied the wine list. He ordered a bottle of a pinot noir and handed her the menu. "A few minutes before we order, then, yeah?"

After the server disappeared, he seemed engrossed with the condensation on his water glass for several breaths.

"I know last night was probably really wild for both of us," I said, addressing the elephant sitting on the table, "but I hope you don't regret it. I would feel terrible."

His head shot up, brow tight. "Not at all," he said, and I exhaled in relief. "I was the one who came to your room, if you recall."

I *did* recall.

The seconds ticked by as he looked back down at his hands and failed to say anything else. With each passing moment of silence, I couldn't help thinking, *That's it?* I gnawed at my lip, studying him.

He took a calming breath, laughing a little self-deprecating laugh. "This is all very new to me, Ruby; forgive me if it takes a while to find the words."

I wanted to be patient, but the quiet was torture. In professional situations, Niall was entirely self-possessed and capable. The few times he'd relaxed enough to touch me, he was all confidence and command. But when it was like this—personal and relying on expressing things verbally—he seemed unable to communicate a single private thought. Maybe Pippa was right and this sort of emotional reserve was only sexy in a book or movie. Here it was torture to my hammering pulse.

"It must have been weird," I said, unable to take the

silence anymore. "To do that. I mean, to *watch* me do that."

Oh, God.

He gazed at me, waiting to see where I was going with this. Hell, *I* was waiting to see where I was going with this.

"With someone totally different, after the divorce," I babbled. "Or, to just be back in the swing of things . . . Like *that*. With me."

Gah, if this were a football game, it would be the kind where I fumbled the ball, it exploded, and the entire stadium burst into flames.

He ran a finger over his eyebrow and gave a tiny smile. "Back in the swing of things," he repeated. "Not sure what I've done since the divorce could be classified as such."

The server stopped by our table to take our order, and we both opened the menus, scanning quickly.

I ordered the first combination of words I could coherently string together. "I'll have the salmon."

Niall stared blankly at the choices before he snapped his menu closed and handed it to her, saying only a distracted, "Steak." She opened her mouth to begin listing the choices and he cut her off with a gentle "Whichever you recommend. Medium rare, please."

We waited patiently for her to leave and then our eyes met again.

"Where were we?" he asked.

"We were breaking down the meaning of 'back in the swing of things.' "

He laughed. "Right."

"You don't date much?"

Niall considered this, straightening his cutlery and wiping a bead of condensation from his water glass. "I haven't, no."

"Why? You're gorgeous and successful. You—" I stopped, wishing someone would tape my mouth shut. "Let's just summarize: you're a catch."

He let out a small laugh. "I've never really, I mean I know I'm not . . . but I'd never describe myself as such."

Was he kidding?

"You must be joking. Have you looked in a mirror? Listened to yourself speak? Maybe I could get the server to come back and you could read her the menu. I'm sure she'd propose before you got through the salads."

When he smiled at this, one dimple flirted shamelessly with me. "You enjoyed last night, then?" he asked.

Ah. There it is. "I'm pretty sure we both know I *enjoyed* last night." Fighting the heat of my blush, I continued on to the more pressing matter: "But then today, when you were touching me and . . ." I took a sip of my wine, mouth suddenly dry. "I wasn't sure all day where your head was."

"I'm not sure where my head was, either," he admitted. "My body kept pushing me forward, but I'm still hesitant. Not because I'm not attracted to you. I am— hopefully that much is obvious. But I'm not sure I trust my navigational skills in relationships."

"There's only one way to learn," I told him, honestly. "I'm not sure I have it any more figured out than you do. Besides, your marriage lasted over a decade. You had to have done *some* things right."

"I'm afraid that even when Portia and I were together, it wasn't always . . ." He trailed off, clearing his throat before starting over. "With Portia, one has the sense that one does most things wrong."

What had she done to him? I imagined straight blond hair pulled tight, pinched features, and a constantly sour expression. A husband who felt he could never do any- thing right. "Well, her name is *Portia*, for starters."

He gave me a small smile to acknowledge this. "We found a rhythm in day-to-day life, I suppose. It was quiet, but it was predictable." He took another sip of wine. "But with you, when everything feels so intense and overwhelming . . . when I'm alone afterward, I find my- self overthinking it all, and floundering."

God, he was so adorably stuffy I could hardly stand it. I'd seen glimpses of how much fun he could be—when he'd caught me in the hallway, taking a selfie in front of Radio City, talking about his niece—he just needed to loosen up a bit. "I think it's best between us when we both *don't* overthink it. When it's just us hanging out, it's been really good."

"Agreed. Yet . . . with matters of intimacy, I'm less well versed. So—"

"You mean sex," I said, trying to put it plainly.

He shook his head at me, a patiently amused smile curling his mouth. "Not just sex. Intimacy including and beyond that. We didn't have sex last night, but it was one of the most bare, intimate experiences I've had. I'm still digesting that a bit."

I held my breath, nodding slowly. So he *did* understand how different last night was, how much deeper it went than a quick tumble on a hotel bed.

He scratched his jaw, contemplating his wineglass. "You'll find," he began carefully, "that much of this may feel like a retread for you, if you're used to discussing up front what a relationship will be, or how it will proceed. But for me, this is all unfamiliar. Portia decided we would be together, and then we were. After that, she and I were more likely to discuss the weather than emotion. As far as sex . . . to discuss *that* was unheard-of. So the mere fact that you and I are sitting here, discussing what we did last night—and yet we haven't really kissed or even touched . . . it's a bit of a revelation for me."

"A good one?" I asked, not able to hide my hopefulness.

"A good one," he agreed, nodding slowly. "I enjoy your company. I just want to explore this in the right way." He paused, meeting my eyes. "We've been quite intimate already without really knowing each other."

I nodded, swallowing a heavy lump in my throat. The

oddest twinge came over me, because I felt like I *did* know him. But upon reflection, it was true; he didn't know *me* yet. "We can take a few steps back. Learn about each other."

Shaking his head, he murmured, "That's just it. I'm not sure I want to move backward, or that I *need* to. Why do I need to know everything about you before we enjoy each other physically? I like you. Isn't that enough?"

I shrugged, feeling my stomach twist as I watched him work through it all. "It is for me. It doesn't have to be for you."

"I want it to be. There is a unique freedom I feel near you."

Smiling into my wine, I asked, "Yeah?"

"You make me feel adventurous and interesting . . . and *fun*."

"Fun?" I repeated, with feigned shock. "Mr. Stella, you must banish the thought."

His answering laugh was deep and warm, sending a shiver across the surface of my skin. "You also make me think about things I don't consider gentle, or chaste or very proper."

"Like what?"

He blinked up, met my eyes. "I believe I'd prefer to *show* you. I just have to give myself permission, if you'd agree."

It didn't seem possible that my chest could grow any tighter but it did. I barely managed a hoarse "Okay."

His eyes were so earnest, so expressive when he asked, "Will you continue to be as open with me as you were last night?"

I nodded, lifting my glass to my lips with a shaking hand. How was this happening—

How?

"In that case," he said, seeming to tamp down some renewed nervousness, "I know it may be hard to explain such preferences, which is to say, it is difficult to *vocalize* things that are more a matter of physical reaction . . ." He babbled helplessly, finally looking up at me. "But it helps to know."

He'd completely lost me. "To 'know'? To know what?"

Niall swallowed, blinked to his left to confirm the couple beside us weren't listening in. "To know what feels good," he said, hesitating. "To be frank, I'm not sure she ever . . ."

"Came?" I guessed.

"Ah, no . . . she always came," he said, rubbing his jaw with his index finger. "But I'm not sure she ever *wanted* sex. Wanted *me*."

It felt like an elevator car dropped through my stomach, and I needed a moment—and a little wine—to clear any heartbreak from my voice before I could answer him. "Well, then she really is a beast. Like I said earlier, have you looked in a mirror lately?"

He laughed and then seemed to instantly regret it. I felt terrible. "Ruby, I don't want to malign her. You must understand that she's the only woman I've been with. What

I'm trying to say is that we didn't explore very much. There's a lot of mileage between getting somewhere and enjoying the journey." He looked up and grinned, eyes dancing. "Last night—and your uninhibited show—was a completely new experience for me."

I paused, looking out over the water while I considered how to respond. No wonder he had such a wall up. She'd built a fortress around their sex life a decade ago.

"Do you still love her?" I asked.

"No. Heavens no. But without a doubt our relationship shaped me. I was made very aware of the fact that she had sex with me, for *me*. Never for her."

I raised my glass. "Well, I'm fine having it be all about my pleasure, if that helps," I said, hoping to lighten the mood.

"How very generous of you," he said with my favorite, dimpled smile. "That's just it, though. What do women really like? Pornography is rather unhelpful in this way."

"Not always," I corrected. "We *do* like big dicks and dirty talk."

It was a testament to his newfound comfort with me that he barely flinched.

"But oral sex, for example . . ." he began and then left the rest unsaid, simply raising his eyebrows.

"Most women, you'll find, tend to be a fan of the oral sex."

He was straightening his silverware, and looked up at me from across the table. "Receiving?"

"Is that a serious question?"

"It is, unfortunately." He grinned at me, and in that moment—just a heartbeat—he looked so young and playful. "And giving?"

I bit my lip, imagining how good it would feel to drag my tongue around the tip of his cock, hear his quiet groan. "Oh, yes."

He took a moment to look around the room, just long enough to make sure we weren't at risk of being overheard by the other diners. "Do women like to swallow?"

This conversation had leapt off the cliff and was sailing through the air. I could barely hold on. "I'm going to make a completely unscientific guess and say it's seventy-thirty, in favor of *not* swallowing."

His eyes lit up with a teasing smile. "And which category do you fall into? The seventy or the thirty?"

"With you?" I said in a whisper, leaning in, "I will."

Niall inhaled, his head jerking back slightly. The room seemed to shrink until I felt like it was just the two of us at this table, looking at each other. "I want it, too," he admitted.

The image, the idea seemed to take up the tiny remainder of empty space between us until it was this alive, pulsing thing.

"Say something filthy," I whispered, feeling brave. Feeling *wild*. "Tell me the craziest, dirtiest thing you can think of. Render me speechless."

He nodded as if I'd given him a normal request, and

glanced at his clasped hands on the table for several breaths before blinking up to me. His brown eyes were so thickly lined with lashes and once again he looked just like a *man*, and less like the intimidating conquest I'd idolized for months.

I wanted him even more.

He leaned closer, saying, "I very much enjoy—"

"Dirtier," I cut in, breath catching. "Stop thinking so much."

His eyes seemed to darken as he looked down at my mouth. "I *want* it."

"Want what? Don't filter."

"For you to suck my cock, and suck it so hungrily that you beg me with your eyes to let you swallow."

Oh.

Niall Stella was a fast learner.

The waitress came by with our food, setting it down before asking us if there was anything else we needed. I wanted to ask her for a bucket of ice. For my lap.

I bit back a laugh, but Niall replied with a smile, "We're good. Cheers."

"Wow. Well played," I mumbled when we were alone again, still dazed. "I'm not sure how I'll eat now."

The noise around us seemed to return in a roar, reminding me that we weren't alone in a hotel room. We were leaning toward each other, nearly kissing across the table.

"What are we doing to each other?" he whispered.

I shrugged. "We're . . . trying?"

He lifted his knife and fork, cutting into his steak. "I'm actually famished now."

"Postcoital?" I joked.

"Not hardly," he growled, taking a bite.

He looked up at me as he chewed. I watched his sharp jaw flex with the motion, his lips press together. How did he make *eating* sexy? Not even a little fair.

Swallowing, he asked, "What?"

"Nothing. You're just a sexy eater. It's distracting after what you just said about oral sex."

He pushed his lips together in an adorably dubious reaction before asking, "Normal topic then?"

"Good idea." Finally, I took a bite of my salmon.

"Favorite word?" he asked.

"*Cunt*," I said without hesitation.

He gasped in mock horror. "You stole mine."

I nearly choked. "I can't even imagine you *thinking* that word, let alone saying it."

Laughing, he shook his head as he cut another bite, chewed, and swallowed. "I imagine there are a great many things I think but never say. I love that word. It's true I rarely say it aloud."

"What's your favorite context for it?"

Humming in thought, he finally said, "I like it as an insult in a game of footie, you know? Like, 'Stop grabbing me shirt, yer cunt.'" He bent, taking a bite of green bean and oblivious to my wide-eyed swoon at his thick northern accent when he said it. He swallowed, wiped his mouth with his napkin, and then said, "What's your favorite context for it?"

I gulped down about half of my wine. "Probably something a bit cruder than that."

"Yeah?" he asked, grinning in understanding. "I thought Americans hated that word."

"*I* don't."

Niall lifted his wineglass to his lips, and took a long swallow. "I'll remember that."

EIGHT

Niall

The playful banter slipped into something a bit quieter after we'd finished our meals. Conversation flowed as easily as did the wine. Ruby had youthful attitudes about sex, but surprisingly traditional attitudes about relationships themselves. She admitted, between dinner and dessert, that despite all the flirting, she didn't like the idea of sex without some sort of understanding.

I studied Ruby—soft mouth, wide eyes, hands gesturing sweetly in front of her to punctuate every thought she shared—and marveled over how effortless it seemed for her. She was patient with my inexperience and hesitations. Indeed, they didn't even seem to surprise her.

Our dinners finished, our drinks consumed, Ruby picked up her clutch and stood from the table. I watched her hands wrap around the leather, watched her neck stretch as she reached up and untangled her necklace from where it caught on the neckline of her dress. I watched her tuck her hair behind her ear and then turn to look up at me.

She caught me staring; I was mesmerized with every movement she made.

"That was delicious," she said, giving me a cheeky grin.

Dear God in heaven.

"Every bite," I agreed, helping her with her coat.

"Do *you* bite?" she asked, making her way through the restaurant and out onto the street.

The air was bracing between blasts of steam from vents, and a cacophony of noises rose from the street.

"I imagine I might," I began, and we turned onto Greenwich. "Depending on the circumstances."

My skin hummed, my fingers twitched at my sides until, finally, I gathered the nerve to place my palm at the small of her back. Beneath my touch, she straightened and then shivered, before reaching behind her and taking my hand.

Her long, thin fingers weaved between mine and she pulled me into step with her. "Are you worried about work?" she asked quietly.

"About work . . . ?" I asked, confused.

"About *this*, and work."

I felt my brow lift in understanding. "Ah. Well, no, not at the moment." I raised a hand and hailed a taxi, holding the door for her. "I think we'll need to be clear on what we're doing, and then make sure that it doesn't interfere with our ability to do our jobs but"—I followed her into the car, noticing her amused smile as I babbled—"I don't think what we're doing is forbidden according to company policy."

"It isn't," she said, leaning into my side and looking up at me. "I checked forever ago."

" 'Forever ago'?"

She pulled her lip between her teeth and bit down as she smiled. "Maybe four months ago?"

We drove in silence for a few blocks. "Four months ago I didn't . . ."

"Know I existed," she finished for me, "I know. I think I was hoping to talk myself out of liking you," she said, laughing. "Maybe I'd see it was forbidden and, well, that would be that."

"Or maybe you'd want it more," I said, and ran my thumb along the side of her jaw.

"Maybe," she asked, turning into my palm. "When did you notice me?"

"The day Tony told me you'd be accompanying me in his place was the first day I *really* noticed you—"

She touched her finger to my chin, drawing my eyes back to her face. "You're getting nervous needlessly here. I know you were oblivious to me before. It doesn't hurt my feelings."

I swallowed, studying her sweet, pink mouth, her calm, green eyes. "I wasn't oblivious to you but, ah . . ." I struggled to hold her gaze. "You see, and this stays strictly between us . . . Tony may have suggested I use this trip to get a leg over."

" 'Get a leg over'?" she repeated, shaking her head.

I stared at her and smiled wanly as realization struck and she burst out laughing. "He is such a pig."

Her reaction calmed me immediately, until a thought occurred to me. "He's never touched you, I hope."

Tilting her head, she said, "No, he's just a creep. The way he looks at me and Pippa sometimes . . ." She shook her head, shivering.

I grimaced, not wanting to confirm that much of the time I felt the same way about how he looked at women in the office. On more than one occasion I'd been inclined to carefully request that HR keep an eye on him.

"But I do love that phrase," she said, blinking away. " 'Get a leg over.' It's hot in a crude sort of way. I like the idea of your long legs over mine, pinning me down."

I closed my eyes, steadying myself with a deep breath. "I assure you his suggestion carried little weight with me. But I'm a man, after all. And even if he hadn't said that, just knowing we would be traveling together would have sent me into a spin." She laughed, and I registered again how well she seemed to know me, how much she had picked up simply by observing. "I ran into you in the lift and—"

"And I was a *maniac*."

"Yes, you were. A menace, really," I teased. "But I wanted to get out only because I felt somewhat disoriented being that close to you."

"My derpy awkwardness overpowered you?"

"Without a doubt," I murmured, reaching to tuck her

hair behind her ear. "You're joking, but I'm not. Something about you . . ."

She closed her eyes and I let my fingers linger at her neck, drawing them down to her collarbone. Beneath my fingertips, her skin was cool from being outside, and so smooth. I could scarcely imagine how intense it would be to kiss her, let alone make love to her. I would likely tear her clothes, as she suggested only last night. I would most definitely bite.

"But I'd noticed you before. In meetings, we'd a shared look once or twice . . ."

Ruby opened her eyes again and her expression grew dubious, as if I'd begun to toy with her. "It's okay if you didn't notice me. It's also okay if this is just an experiment in seeing someone other than Portia. I promise I have my big-girl pants on."

"It's not . . ." I started, but then stopped when the cab pulled up at the curb.

I led Ruby inside the hotel and into a crowded lift. We exited on our floor in silence and walked down the carpeted hall toward our rooms, our steps echoing in the quiet.

Once we stood outside my door, I told her, "I have never considered having a fling. One drunk, fumbling interaction aside, sex purely for the sake of sex is not interesting to me."

She licked her lips and gave me an impish smile. "Then you need to have better sex."

As she continued to look up at me with her patient, playful eyes, the moment grew heavy.

"I think without a doubt I need to have better sex," I admitted quietly.

Her brows slowly inched up in suggestion and she tilted her head toward her hotel room door. "I had a really nice time at dinner . . ."

Ruby gave me another ten seconds to do or say more before she stretched to kiss my cheek, just barely missing the corner of my mouth. "Good night, my tentative, sexy, secretive crush."

I watched her turn and walk the ten steps to her room. She let herself inside, and the door clicked shut quietly behind her before I murmured, "Good night, my beautiful, exuberant girl."

———

"What brand of imbecile are you?" I asked my reflection in the bathroom mirror. "You could have kissed her. You could have *enjoyed* her tonight. At the very least you could have asked her in." I closed my eyes, taking a deep breath through my nose. It felt a little as if my skin were on fire, and short of walking into the shower with all of my clothes on, or barging into her room and deciding once and for all to have a go, I wasn't sure how the feeling was going to diffuse.

I swore I could remember every time she smiled tonight, or her openmouthed laugh, head back, eyes closed. Ruby seemed to enjoy every tiny instant of her life. There was something about her that made me want to be near her, put her up on a pedestal, bask in her energy and uninhibited sweetness.

Say something filthy, she'd said. *Tell me the craziest, dirtiest thing you can think of. Render me speechless.*

Walking to my closet, I pulled off my jacket, my tie, my shirt. I hung up all of my clothes, feeling overheated and sensitive and wound up to the point I thought I might burst. And I felt stupid, really. Ruby wouldn't have said no had I stepped forward, cupped her lovely face, and kissed her. She wouldn't even have said no if I'd simply asked her, "Come inside, show me how to do all of this for real, now? I'm afraid I'll bungle it."

Because, sincerely, I'd never taken a leap like this. Professionally, yes: I put myself out there, drove for what I wanted. But my personal life had sort of fallen easily into place. When we were sixteen, Portia found me in the woods near my home and suggested I kiss her. When we were eighteen, she informed me that she was ready to make love. Being Portia, she was unable to resist telling her mum what we'd done, and being Windsor-Lockharts, her parents had immediately *suggested* we marry. From there, it all unfolded rather obediently: a grand wedding, a flat her father loaned us the money to buy (and which I repaid in under four years), a car, a dog, and a marriage built on suggestion.

Things I never wanted again.

A new plan, then. I would take this side of me—the secret side that had long been dormant: romantic, passion-ate, desperate to find adventure with someone just a touch wilder than I could ever be—and not let it slide back into politeness, into convenience, into routine.

If Ruby wanted me to open up, I would do everything I could to do it.

I would ask for what I wanted with her.

I would learn how to play.

I would show her that I could give her what she needed.

With this sorted, an unwinding sense of relief passed through me and I sat down in my boxers at the desk, intent on going through my piles of voice mails from the London office. Pulling out my small voice recorder, I set to making notes after each call: which required immediate follow-up, which I could have my assistant attend to, and which only provided information of note. But after only fifteen mes-sages, my mind wandered back to dinner.

Ruby's habit of smiling with her tongue trapped between her teeth combined with the sweetness of the pineapple sorbet she had made me nearly dizzy with curiosity: Was her tongue cold? Cold and sweet? Did she like to have her tongue sucked and licked?

What would it feel like if she tasted her sorbet and then licked me, her tongue chilled, sliding around . . .

I let myself imagine Ruby at my door, in her tiny silken sleep shorts and tank, her breasts hard at the tips, the curve of her hips narrow and smooth. She steps inside, holding a glass of ice water in one hand and using the other to press on my chest and walk me backward to the bed.

"Don't sit," she warns me.

Wordlessly, I nod. I'm wearing only my boxers, and she doesn't say anything else, she doesn't even kiss me; but she traps that pink bubble-gum tongue between her teeth, smiling up at me, and slides to her knees, pulling my pants down as she goes.

I slid my boxers down my hips, letting the fantasy build.

I'm hard, jutting thick toward her, and watching transfixed as she takes an ice cube in her mouth, sucking it, sliding it down my stomach, over my hips.

"Ahh," I gasp as she slides her free hand up the inside of my thigh, cupping all of me—testicles and cock together in her grip—holding me crudely. I'm finally brave enough to put my hand on top of her head and then slide my fingers into her hair. It's soft, just like I imagined, and she gasps a little when I fist it, when I tug it.

She didn't expect that. She lets the ice cube fall from her mouth.

I wrapped my hand around my cock, pulling down and tight, groaning. "Lick it," I managed, my voice feeling oddly loud in the empty room.

Ruby's eyes go from bright and mischievous to half closed and sweetly obedient. I can feel her pull against my grip in her hair, struggling to reach me.

"You look so bloody gorgeous," I growled, moving my hand faster, imagining how it would feel for her to wrap her fist tight around the head of my dick, and swipe that soft, cool tongue around and around . . . I groaned. "Go slow," I hissed. "I want your tongue to play with me before you show me what you look like when you beg for it."

Her tongue peeks out, licking away the liquid there, sucking for more. Greedy, wicked little thing. I pull back, swiping myself across her lips, asking,

"Did you think about this earlier? When you licked your dessert from your spoon or sucked the sauce from your thumb, did you imagine you had my cock perched between your lips?"

She nods, opening her mouth and looking up at me with her lips suspended like that—parted for me.

"You want it?"

Nodding again, she lets her lips meet only long enough to whisper, "Please?"

With a tight moan, I slide in deep, relishing the feel of her tongue, of her mouth sealing around me and the rippling vibration of her surprised moan. Her eyes widen only for a heartbeat at the abrupt invasion before she relaxes, licking and whining sweetly, eyes fixed on mine. I slide in, and out, my breath choppy and rough as I tell her,

"Like that,"

. . . and . . .

"Oh, sweet girl . . . suck me . . ."

. . . and . . .

"I'll never get this sight out of my head. Never."

Her hands reach up to cup me lower, to tug and pet—

and it's heaven. It's too good, and it's too soon and I want to watch her face when she feels me come.

I closed my eyes at the fantasy. I hadn't received oral sex in nearly seven years and I was obsessed with Ruby's mouth and her tongue and her filthy, brave words.

I touch a finger to her chin, whispering,

"I'm coming. Ruby. Ruby. Please . . . please let me come inside."

And with a jerk against her tongue I do—the pleasure crawls up my legs and down my spine until it's pulsing and hot and my skin flushes with a tingle along every inch and

and

and

"Ohhh . . ."

I came against my fingers, groaning her name.

It took nearly a minute before my vision cleared and I could use my discarded boxers to clean my hand and the floor in front of me. The room felt startlingly quiet, as if I'd been on a stage somewhere, performing.

On the desk, my watch ticked loudly in the silence.

I glanced down at the desk and felt my face heat in embarrassment.

My voice recorder had been on the entire time.

My finger hovered over the rewind button. Nothing in the world could be more mortifying than listening to myself masturbate. I could rewind it all, erase everything.

But something in me dared to hesitate, and I put the device back down on the desk, staring silently at the wall separating our rooms.

The opportunity to move forward with Ruby got away from me tonight, but I wasn't going to let it happen again. Ruby was my safe space; oddly, after only a handful of days I felt we knew each other better than I knew Portia after nearly eleven years of marriage.

I *could* give Ruby what she needed.

I hit record again. Picking up my phone, I dialed her mobile and waited as it rang once,

My heart is beating so hard

twice,

Do this, Niall. Do this

and then she answered, clearing her throat before saying, "Niall?"

"Hello, Ruby."

Pausing, she whispered, "Is everything okay?"

My heart thudded in my chest and it occurred to me that I was standing in the middle of my hotel room, *stark naked*, on the phone with her. "Everything is fine," I murmured. I closed my eyes, imagining her listening to the recording of what I'd done, and then realizing I called her just after. Smiling, I said, "I just wanted to confirm that you'll be present at the meeting tomorrow at eight thirty?"

Another pause, and when she answered, she sounded slightly disappointed. "Of course. I'll meet you in the lobby at a quarter to eight?"

I glanced at the clock. It was nearly midnight. Only a matter of hours before I would see her. "Quarter to eight," I said. "Perfect."

"Good night . . ."

"Good night, darling."

I hung up, and reached over to hit stop on the recording.

Nine

Ruby

The next morning, I was holding my breath the entire time the elevator was descending to the lobby. It was 7:43 and I knew without question that Niall would already be downstairs—suit: immaculate, hair: perfect, body: banging. What I didn't know was exactly *which* Niall I would encounter today.

Would it be the teasing, flirtatiously forward maybe-almost-my-boyfriend-Niall from dinner last night? The one that sent my hands straight down my panties within seconds of closing the door? Or the strangely terse, abrupt Mr. Stella from the phone call only an hour later?

Niall's brain seemed to be his own worst enemy, unable to shut down or stay silent long enough for him to just have *fun*. At dinner he'd let the walls down, teasing and being downright filthy across the table from me. But give him an hour in his room, alone with his own thoughts, and any afterglow I'd been experiencing was doused like a bucket of ice water.

A tiny voice warned that I should pay attention, that

I should heed the warning bells—however dim—inside my head. Although he *looked* like a man who carried the world in the palm of his hand, Niall was also a hyper-cautious overthinker, and maybe I should rein in my desire to dive headfirst.

Good advice, I was sure.

But when the elevator doors opened and I saw Niall Stella himself across the lobby, that advice was all too easy to ignore.

Like always, my pulse sped up at the sight of him, my skin prickly and almost hot to the touch. He looked over and met my eye. People filed out in front of me and the seconds seemed to tick by while I waited for a reaction from him—any reaction. My shoes clicked on the marble floors as I walked, and I had to look away, adjust the belt on my trench coat, and force myself to keep my shoulders straight. Niall was just a man, after all, and from what he'd told me last night, I had more experience in this sort of situation than he had. *I* had the upper hand.

Keep telling yourself that.

His overcoat slung over his arm, he checked his watch, his brow lifting when he glanced back up at me. "Punctual, I see."

Teasing. My breath eased out of my lungs and I straightened my shoulders. I could do teasing.

"Punctuality is a critical virtue," I told him.

"Couldn't agree more. I happen to find it *very* attractive." His voice sounded deeper this morning, more confident. There was something about the way his accent sharpened *very*, shaping it into something dirty that sent goose bumps up and down my arms. If this was anyone else, I would have questioned whether he was up to something, but this was Mr. Straight and Narrow. I was fairly certain he wouldn't be ravaging me in a hotel lobby, or while meeting with the New York Transit Authority.

I knew he'd be careful to keep everything between us strictly professional at work, but after last night, when he'd suggested he wanted to show me all the things he didn't consider "gentle, or chaste or very proper," the question of where we stood was still largely unanswered, and I was trying my best to let him tell me how fast we should move. One would *think* he would have wanted to start right away. One would *think* he would have even simply kissed me good night.

I looked at him expectantly as he slid his arms into his coat and motioned for me to lead the way. "Shall we?"

Halfway through the first meeting, we adjourned for a break. I felt pretty useless during these discussions about budget and public perception rather than the cogs and wheels of the actual structures themselves. But I listened, knowing the conversations that felt challenging right now were actually the ones I needed to grasp the most.

Still, even Niall seemed to be distracted, staring down

at the same page of his agenda repeatedly, and twice needing to be nudged when called on to answer a question. He barely glanced my way, but there were lingering touches as I'd handed him a stack of papers. His calf rested a bit too comfortably against mine to be written off as anything but intentional.

In fact, his lack of focus was bordering on unnerving, and so I was grateful when he pulled me aside, asking if I'd mind sitting the rest of the meeting out.

"I know this is terribly rude of me," he said, motioning to the phone in his hands. "But I've just checked my mobile and I've a few things that need attending. Nothing too urgent, but Jo's called with some names and dates I need for a conference call with Tony. Would you—" he paused, eyes apologetic. "I know you're not my assistant, or under my report in any way, but would you mind listening and jotting the information down?"

I heaved a sigh of relief, both that there seemed to be a reason for his distraction, and that I might be spared the pain of another two hours of this.

"With pleasure," I said, taking his cell. "These team meetings have nothing to do with my department. Give me a job, *any* job, before I lose my mind."

The wall separating the conference room from a smaller waiting area was about twenty feet long and floor-to-ceiling glass. Inside the space were a pair of white leather couches, a handful of sleek iron tables, and two matching chairs. A wall of exterior windows looked out over a street lined with restaurants and newly flowering trees. I deposited myself on the couch, pulled out a notebook and pen, and began opening his phone.

"One more thing."

I startled at the sound of his voice in the doorway.

"The passcode is my birthday—"

"Oh-six-oh-nine, I know," I blurted, and then blinked up to see him staring at me in surprise. I gave him a slow, wincing smile. "You should probably know I want the floor to eat me now," I said. "Because, hello, stalker."

He laughed. "Perhaps I'm not very clever with my passcodes."

"I guess if you stare at a person enough you pick up all sorts of things," I said, throwing in an awkward cough for effect.

But Niall only laughed again, shaking his head and throwing in another "thank you" before turning to leave. "Oh and Ruby?" he said, pausing just at the door.

"Yeah?"

"Be sure you listen straight through. Some of them are quite long and . . . there's one at the end that's particularly important."

"Got it," I said, and didn't even pretend I wasn't watching his butt as he walked away.

⌐━━━━⌐

From the sofa, I could see him perfectly. He'd stopped at the refreshment table for a bottle of water before taking his seat, and I wondered if it was a trick of the light that made him look slightly flushed.

Given that some of the voice messages were apparently on the long side, I reached for my purse, happy when I found my earbuds tucked away near the bottom. I inserted the plug into the jack and placed one of the buds in my ears, then keyed in his password. Four messages. The first, predictably, was from Jo, and I listened while she rattled off a list of names and corresponding dates, and carefully wrote each one down. The second and third followed along the same lines, and within three minutes an entire sheet in my notebook had been filled.

I looked up and checked into the meeting again, catching him discussing something with a person seated nearby. Without the benefit of his voice, I could *see* the way his mouth formed the words differently than those around him, his accent visible at a distance. He used his lips more, held the shape of the words longer. I wondered what it would be like to hear that voice at home, in my ear while it panted out commands, telling me what he needed.

One day I should write a novel full of all the things I wondered about that man.

Pressing play again, I caught Niall's eyes for just a second before he blinked away. The last message started, and I waited, trying to discern exactly what I was hearing. Someone breathing . . . the hum of an air conditioner . . . faint traffic? The shuffling of fabric filled the line—

almost as if a piece of clothing were being dragged over the receiver—and I picked up the phone again, checking the connection to make sure I hadn't knocked something loose.

But then I heard, *"Ahh,"* and *that* . . . well, I definitely wasn't expecting that.

"You look so bloody gorgeous."

I knew that voice. I'd spent the last six months with my ears straining to hear him step out of the elevator and onto my floor, to speak during meetings. For him to speak to *me. This* was Niall, and he was . . . I think . . .

"Go slow. I want your tongue to play with me before you show me what you look like when you beg for it."

OH MY GOD.

I blanched. Had I somehow stumbled onto something I wasn't supposed to have? Was this even Niall? It seemed impossible that he would record anything like this, let alone give it to me to hear.

Unless he didn't know it was being recorded. Was he . . . *with someone?* Should I tell him I had this?

"Did you think about this earlier?" he said through the tape. *"When you licked your dessert from your spoon, or sucked the sauce from your thumb, did you imagine you had my cock between your lips?"*

Dessert? Was he talking about . . . ?

I straightened and glanced toward the conference room, not sure if I was surprised when I found him already looking at me. I didn't know how long he'd been watching, but when he nodded, slowly, I was certain he knew exactly what I was listening to, and that he'd orchestrated this entire thing so I could.

"You want it?"

"Like that."

"Oh, sweet girl . . . suck me . . ."

He was getting himself off, thinking about me going down on him . . .

He must have done this last night after dinner—*Holy shit!*

It was sixty-eight degrees in that office, and I was sweating.

Niall didn't look away from me once, and I swear this situation could only have felt dirtier if he'd had me spread out naked on the floor. And then, only barely. How did he do that? We'd hardly touched, and yet it felt like he'd touched me in ways that nobody else ever had.

"I'll never get this sight out of my head. Never."

I crossed my legs and pressed them together, shifting in my seat. I could feel how wet I was, how ready my body felt to do exactly the things he was talking about.

"I'm coming. Ruby. Ruby. Please . . . please let me come inside."

<hr />

When the group broke for lunch, I noted the way Niall hesitated to leave. He'd have to face me now—now that I'd listened to his hit single—without the safety net of twenty feet, a wall of glass, and fifteen engineers and transit authority workers between us. He was nervous, and fuck if it wasn't the most endearing thing I'd ever seen.

Unable to put it off any longer, he gathered his things and stepped out.

"Hungry?" he asked.

"Starving," I told him, wondering if—*hoping*—he got the implication of my words.

Judging by the way he reached up and began to fidget with the knot in his tie, I was guessing he did.

I tilted my head toward the hallway. "Walk with me?"

I led us out of the office and down a slowly emptying hall. A man from the meeting stopped us on our way.

"There's lunch on the floor above us. It's National Taco Day or something, if you're hungry. Should be . . . interesting."

Well, the most interesting thing *this guy* was going to have happen today, anyway.

"We need to touch base with the London office," Niall said smoothly. "But we'll be up as soon as possible."

And I had to admit, I was impressed.

With a nod, the intruder was off and we continued on, down one hall and then another, until the sounds of voices were just a hum in the opposite direction.

"We're calling London, are we?" I asked.

"Not exactly." He glanced over at me, smiling. "I assume you're taking me somewhere quiet to talk?"

"*Talk?*" I said with a little smile.

He pursed his amazing lips. "Perhaps."

"Speaking of 'talking,' here are your notes," I said, handing him the notebook.

"Ah. Thank you."

A dark room stood at the end of the hall, and I led him inside, closing the door behind us. Then, leaning back against the cool wood, I said, "Your messages were very . . . engrossing."

"Engrossing, you say?" He took a step closer.

"They affected me," I said through a giggle. "Deeply."

Tilting his head and wearing a smile that tilted half of his mouth deliciously, he murmured, "How so?"

I moved to answer, to give him something playful and coy, but when our eyes met, every coherent thought left my brain. My heart started beating so hard with the sudden, surreal understanding that this wasn't a fantasy, this wasn't just flirtation. I wasn't sitting in the middle of a Thursday meeting imagining all of this.

We'd blazed past so many Niall Stella Moments that I'd stopped keeping track.

The Number of Times Niall Stella . . . Touched My Calf, Tucked My Hair Behind My Ear, Looked Me in the Eye and Asked If I Came.

Told Me He Wanted Me to Swallow His Come.

Recorded Himself Masturbating to Share with Me.

Was About to Kiss Me.

This was a thing. *We* were a thing.

"Answer me."

I lost the ability to play for the moment, ducking my head. "I *ache*."

"Tell me." His voice was somehow both commanding and gentle as he bent, kissing my neck. "When you ache, what does that mean?"

He knew. He had to know. He wanted me to say the words. "It means I'm wet."

He inhaled sharply through his nose, running it up my neck and along my jaw. "Bloody hell, Ruby, will you look up and *kiss* me?"

I tilted my head, completely out of breath and heart crashing around the cage of my lungs. The smell of his cologne permeated the darkness and I felt almost drunk on him, on his nearness and the realization that I was actually going to touch him. *Kiss* him. And he would kiss me back.

He bent to meet me, lips parted with a shaking exhale. He'd been expecting a small kiss, a quiet slide of his lips over mine. I could tell because I knew him better than maybe I should at that point, but also because of the careful way he bent to me and the gentle brace of his hands on my waist.

But I couldn't do small and quiet. I'd wanted this for too long. The relief—the *awareness* of him, his scent and the warm Stella skin—clawed up my spine, jolting through my arms, and I pulled him down into me. I gave him anything but small and quiet. My lips slid over his, pulling his bottom lip in between and he huffed a little breath against me, groaning.

I wanted to swallow it up, wanted to consume his sounds and keep them inside me so I could save them for later and listen to them on a loop, again and again.

His mouth was unreal: firm lips and that perfect man combination of soft and hard, giving and commanding. My world was *spinning*. I dug my hands into his hair, pressed my breasts into that solid wall of his chest, and let loose the most ridiculous sound of relief and need I'd ever made.

He groaned louder now, surprise and thrill making his hands grip me reflexively before sliding around my back and clutching me close.

Close enough I was bent backward as he curled over me, his lips parting only enough to let loose another deep sound as his tongue slid into my mouth, tasting me.

Close enough that I was positive he felt my heart hammering through my chest.

Close enough for me to feel him growing hard, longer, pressing into my stomach.

I was so wildly, deliriously hungry for him, for this, that I let out tiny gasps, a tight moan at the feel of his tongue sliding over mine. I barely had time to process what I was saying before "Niall. *Please*," escaped.

"Please what?" He slid his lips to my ear, kissing, exhaling in a shaking gust of air. "Anything."

"Just . . . kiss me."

I felt his small laugh. "I believe I *was* kissing you."

"Then touch me. *Something.* I feel . . ."

"Show me," he whispered against my mouth. "Show me where you ache."

I couldn't stop the small whimper that escaped my throat, and I pulled back, just enough to meet his eyes.

Turning my hand so that our palms touched, I twisted my fingers with his, bringing them up to place a single kiss on the back of his hand. His gaze flickered from my eyes to my mouth, and back again, before he nodded, slowly. Hands still entwined, I brought them between us and down until together they slipped beneath the hem of my skirt.

"Yes," he groaned, feeling bare skin as we moved up together, finally brushing the damp fabric of my panties. I took a step back, and then another, bringing him with me until my back was pressed against the door.

He followed my lead, fingertips slipping beneath the lace to skim along my skin, slick from wanting him.

"Already," he gasped moving back and forth so easily.

I nodded but couldn't form even a single word in response. I wanted him so much it hurt, and now he was touching me, *finally*, his long index finger smoothing along my bare flesh to slip over and between, finally to where I wanted him most of all.

Right there,
Oh, God, there,
Oh, it's so good.

I gave him every thought before I was even conscious of it.

He traced the same path again, along my entrance and back up to my clit with a surprisingly competent touch for someone who wasn't even sure whether the woman he'd spent over a decade with had enjoyed the nights they shared together. His lips moved from the corner of my mouth to my jaw and then up, finally tracking the shell of my ear.

"This is what I've wanted," he whispered. "What I think about. What I thought about last night. I thought about your soft tongue, how you would feel just here. What it would feel like to slip into your body, your mouth. I think about it nearly to the point of obsession."

I pushed back into the door, wanting to escape the increasing urgency of his touch, or needing the support it offered me, I wasn't sure. I only knew that I was lost, only a breath away from falling apart so completely he might never be able to put me back together.

"Inside," I whispered, voice breaking. "Want to come with you inside me."

"When you speak this way . . ." he said, but did as I asked. He pushed one finger into me, and then two, pumping deeply. "Bloody hell . . ."

Sensation built, making my legs weak and my kisses distracted and wet all over his lips, his chin. My desperate sounds carried only so far as his mouth before he consumed them. His thumb circled, firm and sure, as fingers slid in and out. I could swear he was pushing deeper with every stroke, reaching something inside me that was wild and untouched.

And then, the feeling built until it was spilling over and I came, my body arching into his hand. His mouth found mine again, and he whispered things I only barely understood.

"Give me your sounds," he said. "Let me keep them to think about tonight."

But we had all night together, I remembered. No meetings and no dinners planned with anyone from the conference. Nobody that would interrupt us. I wondered if he knew that, too. Maybe doing this here was easier, with the distant sounds of office life coming from the other rooms around us, reminding us both that we couldn't take it too far. Maybe—

"I can't believe I'm the one saying this," he said, rubbing his nose along mine, "but stop thinking."

"Just . . . wow," I said, wanting to slip like warm honey down to the floor. Regretfully, he pulled his hand from my skirt and wrapped his arms around me, keeping me upright.

" 'Wow' is good. I'll take 'wow.' "

"We should do that again," I said, feeling my stupid grin.

"Just seeing how quickly you fell apart in my arms . . ."

"No kidding."

He glanced at the door, his expression falling the

smallest bit. "But we've been gone for some time; we should join the others."

"You—" I started, eyes flickering down to his cock.

He was still hard—impressively so—but he stilled my hand when I reached for his belt. "Quite used to it by now, I can assure you."

I frowned. "But I can—"

As if on cue, a voice called out from the other end of the hall. Time was up.

For now, I thought. We had an entire night, and I planned on enjoying every second of it.

TEN

Niall

I could sense from the way Ruby kept glancing at me that she was up to something.

"What?" I mouthed when she'd trapped that full pink bottom lip between her teeth and finally looked up at my face after staring at my neck, my arms, my hands.

She shrugged. "Nothing," she mouthed back, her tongue peeking out between her teeth with the single word.

She *knew*. She had to know what that tongue did to me. So soft and pink and teasing.

I tore my eyes from her and back to the woman leading today's discussion on hurricane disaster relief budgeting. All around the room, eyelids drooped or hands doodled on notepads. For my part, I'd found the meetings all week predictably intense but fascinating. I loved my job, loved the topic of disaster preparedness and the details we had come together to scrutinize. I enjoyed work in a way I suspected many of my colleagues didn't: it was my escape, my passion. So it threw me somewhat when I found my eyes wandering to the clock, my mind drifting to Ruby and what would happen between us tonight.

We had no meetings, no social obligations. From 1700 until the following morning, we had nothing but time . . . together.

With Portia, we'd had all the time in the world, eleven years' worth. And yet, even in the beginning, more time in each other's company was never something either of us particularly yearned for. Everything felt more important than having lunch together; even something as simple as a few hours side by side watching television was always passed up in favor of working independently or catching up on odd projects. But Ruby seemed to practically vibrate at the prospect of a handful of hours alone—with *me*.

Clearly what had happened over lunch was an admission that we both needed to move forward, away from the flirtatious games we enjoyed during the day into something more personal and intimate at night.

I simply didn't know how well I could do it. I had little practice being forthcoming about emotions, and even less experience being bare sexually with another person. I knew I'd made her come. I knew I could give her far more pleasure than what I'd done today. That wasn't really what worried me. What worried me was knowing she would give me exactly as much as I wanted from her.

If I wanted to make love to her tonight, I could. If I wanted to feel myself deep in her throat, I could. If I wanted limits,

I would need to be the one to set them. But did I truly want limits, or did I think I *should* want them?

My stomach cramped and I looked back to the woman at the head of the table. Out of the corner of my eye I could see Ruby tilt her head and glance at me, and I suspected she was watching my every thought pass across my face. I was starting to believe she had a decoder ring and was the one person I'd known other than my brother and younger sister who could take one look at me and know just how much I was hiding.

I blinked up, met her eyes.

She studied me briefly, her expression softening as she smiled, mouthing the words, "Don't worry," before looking down at her notes and then up at the moderator.

At once, my shoulders relaxed, my jaw unclenched.

Let go, her voice whispered in my thoughts. *We'll figure it out together.*

We walked back to the hotel, and Ruby babbled sweetly about the meeting, the oddly warm weather, the band she'd been dying to see live that was in town. She talked to me about all the wonderful nothings I wanted to hear, distracting me from my own neurosis about the impending evening.

At the Parker Meridien, Ruby steered us to the elevators, down the hall, and stopped in front of the door to my room. Turning her green eyes up to mine, she whispered, "So. Decision time. Do you want to hang out with me tonight?" She placed her palms flat to my chest. "No pressure. I can go to my room and masturbate to a Ryan Gosling movie, and you can go back to your room and beat yourself up for not getting me topless, but the choice is entirely yours."

I swallowed, taking a few calming breaths before giving her a kiss that started at the corner of her mouth and slid over to her cheek, then to her ear. "Yes, please," I murmured.

"So," she said, managing to stretch the word into at least three syllables. "Dinner out, or in?"

It took no more than three seconds for me to answer, "*In*," and with a bright smile, she took my keycard from my hand and let us in, bounding across the room. She kicked off her shoes, jumping on the bed and rolling until her face was in my pillow.

"Dammit, they changed the sheets. This pillow doesn't smell like you." She flipped back over, hugging it to her chest anyway.

"I'll make sure to have them leave the linens tomorrow."

Then, in a Niall Stella voice, she said, "An excellent notion," and nodded once crisply, bringing a smile to my lips. Smiling back at me, she reached for the room service menu off the bedside table and flipped it open. "What are you in the mood for?"

I leaned against the desk, watching her. Loving seeing her in my room, on this bed, so easy and comfortable in this role as . . . *girlfriend*.

Sitting down to unlace my shoes, I murmured, "Hmm. Maybe a burger?"

"Are you asking me?" She looked back down at the menu. "They have a few choices. Cheeseburger and fries?"

"Perfect. And whatever dark beer they offer."

She chucked the menu to the floor and grabbed the room phone. I heard the quiet echo of a voice on the other end of the line and Ruby laughed, cupping her hand over the receiver. In a playfully scandalized voice, she said, "They called me Mrs. Stella."

I smiled, slipping off my shoes. Mrs. Stella was my mother, or—once upon a time—Portia. "Mrs. Stella" wasn't this vivacious creature sprawled on my bed with her skirt slowly inching up her long, slender thighs.

But that was the problem, wasn't it? I was stuck thinking Ruby was just a little too fun, a little too pretty, a little too adventurous for the likes of me. I had a picture of what I thought I deserved, who might like me, and it wasn't ever someone like Ruby.

If she'd been able to hear this thought, I'm quite certain she would have ripped the phone out of the wall and hurled it at me.

I listened, watching as she ordered, confirmed our selection, and then hung up. All of this was so commonplace, so easy, so comfortable; my shoulders unknotted, stomach settled.

She patted the bed, lifting her eyebrows and giving me a

seductive little smile. "We have approximately forty minutes for mischief."

"Ruby . . ." I began.

Her smile slipped a little before she picked it up again. "Why are you so afraid of being on a bed with me?" she said, and I could hear the embarrassment just beneath her laugh. "I'm not going to steal your virtue, I promise."

"It's nothing about being afraid. I—" I stopped, pulling my tie from the collar of my shirt and draping it over the desk chair. Whenever I wanted to explain myself, say something important—something *personal*—the words in my mind scattered into disarray. It's why, with Portia, I'd long since given up.

I knew I needed to stop comparing everything to my marriage. Ruby was trying to help me find who I was again, and I needed to let her.

New relationship. New pattern.

"Tell me."

I closed my eyes, putting together the sentence before I said anything more. "I feel like I've barely processed the idea of being with you and what that entails, and yet here we are, in a room with a bed. Although there is no 'normally' to be found in my dating experience, I like to think that 'normally' I would take you out to dinner a few times, kiss you at your doorstep, be far more measured in my interactions. At least that's what eighteen-year-old me would have done all those years ago," I said with a quiet, sheepish laugh. "Yet, here we are in a hotel room, I put my fingers inside you earlier, and all I want to do now is join you and relieve the ache I've felt all day long. I suppose it surprises me that my body and my heart are so far ahead of my brain here."

Ruby rose up on her knees so she could crawl to the foot of the bed. Reaching out, she slid her finger through my belt loop and pulled me closer. "Why do people act like the heart and body aren't part of the brain?"

She worked the top button of my shirt free and moved to the next. And the next. Her fingertips tickled as they brushed over my breastbone.

"When you want me?" she began. "That's your brain. When you like being around me? Hey guess what?" She looked up at me, sweet tongue-trapped smile in place. "Also because of your brain."

"Do you know what I mean, though?" I asked in a whisper. Our faces were only inches apart; I'd need to only duck down to kiss her. "I worry you're young. That I'm neurotic. How can it work away from all of this?"

"In fact," she said, pulling her brows together in mock seriousness, "I would think it would be easier for you to do this with me back home. In your space, with your routines. I would think what's hardest about this for you is that you're away from all of that, and I'm just another piece of chaos thrown in the mix."

Her words eased my mind, massaged away the growing wave of anxiety. "Are you sure you aren't really a sixty-year-old bird with a fantastic plastic surgeon? You seem remarkably wise."

"I am definitely sure," she said, smiling prettily up at me. "But I'm also sure that you don't have to do a single thing you don't want to, Niall. You're allowed to not want this."

I looked down to her pulse point, wondering what it would feel like beating against my lips. "I'm quite sure . . . What I mean is . . ." I sighed, frustrated by my own thoughts. "I do want this," I said finally.

Ruby giggled, falling backward onto the bed and pulling me down over her. We landed softly, bouncing off the mattress, and I easily rolled beside her, shrugging out of my dress shirt. Almost as if we'd planned it—or had been doing it for decades—she bent her knees, lifting her legs over mine and tucking her feet down behind my thighs as I curled on my side into her.

I stared down at our position, speechless.

"We fit," Ruby observed quietly. "And look. I got you on the bed with me this time." She reached up to smooth away the lines that had formed on my forehead. "To be clear, I want to spend time with you, and cuddle while we talk," she assured me. "We don't have to get naked before dinner. Or after."

I smiled, reaching forward and running a palm over her stomach to her opposite hip. "Tell me about your family?"

"Let's see . . ." Her hand reached up to run along my neck and into my hair. "I have one brother, my twin—"

"You have a twin brother?" I asked. How could I have kissed her, watched her bring herself to orgasm, given her another one with my hand earlier and spent the last five days with her without knowing such basic information?

"Yeah, he's in med school at UCLA. His name is Crain."

"Crain? That's not a name you hear every day."

"Well, everyone calls him by our last name, Miller, but yeah." She ran her fingers over my scalp, lost in thought. "He's good people."

"And your parents?"

"Are married," she said, meeting my eyes. "They live in Carlsbad, which is just north of San Diego. I think I mentioned they're both psychologists."

I pulled back to study her. "How is it possible *both* of your parents are psychologists and you seem so . . . normal?"

Laughing, she pretended to shove my chest. "That is such a stupid stereotype. One would think if the parents were both very good shrinks, their children would be better adjusted, not worse."

"One would think." I felt my lips press together in an amused smile. She . . . she was *unbelievable*. "So you grew up in Carlsbad before attending UCSD?"

"Mmmhmm," she said, focusing on where she drew her finger back and forth across my collarbones. "Happy childhood. Cool parents. Twin brother who only occasionally dated my friends . . ." She seemed distracted, and confirmed it when she stretched up, kissing my throat. "I'm a lucky girl."

"No demons, then?" I murmured.

Ruby pulled back slowly, her eyes clouding for a heartbeat. "No demons."

I studied her face, sliding my hand up to her ribs before telling her very quietly, "That wasn't very convincing." I had no idea why I'd asked that, but now I needed to know. My chest grew tight with this feeling of diving deeper, of making this into more than flirtation, kissing, groping. This here was what I needed but was also most terrified to seek: intimacy in words before action.

"Fine," she said, smiling a little. "But you first."

I blinked, surprised. Despite having asked her this, I hadn't really expected the question to be turned back on me. "Well, I suppose my childhood was fairly happy as well. Looking back I realize we were rather poor, but children don't often notice things like money shortages when they have everything they need. My marriage, as I may have mentioned, was rather . . . *quiet*. Especially compared with a childhood filled with rowdy brothers and sisters. We didn't argue much, we didn't laugh much. There wasn't much left holding us together at the end."

She brought her hand to my jaw, following the shape of it with her fingertip as she listened.

"I suppose my demons are my reserve, and how I fear I spent the better part of my teens and all of my twenties with a woman I probably won't know for the rest of my life. It feels like a bit of a waste."

"Your reserve?" she repeated quietly.

Nodding, I murmured, "I always wonder if I come across the way I mean to with people."

"How do you mean to come across?"

"Friendly. Interested," I told her. "Responsible."

"You come off as responsible." Her lips tweaked into a smirk. "Maybe a *little* aloof."

Laughing, I admitted, "That's fair. I've always been the quiet one, a bit awkward. Max and Rebecca, who are closest to me in age, were the clowns. I've been the contained one, but it also meant I got away with things they didn't."

"This sounds like a story I need to hear . . ."

Shaking my head, I bent to kiss her jaw, speaking into her skin, "Your turn."

When I pulled back, she looked at my chin, her finger drawing lazy circles at the hollow of my throat.

"Ruby?"

Blinking up to meet my eyes, I watched as she took a deep breath. "I had a bad boyfriend my freshman year," she said, simply. The words were just vague enough that I wasn't sure how she meant it. Was he violent? Fickle?

"What do you mean—"

"Maybe calling him a boyfriend isn't exactly right," she said, tilting her head on the pillow as she considered her words. "We went out a few times and he wanted sex before I did. He got his way."

When I understood what she was telling me, my heart seemed to try to claw its way up my throat, so my words came out strangled. "He *hurt* you?" As I looked down at her thin frame, her delicate jaw, full lips, and wide, honest eyes, a fire-red tempo took over inside my chest; I was consumed by a rush of anger and vengeance I'd never experienced.

She shrugged. "A little. It wasn't very dramatic or violent, just unpleasant. It wasn't my first time, but . . ."

My brow lifted in understanding. "It hurt anyway."

She nodded, focusing her attention on my chin again. "Yeah. So, you asked about demons. I guess that's mine."

I was at a loss. I felt my mouth open, and close again. I wanted to punch a wall, wrap her up in my arms, and cover her body with mine. And then I pulled my hand back from her ribs, instinctively worried.

"Stop," she said through an uncomfortable laugh. "That's why I don't like talking about it. It was a bad night, but one of the many benefits of having *good psychologists* for parents is that you learn to talk about things, which helped me out with this."

Ruby seemed so wholly healthy, so composed, weathering my fits and starts easily. That said, it was all well and good to embrace the idea of being adventurous sexually with someone, but it made me regard her a bit more earnestly as someone with good and bad experiences, who not only wanted to handle me carefully, but also required careful handling of her own.

"Just ask me," she said, correctly reading my expression. "If we're going to do this"—she gestured between us—"then you need to know these things about me."

"You're not . . ." I began, feeling awkward, like I was trying on a child's glove. I swallowed, and then swallowed again, coughing.

"Niall," she said, stretching to kiss me, letting her lips linger at the corner of my mouth. *"Ask."*

"Sex . . . isn't an issue for you." It wasn't a question, and I wanted to close my eyes and vanish when I felt the hot flush of embarrassment rise over my skin. She was just so open, so comfortable being sexual.

She didn't seem to notice, and didn't even seem bothered by my blunt words. "It was at first," she began. "I mean, maybe it still is sometimes. For the first year or so after I was a little . . . freaked-out. I slept with a bunch of guys, almost like, 'Hey, universe, I choose to do this. And *this*, and *this*.' But my therapist helped. What Paul did wasn't really about sex. He was a mess. The times I've been with guys after him weren't anything like that. I don't feel like he broke me, but he did show me that some people are just . . . bad."

"Do you think of it often?"

She smiled up at me and touching my lips with her index finger in a gesture that was at once sweet and maddeningly seductive. "I guess. It depends on what's going on in my life, really."

I felt myself instinctively pulling back.

"But especially times like now, where I'm worried it's going to make you careful with me, or hesitant to let go . . ." Her eyes searched mine, pleading. "Promise me you won't be."

I wanted to promise her this, but what she'd told me simply reinforced my desire to take this slowly. "I—"

We were interrupted by a knock at the door: our food had arrived. I stood, slipping on and buttoning my shirt to let a man with a rolling food-laden table into the room. He placed it beside the bed as I signed the ticket. The room ticked in the silence; the remnants of our conversation seemed to dissolve out of the air.

Ruby sat on the mattress, curling her legs beneath her as she lifted the silver domes off our plates. The door closed behind the waiter, and I sat beside her at the table.

"Hungry?"

"Starving," she mumbled, pouring ketchup on her plate. She leaned over, kissing my cheek. She was relentlessly right-minded. "Thanks for dinner, hottie."

And as she tucked into her meal, it was clear that, for the time being, our conversation had moved on.

———

Ruby fell back against the mattress with a satisfied groan. "Whatever happens tonight, just know you're in competition with that cheeseburger for best in show."

"I fear Burger Joint has a bit more experience with cheeseburgers than I do."

"Then bring your mad seduction skills, Mr. Stella," she teased.

Dinner had been good, but I hadn't paid much attention, moving mostly on autopilot. I knew without a doubt that I didn't want to move too fast, and given her honesty with me tonight, I wanted to be particularly careful with her emotions, too.

I moved the table away from the side of the bed and returned to her, maneuvering so that I lay beside her, hovering above.

"Good start," she whispered, hands moving to begin unbuttoning my dress shirt. Again.

My fingers played with the button at the top of her silk shirt.

"Are you having second thoughts?" she asked, perhaps after I lingered too long on my action.

I shook my head, thinking. Her green eyes scanned my face, patient but intense.

"I suppose I just want it to be clear what we're doing tonight," I admitted at length. "I'm a bit thrown by what you've told me."

Her forehead relaxed in understanding and she pushed her head back into the pillow a bit to see me better. "About Paul."

"And your reaction after of running headlong into sexual relationships."

A flash of hurt crossed her face but she hid it away quickly. "I haven't done that in a long time."

I smiled at this. She was twenty-three. *A long time* was such a relative thing. "I'm not trying to judge you, Ruby. Perhaps it's a good reminder for me, as well, to take this slow."

"No sex, you mean."

Looking into her eyes, I nodded. "I'm old-fashioned, I realize, but that's something I do want to do only when I'm in love."

Her face registered some unrecognizable emotion and she looked like she was going to say something but instead, she simply nodded.

I wanted to clarify my words, knowing how she may have interpreted them—that ours wasn't that kind of relationship, that we weren't headed in that direction—but how was I to know whether or not we would? In my lucid moments near her, it occurred to me that all of this seemed so impossibly easy. I wanted to enjoy her for whatever this was, and not expect too much. My default always seemed to be so bloody *sincere* about it all. Maybe this was just meant to be something lovely, and easy but, ultimately, primarily sexual.

And temporary.

Most people had several relationships in their lives; I liked the idea that Ruby could be something more permanent, but I'd known her just two weeks.

"I can practically hear you thinking," she whispered, pulling my head down so she could kiss me once, sweetly. "Why does being alone with me in this hotel trip your panic button? No one is labeling this." It was as if she read my thoughts. "I like you. I want to be close to you, whatever that means right now."

Whatever that means right now.

The words liberated me, and I leaned into her touch, relishing the feel of her hands sliding up my neck and into my hair. I loved the tugging, the nails scratching. I loved the signs of passion that had always been absent from my romantic life.

Ruby's lips were full, and warm, tasting of Sprite and the little chocolate mint that had been placed beside our dinner plates. Her mouth opened, tongue sliding out across her lips to mine, dipping into my mouth and letting me feel the small, sweet vibrations of her moan.

I *was* thinking too much; I was always thinking too bloody much. I slid my hand up her ribs, over her breasts, and back to the button that had made my entire brain hit pause.

I slipped the first one free, and then the next, and the next, until Ruby was shrugging out of her shirt and lying beneath me in a pale yellow bra.

Sweet Lord, I could lay my face on that skin and never need for anything more.

"You have the most perfect breasts I've ever laid eyes on."

She stilled beneath me and then brought her hands to her face, hiding.

I stared down at her. What had I said? That she had perfect breasts? Were we meant to do this without comment?

"Ruby?"

"I'm having a moment, just give me a second," she said, her voice muffled by her palms.

"Was I too forward?"

"No," she said, dropping her hands and looking up at me with these crazy, beautiful eyes. "I just had an out-of-body experience. Niall Stella just took off my shirt and admired my chest."

"Do you need to text someone?" I said, stifling a laugh.

"I just need to remember to add it to my spreadsheet of Niall Stella Moments," she joked, and reached for my head again, pulling me down.

I traced the straight line of her collarbone, across to the middle and over to the other shoulder.

She arched beneath me. "*Niall.*"

I made a faint tsking sound before saying, "Patience."

Her bra strap was silky and thin, a wisp of fabric holding up such plump, perfect breasts. I almost didn't want to reveal them; the anticipation was too sublime.

"You've seen me completely naked," she reminded me.

"But I haven't *touched* you when you were completely naked." Looking up at her face, I smiled. "I have never been directly responsible for *making* you completely naked."

She gave me a playfully exasperated look, but behind her eyes I could see her urgency and it set a fire inside me. "Can you make me completely naked *now*?"

"You aren't something to rush through." I bent, smelling her neck. "Your skin is meant to be savored. Your pleasure is meant to be drawn out, stretched thin, seduced from within you." Looking up at her I told her, "I'm not making love to you tonight with anything but my hands—but I want you to come so violently on my fingers that you'll wake in the middle of the night, desperate to re-create it . . ." I kissed her shoulder, murmuring, "only to fail."

Her mouth fell open.

"You won't have the right angle, you see." I ran a finger along her jaw. "Or the right size of finger, or depth. But mostly you'll fail at making yourself feel as good as I will because you won't be *patient*."

She growled, digging her hands into my hair and pulling.

I drew my finger down from the hollow of her throat to her breastbone. "You won't want to linger at these perfect spots: the warm skin here, the sole freckle on your torso just there. You won't be able to kiss your own rib."

I bent kissing her just beneath her bra before sliding my hand beneath her, releasing the clasp and leaving it there to loosen as she arched for me, as she wiggled and whined on the bed. The left strap fell from her shoulder, looping down over her bicep, and I kissed the tiny new spot it revealed.

"Take it off?" she whispered, back lifted from the mattress.

"Not yet."

She paused, breathing heavily while I sucked at the skin just beneath her breast, my hand working to unbutton her skirt, to slide it down her hips. "Niall?"

"Hmm?"

"I *ache*."

My laugh came out as a small breath on her skin. "Do you?"

"You can *linger* all you want just put your *hand* on me."

"I'll put my hands all over you when I'm ready. Trust me." I'd never been able to take my time like this, to enjoy and relish and taste. Compared to my time with Ruby, my sexual experience to date felt like digital code entered bleakly into a program.

I bent, sucking at the top swell of her breast. So full and firm. I pressed my teeth into the skin, groaning. I wanted to bite and suck and *consume*. Her breasts made me want to turn savage, groping and biting and . . . Christ, just *fucking*. I imagined myself crawling up her body, pressing her breasts around my cock, and shifting over her, selfishly chasing the pleasure I craved being this close to her skin, her scent, her hoarse, gasping noises.

A small part of me curled instinctively at such a crude, bare thought, but Ruby's voice in my mind was louder: *Let go*, she said. *Show me what you need. Take what you want.*

With a growl, I climbed over her, cupping her breasts over her bra and pressing them together, sucking at the skin where they met, sliding my tongue in and around the delicious crevasse.

Beneath me she gasped, arching, her hands working their way back into my hair, her legs wrapping around me, pulling my hips to hers so she could rock up into me.

I pulled her bra straps down her arm, tossing the garment aside before returning to her. Her nipples were the same warm pink as her lips, and without thinking—without even a moment of hesitation—I bent, pulling one into my mouth, sucking hungrily while my palm gripped her other breast.

Ruby arched from the mattress, crying out and pulling so

hard at my hair that the sensation teetered between plea-sure and pain. "Niall," she gasped. "Oh, God. Oh, *God*."

The intensity of her response threw me; *I* was causing this simply by licking her breast and covering her body with mine. I wanted to own this reaction, wrapping it carefully and hiding it away. My thoughts shifted away from relieving my own ache, to giving her more of this pleasure. I needed to feed on her reactions until she was sweaty and scream-ing beneath me.

Her skin seemed to glow under my touch; my lips fol-lowed the fit lines of her abdomen, the perfect circle of her belly button, the sharp spike of her hipbone. I drew my teeth over each of these discoveries, following with my fingertips, hungry to know every inch. Pushing my hips into the mat-tress, I grew desperate for relief.

Beneath me, Ruby rocked up into my hands, mindless and begging; a fine sweat had broken out on her chest. My hair was a mess from her hands, tugging fingers and scratching nails.

Oh, she was a fucking wonder.

"Let me taste you," she begged. "Let me *touch* you."

Her words sent a spike of electricity down my spine and along my cock. "Wait, darling."

"I *can't*."

I pushed the top elastic of her knickers aside, kissing the softest skin of her navel, just above her pubic bone.

She hissed out a *Yes* and gasped when I slid the light yel-low lace down her hips and thighs, undressing her entirely.

Ruby was completely naked and she was fucking *perfect*.

I felt her eyes on me as I slid my hand up her leg, watching my fingers move over her skin, mine darker than hers, tan against pale. Her inner thigh was the softest skin I'd ever felt, and my fingers trembled slightly as I moved them higher. Inside my chest, my heart hammered. I'd touched her between her legs before, of course, but it was different at the office: rushed and intense. Here, I had hours. I could keep her up all night with my hands giving her pleasure and my mouth on her breasts, her ribs, her stomach.

My fingers reached the juncture where hip met thigh and I lingered, barely an inch away from where she wanted me. Under my hand, she shook, pushing her hips off the bed.

"You're killing me with the teasing," she whispered, reaching to wrap her hand around my wrist. "I swear I'm going to come the second you touch me."

The way she said *come*, and the idea that she was this worked up—that my touch could do this so easily—rocked me. With a smile pressed to her hip, I slid my fingers over her, groaning at the sound of her sharp cry. She was *drenched*, and slick and warm and it was all I could do to not bend to kiss her there, or—even more tempting—lift my body over hers and simply slide inside. I couldn't begin to fathom how it would feel to be inside her.

I was grateful for the barrier of my trousers, and of the kernel of hesitation still residing in my thoughts, the constant reminder to *take this slowly*.

It was impossible not to compare this experience to

the only other one I'd really had—late-night pub fumbling aside—even though guilt tried to shove the thoughts away. I knew I shouldn't think of Portia right now, not even in relief of my independence from her, but with Ruby naked against me and my brain fried to bits at the thought of giving this sublime creature pleasure, I didn't have the discipline of thought to which I was accustomed. Ruby unraveled me, opened something inside me, and made me want to be more transparent with myself, with her.

And as I touched her, and gave her pleasure with first two fingers, and then three, I let my thoughts flap wildly in my mind. *This is what it should feel like to be intimate, giving pleasure to someone who wants it hungrily, both partners wholly giving in to it.* She'd opened up to me tonight—it was the entire purpose of her admission, I realized—and in turn it had given me some freedom to relax with her, with *this*. With each circle of my hand and each moan that pushed past her lips, my confidence multiplied until I was convinced no man had ever wanted a woman more than I wanted the one beside me just now.

I wanted to kiss her and lick her and fuck her, but a baser part of me—a dark piece I'd never acknowledged—wanted a greater ownership over her lips, her glowing skin, aching sounds, soft thighs and—I let myself admit it—the most beautiful, soaking-wet pussy I'd ever dreamed of. I wanted to look at her and have a deeper sense that she was *mine*.

She started to clench under my movements and my insides began to simmer, thrilled. *How odd it is*, I thought, *that my whole body should ache for the curve of her shoulder, the straight, downward slope of her navel, the pounding pulse at the side of her neck.*

Watching her unravel under my touch seemed to literally bring my heart into my throat. I lifted my gaze from where I touched her to move up and suck savagely at her breast as she first seemed to calm—her breaths came out slow and deep—and then she pushed her head back into the pillow and nearly screamed as her orgasm tore through her and pressed down against my fingers inside.

She stilled for only a breath before pulling me by my hair so we were face-to-face and I could lick away the quick, re-lieved exhales falling from her lips.

"*Holy shit.*" She closed her eyes, going limp beneath me. "I just . . ."

"You're exquisite when you come," I whispered, sucking at her jaw, her neck, her mouth.

"That . . ." she began, looking up at me. "Right now you seem like something I made up when I was lying awake at night."

I ran my wet fingers up over her stomach, to her ribs, quietly giving voice to the crude thought that slipped into my mind, sharing my most exposed self: "I love the way you smell. I fear I'll lose my mind when I finally feel you on my tongue."

After the words left my mouth, Ruby pulled me back to her with eager hands and renewed desire. I was wild and she was nearly out of her mind—sweaty, mouth wet and messy over mine. Teeth scraped chins, kisses turned sloppy, and she whipped my belt across my stomach in her haste to get my trousers off.

Oddly, the sharp sting only made me more unhinged.

With my pants pushed to my knees, Ruby reached for me, her hand strong and warm as she gripped my shaft. "Holy shit," she said. "You're . . ."

I pulled back, looking down at her with what I was sure were savage eyes. She was only the third woman in my life to have touched my cock, and I honestly didn't care what she was going to say to finish the sentence; I pulsed in her palm, practically begging her to give me relief.

"Big," she said, looking down at me. "*Jesus.*" And then she slid her hand over the head with such perfect pressure that I nearly missed her words through my loud, relieved groan: "I've never been with a guy who wasn't . . ."

My mind fogged with the feel of her slowly stroking up, and slowly stroking down. *Wasn't what? American? Willing to take his time? Experienced with scores of women?*

And then it occurred to me, where her hand lingered, exploring. "Wasn't circumcised?"

She nodded, ducking her head to press her mouth to my neck.

"I imagine it's much the same, only perhaps easier in some ways."

"Easier?" She sounded as dazed as I felt.

If you moved your bloody hand a bit faster, maybe you'd see what I mean.

I reached between us, wrapping my hand around hers to make her move. I could feel the hot tension in my lower back, my growing need to fuck into her, fuck her fist, fuck *something*, and she whimpered a little as I think my words registered: my foreskin slid easily over the head of my cock as she worked me.

"It's so fucking *hot*," she groaned. "Oh fuck, I can't believe I'm doing this. I can't believe—"

"Shh," I whispered, wanting her lost in me, not the *idea* that she was doing this. This was a reality: I was over her, my cock in her fist, my mouth on her neck, and my heart slowly bleeding into hers. "Stay with me."

My words transitioned from this to a steady mantra of *give me*

Give me

Give me

Oh, fuck, Ruby, Ruby

Give me

Give me—

—I wasn't even sure what I meant.

Give me pleasure and your achingly honest words and the reassurance that this is real. Give me the freedom to let my words fall easily. Give me permission to let go and lose myself the way I've needed to for so long. Give me a place to be safe and open and unguarded.

Her hand slowed, thumb sliding over the taut, slick head, eyes wide as she watched herself. And I watched, too. The sight of her hand wrapped around me caused me to groan, jump in her palm.

"I love that I made you hard," she barely whispered.

"You do," I admitted. "Hard enough to feel nearly mad, all the time."

I sounded desperate. Hell, I *felt* desperate.

She looked up at my mouth and I bent to kiss her, sucking at her wet, plump lips.

Her nipples grew tight, skin pebbled, and it struck me that she behaved almost as if this was all for her, that my pleasure was a gift in some way. I had to admit it made me high to be wanted like this, with such awed abandon. At the same time, I wanted her to feel the same ease with me when we were intimate like this as when we were conversing or simply walking down Fifth Avenue in easy silence.

I ran my finger over her lip, trapping it with a kiss and hissing at the taste of her on my skin.

Her fist stroked up, down, sliding and gripping perfectly.

"I can taste you on my finger," I murmured into her mouth, shifting, beginning to move my hips as I kissed down to her chest.

I swelled in her hand, feeling the pleasure climb my legs and descend along my spine until I was savagely fucking her fist, my mouth sucking ferociously at her breast until the blood pooled beneath the skin and her tight breaths in my ear begged me to *come, come, come, come* . . .

With a deep groan, I let go, spilling into her hand, her hip, her navel, and even across the breast I'd marked with my mouth. Even after my orgasm dissolved and the only sound in the room was my heaving breaths, she didn't let go of me. Instead, with her other hand she reached up, pressing her palm across where I'd come on her skin.

Only once I stilled over her did I realize how wild we'd been, how savage in our touches and kisses. Her chest was red from the scratch of my stubble; her lips looked swollen and abused. Sweat covered the surface of our skin. Without having kissed her between her legs, without having made love to her, I'd just had the wildest sexual experience of my life.

She closed her eyes, chin wobbling slightly before she admitted, "I'm terrified that what I feel for you is going to get too big for—"

I quieted her words with a kiss, sucking at her full bottom lip and reaching to distract her, my fingers sliding between her legs again.

I was barely able to escape the chaos of my own thoughts. This was more intense than anything I'd experienced in my marriage. This was more intense than anything I'd experienced, *ever*.

Something about that felt terrifying, and wrong.

I needed to dive back down into sensation before panic over this enormous emotion swelled and made me mute.

Eleven

Ruby

I expected him to sleep like he worked—stiffly, everything about him as adult as an adult can be. *Adult* as a verb and adjective. But he didn't. He was asleep on his stomach, hands dug under his pillow, curled around it and with his face pressed to his arm. Like a kid or a drunk frat boy, complete with the occasional mumbled word and soft, snuffling breaths.

The arm I was propped up on began to fall asleep, and with a quiet groan I rolled to my back, careful to not jostle him. I wanted to keep watching him. I wanted to keep this feeling—completely blissed out—alive just a little longer. If I thought keeping him primed on a steady dose of sleeping pills would make this moment last, I might have considered it. The sheets smelled like him, my skin still hummed with the memory of his fingertips, and lips and—*holy shit, his come*—everywhere. If I closed my eyes I could still feel the faint press of his fingers pumping between my legs.

But with the quiet, soft sounds of Niall sleeping came

the familiar doubt. It was still faint enough to ignore, like hearing someone shout from the other side of a wall, but I wondered how long it would stay that way. If there was one thing my parents encouraged us to do, it was to listen to our gut, to take note when something felt worrisome or scary. And this definitely felt scary. It was fucking terrifying.

Niall seemed to approach our relationship with fits and starts. I knew he was hesitant about his ability to be a good partner, but was that all it was?

The room was still dark, and I rolled over again, tucking myself back into the warm space at his side. His skin smelled faintly of soap and his breaths were soft and even. I closed my eyes, rationalizing that it was too early to worry about things I couldn't control. There would be plenty of time for that later.

When I opened them again, I was alone, blinking up at the ceiling overhead.

The blue curtains glowed, backlit from the morning on the other side, and the bathroom light flooded the carpet near the hotel room door.

I could hear water running and the faint *tap tap tap* of something knocking against the sink.

"Niall?" I called out, pushing up onto an elbow. The water shut off and a head of dark hair peeked out the doorway.

"Good morning," he said, one side of his face still covered in an even layer of shaving cream. "I hope I didn't wake you?"

I frowned when I realized that he was shirtless—*yay*—but he was wearing dress pants—*boo*. "Where are you going?" I asked through a yawn.

He'd stepped back into the bathroom, and I heard his voice over the running water. "I woke to a message from Tony," he said, and I felt the involuntary eye roll that somehow always accompanied that name. "He's set up an early meeting across town I need to get to."

"At . . ." I glanced at the clock. "Seven in the morning?"

"Sadly, yes."

I was hoping we'd have breakfast together. Actually, I'd hoped we'd have room service and maybe feed each other bite-size pieces of fruit followed by rigorous shower sex.

"Okay," I said instead. The bed suddenly seemed less empty as my doubts from last night resurfaced and slipped back between the sheets.

Niall walked out of the bathroom and slid his arms into the sleeves of a dress shirt. I stared as his torso disappeared with each button slipped through its hole. "You'll meet me at the office later?" he asked.

"Of course." I propped myself up on two pillows, and a thought occurred to me. "Last night—?"

But what had I meant to say? *Last night was amazing? Confusing? Terrifying?*

Pretty much all of those.

"Was it enough for you?" he asked, and I knew he wasn't looking for false praise or ego boosting, he was simply wondering.

"More than enough. I don't think people appreciate the awesomeness of a good fingerbang."

He laughed, shaking his head as he focused on his hands knotting his tie. "The things you say."

"I'm serious. When we're young, each step is a milestone. First kiss, first base, *second*," I said, ignoring the way he watched me. I brought my knees to my chest and wrapped my arms around them. "If I could go back and tell Teenage Ruby anything . . . well, first I would say to wear more sunscreen, but the second most important thing would be to slow down and enjoy all those firsts. *Enjoy* the anticipation. Once you have sex, all the good stuff becomes a means to an end. Nobody wants to *just* make out anymore."

Niall looked up and smiled at me from across the room. "Thank you."

"For what?"

"For being patient with me, with all of this. I know I come across as . . . uptight at times. But I assure you . . . I've grown quite fond of you, Ruby."

I bit my lip through a smile. "I'm *quite fond* of you, as well, Niall Stella."

He walked over to the bed and bent, kissing my forehead. "See you in a bit, darling."

I took my time getting ready back in my room—slim black dress, smooth, straight hair, and my favorite special-occasion lipstick—and grabbed a quick breakfast at Norma's before heading to the office. I needed an extra layer of confidence today and this outfit always did the trick. Manhattan was chilly, and I tugged at my coat—red, to match the lipstick—bundling it a bit higher against my throat.

I'd decided to walk this morning, opting for a different route than I'd used before, having googled a landmark I knew my mom would love to see in a photo. I remembered an old copy of *Love Story* on her bedside table, while growing up, and that the cover was inspired by a version of the sculpture located on Sixth Avenue.

It was easy to find. Groups of tourists crowded around it, re-creating iconic poses while they took each other's photo. It was simple: red capital letters with blue accents, the *L* and *O* set on top of the *V* and *E*, and I pulled out my phone, hoping to snap a quick photo to send to her.

"Well, hello there, Miss Miller," I heard, in an accent so familiar it sent goose bumps up and down my arms.

"Max!" I said, and *dear God* the men in this family were gorgeous. It was obvious Max and Niall were brothers, even if Max's hair was a bit lighter and he had more green than brown in his eyes. They had the same straight nose, the same sharp jaw, and the same dimpled grin; Max's just made far more appearances. And wow, were they both tall.

I hoped he'd assume the blush that warmed my cheeks was because he'd just caught me taking a photo of myself on the streets of New York, and not because I'd just realized how insanely gifted his family's gene pool was. Then I noticed Will—*sweet Jesus, Will looked like sin in a suit*—standing just behind him on the phone where he offered me a small wave.

"Where's baby brother this morning?" Max asked.

"Something last minute came up. I'm meeting him at the office later."

Max winked and tugged a leather glove on over his left hand. A thick wedding band gleamed in the morning light. "Don't suppose I could talk you into joining us for coffee, then?" he asked.

Will finished his call and stepped up beside him, smiling and nodding in agreement. I had no idea how the women in their lives got anything done.

I'd already had a cup but how could I pass this up? "Sure. Let's do it."

"Excellent. William?"

"Hmm?"

"Ready?"

"As I'll ever be," he said, offering his arm to me.

I took it in sort of a daze, even more so when Max took my other arm. What in the world had I just agreed to?

At a small café just up the block, I followed them both to a table near the back of the room, crowded with tourists and businesspeople grabbing breakfast before work. Our drinks were brought out almost immediately, and I couldn't help wonder what Niall would think of my having coffee with his brother.

"I saw a picture of Annabel," I said. "She's absolutely stunning. Congratulations."

Max, who had been unwinding a scarf from his neck, beamed at me. "Niall showed you my little miss?"

I nodded. "She looks so much like you."

Will frowned as he tore open a sugar packet. "No way, not this guy," he said. "Sara's a knockout and that little girl is the most beautiful thing I've ever seen. She's going to have her uncle Will standing at the door with a shotgun, ready to blow the balls off any boy who even looks at her wrong."

"Ta, William. Couldn't have said it better myself. Her mother, Sara, is stunning. If my little Beloved is even half as vivacious and charming . . . I am well and royally fucked."

"Oh, you are," Will said, holding up his drink.

"Do you have any children?" I asked Will.

Max snorted into his water glass.

"Uh, no," Will said, his smile softening. "None for us, yet."

"Not for a lack of practice though, mate," Max said.

"This is true," Will said, looking appropriately thrilled.

Pouring cream into his coffee, Max turned his smile on me. From what I could tell, Max was *always* smiling—especially when he was teasing someone—and he had a rare kind of charm that made me want to spill all of my secrets, talk about *everything* . . . because something told me he was dying to hear.

"So, how's Niall treating you?" he asked.

"Great," I said, stirring my drink. I kept my eyes on my cup, watching foam disappear into caramel-colored liquid, hoping I could pull off casual and completely un-affected. I had nothing to say. Nope, no dirt to spill here. "He's great—I mean, it's great—he's treating me great."

Nailed it, Ruby.

"Is he, now?" Max drawled.

"Stop that," Will said, pointing his coffee stirrer at Max. "Don't think I don't see that face. You're worse than my mother; leave the poor girl alone."

Max's eyebrows lifted with exaggerated innocence. "Your mother's a lovely woman. I find that comparison rather complimentary."

"Ignore him," Will said to me. "He's a busybody who loves nothing more than knowing what's going on with every person he meets so he can give them shit about it. Don't tell him a thing. Make him suffer."

Max reached out to stop a waitress who was passing our table. "Sorry, love. Think you could bring this one 'round a bowl of bran?" he said, motioning to Will. "He's a wee bit irritable this morning and a bit of fiber might help to sort him out."

The waitress looked between them and nodded awkwardly, before walking away. For his part, Will just chuckled into his cup.

I was beginning to see that this was just their *thing*, and exactly what Niall had meant when he'd said his brother was a character. I could stay here all day and watch it.

"Would you like me to leave you two alone?" I asked finally. "I could let you have my hotel room for the day?"

They both turned to me; Max was already laughing.

"This one's got your number," he said to Will. "Quite like to keep her 'round."

"You sure your guy's ready for her?" Will said, lifting his chin to me. "She's got some fire and Niall—"

"Aw, he's all right, in't he?" Max cut in, sounding sweetly protective. "Just needs to clean his system of the other one. Bloody nag, she was. Niall likes adventure as much as the next bloke."

I nodded in emphatic agreement.

"I think you're right," Will said. "What was it you said about repressed sexual energy?"

"Enough to power the whole bloody city, if you ask me," Max said. "That's where his real urban planning skill would come in—hooking himself up to the grid . . ."

Will laughed into his mug. "Well, it worked for Chloe and Bennett. A little boss, a ball-busting intern—"

"Niall is *not* my boss," I said, with perhaps a bit too much conviction. It was like someone gathered up all of the awkward in the room, wrapped it up in a bow, and dropped it right in the middle of our table.

Thankfully, they were each polite enough not to acknowledge it. Instead they took sips of their coffee, straightened their silverware, and checked the time. Subtlety was not their strong suit.

"Okay," I said with a sigh, unable to take their dramatic silence any longer. "I like him. A *lot*."

Max's enormous grin was back and *God*, just like his brother, so damn endearing.

"Now you've done it," Will said. "This limey'll never butt out. Might as well invite him to move in. Plan all your dates, your wedding. Name your children—"

"Just be patient with him," Max said, ignoring Will. "He's a tough egg to crack."

"I'm discovering this," I said. "He is not skilled in the art of the overshare."

Max laughed and lifted his cup in reply. "He may not say much, but I can assure you that for every one thought Niall verbalizes, there are at least six running through his head. Been like that his whole life."

"Great." I dipped my head, staring at what was left of the foam floating at the surface of my latte.

Across from me, Max set down his coffee. "Allow me to be protective big brother for a moment though, yeah?"

I looked up and his expression softened when I murmured, "Of course."

Even Will, who seemed to realize the serious turn the conversation was taking, leaned forward to listen.

"My brother is loyal to a fault, always has been. Whether to us, or his job, or a woman. I'm not sure how much you know about his divorce . . ." he said, letting the implied question—*what has he told you?*—hang in the air.

"We've talked about it," I answered, wanting to be honest but not wanting to betray Niall's fragile trust. "A little. I get the sense she was . . ."

How to finish that sentence?

"Maybe a little difficult?" I said delicately.

"Well put," Max said with a knowing wink. "I think his loyalty is why he stayed for so long. And why, I think in many ways, he feels like he failed . . . or should have done something different, left sooner. She wouldn't have been happy no matter what, but that's a tough truth to accept. He's had a rough go of it this year."

"I sense that."

"Give him time. Might have to chip away at the outside, but I promise it'll be worth it."

⎯⎯⎯

Niall was at his desk when I walked in, and I closed the door behind me. His pen stopped moving midsentence, and he set it down, slipping off his glasses to look at me.

His eyes moved from the tips of my patent leather pumps to the top of my hair. Heat curled in my stomach and slithered lower.

"Where have you been?" he asked. Not accusing, not upset. Just wanting to know.

"I had coffee with Max and Will." When his eyebrows rose, I added, "They found me taking selfies in Midtown."

"Did you have a good time?" he asked.

"They're . . . nice." Tucking my hair behind my ear, I added quietly, "We talked about you. He's quite a fan, that big brother of yours."

Niall's smile curled one side of his mouth and he pushed back from his desk and stood, walking around to face me. I expected him to ask what we'd said, but he didn't. He simply let his attention move over my face. I'm sure it was obvious that we'd talked about my feelings, about Niall and me together; I could feel how warm my cheeks were.

"How was your meeting earlier?" I asked, out of breath. I'd taken the elevator; it wasn't from exertion. It was the nearness of him, the way he was looking at me as if he was reeling through every touch from last night. This morning he'd been so brusque, and with the intensity of his stare now, I was able to acknowledge without triggering an internal panic that Niall had seemed to be freaking out—as if fleeing the scene of a crime.

But had I misread him entirely?

Had he simply wanted it to feel familiar? Or had he needed to know that I was okay, that *this* was okay?

"It was good," he said. "We're very nearly done with our proposal." His eyes barely strayed from my mouth.

"That's good," I agreed.

"Quite."

I bit my lip, pulling in a nervous smile before saying, "You seem a bit distracted."

Niall nodded, reaching up to carefully touch my bottom lip. "I've never seen you wear this color."

"Is it too red?" I asked.

He blinked, shaking his head in two tiny movements. "No. Not too red."

Was this how I chipped away at the outside? By reminding him again and again that I wasn't Portia, that I wanted him, and that it was okay to want *me*, too?

My heart hammering, I turned to the door and locked it as quietly as possible before turning back to him. Pulling my purse up, I dug inside it for my lipstick. I still had no real idea what I was doing, only that he was transfixed by the color of my mouth and I felt physically unwilling to redirect his attention.

While he watched, rapt, I uncapped it, rolled it up, and reapplied it.

"You can't be real," he whispered.

My pulse pounded so powerfully beneath my breastbone that I still couldn't catch my breath. I set the lipstick behind him on the desk and then reached up, undoing his tie, releasing the top two buttons of his shirt. He stood completely still as I bent, pressing my mouth to the warm skin just over his heart.

I lifted my head to look up at him, catching his expression of wonder.

"Again," he rasped.

I leaned forward, kissing lower, releasing another button, and then another. I kissed over his rib, bending to kiss again where chest turned into stomach.

He remained silent, breaths coming out in sharp exhales that jerked his abdomen beneath my mouth.

I looked over the red marks along his chest and stomach, starting to relish the idea of Niall walking around the rest of the day wearing me beneath his clothes. But I didn't want to be done with this, and he didn't seem to want it, either.

"I can keep going," I told him.

He wants my kiss there. I can see it in his eyes.

My fingers toyed with his belt, eyes studying his expression. If it tightened, if I saw even an inch of retreat there, I would back off.

Instead, I saw relief, acquiescence, something just shy of desperation.

His belt came free with a tiny clang of metal on metal. His zipper ticked down in the silent room. And then I waited, my fingers holding the open fabric of his dress pants. The straining tip of his cock pressed up against the elastic waistband of his boxers. The quiet was sliced apart every time he exhaled in a gust.

I saw his eyes flicker to the door and then return to my face.

I shook my head. "I can st—"

His "*no*" was sharply hissed.

With a little nod, I kissed the soft trail of hair on his abdomen, licked it.

"Dear God," he gasped.

I slid my hand into his boxers, nearly undone by the dip of his Adam's apple as he swallowed, let his head fall back. I was struck all over again by the weight of him, the heavy length I pulled free as I kneeled in front of him.

"I probably need more lipstick," I whispered.

With effort, he raised his head, looking down at me, and then blinked into awareness. "Of course." His fingers fumbled behind him on the desk, knocking pens and papers to the floor before finding the silver tube.

The cap came free with a tiny pop and Niall blinked away, to his own hands shaking in front of him as he twisted the lipstick to reveal the brilliant red.

With one hand cupping my chin, he reached down and pressed the lipstick to my bottom lip, carefully sliding it from middle to left, middle to right, before even more gently repeating the action on my top lip. "Ruby."

I smiled, holding his gaze as I bent to kiss the underside of his shaft, just in the middle.

Niall's grunt was rough, hands grappling behind him to grip the desk. "*Christ.*"

"Okay?"

He nodded.

I kissed lower, leaving perfect red prints down to the base.

I studied him in a way I hadn't bothered to last night, looking at how he strained forward, filling my hands. "You're so perfect I'm not sure what to do with you."

Tell me, I meant. *Direct me.*

"L-lick," he rasped. *He understood.* "Please, darling."

I smiled, darting my tongue out and sweeping it along his shaft. Niall groaned, low and broken.

"There?" I asked.

"No. No, please."

I smiled into another kiss in the middle of his cock. "Where?"

His eyes closed for a second as he swallowed, and then said, "The head." His eyes met mine again. "Lick the head."

I felt nearly liquid, chest thrumming with need, desire a wild pulse between my legs. When I slid my tongue over the wide crown of him, I tasted sweet and salt, earth and man, and felt more than heard his relieved moan vibrate through him.

Long fingers ran over my jaw and into my hair, turned into a fist when I opened my mouth and took the entire tip inside, sucking down a few inches and back, surrendering the game in favor of giving him what I suspected was his first blow job in years.

And what a tragedy. He was thick, intimidatingly long, but where his cock felt nearly savage in its size and need, his hands were gentle in my hair, shaking as he sweetly encouraged me.

Down and up, sucking, wet. I didn't care about the sounds I made or the way I lost my breath when I took him deep, coming back with watery eyes and a gasping, wet mouth. He stared at me as if I was a glowing star in the middle of this room, and it made me want to give him every drop of pleasure a man could possibly feel.

My hand cupped him lower, the other gripped his hip, silently telling him *take take take*. I urged him to flex forward and he did, first a shallow thrust of relief, and then deeper and deeper with careful precision, helping me work him in and out of my mouth, across my tongue, between my lips.

I wondered if he loved the crude sound of it as much as I did, my unintentional gasps and moans when he went deep, when he jerked forward in a small loss of control, when he pulled my hair in tiny flashes of frenzy. It sounded wet, and good, and the tiny pop of him in and out of my mouth seemed to make us both frantic.

He let himself enjoy it—slowing down, speeding up, slowing down again—until he grew determined: knees bent, hips rolling easily. I watched his face as, against my tongue, he grew tighter somehow, his brow tight with what almost looked like pain, his fingers finding handfuls of my hair.

"Oh," he gasped, and I remembered his words, could see in his eyes that he did, too: *I want it. For you to suck my cock, and suck it so hungrily that you beg me with your eyes to let you swallow.*

I held his eyes with mine, and begged.

"Oh, darling, I—oh. *Oh, God.*"

Yes

Yes

"Oh. Oh, God, here I—oh I'm—"

His eyes rolled closed, cock swelling hugely against my tongue before he spilled with a helpless groan, warm and deep inside.

Niall's hands went limp before falling to my shoulders. I pulled away, swallowing as I kissed the head before kissing his hip and sitting back on my heels.

He opened his eyes, taking a deep breath as he stared down at me. "Well. Right. That was . . ."

I stared up at the still-hard cock lying free of his pants, the bright spots of lipstick down his torso, the look of bewildered bliss curving across his perfect mouth.

Looking up at him, I said, "I feel like a criminal with a very obvious trail of evidence here."

He laughed, staring down the length of his body. "I certainly do not feel like the victim of a crime." His broad hands came down, maneuvering himself back into his boxers and fastening his pants. "I'm quite at a loss for words."

"Good." I ran a fingertip along the side of my mouth, grinning proudly up at him.

He reached down for my elbow, helped me up. "Your knees . . . ?"

"Are fine."

In silence, we worked together to button his shirt, and then I smoothed my hands across his shoulders while he carefully reknotted his tie. I wanted him to pull me into his arms, kiss me, taste his pleasure on my lips.

"Ruby?"

I looked up at his face. "Hmm?"

"Thank—"

I reached for his lips, my heart drooping. "Don't."

"Don't say thank you?" he asked from behind my fingers.

"No."

Niall looked momentarily at a loss, before reaching up and gently pulling away my hand. "But it was astounding."

"For me, too."

His gaze flickered back and forth between my eyes. "Truly?"

"When you want someone as much as I want you, giving pleasure is almost better than getting it."

He fell silent; his thumb coming up to stroke a bottom lip that I'm sure no longer had a hint of lipstick remaining.

"Am I a mess?" I asked.

"Mmm," he hummed, bending and kissing me once. "Quite. I rather like it."

He returned, kissing me deeper, lips parting and sucking, and, finally, tongue sliding along mine.

When he pulled back, he watched where his index finger drew small circles at the hollow of my throat.

"I'm still a bit amazed at the . . ." he began, and then shook his head a little before pressing his lips together.

"Intensity?" I asked.

"Yes. The intensity. But then I'm never sure . . ."

I waited for him to finish, but he simply nodded and said a quiet "*Well.*"

I suddenly knew what Max meant about chipping away at the outside. It wasn't about seducing Niall in the first place. It was about keeping him from turning back inward immediately afterward.

"Let me go clean up." I stretched, kissing his cheek and then turning for the door. Opening it, I took a peek in the hallway before making a dash to the restroom.

Inside, I stared at my reflection: at the swollen pink mouth, the hint of red in a halo all around it, the mascara blurred from my watery eyes while I sucked him.

I didn't really need Niall to finish that thought. I knew what he would say even if he didn't know it himself: *I'm a bit amazed at the intensity . . . But then I'm never sure what to do with you afterward.*

————

If Niall was as distracted as I was that afternoon, he didn't show it. His attention barely wandered from the speaker as she unveiled one plan after another. He took meticulous notes, and barely spared a glance in my direction. I could still remember the shape of him against my lips, could hear the choppy, gasping breath he took just before he came. But I could *not* believe I'd done that in our office. My recklessness was escalating.

I'd be damned if I ever apologized for wanting something sexual, but I didn't want to let it make me irresponsible.

Still . . . after this morning, then the blow job, then his retreat back into his own thoughts, I felt insecure. And I *hated* feeling insecure.

Beneath the table, I slid my foot closer until it touched his. Startling, he looked over at me and I could see in his expression when he understood that *I need to know that what I did was okay with you.*

And in the same way my kisses were hidden under his expensive clothes, his ankle wrapped around mine beneath the table. A secret only the two of us shared.

I'd never considered how many nerves might exist in the human foot before, but for the next two hours I grew aware of every single one. I noticed every shift of his leg and every brush of fabric. I could feel the heat of his body so close and yet I couldn't *do* anything. It was maddening. When he stood to take the floor himself, my eyes bore into the places I knew were marked with red. I kept my face impassive, but inside, I burned.

Being back in the States didn't mean my responsibilities back in England had lessened. In the time I wasn't with Niall, I had to put in extra hours. My coursework was finished, but if I hoped to get into Professor Sheffield's program in the fall, I had some catching up to do. Nothing could suffer at this stage, which was exactly why, at the end of the day, I decided to opt out of a group dinner that night, even if it would have meant time with Niall.

As the global lead on the team, Niall couldn't back out. So, with a small, apologetic glance in my direction, he told everyone he would meet them in a half hour at the restaurant.

I moved to the elevator and shivered a little when he came in behind me. We'd been able to spend nearly every second together the past couple of weeks but would be apart tonight. I felt a little petulant in my unwillingness to share.

"All right?" he asked quietly as a few other people came in after us.

"I'm good." I smiled at him over my shoulder. "Just

need to be an adult for a few hours and feeling bratty about it."

He couldn't exactly kiss me or do anything even mildly physically reassuring. It was just that everything still felt so precarious. Our relationship was starting to feel like a towering house of cards, and in a way I understood why he was inclined to take the physical side of things slowly: there was no established *us* yet. No moments where I felt like, *wow, this guy is totally my boyfriend.*

There was also a tiny part of me that suspected I'd complicated his thoughts further by telling him about Paul. I was being truthful when I said I still thought about what happened from time to time, but what I gathered most from those moments was a sense of pride that I had worked through it, and that I hadn't let it dictate how I felt about myself or who I would be. I needed to make sure he knew that.

"You'll be at the hotel working?" he asked.

I nodded and he followed me out of the building. "I'll walk you there."

Smiling up at him, I whispered, "Thanks."

Cabs jerked past us, honking. The cold March wind seemed to lash us with sharp fingertips. Niall put an arm around me, awkwardly maneuvering us through the crowd, bending to speak close to my ear. "If I ever forget to tell you, it helps me immeasurably that you're so honest. For the record, I don't think you're being bratty. I'm pouting on the inside."

And like that, butterflies. Lots of them.

We chatted about the meeting, about what was coming up in the summit over the next few days. He held my hand and I realized with some pride that I'd grown accustomed to his long strides; we walked easily in tandem. But there was still the *thing* between us.

"You wanted honesty?" I whispered during the elevator ride in the hotel, using the excuse to lean into him.

"Yes."

I tilted my head to look up at his face. "Was today too fast?"

He swallowed, immediately understanding. "Maybe a bit. But I'm not sure I wanted to stop you, or whether I could have."

I closed my eyes, feeling faintly sick.

"Or whether I *should* have," he added quietly, placing his finger under my chin to turn my face back up to his. "Ruby, it was amazing."

I nodded, forcing a smile. "Will you come by my room later? When you're back from dinner?"

He looked at me for a long moment, eyes meeting mine and holding there, and then he nodded in agreement, bending to kiss me once, sweetly.

"Let yourself in, if you want to," I said, placing my extra keycard in his hand. "I have a ton to do so I may be up all night or . . . who knows, maybe I'll fall asleep at the desk in a puddle of my own drool."

He laughed and I adored him so much in that moment

it was like a punch to my stomach. With one more kiss to my lips, he slipped the key into his pocket. I got out of the elevator at our floor and waved, watching him disappear between the closing doors.

———

I woke to the electronic sound of a lock turning, to a slice of light that cut across the room and was swallowed behind the closing door. Just like I'd told him, I worked until I couldn't keep my eyes open, dragging myself away from the desk just long enough to undress and throw on a T-shirt before climbing into bed.

The door closed and I watched Niall's silhouette move in front of the window, quietly slipping out of its jacket and shirt before taking a seat near my feet. I felt the mattress dip with his weight, and waited for him to say something. The silence ticked on right along with his watch again before he spoke.

"You awake?" he whispered into the darkness. The stillness in the room knotted my stomach. What had happened after I'd left him in the elevator? Had he spent the night thinking and overthinking and second-guessing what was happening between us? I felt frozen in place, my words locked in my chest, and wondered briefly what would happen if I didn't answer. Would he crawl into bed and wrap himself around me? Or would he stand, redressing before heading back to his room? I was afraid to find out.

"Ruby?"

"What time is it?" I asked finally.

"Around one."

I sat up, pulling my knees to my chest. "Are you just getting back?"

"No," he said, and though I couldn't see his face or the expression that accompanied it, I saw him run a hand through his hair. "I've been sitting downstairs for the last two hours."

My heart pounded and I wasn't sure if the darkness was a blessing or a curse. He'd been downstairs for two hours? "Why?"

He laughed a little dryly. "I've been thinking about what we did earlier."

"Oh."

"You're not surprised?"

I pushed the hair from my face and wondered how honest I should be. "I think I'd be more surprised if you weren't."

"Am I that predictable?"

"I'd say *consistent*," I told him. Silence stretched between us until I couldn't take it anymore. "Do you want to talk about it?"

He stayed quiet for a moment before I sensed him nodding. "I think so. Yeah."

I smiled into the darkness, realizing what a leap this was for him.

"I was thinking about how confusing this must be for

you. And how I've probably got you turned upside down with mixed messages about our physical relationship." He paused and took my hand in his, brushing a fingertip over my palm to stop at my wrist.

"I told you I wanted to take things slowly, and then . . ." He turned, pulling his knee up onto the mattress to fully face me. "And then I reacted how I did, put the lipstick on you . . ."

"I didn't mind that," I admitted. "I know we can't always script these things. Sometimes you might do something in the heat of the moment and then find yourself questioning it later. As long as we're honest with each other, I don't think there's any right or wrong way for this to go."

He considered me for a moment before offering a simple, "Thank you."

"And you're not the only one who has a tendency to overthink things," I told him. "I might just be better at blurting things out or running ahead."

"That actually makes me feel better."

There was a beat of silence. "As long as we're being honest, can I ask you a question?"

He squeezed my hand. "Of course, darling."

"Does part of you wanting to go slow have to do with what I told you last night?"

He was silent for another moment and I felt him shift on the mattress.

"After what he did to you," he said, "I feel like I *should* be—"

"I need you to stop right there," I said. I was right. It wasn't just about his hesitation to dive in; he didn't want to rush *me*, either. "I told you what happened with Paul because I trust you, and because you *asked*. I want you to have an idea of the pieces that make me who I am, just like I want to know about you. What happened to me will never go away, because it's a part of my past, but I don't want you to handle me differently because of it. I'm not delicate and I don't need you to be careful with me. Not like that. You need to trust me to tell you where my limits are, just like I need you to tell me yours."

He leaned forward, rubbing his hands over his face. "That's just it, though. I feel so out of my depth," he said. "That we can so readily communicate these things is still a bit of a revelation. My marriage was a lonely place, for both of us, I'm sure," he added quickly. "And I'm terrified that that wasn't just a Niall and Portia thing, that it's *me*. I know I don't say enough and what if y—*someone*, tires of having to pull every little thing from me?"

"Niall—"

"And what if after the rush of conquest wears off, you'll realize that I'm not what you've built me up to be? I . . . I'm not quite sure how I'd deal with that."

"I know how different we can be in that way," I told him. "You feel like you don't share enough and I'm the opposite." He laughed, reaching out to brush the backs of his fingers along my cheek. "And if we're being honest here, it *is* frustrating when I have to try and decipher what you're thinking. Like this morning? I'm not saying I'd need to be privy to every thought in a man's head . . . but I do need someone who can talk to me. Who can step outside their comfort level and meet me halfway. I want that for myself."

The room filled with a silence so heavy it was like a third person, towering above us.

Those moments where I'm trying to decipher his thoughts? This was one of them. Then it hit me and I wondered if I needed to take his insecurity into account, and clarify that when I said *someone*, what I meant was *him*.

But Niall seemed to be ready to take a leap. Leaning forward, he pulled me by the back of my neck so that our foreheads pressed together.

"I'll try," he said. "For you, I'll try."

TWELVE

Niall

I'd truly never known a woman like Ruby. Instead of needing giant leaps to prove my commitment, over the next week she seemed to revel more in the small things: the pressure of my palm on her lower back while we waited on the subway platform, a lingering glance while queuing for lunch at a street vendor, doing nothing more than kissing for hours at sunrise. But while our physical relationship seemed to have taken a few calming steps backward, she never pressed, and she never asked me to explain myself beyond what I'd told her that night in her hotel room.

I *did* want to try. Knowing that, she seemed content to simply be near me.

Ruby surprised me in other ways, as well. She was smart, far smarter than I'd initially given her credit for, and absorbed details like it was some sort of superpower. I was a note taker myself, and could usually gather any piece of information needed quickly enough when called upon, but over the following week I was blown away on more than one occasion when a question was posed during a meeting and Ruby would pull the answer seemingly out of thin air. It was truly remarkable.

We fell into a rather easy routine of work and meals, and at night an unspoken ritual of pillow talk in between kisses until we were nothing but mumbles and nonsense and her soft sweet skin curled around me as we fell asleep. It was a flash of a fantasy life—I suspected we both knew it—where we lived in a gorgeous hotel, ate wherever we wanted, and could spend the entire workday as a couple, out in the open, managing quite functionally together.

So it was odd to find myself deep in a Tuesday without having seen Ruby once since she'd left my room early that morning. I'd been in an endless loop of discussions and conference calls to wrap up the first phase of the summit. From here until we left for London, my days would be far more relaxed than they had been, since I would essentially just be on call. I both feared and welcomed it. On the one hand, I wanted more freedom in my daytime hours to ponder everything that was happening between us. On the other hand, I wasn't sure that I needed more time in my own head thinking about this new relationship, its stark difference to my life before, and how I would manage this abrupt change in my life when we returned to London.

Finally Ruby found me in the hall, talking to one of the city's head engineers. In my peripheral vision I could see her waiting to talk, and it seemed to me she was practically vibrating where she stood. When I said goodbye to Kend-rick and he'd stepped away, she lifted her hand from where she'd hid it behind her back.

Clutched in her fist were two tickets.

"What is this?" I asked, pulling one loose from her grasp.

Bitter Dusk, Bowery Ballroom, 8:30pm March 29.

A concert, scheduled for tonight?

"What is this?" I asked again, looking up at her enor-mous grin. Surely she didn't expect me . . .

She turned to start walking toward the lift, pushing the down button. "It's the concert I was telling you about. By *huge* coincidence, it is also what we're doing tonight."

I winced a little, already imagining a roomful of sweaty bodies, rocking and swaying next to me, pressing into us as loud, screeching guitars assaulted our ears. "Ruby, I really don't think this is my thing."

"Oh, it's definitely not, and it's every bit as bad as you're imagining," she said, tapping my forehead with a laugh. We stepped into the lift, and I was happy to note we'd enjoy this quiet ride alone together.

"Worse maybe," she continued. "The club is small for such a big band and it's going to be packed. Sweaty, drunk Americans *everywhere*. But I still want you to go."

"I confess I find your sales pitch to be somewhat lacking."

"I'm going to get you liquored up, because you don't have to work tomorrow, and," she stretched up to kiss my chin, "I bet you a hundred dollars you have an amazing time and want to reward me with orgasms afterward."

"I want to reward you with orgasms *now*."

"Consider the concert motivation, then." She gave me a look, one that I knew said, *This is exactly what we talked about. Do this with me.*

I sighed in mock annoyance, stepping out after her into the lobby. As much as my skin burned to feel her sliding under the sheets beside me sooner rather than later—and as odd as it was to admit it—it was nice to think about going *out*. "Will I know a single one of their songs?"

"You'd *better*," she said, turning to glare playfully at me over her shoulder. "And if you don't, you will soon. This is my favorite band in the world."

As I moved into step with her, she looked up at me, singing a few lines from a song I did actually recognize from the general popular music osmosis one gets in public settings. Ruby's voice was thin and off-key—bloody awful, really—but she didn't care at all. Lord, would there be a single thing about this girl I didn't find endlessly endearing?

"You're thinking right now that I'm a terrible singer," she said, poking me in the side.

"Yes," I admitted, "but I *have* heard that song. I'll tolerate the evening's activity."

She threw me a mock exasperated look. "How noble of you."

———

The exterior of the Bowery Ballroom reminded me of an old firehouse: simple sandstone, wide central arch, with a green neon sign illuminating the entrance to the side. As we emerged from the subway station just outside the venue, Ruby bounced beside me, pulling me toward the entrance. Inside the space expanded into a much smaller floor than I'd been expecting, positioned less than a meter below a narrow stage lined on the sides with heavy velvet drapes. I could see in an instant why Ruby was so excited for the tickets: in a venue such as this, she would be closer to her favorite band than she'd likely ever been.

Upstairs, a balcony lined the sides and back of the room, looking down on the action, and had begun to fill with a few people holding cocktails. Already the floor had started to fill, and the humid air created by over a hundred bodies tripped my claustrophobic wire. As if sensing my impending panic, Ruby tugged my sleeve, pulling me to the bar.

"Two gin gimlets, tons of limes!" she yelled to the bartender. With a nod, he grabbed two glasses, filling them with ice. "I mean a *lot* of limes," she added with a charming smile.

The oily hipster bartender smiled back at her, eyes stalling at her mouth before glancing at her chest and lingering.

Without thinking, I reached an arm around her shoulders, jerking her back against my front. The move surprised her. I could tell in the way she caught herself by wrapping both hands around my forearm, by the way she broke into a delighted laugh. Arching into me, Ruby slipped her hands behind her and around my lower back to hold me closer.

She turned her head, leaning against my chest and I bent so that her mouth was closer to my ear. "I've been crazy for you for months," she reminded me with a small bite to my jaw. "Seeing you jealous like that just completely made my life."

"I don't share," I warned her quietly.

"I don't either."

"And I don't flirt."

She paused, as she seemed to understand the depth of my reaction. I wasn't even sure *I* understood the depth of my reaction. I'd never been jealous with Portia; even when she tried, by dancing at parties or getting drunk and flirtatious with friends. But with Ruby . . . there was an instinctive pull, some desire to claim her that made me at once uneasy and thrilled.

"I know I'm flirty," she admitted, her eyes searching my face, "but I'd never betray anyone like that."

And somehow, I knew that. In the dim light of the bar and in the midst of such a bustling crowd, our conversation felt even more intimate.

"I'm having more fun with you than I can remember having," I told her. "I trust you, even though sometimes it feels like I know so much about you, and other times I remember that we're barely acquainted."

I had to remind myself that Ruby was only twenty-three, that she had broader sexual experience than I did, and far more experience with flirting—but no long-term relationships, nothing showing her how to enter into something to be treated initially as fragile. I wanted to balance her tendency to run headlong into things against my tendency to hide my head in the sand.

"We are not 'barely acquainted,'" she growled, pinching my backside in her hand. "Just because this is a new relationship doesn't mean I don't know you in ways no one else does. How else are we supposed to start? You can't know everything at the get-go."

The bartender returned with our drinks and I released Ruby from my hold and paid before she could get her wallet out of her small bag. She offered me a petulant glare, and then turned, stretching to pull me into a kiss I expected to be only a small brush of her lips but immediately turned deep, her tongue sliding into my mouth, claiming me in the playfully brazen way she had.

And for a moment, I forgot that we were away from the privacy of our hotel or the safety of London. With my hand cupping her neck and her palms pressed flat to my chest, it was just Ruby and I, as lovers, falling forward into this *thing* that had captured me so immediately.

I pulled away to catch my breath and slow my pulse, jerking back into awareness of the press of bodies all around us at the crowded bar, the eyes on us attempting to not stare, the hint of a smartphone capturing a public flash of our passion. The bartender deposited my change on the bar with a smack that told me he'd been watching us, too. And Ruby couldn't care less. She lifted her drink, raised her eyebrows cheekily at me, and took a long swallow.

"You kiss like it's your goddamn job," she said.

With a little smile, I pulled out a few of the multitude of limes in my drink to drop onto a bar napkin. I liked limes as much as the next bloke, but my Ruby seemed to want her gimlet as limes with a side of gin.

My Ruby.

I swallowed, staring at her as I licked the juice from my fingers. *My Ruby.* She watched my tongue slide over my fingers with wide, fascinated eyes.

"Right now," I began with a grin, "are you imagining how far I could work my tongue inside you, or how many of my fingers would fit?"

Her breath caught, and her eyes went wild for a flash before her confident smile took center stage. "I'm actually wondering if you would like to watch me lick your fingers as much as I like watching *you* do it."

I swallowed thickly, staring down at her slightly parted lips. They were shiny from her drink and from her habit of licking them often, and I was immediately reminded of the way they looked around my cock the only time she'd done that, swollen and slick.

"I'd rather like to watch you suck something else entirely," I admitted, feeling a heated flush run down my chest, adrenaline pumping to the tips of my fingers, adding, "Again."

While she stared at me, I heard a woman's voice mutter just behind her, "Right? I bet they have sex every fucking day."

Ruby's eyes widened, a smile spreading over her face as she tilted her head slightly to listen.

"I bet she *lives* with his dick inside her."

Her brows shot up and I blinked away for just a moment to keep from laughing. Ruby was still grinning when I looked back. "Are they talking about us?" she mouthed.

I nodded. They were definitely talking about us.

She looked down the length of her body and then up to me, whispering. "Nope. Not inside me right now."

I slid her hand down my stomach and over the shape of my cock. "Not right now, no."

But Lord, there were few things I wanted more just then.

The opening band filed out onto the stage and a portion of the crowd immediately began migrating away from the bar. Ruby grabbed my hand, downing half of her drink in a few swallows and motioning for me to do the same. As she watched, I finished it, set the glass down, and raised an eyebrow at her. With a tiny shake of her head, she tilted her drink back and downed it, wincing as she slammed the glass down on the bar.

When Ruby tugged my hand, I held her back from moving to the front, enjoying our time together too much to end it yet. "My condition on this evening is that you spend this opening set talking to me, back here."

She tilted her head, smiling mysteriously up at me. "It's

funny that you don't think you're a flirt," she said, wiping the back of her hand across her mouth.

Signaling to the bartender that we would each like another drink, I asked her, "What do you mean?"

" 'Are you imagining how far I could work my tongue inside you,' " she quoted in a British accent, " 'or how many of my fingers would fit?' " Resting her chin on my chest and gazing up at me, she said, "That, my *darling*, is perhaps the flirtiest and filthiest thing anyone has ever said to me."

I held her gaze as I slid another twenty onto the bar to cover the drinks, saying, "Aw, dove, you can't have a go at me for asking a simple question."

She laughed pulling away and playfully thumping my chest. "Don't play innocent with me. I'm onto your act. The calm stoic man in public, and behind closed doors, you're wicked."

I stilled, looking down at her. Was this how she saw me? I reflected back on the past week with her in this new, easy relationship and had to admit my behavior was so far out of character for me I could hardly recognize myself. And at the same time, falling into the role with her had felt nothing but natural.

"When you let yourself enjoy it?" she started, her voice quieter now as the crowd hushed to watch the band assemble up front. "You're almost too much for me to take. I didn't think men like you really existed." Reaching down to wrap her fingers through my free hand, she said, "Tell me what you're thinking right this second."

I blinked away, swallowing my reflex to inwardly recoil at this type of question and reminding myself how important it was to her that we were open with each other. "I'm glad you made me come here tonight."

She waited, clearly hoping for more.

"Honesty, yeah?"

Nodding, she said, "Of course."

"The last week, since we've settled into each other, has been lovely. Part of me worried initially that you viewed this relationship as only sexual."

"I want a lot of sexual things from you," she admitted, "but I want that because I want you, and *this*. Not because sex is the most important thing or I'm working through something." She looked away, out over the crowd and to the stage.

It took me a moment to realize I'd tested her patience, that what I'd said had actually hurt her feelings.

"I don't question that you genuinely care for me," I told her. "I hope you feel the same keen fondness from me."

She laughed, stretching to kiss my jaw. "You are so adorably proper, I can't handle it."

We drank our second round only a touch slower than the first, and by the time I ordered our third drink, I could feel the warm flush of alcohol in my blood. Ruby's cheeks were pink, her laugh bursting readily from her lips as I told her stories of my childhood in Leeds: Max running home trouserless at fifteen after getting caught shagging the daughter of the chief executive of Leeds City Council in the middle of Pudsey Park, my oldest sister Lizzy's wedding, where her chief bridesmaid spilled a full glass of red wine on her wedding dress and Uncle Philip got so pissed he fell into the wedding cake, my other sister Karen's famous temper and her high school reputation as the best (unofficial) boxer in Leeds.

As the opening band—an absurd group of screeching men calling themselves Sheriff Goodnature—wrapped up, people started to gather at the bar again, refreshing their drinks before the main act appeared. Ruby swayed a little in front of me, putting her half-finished drink down on the bar and excusing herself to the restroom. I followed her into one of what appeared to be a number of small corridors, and met her back in the hall when she emerged, taking in the sight of her excited grin as I bent to kiss her.

"Couldn't wait for me to come back?" she asked with a giddy flush.

"Guilty," I murmured into her mouth. "You're absolutely lovely."

With a little squeak, she pulled me back to the main room and deep into the throng of sweaty, pulsing bodies, all anxious for Bitter Dusk to appear onstage. The band members came out, plugged in their guitars, tested the mics, and ducked in and out of the backstage area. I could feel Ruby trembling excitedly against me and watched as she absorbed every move they made. It was too loud to speak to her, but even though the packed room wasn't my scene and I was sure to complain later about the noise, seeing her this happy erased any reserve I felt. I could watch her all night and enjoy each and every second.

A hush fell over the crowd as the lead singer approached the microphone. He didn't say a word, only looked behind to his bandmates and nodded. The drumsticks met in a sharp crack once, twice, three times.

And then the room exploded into noise.

It was drums and bass and raw guitar layered together in a way that could only be described as pure beauty. In an instant, it fed into my blood, made the hairs on my skin stand up. The music was wonderful: full and rich, clean bluesy guitar and precise drums with vocals that astounded me. I knew at the end of the night my ears would ring and Ruby would need to shout into my brain to be heard, but it was a kind of magic I'd never imagined: I felt the music as a physical presence all along my skin and inside me.

Ruby hadn't said anything about what to expect, and maybe she'd assumed I'd done this before—but the truth was, I never had. I'd seen the symphony, the ballet, and endless musicals with Portia over the years in the London theater scene, but never had I experienced anything as visceral as this.

The lead singer's voice in one song was smoke and rough pavement, and then in another was honeyed and smooth. The lyrics made my imagination do things I'd never expected, made things like regret and guilt, anticipation and relief bloom thickly in my chest. I felt oddly nostalgic for my wasted years of misery, and massively hopeful about what life could be, starting from this very point in time and onward. It was nearly too much, too intense with the lights bursting across the crowd, and Ruby lifting her arms over her head and singing along to every word of the song.

In front of me, she danced in a hip-swaying, shoulders-dipping move that had me mad for her, wild to grab and pull her backside directly against my lengthening cock. My fingers gripped her hips, my eyes rolled closed, and I relished the sound penetrating every inch of space in the room, relished the seductive movement of her against me. Her hands reached up behind her, tangling into my hair and pulling my face to the side of her neck.

I sucked and bit, groaned into her, and then—when I began to harden, my mind turning away from the song and focusing solely on the gorgeous creature in front of me—I had to decide whether to pull her into one of the many tiny alcoves or let her remain here to enjoy the music. I stood up straighter, deciding to simply let the moment wash over me.

The band tore through the set, barely stopping to greet the crowd or take a sip of the beers precariously perched on their amps. It was unlike anything I'd seen or heard, and I felt as if I was getting a glimpse into Ruby's heart: her love for energy and adventure, spontaneously nabbing tickets to see her favorite band in an unfamiliar city. I admired the trust she put in her own instincts, bringing me here. She knew all along that my reaction to the music and the lights and the pulsing rhythm of a hundred people jumping all around me would be profound.

At nearly six foot seven, I'd grown accustomed to bending to hear others speak, to instinctively ducking through doorways, to standing on the outside of circles to not feel as if I was crowding anyone away. But on the subway home, as we stood rocking with the motion of the train, I could tell Ruby wanted me stretched to my full height, holding the bar overhead so she could lean into me, wiggling and practically climbing me in her post-show excitement.

Her belly rubbed my cock again, and again, while her hands slipped beneath my open coat and under my shirt so she could press her cold hands to the flat of my stomach. Fingertips teased at the hair on my navel, at the buckle of my belt. I felt her slip an index finger just below the waist of my jeans.

And fuck, she knew exactly what she was doing to me. I could see it in the mischievous twinkle in her eye. Her smile was a sly thing, sliding in from the side, pushing her lips out into a flirty smirk and I listened to her chatter on about the show, the crowd, various songs, my mind bending with each scratch of her nails down my stomach, with every press of her soft body to my hips. I weathered the torture in silence, eyes never leaving her face, absorbing the treasure offered with each giddy word. With every jolt of the subway, every sway along the tracks, I mentally calculated how long it would be until I could devour her.

We rose from the station and she seemed to pause for

air. Long enough, in fact, that I could press her against the wall of a building just down from our hotel, bend to inhale the honeyed rose of her skin and hiss, "What are you doing to me?"

"Hmm?" She stretched, catlike in my arms.

"Where is the order in my brain? Where is my sense that I need to tread carefully with you?"

"You *don't*."

"You're muddling my every thought. We were doing so well taking our time."

Her hands slid up around my neck, pulling me into a kiss so intimate I felt something turn over in my chest. The soft slide of her mouth shattered me, the way she offered up her lips and tongue so earnestly, her quiet whimper when she felt me licking her bottom lip, sucking it between my teeth.

"We're still doing so well. I won't make love to you until it *is* love for you," she said.

No, not said—*reassured*. She was telling me that she knew she'd stolen my mind, possibly my heart, and would treat both things with care.

Somehow this promise that we wouldn't make love until I was sure only heightened my delirium. I drew away, pulling her down the street.

Two seconds inside the hotel room and I'd jerked her coat off, thrown mine across the room, and had her flat on her back just inside the door. Her trainers landed some-where near the bed; her jeans were roughly tugged down her legs and tossed aside.

I'd never known a hunger like this; my skin was tight and practically vibrating. Ruby stared up at me, washed only in the streetlight coming in the window, her eyes wide with thrill. Her expression of anticipation and the rigid ache of my cock pressed equally in my thoughts. Somewhere far in the back of my mind I knew I needed to temper myself but in the moment, with my heart drumming so hard I could hear it in my ears, I couldn't be fucking bothered to slow down.

"What are you—" she began before I shoved my own jeans to my knees and fell heavily over her, my boxers and her knickers the only thing keeping me from taking her for the first time on the floor.

Between her legs, my cock pressed against where I could enter her through the thin material, and I felt how slick she was beneath the satin. Groaning, I thrust my hips against her again and again, hurried and desperate, shoving her top and her bra up over her breasts to grip her, plump her in my hand.

I could imagine how it would be—*how it will be*—her legs around my waist and her eager hips pressing up and around, up and around, meeting every single one of my greedy thrusts. Ruby's hands gripped my backside, urging me faster, crying out.

I held my weight from her, perched on my elbows but kissed her madly, too frenzied; my teeth slid over her skin, mouth sucking at her tongue, her lips, her neck. She didn't seem to mind my recklessness—it seemed to thrill her, rather—and her sounds and lips and grabbing hands made me feel bloody *savage*.

I was close so soon—*too* soon—but I could take my time with her after. I needed relief from the wildness that built in me being so near her, tasting her, feeling her under me. Aching relief gathered in my back, shooting electrically down and building until, with a deep rock of my hips forward, I came, shouting into the dark room.

Ruby gasped, hands in my hair as I immediately pulled away, jerking the satin down her legs and off, bending to press my mouth to the sweetest slickness, burying my tongue between her legs.

Oh, the relief of it, of taking her, of tasting her this way.

Her cry came out choked, her hips left the floor and somewhere in the back of my mind I knew I needed to be gentle and loving but as I spread her open with my fingers, sucked her and fucked her with my tongue, she only grew more frantic.

"Niall—" My name disintegrated into a gasping, breathless cry. She tugged at my hair, pulling my mouth from her. "Put me on the bed," she managed. "Let me watch you."

I stood, kicking out of my pants and pulling my shirt over my head before lifting her, carrying her to the mattress and helping her out of the tangle of her rumpled top. My body had slowed enough that I could stop and gaze down at her, kissing her neck until she pulled me up to her face.

"I love this," she whispered between kisses, repeating my words to her the other night, our first intimate night in her hotel room. "Love to taste myself on your tongue."

I felt her goose bumps beneath my palms and closed my eyes, let myself enjoy the sweet sucking kisses she gave me, the way she took my hand and led it down her body and between her legs.

Pulling my lips away, I moved to her neck, her chest, giving attention to her breasts and stomach, before settling between her legs, kissing her hip.

She ran her fingers into my hair, studying my face as I let my eyes move up and down her naked body.

"You're so quiet all of a sudden," she whispered.

I spread her with my fingers, and relished the feel of the pad of my thumb, wet from her, tripping back and forth over her clit. "I'm concentrating."

And why would I want to speak over the sweet, rasping sound of her breath catching, of the sheets pulled tight in her fists?

I made pressing, steady circles and her hips rose slightly up from the mattress, rocking.

"I . . ." she started, words falling away in a strangled gasp.

"Shhhh . . ." I bent, pressing my mouth over my thumb, licking and stroking her in tandem. I'd stopped letting myself fantasize about oral sex—giving or receiving—as it was never something Portia wanted to do after our first few years together. She wanted missionary sex, music in the background so our noises weren't so obvious, eyes closed, lights off.

But I loved the taste of a woman, loved the way this act felt at once sweet and devious. Kissing a woman here always seemed like the pinnacle of fevered sensuality: a man wanting to taste the source of his pleasure. And here, on the bed, Ruby pushed herself onto her elbows to watch me with wide eyes, her lashes so thick and dark and seeming to draw her lids down under the weight.

As I swirled my thumb and circled my tongue, her chest rose and fell under sharp breaths, her mouth opened slightly, her tongue sliding back and forth over her bottom lip.

"Do you like doing this to me?" she asked, voice barely audible.

"I don't think *like* is the word I would use," I told her, kissing her, teasing. "I don't think anything in the world would give me more pleasure right now."

Her breathing slowed, hips pressed up and froze when I pulled my mouth away. *So close.*

"*Niall.* Please."

"Please what, darling?" I nibbled her hip, the delicate skin beside my hand, slowing the movements of my thumb.

"Put your mouth back . . . *there.*"

I fought my smile. "Where, exactly?"

Her eyes met mine, softening. "You know where."

"Your cunt, darling?" I whispered.

She squirmed under me. "I need it."

"You still only *want* it," I told her, relishing this return to our game when I could actually touch her, taste her, and make good on my promise to let her come against my kiss.

I saw her lip shake before she trapped it between her teeth, her eyes pleading with me.

It was so easy to bring her here, to this point. Nothing made it sink in more fully that she'd fantasized about this hundreds of times than the way her body fell so easily into pleasure under my touch.

"Tell me," I whispered, bending to exhale over her clit.

She squeezed her eyes shut, reached out to wrap her fingers around my wrist, urging and needful. She was so wet; she shook against my hand, her body clenched so tight, breath trapped in her throat.

I was delirious for her pleasure, lost in the sight of her mouth parted, her pulse ticking wildly in her throat, the taste of her still on my lips. "Tell me, dove."

Bending, I slid my tongue over her, again and again, and again.

Her thighs shook beside my head. "I'm so close."

"No, *tell* me," I repeated into her skin, pulling away again.

She seemed to have to force her eyes to open, and they looked down at me, confused. "Please, I—"

"I have all of these idle fingers," I observed, giving her a tiny smile. "That seems incredibly wasteful. Tell me . . . is there something I should do with them?"

She groaned when I bent and licked her in earnest, her

entire body shaking, and I could feel the way my question sent her tumbling over the edge.

I'd simply wanted her to know what was coming, and without hesitation, I pressed my fingers together and into her, deep—hard—as I sucked her into my mouth and nearly lost my mind when she screamed, back arching sharply from the bed and she came violently, legs closing against my shoulders, thighs trembling beside me.

————

I carried her into the bathroom, her legs wrapped around my waist and lips on my neck, kissing, scratchy voice quietly confessing she'd never felt anything like what I'd given her just now.

I hadn't, either.

Ruby shook in my arms, weak and overwhelmed, and I carefully lowered her into the shower, shielding her body from the pounding spray as I followed after her and lathered every inch of her skin. She braced her hands on my waist, watching me silently, with eyes full of an emotion I was suddenly terrified she would name aloud. Ruby's eyes hid nothing: I knew, without a doubt, that she was in love with me, and that it wasn't just the pleasure of my mouth just now, or the idea of my stoic reserve melting under her charm, but honestly in love. With me.

And if it were that simple, I would be making love to her right now, for I knew my feelings had quickly crossed over from initial attraction to a far deeper emotion. Love, maybe. But having stayed with Portia for so long under the pretense of what I sincerely believed was love, how could I trust my own definition? I was dedicated to her, yes. Loyal to a fault. But love? I wasn't so sure anymore.

A memory burst through me, from the evening of my wedding, while we danced in front of every guest, and when I felt oddly effervescent, brightly hopeful.

"Why is it so alluring you're wearing white? It's like a secret." I'd bent, kissed Portia's neck. "*Our* secret."

"What do you mean?" she'd asked, and if I were a smarter man then, I might have caught the edge in her voice, the look I would come to know so well that suggested I tread carefully.

But I was not a smarter man. "I've already had you, love," I said. "I'll have you again and again tonight."

Portia fell still in my arms, letting me sweep her 'round the floor. The song ended, and guests broke out into applause.

I looked down at her face, steely and cold in the warm glow cast from the overhead tent lighting. "What is it?"

She smiled stiffly at me, stretched to kiss my cheek and said, "You just called me a trollop at our wedding."

The beginning. Though it hadn't always been like that, just mostly. I had proposed to Portia with a ring I'd bought in a sweet shop and she'd laughed so hard she'd cried and then kissed me properly in front of whoever may have walked by at that moment in Piccadilly Circus.

Our engagement was a memory that often got lost in the shuffle of all of the flat, emotionless ones that followed. I struggled to remember the brighter times whenever I spoke with Portia lately, held on to them with an admittedly strange fever for a man who had no desire to reconcile with his ex-wife. I replayed them because I needed to remember there had been a time when marrying her wasn't only a clear expectation, but a rather lovely idea.

It was jarring to feel things for Ruby—crippling lust, admiration, worship, and a willing defenselessness—that I'd never before felt, even with the woman I'd married.

Guilt lingered in my chest—guilt that I'd wasted time, that I'd had more to give Portia than I'd bothered to. Guilt that I was thinking about all of this while I washed the body of the woman I was falling for.

Ruby left me feeling exhilarated, but I was terrified. Terrified of the speed at which it was happening, terrified that it wasn't in fact fleeting.

I smoothed my hands over her breasts, her hips, her backside, and down each leg, washing her feet. My body stirred for her again, insatiable, and more than anything I was terrified that I'd already grown addicted to the way she looked at me, that I'd come to rely on her affection and devotion in a way I never had with Portia. That I knew I never would have, no matter how many years we suffered through.

I stood, turning Ruby into the water to let her rinse and unable to keep my hands from roaming over her curves, and—when she'd finished—guiding her hand to stroke where I'd stiffened painfully between us, bending and practically begging without words for her mouth on mine.

She stretched to kiss me, pulling me with one arm down until our mouths met beneath the water, her other hand moving sensuously along my length.

With her eyes squeezed closed and tiny whimpers escaping from her mouth into mine, her lips shook when she kissed me. I wouldn't be able to distinguish tears from the water running down her face, but I knew I loved her when it registered how desperately I cherished seeing her so overcome. And the twin realization followed, with a single, stabbing heartbeat, that if Ruby's affection for me ever cooled, it would break me.

Thirteen

Ruby

That I was in love with Niall Stella was only a secret in theory. He knew it, I knew it. The fact that the actual words had yet to be said was nothing more than a mere formality. I saw the realization as it flickered across his face—expression adoring if not slightly wary—behaving as if I were a glass he might drop, then be left to pick up the pieces.

The sentiment hung in the space around us and it was hard not to feel even the smallest flash of irritation. My wild adoration, his almost constant wariness—I wasn't sure which was worse. My silent admission was as good as graffiti across my chest, and yet he didn't say anything.

So neither did I.

Niall had toweled us both off, and we'd fallen almost immediately into bed. His? Mine? I wasn't even sure anymore. Did it matter? My orgasm had left me boneless, but I was still wide-awake.

"If you could be anywhere right now, where would you be?"

We'd been quiet for a while now, lights off and only the sounds of traffic, or the occasional bump or voice from down the hall to break into our thoughts. He'd assumed the position—stretched out on his stomach, pillow clutched tight—and looked up at me in the dark. I loved that I knew how he slept now. It was such an intimate thing, to know the way a person arranges themselves to depart at night, and a part of me delighted that I was one of the very few who knew this tiny, secret thing about him.

"And you can't say 'right here,'" I added, running a finger along the back of his arm. His skin was smooth and still warm from the shower. I dug in a little, kneading the muscle, and he sighed in pleasure. "Anywhere else."

The moon was high in the sky, and a swath of light cut across the bed, angling up and over his body. I watched him frown in thought as he considered my question.

I wasn't even sure why I'd asked. It might have been that I was feeling vulnerable after our shower, and that tiny seed of doubt was making me homesick. Maybe it was the wall I felt had been knocked down tonight, seeing him lose himself to the music and the crowd moving all around us. Or maybe it was just my way of trying to get inside that maddeningly complicated head of his. I didn't even know.

"Hmm, anywhere?"

I nodded from my spot next to him. The sheets were cool against my naked body, but I could feel the heat of him next to me.

"Why can't I say 'right here'?" he asked, reaching out to brush the tip of my nose.

I shrugged and he moved his leg, hooking it over mine to bring me just a breath closer. It was a tiny thing that had me smiling into my pillow.

"When we were small, our dad had a friend who worked at Elland Road, the football stadium in West Yorkshire. Max was old enough to drive and sometimes he'd bring me with him—the irritating little brother. Drive us both down there to kick balls 'round on the pitch. Leeds United play at Elland Road," he said with reverence, "the club I've watched my entire life on telly at home. I'd been up in those stands, cheering them on, and here I was, standing on the same green as the men I'd worshipped. I'd like to go back there someday with my brother. See if it still felt as big."

"I'd like to see that," I said, grinning now. "You and Max as teenagers, running up and down the field. You'd both be shirtless in this scenario, yes?"

Niall pinned me with a glare that had me erupting in giggles.

"And what about you, where would you be, Miss Ruby?"

"I miss San Diego."

"Do you not enjoy London?"

"I *love* London, getting to live there has been sort of a dream, but it's expensive, it rains a lot, and I miss everyone."

"Everyone?"

"My roommates, Lola and London. And especially my brother."

"It must have been hard being away from them."

"The time difference sucks," I said, groaning. "It's like we get four hours to be awake in the same day and those are early in the morning or late at night."

Niall nodded, continuing to run his fingers through the front of my hair. I began to feel my eyes droop. "But you'll stay in London?" he asked, and I wondered if I imagined the hint of anxiousness there.

"Through school, at the very least."

"So a few years."

The words burned on the tip of my tongue. "Hopefully," I said at last.

"And tell me about San Diego. What was it like growing up there?"

"Have you ever been to California?" I asked.

"I've been to Los Angeles," he said. "Perfect weather and palm trees. Lots of blond people."

"LA is *not* San Diego," I said, shaking my head but feeling my chest warm just thinking about home. "LA is cement and cars and people. San Diego is green palms and blue sky and ocean everywhere. When I was younger, Crain and I would head over to a friend's house just a few blocks from the beach. We'd load everything up in the baskets on the front of our bikes and just stay there, all day."

"What would you do?" he asked.

"*Nothing*," I said blissfully. "We'd just lie around in the sand all day, play volleyball or read or talk, listen to music. When we got hot we'd jump into the water, maybe take turns on someone's paddleboard, when we got hungry we'd eat the lunch we packed. My mom would see us in the morning and then not until the sun went down."

"Sounds brilliant. I quite like the image of teenage Ruby," he said, wrapping a finger around a piece of hair and tugging. "Hair bleached from the summer and freckles across your nose. Tan skin and tiny bikini." He seemed to consider how this sounded for a moment before clearing his throat and adding, "We're going to imagine I'm teenage Niall in this scenario, as well."

I laughed, pulling the sheet up around my body. "Carlsbad was an amazing place to grow up, you know? Before I left the States I was sharing this great apartment with two of my best friends. We could see the ocean from our dining room window," I said, missing them so much in that moment it was like a physical ache. "Between our work schedules it felt like we hardly saw each other, but when we finally managed to all be there at the same time we'd make cappuccinos so we could stay up late and talk, sometimes watching the sun come up over the marina. Maybe that's why it was so easy to leave . . . We'd all grown so busy we barely saw each other anymore."

"Maybe. Or perhaps, you knew something bigger was on its way. Waiting for you."

I looked at him for a long time when he said that, wondering if he meant school and work, or more. "You should go there someday. Lie on the beach, go to Disneyland, ride Space Mountain."

Niall scrunched up his nose in distaste, but I leaned in and kissed him anyway. "Disneyland?"

"You didn't think you'd like the concert, either. Remember? Sometimes it's fun to just be silly."

He was quiet for a moment before nodding once and tilting his chin toward me for another kiss. "You're right, I suppose," he said against my mouth. "And what do you think of New York? Do you enjoy yourself?"

"It's big and loud, but . . . sort of exhilarating. I'll never forget it," I said, eyes still on the comforter.

"Maybe you'll come back."

I lifted a shoulder in a small shrug. "Maybe. Might not be the same without the company, though."

"Who would buy you hot dogs and tease you about mustard?"

"Or grope me on the subway?"

"Exactly. So school first and then you'll what? Go back to San Diego?"

We'd been so honest tonight and I didn't want to give that up. "I'm not sure," I said. "It depends on a lot of things."

"Such as?"

School, finding a job, finding a flat. You. Me.

"School," I said. "A job that pays enough to live there."

"I'm fairly certain neither of those things will be a problem."

"I still have to actually get into Maggie's program, you know."

"You will. Margaret Sheffield would be nutters to let someone like you go. You're quite brilliant, Ruby."

"I'm *distracted*," I corrected him.

He smoothed a hand down my back and over the curve of my ass, to rest at my hip. "Ah, but we go home soon, yeah?"

"I think we both know that New York isn't the distraction," I said honestly.

"I think that may be true for the both of us," he said, pressing his thumb into my skin.

"What *will* happen when we get home?" I asked, voicing the question we'd both been avoiding. We were due to leave in two days. The tickets were bought. The email telling me to check in to my flight would be arriving in less than twenty-four hours. Everything had happened so fast, but would it continue? We wouldn't take the physical side of our relationship any further until he knew he loved me, but what did that mean for the rest? Were we an actual couple? Would we tell anyone?

He blinked up to my face, and I could tell he hadn't been expecting that, for me to just come right out and ask. "We'll plug along," he said. "Things will of course be different at work, but outside of that, things can stay as they are."

His expression tightened into one that I'm sure mirrored my own. I wasn't sure which of those sentences I hated more. *We'll plug along* made it sound like we were barely surviving this, that *we* were something to be endured. *Things will be different at work*. Of course they would, how could they not? *And things can stay the way they are.* I was greedy. I didn't want things to stay the way they were, I wanted more. I wanted all of him.

❦

Nearly three days later we stepped onto the curb at Heathrow, bags rolling to a stop behind us. The sky was a dingy gray, the air cool and smelling of damp stone and exhaust, but it felt like home. Niall had held my hand throughout most of the flight, growing more confident in how he allowed himself to touch me, and even now stood close enough that the side of his body was in constant contact with mine.

He'd suggested we head to his flat, but we were both exhausted, and, realistically, we wouldn't get any sleep if we were together. We'd each been gone for weeks, would have people to catch up with, a stack of mail to sort through, and, after nine hours of traveling, there was nothing I wanted more than a shower and my own bed. Especially given that Tony had requested I come into the office the next day to debrief him and because, he "hasn't seen my lovely face in a month."

Niall and I definitely should have talked more, at least discussed some kind of game plan for work, but instead we leaned heavily into one another, both of us trying to enjoy just a few more minutes. He kept my hand tucked between both of his as the view outside the windows shifted from the M4 to surface streets, and by the time the taxi stopped in front of my building, it was all I could do to kiss him goodbye—albeit a bit enthusiastically, considering we were in the back of a cab—and stumble with my bags through my front door.

Rain pounded on the street outside my apartment that night, tracking over the windows like leaded glass. It felt right somehow that it would rain our first night back in London, a welcome return to normalcy of sorts.

I was in bed, fresh from the shower and wrapped in my favorite pajamas, when my phone buzzed from the bedside table.

Miss seeing your face on the pillow next to me, it said, and something sparked, hot in my chest. He was doing it—he was trying—just like he'd said.

Miss hearing those cute little sounds you make while you sleep, I typed back, already smiling at what I knew his response would be.

I am far too masculine to ever be considered 'cute,' Ms. Miller. I laughed out loud at that, and my heart took off.

`I may need to see you fully undressed again`
`soon, just to be sure.`

There was nothing for a full minute, and then the little bubble appeared, indicating he was typing a message. `I can't wait to see you, this bed is far too big for one person.`

My fingers shook on the keyboard as I entered a reply, my cheeks beginning to hurt from smiling. He really was doing this. *We* were doing this.

`I can't wait to see you, too.`

`Tomorrow then. Sleep well, darling.`

If a heart could burst from happiness, mine was well on its way.

I finally fell asleep to the sound of the rain, with a smile on my face and my phone tucked under my pillow. The voice in my head was silent.

FOURTEEN

Niall

It's fascinating how quickly the human mind incorporates new habits. Even though we were back in London, even though she'd never shared this bed with me, waking up without Ruby was odd.

I pulled my phone from my laptop bag and texted her. Did you sleep?

Her reply: Barely. I may need someone to stand behind me and move my arms and mouth for me at work.

I'll see you at the office, my beautiful puppet. I finished breakfast, read the paper, dressed, and left. It could be any other day . . . except it wasn't. My life felt about seven thousand times bigger.

Ruby was in her small shared space when I arrived. I usually got in before eight but doubted I had ever once beat her to the office. This morning, I'd tried, though. I wanted even just one moment alone with her, unguarded before reality descended. Unfortunately it was not to be. The offices already buzzed with Monday morning activity, and I could only manage a small smile, a wink, and a glimpse at her wet, pink lips.

"Hey," she mouthed to me.

I stared at her for a beat longer, wanting nothing more than to walk in and give her a simple kiss on the mouth, but instead I nodded, walking to my office down the hall.

Anthony's familiar sharp, two-knock combination rapped at my office door and, as usual, he stepped in without waiting for an answer.

"All right?" he asked in greeting, walking over to take a seat across my desk from me.

I leaned back in my chair, giving him what I hoped was a relaxed smile. "Good."

He crossed an ankle over his knee and grinned at me. "I trust you had a nice trip?"

Never before had I felt so much as though I were playing a game of chess. "I did."

Anthony watched me with scrutinizing eyes, fingers steepled beneath his chin. I blinked over to my computer monitor under the guise of checking my email. I hadn't decided what I would tell my questionable colleague. On the one hand, I didn't want to hide what was happening between me and Ruby, and if I knew her at all—which I sincerely felt I did—I knew she wouldn't do a very good job playing aloof. On the other hand, I wanted what was private to remain private, and Tony had a way of making everything his new favorite joke.

"Something is different," he mused, pointing a finger at

me. "You have a grin in your eyes just here." He motioned to his own brow. "A twinkle. A little spot of sunshine over your head, I think."

"Do I?"

"You get knobbed in a New York City titty bar?"

His crudeness fell like a weight dropped in the room. "Honestly, Tony."

He hummed. "Bang a Rockette?"

"Frigging hell."

He paused, giving me another once-over, then smiled. "Finally get a leg over on Ruby, then?"

I swallowed, caught off guard, pretending to focus on something on my desk. "Ah, no. That . . . I, well, that is to say, I didn't. No."

It was the truth, if we were being technical. I hadn't technically had sex with her yet.

Tony's hands slapped down on my desk. "You old dog!"

I felt the blood drain from my face. This was exactly the reaction I wanted to avoid. "No, Tony, it's not—"

"You banged the fringe off her, didn't you? You had a go at my Ruby!"

I pushed back slightly from my desk, feeling a thunderstorm build in my chest. " '*Your* Ruby'?' "

"So you did then," he said, clapping his hands once, a violent crack that sliced through the room.

I glanced at the door, hissing at him, "Keep your voice down, you git."

He pretended to wipe a tear from his eye. Tony enjoyed

ribbing as much as the next bloke, but there was an edge to his tone here. "Oh, watching you bumble around the office over this is going to make the wait for the next season of *Game of Thrones* much easier to take."

"Cut the shit."

His dark eyes went wide. "And look at the mouth on Niall! I dare say, she's loosened you up, she has. Think I might step out and thank her."

I took a deep breath, closing my eyes. "Tony, *don't*."

"Aw, come on then, tell me," he said, settling back in the chair, his voice returning to slightly more sincere territory. "What happened?"

I looked at him, feeling the glare slowly drain from my eyes.

"I'm done taking the piss, Niall," he assured me, smiling with genuine apology. "I'm sorry, I've just never in my life imagined—"

"It's not what you're thinking," I cut him off, leaning forward and resting my elbows on my desk. I needed to get back some semblance of control. I had to admit it would be helpful for Tony to be generally aware of what was going on between Ruby and me, but surely he didn't need more information than that. "Turns out she had feelings for me before, and, well . . ." I couldn't find a way to articulate where my head was concerning Ruby, settling only on "I enjoy her company."

Tony could clearly see the understatement in my words. "Ah, sure."

"I'd be grateful if you'd not mention it 'round."

He nodded, making a little X mark over his heart and giving me a conspiratorial wink.

———

Ruby was sitting in the small break room with her friend Pippa when I went in to grab my lunch from the refrigerator. Her eyes met mine and she quickly blinked away, but a bright flush crept up her neck and into her cheeks.

"Ruby. Pippa," I said in greeting.

"Hi, Mr. Stella," Pippa replied, brightly. *Too* brightly. Had Ruby been similarly interrogated?

"Mr. Stella," Ruby said, looking back up with a secret little smile. Her teeth bit down on the tip of her tongue and I sucked in a sharp breath, remembering the last kiss she gave me before we parted ways last night. Her mouth had tasted like the lemon candy she'd sucked on the drive from the airport. I cleared my throat and reached for the refrigerator door handle.

"Adjusting to the time change?" I asked, looking over my shoulder to her.

She smiled wider, shrugging. "Trying."

Pippa stared studiously at her plate of leftovers as Ruby's gaze held mine.

I felt the air draw from my lungs and struggled to inhale evenly. Back here, in everyday life, the reality of *us*—that there *was* an Us—made every part of me seem to ache with longing. With her so close all day long, would I be able to focus on any of the work in front of me? Would I be able to focus on anything?

If I considered her features one at a time maybe she would overwhelm me less. Her eyes were too intense; they communicated to me that she was just as desperate to be alone as I was. Her tongue slipped out, dampened her lips. Her neck was long, smooth, and I imagined taking her to my place, kissing down the slope of that throat as I unbuttoned each of the tiny pearls lining the front of her—

"Um . . . Mr. Stella?" she asked, eyes widening meaningfully as she tilted her head toward my hand . . . which was still wrapped around the handle to the refrigerator door I'd pulled open. Cold air filtered into the room, against my warm chest.

"Ah," I said, jerking into motion and bending to retrieve my salad. I reached for a fork from the drawer and hurried back to my office.

As I suspected, I could barely focus, and knew I needed to find a way to calm my frayed thoughts. This uncertainty wasn't like me; it was disorienting. I needed to know what our schedule would be: Would she stay over at night? How would we be able to take things slowly physically . . . or was it already too late for that? Did I even want to anymore? At this point, sex felt like a formality. Everything we'd done felt infinitely more intimate than that, but as soon as I had the thought I knew that being with Ruby in that way would mean more to me than a simple next step in our physical relationship.

Did I want that? And when I did have sex with her, would

I be able to maintain any sort of cage around my heart, in the event I wasn't what she needed me to be down the road?

I'd assumed Portia was the love of my life, but from the first moment Ruby had stretched and kissed me with such bravery, I knew I'd been wrong.

My phone buzzed on my desk, pulling me out of my obsessive analysis: Are we doing dinner at my place or yours tonight? And before you answer that, remember I have a roommate and a small bed and am the worst cook in the history of bad cooks. PS: stop thinking.

Laughing, I replied, In that case, there is no other option but for you to come to my flat. I live alone, have a large bed, and am perhaps slightly more capable in the kitchen (only slightly; perhaps I will order takeaway).

Just outside my office, I heard a short clip of a cartoonish voice yelling, "Bottom!" and then the same cartoon giggles. A knock landed on my door immediately after.

"Come in," I called.

Ruby stepped inside, smiling down at her phone. "Okay."

My heart swelled at the sight of her again. "Okay?"

She closed the door behind her. "Okay I'll come over for dinner, since you insisted so vigorously."

Just then, I registered that the sound I'd heard outside my office was her text alert. "Was that . . ." I stopped, leaning back in my chair and smiling at her. "Did your text alert say, 'Bottom'?"

She shrugged, all trace of her blush gone now that we were alone in my office. "Specifically, it's *your* text alert. It's the minions. From *Despicable Me*? The movie?" She shook her head as she stepped inside. "We have got to get you out more. Anyway, it fits. You have the best ass this side of the Atlantic."

" 'This side of the Atlantic'? Does that mean when we were in New York you found an ass superior to mine?"

She pursed her lips, pretending to think on it. "I didn't have a chance to do a very extensive survey, but Max's friend Will is pretty fit and—"

I leaned forward, growling, "Finish that sentence, Ruby Miller, and so help me I'll take you over my knee and spank *your* bottom."

She threw her head back, laughing my favorite Ruby laugh. "I love that you think a spanking would be—"

Two sharp knocks landed at my door and Tony burst in, smiling. The smile froze and turned sour, and then slowly straightened as he took in the sight of Ruby leaning casually against my desk. She bolted upright, pretended to find something to pick at on the front of her skirt.

"Hi, Anthony," she said quietly.

"Ruby," Tony said, brows pulling together. He looked over at me, and then back to her. "How're the Barclay Industrial friction calcs coming?"

Her blush was back, and her eyes fixated on the carpet. "They're done, I just need to compose the email. Sorry, I was just catching up with Niall"—she caught herself—"*Mr. Stella* after the trip."

"Ruby, I'm sure it's a relief that he is now aware of your crush," Tony replied coolly, "but Niall is a vice president at this firm, and I'm sure he has a lot on his plate after the trip."

I felt Ruby's wide eyes turn to me, and my jaw clenched in suppressed anger.

What in the bloody hell was he doing?

Tony continued, oblivious. "Perhaps you should leave his office door open when you enter, and leave the *catching up* for your nonwork hours?"

With a tight nod and mumbled apology, she slid past him and out of my office.

"Tony," I ground out, leveling him with an irate look. My blood ran hot through my veins, heart pounded in my chest. "Was that entirely necessary? It's her lunch hour. And 'her crush'? She wasn't in here *harassing* me. I'm just as involved as she is, and there is nothing improper happening between us. She does not report to me."

"No," he agreed, "she reports to *me*." Tony stared, his jaw tight, to where Ruby had left the room and closed the door behind her. "I guess I didn't realize it would be so difficult for her to maintain professional boundaries."

My eyes widened as it struck me: Tony was *jealous*.

"Please tell me you're joking," I said, as nonchalantly as I could manage. Something had ignited inside my chest at his words. Tony wasn't my superior; to the contrary. Technically speaking, I was being actively groomed for the position that would someday make me his boss. "*You*—the one who suggested I get a leg over, who called Ruby fit, who said—and I quote, 'all legs, great tits'—who seems to hire only the best-looking interns for the Oxford program. You're in here lecturing *us* on professional boundaries?"

He blinked, his eyes clearing when he looked back at me. "I'm simply saying I hope I don't find her in here again." With a little nod, he turned and left my office.

It seemed to take ten minutes for my pulse to return to normal. I was livid: pacing my office, contemplating taking this to Richard, to ensure that everyone was aware that nothing improper was happening, and to let Richard know that the way Tony had just spoken to Ruby was unacceptable.

But I was too angry. As a rule I didn't have conversations when I was this worked up: the idea that I would speak out of indignation rather than maintaining a certain professionalism was unacceptable. The issue here was Tony's behavior, and my case would be weakened if I appeared to be speaking from an emotional place.

For this reason, too, I waited another fifteen minutes before texting Ruby again. I didn't want her to think Tony's opinion mattered enough to anger me.

Tony was out of line, I told her simply.

I know, she replied. But it was still mortifying.

I'm sorry, darling.

It took several minutes for her to reply, but when the text arrived, I could hear the words in Ruby's ever-patient voice:

Don't be. Let's just enjoy your roommate-less apartment, your big bed, and the takeout you're going to order tonight.

I smiled at my phone, typing, Looking forward to it.

And I was. I could barely wait to pull her into my arms and remind her that this, between us, extended far beyond the walls of any office.

———

Ruby went to her apartment to gather what she needed for work the following day, and I used the time to pick up dinner from my favorite curry place on the corner.

When she arrived, she looked around the entryway and then stepped past me, into the living room.

My flat was, perhaps predictably, tidy and simply decorated, with a smooth black leather sofa and broad matching chairs, a low marble coffee table, and a large, plush area rug.

"If I had been asked to draw a picture of your place, it would look just like this."

Laughing, I took a step closer to her. "I'm happy to never surprise you."

She turned, stepping into my arms. "The fact that you never surprise me is one of the reasons I love you."

We both froze.

"Did I just say that out loud?" she asked, closing her eyes in a tight, mortified wince. "Please tell me those words were only in my head."

I bent, kissing her forehead. "You're lovely."

Something inside me slammed into my lungs, a self-inflicted punch to the chest for being unable to come up with something better.

I love you.

You're lovely.

It's not that I was particularly surprised by her words, so why hadn't I thought ahead and prepared some sort of response? It was official: I was the world's biggest idiot.

Ruby tensed and began to lean away, but I pulled her back against me, kissing her neck as I madly searched for the right thing to say.

"Ruby."

"It's okay," she said on a quiet exhale, hugging me and pressing her face into my neck. She didn't sound entirely okay. I wanted to look into her eyes and see what I would find there, but I couldn't seem to move. She took a breath and after a moment, visibly relaxed. "I know I'm farther along in the feelings department. I'm sorry I just dropped a bomb of awkward."

"Please, it isn't that . . ." Only I couldn't finish the sentence, couldn't pinpoint what this feeling for her *was*, if not love.

Did I love her?

I had no bloody clue what romantic love even looked like anymore; it felt like a foreign language. I cursed Portia for her coldness, for making me question every gesture, for undoing a childhood full of exuberant declarations of adoration, of wicked tiffs with my siblings, and constant affection from our mother. I cursed myself for managing to become such an emotional midget.

I didn't know what to call my feelings, but I knew they were expanding, and profound, and *frightening*—after all, losing Portia had felt like being unchained, but the idea of losing Ruby felt so hideous it turned something over inside me.

And what it took for her to express her feelings so starkly and then to stay here in the middle of my silence and wait for *me* to find words . . . I wanted to give her everything I had, wanted to let her know how absolutely mad I was for her.

I trailed my lips from her jaw to her neck, sucking, nibbling. *Feel this*, I thought. *Let me show you the things I can't say.*

I pulled her coat down her arms, tossing it aside and lifting my fingers to the buttons of her shirt, silently begging her to meet my eyes. She looked up with hesitation marking her features and then she read something in my face—pleading anguish, some needful hope—and she seemed to exhale a world of tension, reaching to pull my face to hers.

"Are you suggesting we postpone dinner?" she asked against my lips.

I nodded, wrapping my arms around her waist and walking us over to one of the wide, armless chairs in the living room.

My hands were impatient: hastily unzipping her skirt,

pushing her underwear down her hips, hungrily sliding my palms over every inch of her naked skin. Ruby's curves were smooth, pale, utterly flawless, and I bent, sucking at her shoulder, grasping her breast in my palm.

Far more carefully, she unbuttoned my shirt, eyes gauging my reaction. "We don't have to—" she started, but I cut her off with a kiss.

Let go.

She slid my shirt from my shoulders, unfastened my belt, and slowly worked my trousers down my hips until I could kick them away.

Taking me in her hand, she began to lower herself to her knees before me.

I shook my head, in one motion pulling her up and bending to slide my lips over hers, parting them, tasting her. Her tongue was sweet and small in my mouth, pushing against mine with a sudden, aware desperation. Her slim, firm hands pressed against my chest, backing me into the chair, and she followed, climbing over and digging her hands into my hair as she kissed me: messy, biting, moans and tiny pleas escaping as my hands slid down her sides, between her legs, feeling her softest, most vulnerable skin.

"Do you want to move?" she asked, lips wet, eyes heavy.

Did she mean move . . . into her?

"I . . . yes?" I arched beneath her, seeking contact.

She leaned in to kiss me again before whispering, "I mean, do you want to move to your bed?"

I closed my eyes, struggling against the way my brain wanted to pick up that question and consider it too carefully. Getting up and walking to my bedroom would ricochet us out of this place of lust and relief that felt so bloody good. I didn't want to move an inch. I would think too much about what this meant, what I felt, that I'd never had sex in that bed, and that I'd only put a name to Ruby's face just under four weeks ago.

My brain wanted to be sure about all of this.

Stop.

No.

No.

"No." I bent, kissing her neck as my hands on her backside urged her closer, pressing her, slick and warm, against my shaft. "I don't want to move."

Her hips circled and she shifted up until I knew a simple arch of my hips would push me inside her.

"*Christ*," I groaned. I'd forgotten—or maybe I'd never truly known—how desire could be clutching and mindless and *wild*. I wasn't myself. I was a man who wanted pleasure, wanted to *fuck*, and was free to do it for the first time in my life.

"Shit. Protection," I managed.

"I'm clean," she said on a tight gasp. "I'm covered."

Her eyes met mine, the question lingering there.

"Come over me, darling," I whispered.

With a groan, I lifted up as she lowered herself and she

293

choked out a small noise that sounded so much like pain and pleasure I nearly stabbed upward with how savage it made me.

"Wait," she whispered, her voice coming out so small and tight I pulled back to assess her face. She stared at my mouth, her own lips wet and parted . . . and she looked fucking *sublime*.

"Let me . . . just . . . get used to . . ." Her eyes rolled closed and she let loose these delicious, hoarse cries every inch she lowered herself onto me.

I struggled to remain still, my thoughts obscured by the silken feel of her . . . her body tensing so tight around me . . . her splintered gasps . . . the way her hands urged my head down to her chest.

When I was fully inside her she began to shift in perfect, tiny, *maddening* circles. Her nails dug into the back of my neck and she squeezed me, breasts pressed to my face, whispering her broken thoughts right into my ear:

Niall

Oh, God

I won't

It's so

She was getting off, using my body, and began to rise more each time, push harder onto me in her return. Her fingers slid higher and gripped my hair, her hot mouth sucked and scraped at my neck. The smell and taste of her, the warmth of her thighs and her breasts as her skin brushed across mine, the decadent slide and suction of her along my length; it was like being submerged completely, not needing or wanting to come up for air.

And her sounds, *oh.* I'd never heard such honest expression of pleasure, tight and sharp right against my ear. The sound and feel of her—the fucking *bliss* she allowed herself—chipped away at my foggy notion of sex, my frankly laughable experience to date. This was for her pleasure just as much as mine and the reality of it—what sex *should* be: an intimacy to be shared rather than endured—made a fever tear through me, burning across my skin.

I'd also never been so hard, or greedy to grab and feel and consume. Just when I thought there couldn't possibly be more, she moved forward or leaned back, taking me further, drawing me in. I pulled her nipple into my mouth, sucking and cupping the other breast in my hand, wild for her to ride me recklessly, but wanting her to continue to chase the euphoria I could see all over her face, to get there before I would lose it.

Because I knew, with Ruby, I *would.*

I could feel the tension building in my thighs, the need to shove up and *fuck*, and take, and let go. I could feel this raw beast, clawing out of me, wanting sex like I'd never had but always needed: uninhibited and sweaty and *hard.*

Ruby's movements became irregular and she pulled my mouth to hers, lips parted and pressed to mine, simply rocking over me, feeding me her moans and gasps and jagged exhales as she fucked me. Her hips faltered, hands clutching at me, and I felt her tighten just before she arched away, crying out as she came. Her warmth, the slick feel of her stuttering on top of me, and finally—*fucking finally*—the way she rode me hard as her orgasm began to peak unleashed the last bit of my control. The pleasure for me was impossible and I bent, pressing my teeth into the firm swell of her breast, groaning into her skin.

She collapsed into my chest and in a breath I lifted her, lowered her back to the plush carpet, and pulled her hips off the floor, sliding into her with a long, rough stab of my hips.

Ruby's breath caught—she was so tight, a fist around me—and she watched as I began to lose my mind, lose my *heart*. I didn't know myself in this moment: this man who kneeled between her legs and held her hips in my hands to keep from fucking her across the floor. I hardly recognized the man who told her,

Watch

Look right where I'm fucking you

You're soaked so wet so soft

Fucking hell you're so warm and wet you feel so fucking perfect

Pleasure cascaded down my back, clawed out of me and she was reaching between us, touching me where I pulled from her with every stroke, begging me with her eyes to let go, to show her how good it felt.

I couldn't close my eyes. Not in a million years could I close my eyes the first time she watched me come, over her, *inside* her. My thrusts were coarse, exhales sharp and harshly pulling grunts of exertion from my throat. I gave into the spiral, losing my rhythm, as I bellowed into the quiet room.

Never before had I known a pleasure so intense.

I stilled, chest sweaty and heaving as I looked down at her. Her breasts were flushed and glistening, cheeks splotchy and lips parted as she struggled to catch her breath.

"Niall . . ." she said, running a shaking hand up my chest.

Instinct kicked in: a panicky sense of obligation. I pulled from her, standing on shaky legs and jogging to the bathroom to retrieve a cloth, hold it under the warm tap.

Returning to her, I bent, pressing the warm cloth between her legs, soothing and wiping away my—

"Niall," she said, stilling my hand with her fingers around my wrist.

I sat back on my heels, looking up at her face. "Do you hurt?"

Her brow pulled together in confusion. "No?" She took the cloth from my hand and pulled me back over her. "You didn't have to run off to clean me up. I wanted to enjoy some postcoital kisses. I *want* to be messy because of you."

Embarrassed, I winced, bending to kiss her lightly on the cheek. "Right. Sorry."

"Don't be. Seriously, kudos, sir." Her legs slid around my hips and I propped myself on my elbows above her. "Missionary is clearly your superpower. Noted."

I smiled. "It should be. It's all I did for eleven years. Honestly, having you on top—" I stopped, feeling my stomach fall into an abyss when I registered what I'd just said.

Beneath me, Ruby fell immediately still.

"Bloody hell . . . Ruby. That was a terrible thing to say and at the most inopportune moment. I am an imbecile."

She ran her hands up the back of my neck, lifting to kiss, possibly in an attempt to shut me up. "It's okay."

"It's not," I said into another kiss.

"It is," she insisted, her voice uncharacteristically stiff. "I'm sure it's weird to be with someone for the first time after only having been with her before."

"It's not that . . ." I began, and then trailed off, leaving the thought unfinished. I needed to fix this. It was bad enough that I'd gone mute when she'd said she loved me; I couldn't let this be a disaster, too. "Ruby, my timing may be horrendous and I apologize for that, but I feel I need to explain how different this is for me."

She nodded, relaxing a bit beneath me. As I searched for words, I struggled to hold on to the clarity of only minutes before, when I felt completely joined to her, *knowing* her. She'd given me something so rare—true insight into what it was to make love—and I'd fucked it up immediately.

"At some early point in our relationship, Portia read some article explaining that men needed sex at least once a week in order to not cheat. It was bollocks, but it became part of her mental relationship canon. Sex once a week. No more, no less. She was very organized, you see," I said, hoping to add a bit of levity. "Staff meeting Mondays. Sex with husband Tuesdays. Rubbish pickup Thursdays."

Her eyes went soft with sympathy. "Ouch."

"It wasn't so bad," I said, and then tilted my head, considering this. "It simply wasn't very good, either." I met her eyes, swallowing thickly as the words took shape in my mind. "And see . . . that, right there. Please understand I feel uncomfortable even saying this much, particularly given our *current* circumstances." I made a show of looking down the length of our bodies, as if to emphasize the point, to which she smiled. "As a general rule I don't discuss my personal life. But now *you* are my personal life. I want you to know every facet of me, and how different I am with you. And unfortunately that often means knowing things about my relationship with Portia. Somehow her view on it made sex both a special occasion and a chore."

Ruby drew one fingertip across my bottom lip, tracing the shape of my mouth as she said, "Did you ever tell her any of these things? When it ended?"

I felt myself frown. "There wasn't really a chance. Or maybe, more accurately, we'd both grown so weary by that point, that it was easier to just walk away."

Ruby's question pricked at some thought I'd long since buried. Why hadn't we ever spoken of these things? Surely if I was unhappy, Portia had been as well. I could only imagine how self-aware Ruby—with her psychologist parents and need to always express herself—would view the way I'd reacted after the divorce. There was no attempt at reconciliation, no attempts to fix what was wrong, no search for closure. I'd packed up my things and gone. The decision to end our marriage had been filled with as much passion as we'd had during it.

Always able to read my expressions, Ruby tipped my chin back in her direction. "Hey, I'm not saying you should have, everyone deals with things differently. I saw your face before the divorce, and after. I know you're happy with me. I didn't ask that because I'm jealous. I hate to think you didn't get the sort of adoration you deserve, but—and as horrible as it sounds to say it out loud—it turns me on to think about how much *I* can give you." Her hand ran down my stomach and wrapped around where my body seemed to return to life. "You were so different just now. Like"—she closed her eyes, thinking as she absently stroked me—"kind of dominating and rough."

Just as I opened my mouth to apologize on instinct, she stilled me with a look, then said, "I liked it."

Without any words, I returned to her, pressing my chest to hers as we kissed.

I felt her reach for me, guide me into her again, and just like that we were moving together frantically, vocal, grasping. I tried to restrain myself, tried to remain gentle, but the tightness in my chest over her admission made me feel demanding, possessive, and desperate to deserve her.

Fifteen

Ruby

I opened my eyes and blinked in confusion at the walls and ceiling, at the soft dark sheets wrapped around me. Everything looked completely foreign. For a moment I was wildly disoriented. I wasn't in the hotel room in New York. I wasn't in my own flat.

Oh.

I was with Niall, in his bed, *naked*, with his heavy arm slung over my hip.

A glance at the clock told me it was one minute before seven, and in the time it took for the numbers to turn over, I remembered: Niall Stella fucked my brains out last night.

I nearly rolled into my pillow to scream.

I closed my eyes and relished every memory: Niall beneath me, thick and rigid inside me, his hips arching and desperate to get deeper. And after I came: Niall flipping me over, laying me down on the rug, Niall growing so rough and wild with his hands holding my hips off the floor as he drove and drove and drove . . .

My eyes opened wide as I was punched with the memory of the *rest* of it—what had happened before the perfect, obliterating sex. More specifically, the way I'd managed to blurt that I loved him, and the way he'd blinked a thousand times, long lashes fluttering, lips awkwardly forming a hundred different evasions before he kissed my forehead and declared: "You're lovely."

You're. Lovely.

That was easily the most mortifying event of my life. Followed closely by him bringing up Portia mere seconds after being inside me.

Number of Times I Told Niall Stella I Loved Him and He Had Sex with Me to Distract Me from the Fact That He Hadn't Said It Back: one.

Number of Times Niall Stella Ruined Post-Coital Bliss by Bringing Up Sex with His Ex-Wife: also one.

Well, technically, he had sex with me twice.

Carefully, I slipped out from under the weight of his arm. My body was worn-out, limbs and joints stretched, breasts tender in the most amazing way. With each step toward the bathroom, the ache in my muscles and between my legs reminded me *exactly* how good all that pent-up lust and frustration felt when he unleashed it. Max was right, New York should definitely consider hooking Niall up to the grid.

But the feelings after? Not so good. In fact, when he'd initially brought her up—my first instinct had been to knee him in the balls. Niall's marriage had seriously skewed his idea of what relationships could be, and it seemed he was only beginning to realize it. What worked for one couple didn't always work for another, and thankfully, he appeared to be letting those ideas go.

My body . . . my body was exhausted and still humming from what was easily the most mind-blowing, intense sex I'd ever had. My *body* knew it had been good for both of us.

But my heart had its own hesitations. I hated the gnawing sense that if I hadn't declared my feelings last night, we would have kissed, cuddled, gotten each other off, and then happily fallen asleep. Niall was my cautious, courteous giant and I knew that his desire to treat sex with reverence was eclipsed only by his new desire to show me he could try to be what I needed.

It took me only a few minutes to use the bathroom and wash my hands and face. The soap, the towels, the entire room smelled like Niall. I'm sure if I were to press my nose to my skin I'd find that I smelled like him, too.

I tiptoed out of the bathroom and down the hall, where our clothes were scattered all over the floor. The chair sat empty in the middle—a reminder that he hadn't taken me to his bed, but had me right there in the living room. Twice. I tried not to read too much into that. Maybe he simply needed me right then. Or, maybe sex in his bed felt like a new, scary frontier.

My bra hung off one arm, my skirt was a few feet away on the rug. I gathered everything up, a flash of memory replaying with each item I found.

His eyes as he'd slipped off my shirt.

The sight of him sucking my breasts.

The shape of his mouth when I'd pulled off his belt.

The way it felt when he finally, *finally* pushed inside me.

The flash of fear on his face when I'd told him I loved him.

I could hear Niall beginning to stir as I pulled on my clothes, and I wished I'd managed to slip out before he'd woken. I was embarrassed. But I knew *he* would never bring up the fact that we had sex last night way before either of us expected to, so of course I would have to.

But not even I, compulsive discusser of all things, wanted to have the conversation we needed to have.

So, about last night . . . did I unintentionally manipulate you into having sex with me? Or are you just so unwilling to trust your own instincts that you gave in to what you thought I wanted?

"Ruby?" he called out, voice gravelly with sleep.

I walked down the hall in bare feet, my steps muted on the wood floors. He sat up when I entered, the sheet falling to his waist as he took in my clothes, the shoes in my hands.

"Hey," he said, but it was more like a question. His expression still carried the weight of drowsiness but in his eyes was a clear note of confusion. Guilt and irritation wrestled in my stomach and I pressed my hand there, telling them both to knock it off.

"I forgot something," I said. It was a lie, and I could tell by the way his face fell slightly that we both knew it. "I need to run home before work."

"Now?" He sat up at the side of the bed, his hair an adorable mess and miles and miles of bare leg stretching to the floor. Wow. "I can drive you."

"No, it's okay, I—"

"Ruby, stop," he said, voice deep and firm. "Let me just get some clothes on."

He stood, completely naked, and out of some spontaneously polite instinct I looked away—very obviously—instead staring at the far corner of his room.

He noticed, and of *course* he did. I was acting like a twitchy lunatic.

"Are you all right?" he asked, stepping into a pair of track pants. "It's not like you to avert your gaze when I'm nude. In fact, you're usually quite the leering pervert. "

He was teasing me. He was *trying*.

I shrugged, looking back at him but only able to really look at his face. "Just mildly panicking."

Just realizing that I told you I loved you after only a few weeks together and the craziest part is it wasn't a lie.

Just realizing I think you had pity sex with me last night.

Just realizing I'm probably freaking out for no reason and really should just leave right now and get some coffee and food before I do something stupid like overshare all of this.

"Do you want to sit on my bed and tell me what has you 'mildly panicking' after I shagged you roundly until only a couple of hours ago? I would think you'd be too worn-out for conscious thought before seven thirty in the morning. I certainly am."

I looked up at him, at his teasing tone, and smiled weakly. "Maybe over dinner tonight?"

He nodded, eyes narrowed as he studied me. And like that, I'd flipped the switch in him. The overthinking switch. The holy-shit-what-happened-last-night switch. "Okay."

Fuck.

I slipped into my flats and ran my fingers through my hair, attempting to tame it just as his phone rang on the bedside table.

He bent, looking at the screen and then at the clock. Hesitating, he murmured, "I'd better take this. If you'd just . . . ?"

He held up one finger, asking me to wait, and then stepped into the bathroom off his bedroom, closing the door.

Well, that's awkward. If it was a work call he'd have taken it in front of me.

All I needed to hear was his gentle voice saying, "Portia? It's seven in the morning. What is it, love?" before I grabbed my bag and headed out of the flat.

One of the amazing things about London is that you don't have to drive anywhere. Want coffee? There are a dozen shops lining the street. Need to pop into Selfridges at lunch? Oxford Street Tube is across the street. Iconic red buses stop at virtually every corner and there's even the River Bus to take you down the Thames. Need to avoid an awkward taxi ride with someone you may or may not have manipulated into sleeping with you? Thankfully, a short trip on the Tube and the Southwark stop is just a few doors down from my office!

It was still raining when I stepped out onto the street, because of course it was. I'd showered quickly at home but needn't have bothered. My little flats were immediately drenched by the puddles and the constant downpour, and made soppy squishing noises with every step. Cars splashed water up onto the narrow sidewalk and even my umbrella was no match for the storm. Luckily, if I moved close enough to the storefronts, the various awnings offered me some small measure of cover.

By the time I stepped into Richardson-Corbett, I was drenched. I squeezed the excess water from my skirt and jacket, reminding myself that my hair would dry the same as it probably did every day. And besides, the shower at home, the walk to work—it had given me time to talk myself down.

The I-love-you-You're-lovely tic was nothing. It was

us. This is what we did: I dove straight in; he dipped a toe in and then pulled it out to give himself time to consider whether the water was too cold. It's why we worked, and there was no point questioning it.

I also needed to calm down about the way he'd brought up Portia, and then slinked off into the other room to take her call. To be honest, my brain actually stuttered more on that last one and I searched wildly in my thoughts to explain it away. He'd only been with one person, and married to her for over a decade. Of course it would be weird, right?

Pippa met me in the hall with wide eyes that scanned me from head to toe before saying, "Here," and handing me her cup of coffee.

"That bad?" I asked.

"Have you seen yourself?"

"Well, that answers that," I said, continuing on to our shared desk and setting down the coffee. "Thanks for this."

Pippa nodded and took the chair opposite me. "Everything going okay?"

I nodded as I slipped out of my coat. "Yeah everything's fine." I looked up to see the message indicator light blinking on my phone. Picking it up, I punched in my pin and then covered the speaker, telling her, "It's not even nine and today has done a *lot*. I just had a mental meltdown so epic it was like something out of a bad sitcom . . ." I paused, listening to the message and then swearing as I hung up the phone. "Anthony wants to see me as soon as I get in. *Shit.* Why is he here so early?"

"It can't be that bad. I saw the email congratulating the New York team. And that bridge redesign you worked up went off without a hitch. He probably just realized it's still raining and hasn't seen you in that top before." She grinned and rolled her eyes. "Hoping for a little wet T-shirt action, if you know what I mean."

"Gross," I said, dropping down into my chair. I reached into my bottom drawer for my cosmetics bag and emergency cardigan. "Okay, I'm going to clean up a little and then get this over with."

"Go get 'em," she said.

———

"You wanted to see me?" I asked, peering in through Anthony's door.

He'd been arranging something near the bookcase, and turned to look at me. "Miss Miller, yes. Come in."

Miss Miller?

I stepped inside the office and he added, "Close the door, please."

My stomach dropped.

I did as he said and crossed the room to stand in front of his desk, stopping just on the other side of the extra chair. "Yes, sir?" I asked, the sentiment setting off a shudder down my spine.

"I need to talk to you about something very serious,

I'm afraid." He pushed a heavy, leather-bound volume back onto the shelf and crossed to the desk. "You have a bit of a choice to make here."

I'd seen Anthony like this before: serious in an oddly coy way, trying to get me to draw the answer out of him.

I stood across from him, smiling. "What is it, Anthony?"

He looked up at me, eyes narrowed. "'Mr. Smith' is probably best."

I choked on the words I wanted to say, *On my first day here you stared at my tits and told me to call you Anthony*, but instead said, "Sorry. Um, Mr. Smith."

Anthony unfastened the buttons of his suit jacket and took his seat, pulling a stack of papers toward him, contracts that had been flagged with red and yellow tabs where he should sign. "Given your rather unprofessional behavior in New York and since . . ." he began and my stomach evaporated. "Rather, given your *long-term* fascination with a vice president of the firm and your recent pursuit of him—"

"My *pursuit*?"

He flipped through some files, not even bothering to look up at me as he spoke. "I am required to ask you to either keep your relationship with Mr. Stella purely professional, or leave your internship with Richardson-Corbett."

"What?" I gasped, lowering my shaking body into the chair across from him. "*Why?*"

"It is clear to several of us in management that you've behaved unprofessionally," he said, reaching for a pen. "You've been distracted, and your efforts have been mediocre at best. Beyond that, I needn't elaborate."

"But that's not f—"

Fair, I almost said it, but snapped my mouth shut tight. I wouldn't add *behaving like an adolescent* to my growing list of transgressions.

Trying again, I said, "Would you please explain why on earth this has been a topic of discussion beyond just between myself and Mr. Stella? We haven't broken any rules!"

"Miss Miller, please do not presume you have the right to question any decision I make regarding this firm, and whom I choose to employ." He scribbled a signature across a page and the sound was enough to put my nerves on edge. "As an intern, you qualify as a temporary worker in the UK, and therefore I am not obligated to explain anything to you. But seeing as you're young"—and *there* was that thing he did, where he packed a gut punch worth of insult into a single word—"I hope this might be an opportunity for growth. Your conduct of late, though not necessarily qualifying as gross misconduct, has been lacking. Having had this latest . . . distraction with a vice president of the firm brought to my attention—"

"I haven't done anything wrong," I repeated. "Not smart, I'll admit. But not outright against the rules. I do not report to Niall."

"*Niall*," he repeated, smiling down at his papers. "Yes. Well, regardless, this is the type of situation that has a tendency to run away from all of us, and we in management think it best if you end your relationship, or forfeit your internship."

I could feel my face heat with angry tears. *Young* girls cry; I didn't want him to feel justified in his insult. I blinked several times, determined that no matter what happened, I wouldn't give him the satisfaction of seeing what this was doing to me.

"Can I speak to Mr. Corbett?" I said as smoothly as possible. "I think I need someone else to explain what's happening."

"Richard has given me the power to make any and all decisions affecting my department."

Fire lashed through my blood. I couldn't hold it back. "So, to be clear, you urged Niall to *get a leg over* on me, and now you're firing me because you think he has."

Anthony's head whipped up, eyes full of blazing authority. "I dare you to say that again."

"Clearly," I said, seething, "I choose to leave the internship. This has been one of the most unreal conversations of my *life*."

"In that case," he said absently, scribbling another signature, "I'll put a letter in your file. I'll see that you have a copy before you leave."

The rain had stopped and I took a walk to clear my head, far enough away that I could hear the chimes of Big Ben in the distance. Out of instinct I reached into my pocket to find my phone, only to realize it wasn't there. I'd left it on my desk before talking to Anthony, thinking I was just going down the hall but then rushing out before I could get it. I wondered if Niall had made it in yet, if he'd come looking for me, if he'd called.

And that's when I realized how far this had gone, and that maybe there was a kernel of truth to what Anthony said. My first thought wasn't about my job or the fact that I was five thousand miles away from home. It wasn't where would I live? How would I buy food or pay the electricity bill? It wasn't about my fucking spot at Oxford, either, or how long and hard I'd worked, or how much I'd sacrificed to get there.

It was about Niall Stella.

The object of my attention was pacing in his office when I returned and made my way down the hall toward my cubicle. He jumped when he saw me, reaching out to pull me inside.

"Where have you been?" he asked, closing the door behind us.

I must have looked even worse than I thought, because his eyes moved in a circuit from my wet hair and pale face, to my damp clothes and broken expression.

"That depends on what you mean," I said. "First, I walked to work in the rain because I wigged out in your flat thinking I'd inadvertently manipulated you into having sex with me."

He started to speak, eyes wide and incredulous.

But I held up a hand to bid him wait. "Then, I was in Anthony's office being berated. And most recently, I was out for a walk."

"We'll talk about the manipulation thing later. *Honestly*, Ruby." He inhaled, taking a step closer to me. "What's this about Anthony berating you?"

"Nothing I want to talk about here. What I want is to go home, get a little day-drunk, nap, and then have dinner with my boyfriend."

He winced. "About that . . ." Niall wiped a hand down his face and then met my eyes. "I'll need a rain check, I'm afraid."

I slumped down into one of his plush chairs near the window. I didn't want to talk to him here about quitting, and *why*. And I most certainly didn't want to be alone in my own head after all this. "Really? There's no way you can cancel? I need to freak out, with your rational brain on hand."

He sat opposite me, looking . . . okay, if I was being honest? He looked *petrified*.

"What is it?" I asked.

He swallowed, and looked up at me. "You left this morning when Portia called."

"Yeah," I said, wincing. "That was part of the freak-out."

"Completely understandable, darling," he began, leaning toward me a little. "It's just that . . . it may have been a good thing that you left. The conversation went on for some time."

"Is everything okay?"

He didn't answer immediately and I felt my heart squeeze painfully. I'd initially been upset that he didn't say he would call her back. He must have heard the front door close and he didn't even bother to come after me. But it occurred to me only when sitting in his office that something awful might have happened while we were away in New York. Was Portia sick?

Licking his lips, he said very quietly, "She called because she wants to reunite." He pulled a face—like maybe I should commiserate over the awkward unexpectedness of this . . .

But instead my world stopped, split in half, and then splintered into a million pieces.

I blinked, several times. "She what?"

"She wants to reunite," he repeated, sighing heavily. "I'm just as surprised as you are, believe me. She said she's had a lot of revelations and wants to talk to me."

"And . . . ?" I started, feeling like my stomach was climbing into my chest, pushing my heart into my throat. "You *agreed*?"

"Not to reconcile," he hedged. "But eleven years married is a long time. We were together when we were teenagers. After my conversation with you last night, and hearing you ask whether we'd ever actually discussed any of this, I feel obligated to at least hear what she wants to say."

He paused to give me time to reply but I honestly had no words in my head. None.

"Given how things are between you and me, I felt I needed to tell you that I would be having dinner with her tonight," he continued carefully, "and make you aware that Portia wanted to talk to me about why she thinks she deserves another chance."

"What chance *does* she have? An even fifty-fifty?"

He laughed uncomfortably because what I'd said was awkward and sharp. But I couldn't regret the edge to my tone. "God, no, Ruby."

"But you're *going*," I reminded him, aghast. "I mean, we're talking zero chance of reconciliation with your ex-wife, right?"

His expression straightened as if he hadn't really thought about it this way. Clearly, he'd only considered it a courtesy. But if it was just a courtesy, and there was no chance he would take her back, then why wasn't the answer too-little-too-late? Why not just tell her that his girlfriend had just left his flat in a bit of a hysterical state and could she fill him in later—*over the phone*?

"Well, I can't imagine being with her again—"

"So you're going only as a gesture?"

He closed his eyes, exhaling a gust of breath. "It sounds terrible when you say it like that."

"So you're *not* just going as a gesture?"

"I don't—"

"Just tell me!" I cried. "Because right now it sounds like you're telling me that you slept with me last night and tonight you're going back to your ex-wife?" I felt tears burn across the surface of my eyes and by now I was too fucking tired to bother wiping them away.

"Ruby, I'm not having dinner with her tonight to go back to her."

"But you *might*."

He closed his eyes. "I can't imagine that I would, no. But Ruby, I know you're young and that you've n—"

"Don't," I said, my voice frightening, even to me. Unconsciously I had balled my hands into fists; I was at the dead end of my patience with his wishy-washy game. "Don't do that. This isn't about my age. I've *never* acted naïve with you. I've only been understanding while you work through your enormous pile of . . . *baggage*."

He cleared his throat and nodded, looking appropriately contrite. "You're right, I'm sorry. What I mean is that it feels cruel to not at least have the conversation I've felt we needed to have for so many years. You of all people, who are so good at expressing things, must understand this. It might relieve something in both of us to simply discuss things for once."

My heart hurt so horribly that I could barely pull in a full breath.

He leaned forward and took my hand but I pulled it out of his grasp. The pain in his eyes was nearly unbearable. *What was he doing?* We had such a good thing. *Had I scared him off this much?*

"Darling," he said calmly, and something in my brain crawled over the word, trying to excavate any condescension there. "I want to ease your anxiety somehow, but I don't want to be flippant about what it means to meet with my ex-wife to hear her out. I realize now it would feel dishonest if I told you it was nothing and then I still went and listened to her with an open mind."

"*Do* you have an open mind?"

His answer broke my heart. "I suppose I'm trying to. I owe her that, at least."

I nodded, remaining silent. I could see his torment in this moment and my heart hurt for him, too, but it hurt more for me. He wanted to talk to her to ease something in him, to achieve closure. But I knew there was a tiny part of him, the part that couldn't hear her out over the phone, which also wondered if maybe she *had* changed enough. If they might be able to find something comfortable together, and better than what they'd had before.

"I'll see you here tomorrow, then?" he asked. "Perhaps we could do lunch?"

I nearly laughed at the absurdity of it, of "doing lunch" almost like one would with a client. I'd essentially forfeited my job so I could stay with him, and he was going to have dinner with his ex-wife to discuss reconciliation.

Was this really happening?

I nodded, jaw tight, unable to even look at him. "Sure."

Tilting his head, he asked, "Could you tell me what happened with Tony? We exchanged words earlier. He urged Richard to put a rather strongly worded letter in my file. Hopefully I've borne the brunt of what happened between us in New York."

Between us. In New York.

Not last night. Not the night I pushed you so far you're considering going back to a woman who made you miserable, but left you alone in your shell.

"Oh, yeah," I said absently, sinking into an odd numbness. I stood, walking toward the door. "He basically just gave me a letter, too."

Sixteen

Niall

Despite my suggestion that we meet somewhere neutral, Portia insisted I come to her flat—our old flat—for dinner. I'd had an odd weight in my gut since talking to Ruby, some residue of regret about the conversation. I'd texted her as I left the office, saying I would call later, or come 'round if she liked, but she hadn't answered. I knew she was a bit offended that I wanted to talk to Portia at all, and I couldn't exactly blame her. But I hoped, too, that she understood the intent behind it. After all, I wasn't here hoping to reconcile with Portia; I was with *Ruby* now. We were an *us*.

But Ruby made a good point: then why *was* I meeting my ex-wife for dinner? Could I honestly say the only reason I agreed was to let Portia speak her piece so we could both truly move on? Was there a part of me—no matter how small—that wondered if we could find a better place together, with more communication? We knew each other's rhythms, after all. It would be easy to slip back to it.

But the thought turned sour in my mind and guilt clawed its way up my throat. I *had* truly moved on. I didn't look back

320

on my marriage with longing or any type of ache. It had been lonely and passionless. It hadn't even felt like being married to a best friend; it had nearly felt like cohabitation with a colleague.

What could I expect her to say that would change how I viewed any of that? Was I going just because, in my new happiness, I simply *felt bad* for my ex-wife?

I wanted to call Ruby before I went to dinner, to tell her that, no, Portia honestly had no chance, and maybe that was wrong of me to let her think she did by my coming, but a dark and furtive part of me was simply *curious:* Portia had *never* in our relationship sounded as open and pleading as she had on the phone that morning.

It had thrown me enough to forget, for a few minutes, that Ruby had been waiting in my flat for me to drive her home before work. By the time I'd emerged from the bathroom, hand clutched over the receiver to beg her to wait just a minute more, she'd already left.

Even on the steps I could smell the pasta Portia had cooked—my favorite, with sausages and peppers and thyme. I could hear the music playing—my favorite Vienna Philharmonic recording of Brahms. The front door was unlocked and still required the familiar shoulder shove–low kick combination to open.

I bent to pet Davey as he ran across the floor to me, hopping on his hind legs and resting his paws on my knees. "That's a good boy," I said, scratching behind his ears.

Hearing the clang of plates on the counter, I looked up.

Portia stood barefoot in our kitchen in casual cotton pants, a T-shirt, and an apron. I blinked, mouth agape. I'd rarely seen the woman without her pearls.

When she turned to me, she wore her wide, dazzling smile. I was immediately on edge.

"Hello," she said, picking up a second glass of red wine from the counter and walking to hand it to me. She placed it in my grasp and then stretched to kiss my cheek. "Welcome home."

I nearly wanted to turn and leave right then. It was disloyal, being here. I felt like my skin had been replaced with damp wool and I itched all over. It was wrong, and I knew it. Ruby had known it.

"*Your* home," I reminded her, putting the glass down carefully on the sideboard. "I live several Tube stops away."

She waved me off, returning to the counter where she was dishing up pasta into two bowls. "I've still not seen your flat."

"There isn't much to see," I said with a shrug.

Portia nodded to the dining room and I startled slightly. I'd barely been here two minutes and she was leading me to the table as if I'd simply come home from work. No reacquaintance, no small talk. Certainly no playful banter.

I followed her in. It was surreal seeing the table set with candles and flowers, the placemats we'd received from the Wynn family for our wedding. The candelabra her parents had given us for our fifth anniversary. When we lived here together, Portia would cook on occasion, but it was always clearly communicated to be a production and used as a form of currency in the *look-how-much-I-do-each-day* ledger of our marriage.

I felt for my phone in my pocket, now desperately wishing I'd called Ruby before coming here.

We sat. Portia passed me the pepper and then set her napkin in her lap. Davey curled up on the floor, resting his head on my feet. Outside, cars drove by, their tires wet on the pavement. Inside, as always, silence reigned supreme at the dining room table.

"How was your day?" she asked finally, looking down with interest at her bowl of pasta.

My *day*? How about my month, or, better yet, the last eleven years of my life?

"It was . . ." I began and then stopped. The revelation struck me with a nearly physical blow: There was no mystery to be unearthed here. There was no secret to the silent isolation of our marriage. It was, and would forever be, like this between us.

Portia was lonely and having a hard time finding her footing in her new life. It had been true for me, too, in a way. I'd focused on routine, buried my free time in sport. I'd barely looked up long enough to see Ruby watching me, enamored, for months.

And now Portia was watching, waiting for me to finish my thought.

"It was an odd day."

It was a strange thing to say; the perfect opening for her

to ask more. But the quiet returned and I attempted to tuck into my meal. The sound of her chewing was as familiar to me as the smell of the wood from the dining room hutch or the cold stone scent of our kitchen floor.

"How was *your* day?" I asked in return, attempting some stab at a normal conversation. But it wouldn't work. The bite of food I'd eaten sat like a lead weight in my stomach, and my head was full of nothing but Ruby. "Portia, I can't—" I started, but she was already speaking.

She didn't say at all what I expected: "We were terrible together, weren't we?"

Finally, a laugh broke through the unease in my thoughts. "The worst."

"I thought we could . . ." She paused, and for the first time since I arrived I saw a weariness, a vulnerability there. She rubbed a hand over her face. "Honestly, I don't know what I was thinking, Niall, wanting to have dinner to talk. I wanted to see you. I've missed you, you know. Not sure I ever really appreciated you enough to miss you before."

I lifted my glass of wine to my lips and said nothing. I tried with my eyes to tell her that I understood, that a part of me was glad to see her, as well.

Clearly I'd never been good at false sentiment. I closed my eyes, remembering last night. And in this dining room, that used to be mine, with a wife who also used to be mine, I knew the reason I felt so sick to be here was that I loved Ruby.

I loved her.

"It's just that," Portia continued, poking at her dinner, "now you're here, I'm not sure what to say. Where to start. There's too much, isn't there?" She looked up at me. "Too much habit, really, where we don't say very much at all."

It was another needle in my thoughts. Ruby spoke of her feelings, her fears, her dreams and adventures. She wanted to hear mine. She took time to make it a habit of ours that we spoke, and I praised her for it. Told her I appreciated her honesty.

I appreciated it, even when it terrified me. Earlier, she'd told me she needed to talk something out with me—that she'd needed *me*. I'd been unable to get out of my own head long enough to be there for her.

"I don't even have to ask you what you're thinking to know your thoughts are elsewhere," Portia said quietly, pulling me from my revelation. "You're here out of courtesy."

I didn't reply, but my silence was as good an answer as any.

"I appreciate that, I do. I wasn't always a good wife to you, Niall, I know that now. And I was wrong to think we could go back. I wanted to think we could find something we didn't have before, but having you here now, looking so wary . . . I see it, too. It's well and truly done between us."

"I'm sorry, Portia," I said, putting down my fork. "I wanted to hear what you had to say because I felt I owed you that. And I owed it to myself, too, to understand what you'd been thinking the whole time we were married. But it's true: I've other things on my mind tonight."

325

"I can tell," she said. "It's quite a shock to see you looking so . . . upset."

I apologized again. "It wasn't fair of me to—"

"Do you know," she began, cutting me off, "when you moved out, you never once seemed anything but completely sorted? The last thing you said to me when you left was 'Cheers.' I'd handed you the folder with your passport and vital documents and you'd smiled kindly and said, 'Cheers.' Isn't that amazing?"

I bent, putting my head in my hand. "It wasn't sadness I felt at leaving our marriage, Portia, but I did feel *something*. I simply don't know what to call it, or how to express it. Failure, maybe. Or regret." I looked up at her, admitting, "Also relief."

"Oh," she said on an exhale. "I felt that, too. And then guilt, over being so relieved. And I've gone back and forth in the months since. How could I spend so much of my life with someone I was so relieved to leave when he did? How could I have made it better?"

I smiled sadly, nodding in agreement.

"Well," she said, folding her napkin and putting it on the table. "I for one wish—"

"Portia, I'm in love." The words came out so suddenly and raw, I instantly wanted to pull them back in. I bent my head, wincing.

It was several long seconds before she spoke. "Darling?" Without looking up, I could hear her swallowing, hear her finding breath. "Tell me she hasn't hurt you."

"Quite the contrary. I believe I've hurt *her*."

"Oh, Niall."

I leaned my head back, staring at the ceiling. "I'm sorry. I didn't mean for that to come out so baldly."

"It loosens something in me to know you've moved on, even if it's emotional to hear it." She paused to take a deep breath. "I can hear it in your voice, see it in your eyes. This tightness and urgency. I could never have drawn this sort of reaction out of you. I was terrible to you at times, I know that. But you weathered it all with such calm stoicism. Do you imagine how that feels to know, truly, that it would be impossible to evoke a passionate response from you?"

I looked back to this woman I'd mistreated, been mistreated by. "I'm sorry, Portia."

She gave a wan little smile. "Don't be. It wasn't your fault."

"Are you good, though?" I asked quietly.

"In general I am," she said. "It's been up and down. For the first few months after the divorce I was a bit on the wild side. Spending money frivolously, seeing men left and right."

Nothing. I felt nothing when she said this.

"Recently I was seeing someone more seriously." She toyed with the small charm on her napkin ring. "I suppose that's what had me panicking these past few days. It's hard to be with someone different, the fear of repeating past mistakes. We were together so long, Niall, that it felt wrong in a way to go off with someone else, like I was betraying you."

I looked up at her. I'd personally never felt the sense of betrayal, but I understood what she'd said about it being hard to be with someone new. To be afraid. To figure out their rhythms and needs. To worry constantly about failure.

"He's someone I knew from before." She hesitated. "From work."

Something clicked in my thoughts. "Stephen?" I guessed.

Portia sounded guilty when she admitted, "That's him. Stephen."

I caught the way he would watch her. It struck me only then how apathetic I'd been at the work functions, business dinners, and in the office when I'd stop by to drop off lunch or something she'd forgotten at home. Stephen couldn't help but glance at Portia every few seconds, at least when I was near.

If someone regarded Ruby the way Stephen had looked at Portia, I would turn homicidal.

My thoughts tripped, blood running hot: *Tony* looked at her that way.

"Nothing happened before," she said. "I promise, Niall."

"I believe you. And I'm not surprised, Porsh. I saw the way he looked at you."

She laughed. "Yes. Like that one girl at your office, when I dropped off the papers to sign. She had hearts in her eyes, watching you."

I felt something inside me squeeze tightly. *Christ.* Even Portia had seen it.

"Ruby?" I asked, and saying her name sent a heated spike through my chest.

"She's tall, beautiful. American?"

I needed a drink. Nodding, I lifted my wineglass to my lips and said, "That's her."

Portia's eyes widened in comprehension. "She's the one you've been with?" She paused. "The one you love?"

Again, I nodded, not even a hint of doubt lingering.

"She's wanted you for ages and you were finally together?" Portia sounded like a schoolgirl. And it was a testament to our distance that she'd invited me here to discuss taking her back and had so easily let the idea fall away. "Niall, it's so romantic."

"Like you and Stephen?"

"Well, I'm not sure if we're a thing anymore, but it is what it is." She leaned forward, tilting her head as she asked, "Tell me what happened?"

And like this, with my head in my hands and pulse thudding anxiously in my throat, I confessed the entire affair to Portia.

I told her about New York, Tony's not being able to come and Ruby coming in his place. I told her about Ruby's feelings for months before I was aware, her beauty, her humor, and how she put me at ease so immediately. I told her about my fears, my longing, my hesitation. And, although I likely didn't need to, I told her how I knew she needed more from me—more communication, more intimacy—and I sincerely tried to do it right.

"And then I came here for dinner," I admitted. "I couldn't tell her it was nothing without feeling like I was lying— because I did intend to hear you out, Portia—but I didn't want her to think that I was coming back to you, either. She looked *shattered*." I groaned, remembering her vacant expression, the way she'd absently wandered from the room and out of the building entirely. "I've made a terrible mess of this."

"Niall," she said, voice soothing. "You know you've got to fix it."

I nodded, feeling sick. I didn't know if it was that easy. I'd messed up, enormously.

She paused. "I love you, you know?"

Her voice held a rare poignancy. She'd said this only a handful of times during our marriage and here, the words spilled out so much more readily.

Smiling up at her, I said, "Love you, too, Porsh."

And then, the familiar command returned: "Fix it."

———

I jogged down the steps to the street, already dialing Ruby's number.

It rang, and rang.

I'd never heard her voice mail recording before, and hearing her voice while my heart was clutched with an uneasy panic only made me feel more urgent.

"Hi, this is Ruby! Leave me a message and I'll probably just text you back because I'm terrible about calling but if you're calling this number you probably already know that about me and I'm already forgiven." *Beep*.

"Ruby," I began, "it's me, Niall. I've . . ." I trailed off, pulling at my hair. "I've just left Portia's. Ruby, I don't know why I went there. I shouldn't have gone. Please, just call me. I want to see you tonight. This was all absurd. I *need* to see you."

But hour after hour, she didn't call, and she didn't text.

───────

Admittedly I arrived at work early the next morning but I was still surprised that Ruby wasn't yet at her desk.

Her friend Pippa was there, though, and when I approached—knowing full well Pippa was aware of our relationship—she blinked away from me in a scowl.

"Pippa?"

She looked up at me again, eyes level and assessing. "Yeah?"

"Have you heard from Ruby or know when she's expected in?"

Her expression shifted from annoyed to baffled. " 'Expected in'?"

"In to work," I clarified, a bit unnecessarily I felt.

"Are you daft?"

I stuttered out a few syllables, finally settling on "I don't believe so?"

She looked at me silently for a couple of beats. "You really don't know, do you?" she asked, standing up to face me. "Ruby was *sacked*, you dolt."

331

I blinked. "I'm sorry. Sacked?"

"Sacked."

"She was sacked?"

Pippa laughed humorlessly, and shook her head. "She was made to choose between her internship and a relationship with you. She meant to tell you yesterday afternoon that she was done here, but I think you had *other* plans?"

Oh.

Oh.

Bloody . . . fucking . . . hell.

Panic tore through me, causing my heart to squeeze tightly before it exploded into a rapid swing.

"She . . ." I gasped, looking around as if she might actually be there. As if this might be some sort of game.

Tony made her choose between her job and me.

She chose me.

And as far as she was concerned, I chose Portia.

"I'm *fucked*," I whispered to myself.

Pippa snorted. "Too right."

———

I stormed into Tony's office, eyes on fire. "You have got to be bloody kidding me."

He startled, standing abruptly. "Niall."

An intern I hadn't even noticed stood up from the chair across from him, smoothing her skirt and excusing herself with a quiet, "Pardon."

We both watched her leave; her beauty and youth triggered another explosion in my chest. I barely waited for her to close the office door before I turned to him, voice low with fury, "Give me a reason I shouldn't slam your head into that desk right now."

Tony held up his hands. "It's my group policy, Niall. Per the rules I set forth verbally when Ruby started *in my group*, I can't allow fraternization."

"Since when?" I nodded to the door. "Was this rule set forth before or after you hired that one there?" I took a step closer. "Was this before or after you suggested I pull Ruby? Was this before or after you admired her tits, her legs?"

He blinked, swallowing nervously. "I'm not sure what conversation you're referring to, but if you've been able to find it in writing, I'm happy to discuss it with you."

I laughed dryly. "So you've been to HR, then."

Tony closed his eyes, repeating, "Per the rules I set forth verbally when Ruby started in my group, I can't allow fraternization."

Seething, I told him, "You are a bloody joke. I hope Ruby sues your pockets inside out."

———

If someone had told me only a month ago that I would meet a woman from the office, fall in love, and lose her all before spring truly arrived in London, I would consider the prospect ludicrous.

Ruby didn't return to the office that morning, not even to clean out her desk. Her absence was a blaring void: no hint of her silly laugh, no flash of her playful green eyes. Even the interns' office seemed subdued when I walked past. So as late as half past nine—after my blowup with Tony, and as my blood pressure seemed unwilling to return to normal—I could barely focus on a single task in front of me.

Will you not call me back? I asked her via text message. I've made a mess of this. I'm desperate to speak to you.

Productivity at work remained impossible after I hit SEND. I glanced to my mobile nearly every ten seconds, turning the volume up on the ringer as high as it would go. Normally one to leave the device in my desk drawer when I went to meetings, I carried it with me, leaving it just at my elbow on the table. Short of showing up unannounced at her doorstep, it was my only connection to her.

Just after lunch, I heard my text alert, and startled like a madman, toppling a cup of pens on my desk. Hope bloomed, immediate and heavy, making it nearly impossible to breathe. It took no time at all to read it; my heart felt neatly punctured. Her message said, simply, Job hunting.

Typing furiously, I asked her, Darling, please call. Why didn't you tell me what happened with Tony?

An hour passed. Two, three, five. She didn't reply.

I interpreted it as the dismissal I knew she'd intended and turned off my phone to avoid the temptation to plead with her in an unending string of messages. Unable to work, I paced the hall like a lunatic, ignoring Tony's furtive, guilty glances in my direction and Richard's lingering, uncertain ones.

Almost as soon as I set foot in the door of my flat, I moved to the office, dialing her number. It rang once—my heart was lodged in my windpipe—and again, and finally a third time before she answered.

"Hi," she said, her voice small and thin.

Nearly choking on my breath, I managed, "Ruby, dove."

I could immediately picture her wince when she replied, "Please, don't call me that."

I sucked in a breath, pain radiating through my chest. "Of course, I'm sorry."

She didn't say anything in response.

"I wish you'd told me about your conversation with Tony," I told her, absently folding a small piece of paper on my desk. "Darling, I had no idea it had gone that way."

"I was going to tell you away from the office. I didn't want to cry there." She sniffed, cleared her throat, and then fell silent again. Her chatty disposition was notably absent, and the loss of it ached as if a branch of my lungs had been dissected away, leaving me slightly breathless. Indeed, other than the occasional sharp intake of breath on the other end of the line, she was oddly silent; a part of me wondered if she was crying.

"All right, Ruby?" I asked quietly.

"I'm fine," she murmured, "just going through some application forms."

"Ah." So my options were to talk to her while she was distracted, or lose this one connection I had to the woman I loved.

I told her about the fruitless dinner with Portia, and how in the end there wasn't anything to discuss. I knew it as soon as I walked into the old flat. "I'm sure it felt awful for you." I pressed my palm to my forehead, murmuring, "I can't talk through all of this on the phone. I have so much to say." *I love you. I've been a fool.* "Ruby, please just come to dinner."

"I can't," she said, simply.

So, to keep her on the line, I spoke to her until I ran out of subjects, feeling bumbling and lost for the first time with her. I described my day of distraction, the walk home, the bland dinner I planned to prepare. I told her about my conversation with Max earlier in the day, that Sara was expecting a second baby already. I kept talking until I ran out of the normal subjects and babbled on about nothing: stocks, the new construction down on Euston Road, my relief at the lessening rain.

I wanted her to blame me, to rail. I wanted her to tell me all the ways in which I'd disappointed her. Her silence was terrifying because it was so unlike her. I would rather have a million angry words than a single moment of her reserve.

Her opinion and esteem were already fundamental for me, even after only a month. The simple truth was that I'd never felt both so *known* with her, and so wandering even a day without. She was unlike *anyone.*

But eventually, under the weight of her continued silence, I let her go, begging her to call me when she felt ready.

Two more days passed without word from her, and I was

unable to get out of the house, craved nothing to eat, and imagined nothing could be better than sleeping for hours on end. I knew I was facing the type of blood-draining sadness I'd previously—or, rather, blissfully ignorantly—only imagined could be avoided by stoicism itself.

Ruby was the only woman I would ever want, and the prospect of having her in my life for only these past four weeks was so depressing it turned something sour inside me.

———

The first weekend after I took a hammer to her trust and forced Ruby to silently end our relationship, I managed to make it to the office to gather some reports and designs. I wanted to at least present a semblance of getting work done at home. I was long unshaven, wearing the same worn jeans and T-shirt I'd had on for the previous thirty-six hours, and I'm not sure I'd even looked at myself in the mirror before leaving the flat.

It was still dark out, so early in the morning that the streets were wonderfully still, providing a sort of external calm I was desperate to steal and pull inside me. Cars remained parked at the curb; shops wouldn't open for hours yet. The lobby of the building was silent as a vault.

I pulled my keys from my pocket outside the glass doors, curiously peering in at the single light turned on inside the firm.

It was in the far right corner. Near Ruby's old office.

I found my hand moving forward and the door opened

under my robotic push. In the back corner, I could make out the sounds of papers being tapped into order on a surface, of picture frames being set down. Of books being dropped into a box.

"Hello?" I called out, rounding the corner and freezing as I caught sight of her inside the interns' office, hand suspended in midair as she met my gaze.

She'd had the same idea: come in early on a weekend, avoid everyone. But instead of picking up work to numbly sort through in the privacy of a living room, Ruby was packing up her desk.

My stomach crawled up into my chest, clogging my windpipe with emotion.

"Ruby? You're here."

She closed her eyes, and turned back to her packing. "I'm almost done."

"I wish you wouldn't rush off. I've . . . I've wanted to speak to you. To really speak to you, not like that rambling on the phone the other night."

She nodded but didn't say anything. I stood lamely, staring at her and completely at a loss over what to do.

Her cheeks were pink, bottom lip wet and thin beneath the pressure of her teeth biting down upon it.

"Ruby," I started.

"Please," she croaked, holding up a hand. "Don't, okay?"

She'd phrased it as a question, almost as if she wasn't sure continuing this horrible silence was even the right decision. I'd never been heartbroken before, ever, a stark realization for someone who'd spent the majority of his adult life in a single relationship, and the weight of it pressed down on every vital part of my body.

I wanted to walk to her, pull her to face me, and bend to kiss her. Simply *kiss* her, tell her she was the only woman I think I'd ever want again. If she'd let me, maybe I'd be able to offer up some begging. I might, in fact, be able to put a name to these things I felt.

Devotion and apology. Adoration, desperation, and fear.

Above it all: love.

Instinct, however, told me to give her space.

I turned, walking to my office. Behind me, her packing sounds seemed to pick up speed and force and I winced, wishing it was easier than all this. Was I wrong? Was my instinct a constant red herring? I clutched my forehead in both hands, wishing I knew what the hell to do.

Absently, I grabbed a file off my desk, collecting a few more from my cabinet. I was barely focusing on the task in front of me, knowing Ruby was only a few feet away.

Stepping out of my office, I exhaled a long-held breath at the sight of her still in the building, taping up her small box of belongings. Her hair was messier than usual, as if she'd scarcely paid it any attention. Her clothes were loose and drab: a beige skirt, a mud-colored sweater. She looked as if she'd been dragged through a rain cloud.

I missed her. I missed her with a kind of clawing ache that seemed to dig deep scars inside my chest, in a place I couldn't reach, pushing aside things I required for breathing, heart beating, for moving about the world in a way that had once been reflexive. I'd never had the tendency toward melodrama, but in this case my self-pity was crippling. I'd never had to win over anyone before in my life, at least not consciously, and felt utterly unprepared for what was required of me in this instance.

"I know you want to be left alone," I started, trying to shake off the way she seemed to wince at the sound of my voice, "and I realize that I've hurt you in a way that will be impossible to undo. But, darling, I'm so sorry. And if it means anything—"

"I think I'm going to lose my spot at Oxford," she said in the world's quietest voice.

I felt my entire body go still. "You what?"

"I was fired, but Tony also put a letter in my file. He sent me a copy of it—though after reading it I have no idea why he thought I would want to see it—and in essence it says that I was a tolerably mediocre employee because my affections for you had me preoccupied and, he thinks, affected the quality of my work."

I took a step forward, blood pumping so fast in my veins my chest ached. "For one, that is utterly preposterous. I'd heard him rave about you on more than one occasion. And two, he had no knowledge of your affections prior to our trip!"

"I know. Thanks for passing that along," she said dryly, reaching to put the tape back on the now-empty desk.

"Ruby," I spluttered, "I mentioned it spontaneously, like a bleeding idiot, simply because I was still awed that you—"

"Niall?" she interrupted, and I could see tears shining in her eyes. "Don't, okay? I get it. You didn't mean to tell him that, or at the very least you didn't mean for it to come off the way it did. I don't actually care that you told Tony I had feelings for you before our trip; I don't think it matters. Tony is an enormous prick for what he did. My problem with this," she said, motioning between us, "is that he's not entirely wrong. I *was* distracted. I *was* preoccupied. I made it clear I would do anything to be with you . . . and you went back to her."

"I *didn't*. I knew before I went into her flat that I had no intention of—"

"The way you left it last week," she said, her voice thick with restrained tears, "felt like you were giving her another chance."

"Ruby—"

"I *threw* myself at you. I was so in love with you—had been for so *long*—that I ignored all your signs telling me you weren't ready. I told you I loved you after only a few weeks, and you clearly weren't ready to have sex with me, but you did—"

"Ruby, please stop." I felt nauseous. I couldn't keep up, but her words grew brittle and toxic in my ears.

"—and the very next day you went to hear Portia out about *reconciliation*, assuming that I was so desperate for your attention I would still be here if you decided against it." When she looked up at me, the tears in her eyes finally fell. "I think you assumed that because I always want to talk about everything that I would understand how much you wanted to hear what she had to say, and that would some-how override my need to feel important to you."

I opened my mouth and closed it again.

"I think you assumed I would think it was a great idea because—*hooray*—it turns out Portia isn't a robot and actually *does* have feelings and she finally wants to share them." She swiped at her cheek. "But I *didn't*. I *wanted* you to tell her she had eleven years as your wife to tell you those things and that you had a girlfriend now who had the privilege of talking about what was going on in your mind and your heart."

She sucked in a lungful of breath before she continued. "Jesus Christ, I was so eager to hear everything you had to say, even if it meant talking about your sex life with Portia right after we made love for the first time. For fuck's sake." She laughed sharply, without humor. I'd never seen emotion so raw. Ruby wasn't filtering for my benefit; she was just lay-ing it all out in a rush before she could talk herself out of it.

"You could have told her she was welcome to come meet you for lunch if she had things to get off her chest, or to feel free to put it in a fucking *email*. But to go see her the first night after we'd made love? To be unwilling to make it clear that you were with me now?" She shook her head, wiping away more tears. "Even if what we had was raw and weird and sometimes had these awkward fits and starts it was way better. We had something good, we had something *real*, and you know it."

"We did," I told her. "We *do*."

I stepped closer, put my hands on her hips. To my profound relief she didn't pull away, and I bent, kissing her neck. "Ruby, I'm so sorry."

She nodded, her arms limp at her sides. "You hurt me."

"I was an idiot."

Pulling away, she closed her eyes to collect herself and then, to my absolute horror, she picked up her box and walked down the opposite way from me, down a row of cubicles and out of the office before I could gather the right words to make her stop.

———

Bringing home the folders was an exercise in going through the motions. I remained just as useless for the remainder of the weekend.

Sleep. Eat. Drink myself into a stupor. Stare.

My phone was disturbingly silent. I was grateful to receive no calls from Tony, no calls from family, nothing more from Portia. But it devastated me every time I looked down at my phone and had heard nothing from Ruby.

So when it began buzzing over where I'd hurled it a few hours before, on a throw pillow on the floor across the room, it took a few full rings for me to startle out of my trance and answer.

I stumbled over, and cursed down at the screen, answering it anyway. "Max."

"I talked to Rebecca earlier," he said by way of greeting.

"Mm?"

"Mum's in bits over this. Rebecca already told her she thinks Ruby's going to be the one."

My sister. "She's never bloody *met* Ruby."

"Doesn't matter, apparently."

I spoke into my tumbler of gin, "At least you two never dive in to anything headlong."

"You sound pissed."

Staring into my drink, I told him, "On my way. And miserable."

"Aw come on, then. Tell me what's happened?"

"Ruby ended things."

Max fell silent for several beats. "She didn't."

"Yeah, she did. Our affair in New York cost her her job, whereas I got a slap on the wrist. She thinks she might not get into Maggie's program now."

He blew out a heavy breath. "Fucking hell."

"And I went to have dinner with Portia the night after Ruby and I finally shagged, not knowing Tony'd given Ruby an ultimatum: me or her job."

"And she chose you," my brother guessed.

I laughed into the tumbler. "Right-o."

"You *idiot*."

"Exactly." I finished what was in my glass and dropped it onto the floor. "So, needless to say, she's ended things with me quite soundly."

"So you're going to drink yourself into a stupor of self-pity on your couch then?"

"You know what my life with Portia was like," I started.

"And with Ruby . . . I'd never thought much before about children or finding what you have with Sara, but I did with her." I stared out the window, at the sky and the new leaves as they shook in the early spring breeze. "But I will never be okay after this. She changed me and I . . . I don't want to go back." The line was quiet for a moment and I reached for my glass again, refilling it. "So drinking myself into an amnesia of what I've lost—that sounds about right."

"Or," he suggested with a laugh that said, *You twat*, "you could get off that stupid arse and go talk to Maggie. For fuck's sake, Niall, you act as if you've got no resources. Figure out what you can bloody well fix and fix it. This is what you *do*, mate."

————

I had a bit of time to reflect—finally sober—on what I wanted to say while I took the train from London to Oxford. Margaret Sheffield was a bit of a hero of mine, having served on my thesis committee and been more of a mentor to me than my own alcoholic advisor had ever been. Although Maggie's specialty was civil engineering, she had a hand in designing and overseeing the construction of many of the cornerstone commercial buildings in crowded London neighborhoods, and I idolized the way her career easily straddled engineering, architecture, and broader urban planning. One of the proudest moments of my professional life to date had been when a colleague had introduced me at a keynote conference as "our generation's Margaret Sheffield."

But I'd never been to see her on such a personal matter. In fact, aside from the heated moment I'd stormed into Tony's office last week, I'd never really been to see *anyone* from my professional life with a personal matter. So even though the cold wind whipped around me as I trudged down Parks Road toward the Thom Building, I was flushed with nerves.

Maggie had been around long enough to deserve an emeritus office in one of the grander buildings, but preferred being closer to the action, she'd said. Her building was an odd, hexagonal structure but from it she had a beautiful view of the University Park just to the east. Just being here again, close to Engineering and the materials sciences buildings, brought on a heavy sense of nostalgia. I'd been young when I lived here. Young and married, and for that reason always a bit different from my peers who spent their days working hard and evenings partying harder.

I knocked on her open door, relieved when she looked up at me and smiled widely.

"Niall!" She stood, making her way around her desk to give me a firm hug. Maggie had never been a hand-shaker, but with determination had trained me over the years to give in to her affections.

When she pulled back, I asked, "I was hoping you'd have a few moments?"

"Of course." She smiled. "Your email did make me curious with its complete lack of detail."

"And . . ." I began, "if it wouldn't be too much trouble, we could grab a coffee?"

Her eyebrows rose, eyes twinkled with interest. "It sounds like this is not a strictly professional call?"

"It's not. But . . . it is, too." Sighing, I explained, "I'd just prefer the flexibility."

She laughed, retrieving her jumper. "Well, this is a shock of a lifetime. A personal discussion with Niall Stella. I can certainly make time for that."

We walked to a small café on Pembroke Street, using the trip to catch up a bit on the past two years. The topic of Ruby's future hung heavily around me, and despite Maggie's best efforts at small talk, my answers to her benign questions were tight and brief. I was relieved when we reached the café and ordered tea and croissants, before sitting at a small corner table.

"So," she started, smiling across the table at me. Steam curled up from her cup. "Enough small talk, I gather. What's this visit about?"

"It's about a student who has applied to your program, who was an intern at Richardson-Corbett."

She nodded. "You mean Ruby Miller."

"Yes," I said, surprised that she knew immediately whom I meant, but then realizing I'd said "who *was* an intern." Clearly, Maggie had read Tony's letter. "I didn't work directly with her. As you know, she reported to Tony."

"I got his letter," she confirmed with a frown. "He didn't think all that highly of her."

My blood ran hot and I leaned closer, realizing as soon as she glanced at them that my hands had formed tight fists. "Well, that's just it," I said. "I think he may have thought rather *too* highly of her."

"Bloody Tony." Maggie's expression cleared in comprehension. "And you were the distraction Tony mentioned."

"Please understand," I said, with urgency, "I wouldn't ever speak to you about this matter if I didn't feel that it impacted a professional decision on your end. Tony handled this terribly. As did I, I suppose. But in this instance, I worry that you would miss out on a wonderful student if you heeded Tony's advice. Ruby is bright and driven."

Maggie studied me, sipping her tea. "May I ask you a personal question?"

Swallowing, I nodded. "I've imposed on you simply by coming here. Of course, ask me anything."

"Are you coming here because Ruby deserves a spot in my program or because you're in love with her?"

I swallowed and struggled to maintain eye contact as I admitted, "Both."

"So the affection wasn't only one-sided."

"It was, and then it wasn't. I didn't know she had feelings, and she admitted them only after I had some of my own."

She nodded, looking past me at a line of students marching past the café. "I'd never expected you to ever speak on behalf of a girlfriend. I'm not sure if I'm more surprised or thrilled for you."

"She's not," I managed. Maggie turned her face up to me, confused. "She isn't my girlfriend anymore," I clarified. "The loss of her job, the loss of her spot in your program, my inability to handle emotions all that well . . . I suspect in the end it made her reprioritize."

" 'Reprioritize'? The 'loss of her spot in my program'?"

"Tony thought it wise to send Ruby a copy of the letter he wrote for the application. Given that Tony is your former student and completing an engineering internship is generally a critical requirement for your consideration, she said she suspected she wouldn't get in."

"Niall," Maggie began, setting down her tea. "Excuse me for being blunt, but please do not insult me by suggesting I would cast away a good student for having a crush at work."

"Not at all, Maggie, I—"

"Or for being young and unable to always put aside personal for professional. I appreciate you coming here, but the net effect of that was my satisfaction over seeing you actually in love with a woman, not help for Ruby. Ruby's application is brilliant. Her other letters of recommendation are positively glowing. Her grades are perfect, test scores put her at the top of her incoming class. Her personal statement was one of the best I've ever read." Leaning in, Maggie shook her head at me. "You see, her spot was never jeopardized by Tony's letter. Do you think I've known a different Tony than everyone else these last fifteen years? He's a brilliant engineer but a complete arse."

I closed my eyes, laughing. "Touché."

"If I may drop the professionalism *entirely* for a moment?"

"Of course," I said, feeling oddly hungry for her wisdom in a way I hadn't expected. "Please."

"You have known me as an instructor, and then quasi-mentor, and now as a trusted colleague. But I am a woman first, Niall. I was married at twenty, for five years, and then divorced. I married again when I was in my late thirties. With the distance of age and wisdom, I am able to tell you as gently as possible that your reason for this visit is wildly presumptuous. Ruby doesn't need you speaking on her behalf. In addition to all of these accolades I've already mentioned, she's also come to see me." Maggie's eyes smiled. "Quite amazing, that one."

I felt my brows rise to my hairline. "Truly."

"Ruby doesn't need a knight in shining armor. She needs a partner, I suspect. She needs to know that she is seen. And loved. And, occasionally, the inner mechanics of *how* she is loved. She is an engineer. Show her how you are put together. Show her the bolts, and wires, and map of your thoughts when you can."

———

I didn't bother going home or to the office after my conversation with Maggie. The hour-long train ride was a form of torture. I wished for the gift of flight or the ability to teleport. What Maggie had said was true and so obvious: I had to tell Ruby how I felt.

I climbed the slate steps to her flat, hesitating outside the door for a hundred pounding heartbeats, before holding my breath, and knocking.

She opened the door, wearing a smart skirt and fitted

sweater with a neckline that showed the top swell of her breasts. I can't imagine what my expression was when I took her in fully, but when I searched her eyes, I saw a tenderness there that surprised—and thrilled—me.

"Ruby."

"You okay?" she asked, eyes searching.

I tried to draw a breath deep enough to feel calm, but couldn't. "No."

"You look terrible."

I nodded, letting out a short, wry laugh. "I'm sure you're right."

She looked over my shoulder, face tight with anguish. "Why are you here?"

"Because I needed to see you."

She looked back to me, her eyes scanning my face. "Part of me wants to pull you in, and kiss you like crazy. I miss it, and can't pretend I don't still feel it."

"Then don't push me away," I begged her, taking a step closer. "Ruby, I should have told you how I felt that night we made love. I *felt* it then; I just didn't know how to name it, or whether I trusted myself enough to believe it."

She was shaking her head, eyes glassy with tears, and I could tell she didn't want me to say it, but I needed to.

"I love you," I whispered, urgency making my voice thin. "I am desperately in love with you."

"Niall—"

"I knew it at Portia's. I felt sick being there. I don't know why I went, but if nothing else it clarified everything for me."

Ruby laughed, a little humorlessly. "It clarified things for me, too."

I groaned. "Please, Ruby, forgive me."

"I want to. I really *do*. But I don't know how to move past that feeling of humiliation and this deep, exhausted frustration. All of it: trying to figure out what you needed, trying to be everything for you in every moment. Then telling you I love you, hearing you say 'you're lovely' in return, losing my job, and then—the worst—being told you were going to have dinner with Portia to discuss your marriage . . . I just still feel really raw."

"I think I felt like I had to close this one door," I tried to explain. "Or, maybe I just had never heard Portia sound so emotional and a very dark part of me was morbidly curious. But I didn't consider your feelings really until I went, and it was terrible of me. As soon as I got there I knew there was no conversation to be had, no long-buried truths to be shared. I felt unfaithful to you just being there—"

"Because you *were*."

I closed my eyes. It was shattering to see her like this. "I'm so sorry."

"I know you are," she said, nodding. "And I think I get it. But I can't help it. I'm mad at you."

Wiping my hand across the stubble on my jaw, I whispered, "Please let me in."

Looking up at me, she said very quietly, "Is it weird to feel like I need to say no? Like, I need to make sure I *can*?

I gave you time to work through every tiny hesitation. I tried to be understanding and patient, but as soon as you had the chance, you didn't give my feelings the same consideration. I lost myself somewhere in the last six months. I told you to trust me to tell you where my limits are. This is a limit. You disregarded me, and so *obliviously*." She dropped her voice, looking straight into my eyes, and said, "I thought that wasn't the kind of relationship you wanted anymore."

This was a knife to my gut and I pulled back, pained. And even though her lip trembled and her hands shook at her sides, even though I still saw every ounce of the emotion in her eyes that she had only a week ago, she didn't take her sharp reprimand back, not with words or expression.

I could push her. I saw it now, and another man—a more aggressive man—may have stepped closer, taken advantage of the pain in her eyes. If I kissed her right now, she would kiss me back. I could sense it in the way she watched my mouth, the way she continued to shake.

Ruby still loved me as I loved her.

I could press my way inside, put my hands on her body, peel away her clothes and give her pleasure, taste her sweat. With my mouth and hands and words I may even have been able to convince her for a night that I truly did love her.

But she already was struggling with how much she'd lost the sense of herself in her feelings for me. I couldn't manipulate her like that.

I pulled at my hair, completely torn. "Tell me what to do. If I leave, you'll think I don't feel for you. If I stay, I'm not listening to your wishes."

"Niall," she whispered. "I can barely be this close to you without feeling like I'd give you anything. It's your turn to be patient."

I swallowed thickly and stepped back, walking two paces without turning. "Come to me," I said, begging quietly. "When you're ready, I'll be waiting for you. Let me catch up in *my* time spent longing if you need me to. Distance from you won't extinguish what I feel."

She nodded, eyes filling.

"Promise you'll come to me when you're ready. Even if it just means you're ready to tell me it's truly over."

Ruby nodded again. "I promise."

Seventeen

Ruby

April was hell, but May was worse. At least in April
I could replay, again and again, the memory of how Niall
had looked coming to my flat, eyes wild and anxious.
I could still hear how his voice sounded—so deep and
hoarse and desperate—when he'd said he loved me.

But in May, I hadn't seen him in a month, and it was
nearly impossible to convince myself that his affection
hadn't begun to dissolve.

The Number of Days I Needed Niall Stella to Give Me
Space: unknown.

I'd felt like the needy, frantic girl, waiting for him to
have dinner with the ex and then decide if I was the better
option. I'd never been so desperate for a late-night phone
call as I was the night he was at her place for dinner, but
when it came . . . I ignored it. Not until he realized what
I'd known all along—that Portia had never been good for
him, that in fact *I* was the *best thing* for him—did I realize that I was . . . really, really *mad*.

I knew I was capable of taking things in stride in a

way that surprised Niall. It surprised people my whole life. But that evenness didn't mean I couldn't get hurt, be angry, feel betrayed.

Somehow, even with the heavy pulse of heartbreak in every step I took, I had managed to piece little bits of my life back together. I was determined to salvage my chances at getting into Margaret Sheffield's program. So, in early April, after days of sleep and silence, of nibbling sandwiches made from stale bread and hard cheese and sleeping in my clothes, I'd pulled myself together and taken a train to Oxford.

There, Professor Sheffield had assured me that Anthony's letter could only hold so much weight, that my grades and reputation from San Diego were impressive. But although she'd given me no indication that the *distraction* my former boss mentioned in his letter would lead to my rejection from the program, she hadn't said I was a sure thing, either.

While I waited to hear, I stayed in London. I was lucky enough to find a firm on the South Bank in need of an engineer to cover an early maternity leave. It was an easy solution and paid well, but on my very first day I decided to walk home rather than take the Tube, only to then realize I would pass just two blocks away from Niall's flat.

Gut punch.

So of course it became impossible to choose to take the Tube rather than walk. Every day I felt my body tilt that way, as if pulled by some enormous heart magnet.

And when I would press on, heading straight instead of right, it would hurt all over again.

His distance and reserve really had been so impossible to take; everything was logical to him: Portia was ready to speak so he should listen. I had always encouraged him to communicate with me, and so of course that should apply to Portia, as well.

I feel obligated to at least hear what she wants to say.

I suppose I'm trying to have an open mind. I owe her that, at least.

That last day it seemed emotion hadn't come into play for Niall at all, until it felt too late. But for me, it was nearly impossible to get the echoing pain out of my head.

Even when he'd found me in the office, packing up, and begged me to forgive him. Even when he'd come to my flat and told me he loved me.

I was an idiot for sending him away. I knew it at the time. But more than that I knew that if I let him in that day, there would be a proud, resolved piece of myself I wouldn't ever get back.

But the silence seemed unending.

Number of Days I'd Gone Without Speaking to ~~Niall~~ Stella:

~~One~~.

~~Seven~~.

~~Fifteen~~.

~~Thirty two~~.

Fifty nine.

In June I got my acceptance letter to Maggie's program at Oxford.

The innocuous-looking envelope was there waiting for me when I got home from work. Some days it was harder than others to resist the pull to walk toward Niall's flat. Other days I could pretend to be absorbed in a song, or reading some news on my iPhone, and the knowledge that, if I wanted, I could go sit on his stoop and wait for him to get home was only a sharp jab between my ribs. But today the mental debate had been torture. Was I over my anger? And if I was, and if I went to his house, would he open the door and regard me blankly, and then with awkward apology, and tell me I'd been right to end things? That he'd been impulsive to get involved with me in the first place? That his life was better in an ordered system than with such a wild, emotional girl?

The problem was that I could see him rejecting me just as vividly as I could see him embracing me. I knew Niall's schedule, the facts of his life and his preferences for food and coffee and clothing. But I wasn't sure I knew his heart at all.

I tore open the envelope, heart pounding and unknotting in an odd sort of unison, and I read the letter three times, the papers clutched in my shaking hand. For what felt like minutes, I was unable to blink or breathe because *it was happening.* I was going to Oxford, I was studying with Maggie. That shithead Anthony hadn't ruined my chances.

I read through the letter again for dates, and filed through my mental calendar. Michaelmas Term for the program began in September. This meant I could work through the rest of June, July, and into the beginning of August, and use the first part of the following month to find a new flat in Oxford.

Of course my first instinct was to tell Niall.

Instead, I called my girl London.

"Ruby!"

"You are never going to guess what happened!" I told her, feeling my smile for what had to be the first time in more than fifty-nine days.

"Harry Styles is your new roommate and you've purchased a ticket for me to come visit?"

"Very funny, try again."

She hummed. "Well, you sound happier than I've heard in months, so I'm guessing that you finally called Niall Stella, he welcomed you with open arms, and now you're lying in a pool of postcoital bliss. And by 'pool of bliss,' of course I mean—"

My chest ached sharply and I cut her off, unable to play along. "No."

Her tone softened. "But it sounded pretty good, didn't it?"

It did. But the prospect of seeing Niall couldn't be better than what I had in my hand.

It couldn't, could it?

But as soon as she'd said it, I knew that being back with Niall would be *just as good*. I wanted Niall just as much as I wanted to work with Maggie. And for the first time since I'd been fired, I didn't feel embarrassed for it, or that I was betraying some inner feminist thread by admitting how deep my feelings were. If I went back to Niall, some days he would be my entire life. Some days school would. Some days they would occupy the same amount of space. And that knowledge—that I *could* find balance, that maybe I *did* need to separate my heart from my head after all—loosened a tension that had seemed to reside in my chest for weeks now.

"I got into Maggie's group," I told her. "I just got the letter."

London screamed, made clomping noises, which I think might have been dancing on the other end, dropped her phone, and then came back and screamed some more.

"You're going to Oxford!"

"I am!"

"You're going to study with your dream lady!"

"I know!"

She exhaled an enormous gust of air as if she'd just fallen backward on the couch, and said, "Ruby I'm going to ask you a question and you don't have to answer it. Though, let's be real, I've put up with your moping for months now so I sort of deserve an answer."

I groaned, knowing where this was going. "Can't we keep talking about Oxford?"

Ignoring this, she asked, "Was I the first person you wanted to call when you got the letter?"

I didn't answer and instead focused on picking at a loose thread on my sweater.

"Why don't you just tell him?" she asked gently. "He would be thrilled for you."

"He might not even remember me."

She laughed incredulously and it turned into a growl. "You make me *insane*."

I walked to my couch and sat down. "I'm just nervous. What do I say? 'Oh, hey, I'm over being mad, still into all this?'"

"The 'Hey, I'm going to work with Maggie, got any tips?' conversation is a pretty good opener."

Closing my eyes, I told her, "Even with everything I knew about him, I would have no idea *how* he would greet me if I called . . ."

"You don't *call*, Gem. You go to his house like you want to every day on your walk home, and you sit on his porch until he walks up and sees you and his dick gets hard, and you tell him you got into Maggie's group, and oh, by the way, you love him and want to have his giant babies."

"What if I went over there and Portia answered the door?"

"She won't."

"Or, I don't know, he worked through everything I said and decided that, logically, I was right. Boop beep boop, emotions managed."

"Are you listening?" she asked. There was a current of frustration in her voice and I knew London well enough to know she was about to snap. It always took her a while to get there, but when she lost her patience it was done.

"*Yes*, I am. But—"

London began hitting buttons on her phone, filling the line with loud beeps until I was forced to shut up and listen. "Are you done yet?" she asked when she returned.

"Yes."

"Then hear this: This is real life, Ruby. This isn't a movie where two single people come into a relationship with bad experiences that are actually completely hilarious and lighthearted and only made them stronger and healthier. In real life, relationships come with a side order of ex-wives and ex-husbands and stepkids and pets the other person hates. Sometimes people get hurt and they don't have two parents who are shrinks to make sure they come out of everything okay. An ex-wife—especially one that left him feeling less than thrilled with himself—that's a lot to just get over."

Swallowing, I told her, "I know. God, I know."

"Then can you please forgive him for being a dick and wanting to get some closure? You know I'm always here to support you, and I'm head cheerleader of Team Ruby ninety-nine-point-four percent of the time, but I think it's time to go see him, to figure out if you can be together or if you need to move on. You're in love with him. *You're* the one who left it in limbo."

"I know, I know."

"He said he loved you, too," she reminded me because I'd only told her about seven hundred times about the time he said it. "I've never met Niall Stella but I don't think he's the kind of guy who would say that and then talk himself out of it two months later."

I was left speechless, staring at the wall, knowing she was right.

It wasn't as simple as walking down the street and wait-ing on his stoop after all. The idea of seeing him again made me both giddy and painfully nauseous.

Thankfully—or not—work made the decision for me on Monday and Tuesday of the following week: we had a visiting architect and they needed me around to fetch late-night coffee, takeout, and any other after-hours requests it seemed only a temporary employee could manage.

The tension inside me was ratcheting up and I ignored London's calls on Monday night and Tuesday morning. By Wednesday afternoon she was screaming at me in my text message box:

HAVE YOU BEEN TO SEE THE MAN YET? FOR THE LOVE OF ALL THAT IS HOLY, JUST CIRCLE ONE HERE, RUBY: Y / N

With a tiny whimper, I finally replied: I'm go-ing there after work today. I didn't have a chance before now.

Her answer came quickly: What r u wearing

Laughing, I replied, Didn't give it much thought.

HAHAHAHAHA. Seriously though.

I looked down at my outfit and felt the flutters zoom back into my chest before taking an awkward selfie of my short navy skirt and favorite silk navy and red polka-dot tank. It was a weird angle and made me look all-boob but I sent it anyway. London knew my wardrobe as well as she knew her own.

Damn, Dolly. Are you wearing the red heels? she asked.

Yes.

God, she replied, his boner is going to be ENORMOUS.

Smiling at my screen, I typed, Let's hope and then shoved my phone into my bag. I could barely let myself hope we would have that kind of night. I'd be thrilled with even a smile, a kiss on the cheek, an assurance that he was still interested in trying if I was. I had to pretend I wasn't craving more, everything, all of him.

That workday, my God. You know the kind. Seconds are actually minutes, and minutes are hours, and the entire day goes by in the span of a decade. By the end of it I'd thought about the evening so many times that I started to suspect I had made up Niall Stella in the first

place and this entire situation was a figment of my imagination.

Finally, it was five thirty and the office started to thin
out. I slipped into the bathroom in the hall on my way
out to check my makeup and clothes and was jolted out of
my odd fugue into a full-on panic.

My silk top was massively wrinkled and sweet Jesus what
was I thinking this morning? My sassy-short skirt suddenly seemed *extremely* short. Slutty short. What-do-you-
charge-per-hour short. I groaned and leaned in closer to
the mirror. My mascara was smudged . . . basically all over
my face, and my blush had been rubbed off entirely.

I did what I could to fix the mess, but the problem
was that I was so nervous I wasn't sure I would be able
to keep down the water and crackers I'd barely managed
at lunch. *Should I stay in the bathroom in case I'm going to
throw up? Should I carry an extra bag?* Why had I waited
so long to go see him? What if I couldn't manage to get
a word out?

But then the oddest thing happened: I laughed. I was
freaking out over seeing Niall Stella. I was checking
my makeup and contemplating vomiting and worrying
I would be mute or rambling.

This was normal. This was what I did.

Without another look in the mirror, I grabbed my
purse and walked from the bathroom.

Hallway, elevator, street. Seventeen blocks, one bridge,
and there I was. On the corner, making a decision.

That was when my heart decided to explode and my blood evaporated and I lost control of my brain.

He didn't know I was coming. I hadn't seen him or spoken to him in over two months. I asked him to give me time, and he had . . . I was grateful and mad about that at the same time. What if he had moved on? That would break me more, I thought, than the unknown. I could keep walking forward and head home to a quiet flat. I could do cereal for dinner and *Community* reruns until it was time to sleep, then get up and do the same thing tomorrow. I could keep working at this easy, boring job until it was time to move, and then I could disappear from the city entirely without ever having to face this. Someday I might get over Niall Stella.

Or, I could turn right, walk two blocks to his flat, sit on his stoop, and wait for him. I could tell him I still wanted to try and then let him tell me yes, or tell me no. If he said no, I would go home and do the cereal and the sitcom and the eventual painful heart repairs. But if he said yes . . .

There wasn't a choice, not really.

I stared at the sidewalk as I moved, at my bright red shoes on the dull gray concrete. It made it easier to move forward to have something to watch. I counted the Number of Cracks Between Decision Corner and Niall's Flat (twenty-four) and the Number of Times I Considered Turning Around and Going Home (about eighty) and went through what I wanted to say again and again:

Hi. I'm sure it's really weird to find me here on your

steps and I'm sorry for not calling, but I wanted to see you. I missed you. I love you.

Keep it simple, I thought. Lay it all out there and let him decide.

I was pretty sure he wouldn't be home yet when I got there, but rang his flat just in case. When there was no answer, I stared blankly at the steps for a few breaths before sitting down, prepared to wait, repeating my opener.

Hi. I'm sure it's really weird to find me here on your steps and I'm sorry for not calling, but I wanted to see you. I missed you. I love you.

The sun fell in the sky slowly, reluctantly. Cars drove by, or parked, neighbors climbed out and went into their flats after studying me with curiosity for the most brief and British amount of time. The post-work-hours movement slowed almost abruptly, and then lights went on inside. Dinner smells drifted onto the street. And still, no Niall.

Every time I began to think that I should leave—*maybe he was out for the night with the guys?*—I then thought, *but what if he walks up a minute after I've left?*

I expected him maybe a half hour after I arrived, but I sat for an hour, and then two, three, and finally I'd been sitting waiting for four hours without any sign of him when it occurred to me: *Niall could be on a date.*

The thought was so sour, I actually groaned. Resting my arms on my knees and pressing my forehead there, I focused on breathing in. Breathing out.

I may have stayed like that for another half hour or even three more, I don't really know. But when I looked up, it was because of some odd awareness, some change in the atmosphere. The sound all around me dipped and then I could hear it: the faint click of men's dress shoes on pavement. The steady, long strides of Niall Stella.

The Number of Times I Have Listened for Niall Stella's Footfalls: infinite.

I turned my head down the street and saw the long shape of him. What happened inside me had to be described in a medical text somewhere under "lovesick": my heart evaporated and then returned as some beastly enormous thing that seemed to beat far too fast and with too much force. It pulsed in my ears, rushed blood to warm into my hands and feet until they tingled. I was dizzy, narrowing my eyes to see him through blurred vision, and fairly sure I was going to be sick.

He was wearing his navy suit—I could see in the distance, under the regularly intervaled light from streetlamps—and looked . . . amazing. Strong and confident and walking with his trademark posture: shoulders back, arms at his sides, head straight.

Until he was about twenty feet away and saw me sitting on his steps.

And then he stopped, his chest jerking back slightly, one hand reaching up to touch the back of his neck.

On shaking legs, I stood, wiping my hands down my skirt. If my outfit was wrinkled earlier from work,

I couldn't imagine how it would look after sitting on a set of concrete steps for over four hours in the humid June air.

When he took a step forward, the movement was hesitant enough to make me move toward him, too. It nearly *hurt* to see him I loved him so much. I loved his carved features and miles-long legs. I loved the wide expanse of his chest, his deep brown eyes, and the kissable, smooth lips. I loved his hands that were bigger than my head and his arms that could wrap many times around me. I loved that he looked freshly pressed after ten at night, and that I could set a metronome by the pace of his stride.

I wanted to run into his arms and tell him I'd had enough time, and I wanted him.

Hi. I'm sure it's really weird to find me here on your steps and I'm sorry for not calling, but I wanted to see you. I missed you. I love you.

He moved slowly, I moved slowly, and then we were only a couple of feet apart and my heart was beating so hard I didn't know what could possibly be holding my ribs together.

"Ruby?"

"Hi."

"Hi." He swallowed, and only now, up close, could I see that he looked a bit thinner, a bit more drawn. There was more hollow in his jaw, more darkness beneath his eyes. Could he see it in my eyes, too? That I missed him so much I'd felt physically sick for the last two months?

I'm sure it's really weird to find me here on your steps and

I'm sorry for not calling, but I wanted to see you. I missed you. I love you.

But before I could say my preamble, he asked, "What are you doing here?" and I couldn't read his tone.

It was controlled—*he* was controlled—and I swallowed nervously before answering.

"I . . . I'm sure it's really weird to find me here on your steps."

What was the rest of it?

He glanced behind me, asking, "How long have you been here?"

"I'm sorry for not calling," I blurted, robotically.

Ignoring this, he took a step closer, asking again, this time more gently, "How long have you been here, Ruby?"

Shrugging, I answered, "A while."

"Since you got off work at Anderson?"

He knows where I work. He knows what time I leave.

I blinked back up to his face, but it was a mistake. He was the most beautiful person I'd ever seen, and I *knew* his face. His was the face I saw when I closed my eyes, when I needed to feel comfort or thrill, grounding or lust. Niall Stella's face felt like home to me.

"Yes, since I got off work," I admitted.

"That's . . . *hours*," he started, shaking his head. "I didn't know . . . I mean, I don't come home very early anymore. There's no . . ."

Before he could ask me to leave, or tell me why it was a bad idea for me to be here, or any other one of the hundreds of rejections, I started to speak. "Look, I . . ." I glanced to the side, completely forgetting what it was I was going to say. Something about wanting to see him? "See, the thing is," I started, looking back up at him before blurting, "I just really, *really* love you."

One minute he was two feet from me and the next he was against me and I was against the side of his building, lifted from the ground with his arms around my waist. I gasped, staring up at him. Niall was looking down at me with a dark intensity that made my chest squeeze painfully.

"Say it again."

"I love you," I whispered, my throat growing nearly too tight to speak. "I missed you."

His face fell as he searched my eyes one more time and then he bent, pressing his face to my neck. His mouth . . . *oh, God*, with the deepest groan my favorite mouth in the world was on my neck and my jaw and I couldn't catch my breath, couldn't stop the tight lump from rising higher in my throat.

"Niall . . ."

He spoke into my skin, "Darling, say it again. I'm not sure I can believe this is real."

Through a sob, I managed, "I love you."

In a pulse of panic, I didn't know if this was actually happening, either, or I had fallen asleep on his stairs and was having the world's best dream. But then his lips were moving again: on my jaw, my cheek, and then pressing to mine—the best kind of soft, the best kind of hard—and I choked out another cry as I felt his tongue slide inside and his sounds vibrated against me as he groaned into his kisses.

With a desperate sort of babble, he gave me his broken thoughts built of my name, and that he missed me so bloody much, that things had been hell, that he thought he'd never see me again. He cupped my face and his kisses alternated between tiny and hard, soft and sucking, and then his thumbs were sweeping at my face and I knew I was a sobbing mess, but I honestly couldn't find it in me to care.

"You're coming inside," he growled, moving his mouth from mine and over to my ear. "You're staying with me."

"Yes."

"Tonight. And every night after."

I nodded, smiling as I pressed my face to his neck. "Well. Until I move to Oxford."

Pulling back, he let his eyes move over my face. "Yeah? You got your letter from Maggie, then?"

"I got it last week. I wanted to call you."

He smiled a little, seeming to be unable to stop looking at me, even to blink. "You should have."

"I figured I wanted to see you more, so I did that instead."

With a little nod, he looked down, intertwining our fingers. "It's late. You've been sitting here for a long time. Are you hungry?"

"Not really," I admitted. "I just want to . . ."

"Get into my bed?" His voice was a gentle growl.

I whispered, "Yeah. Unless *you* need to eat."

"No. No chance I'm stopping to eat first."

It was really that simple, and there wasn't even a trace of hesitation. I knew I needed to feel him. I needed to be covered in him.

He turned and led me back to his steps and I followed him inside, up the next flight, and to his front door. He pulled me in front of him, pressing my back to the door as he bent to kiss my jaw. "We'll talk later, yeah?"

"Okay."

His teeth scraped at my neck. "Good, because I know we need to talk. But right now I want to put my mouth on you and sing 'God Save the Queen.'"

Finally, a laugh burst from my throat. Oh, the relief of this. I nearly started crying again. "I think you could lose your citizenship for that."

"It would be worth it, though. Kissing you between your legs is like kissing your mouth but softer somehow."

I was tingling from my mouth to my toes. How was it so easy to get back to this place? "Bonus: I orgasm when you kiss me there."

Niall pulled back and gave me a look of mock scandal. "You mean to tell me you don't orgasm from my kisses to your mouth?"

"It's been a little while. Maybe you should try?"

He growled with a predatory smile and here—*here*—

was my playful, sexy man. The version of him only I would get. The world would get his calm, contained exterior. I would get the one here, who reached into his pocket and pulled out his keys, before reaching behind me as he simultaneously bent to kiss me. His hand fumbled with the lock and we laughed against each other's mouth, teeth knocking, sloppy kissing.

I heard the lock give and his groan of relief as he nibbled at my bottom lip.

"Don't fucking leave me again," he said, out of breath as his hand hovered on the doorknob. "It was bloody miserable, Ruby."

"I didn't leave you." I pulled back to meet his eyes. "You did. So if we're . . ." I shook my head. "Don't ever go back to Portia."

I had to say it. Even if it was absurd, it hadn't even been a fear, until it was.

"I *never* . . ." He closed his eyes, pained. "Please believe me when I say I am devoted. It was a terrible misstep."

I gripped his tie and pulled him back down to me, brushing my lips over his. "Okay then."

His arm slid around my waist, holding me to him so I wouldn't fall into his apartment when he opened the door.

I didn't fall, but I was on my back nearly immediately once he got it open, Niall over me as he pushed my skirt up my hips, and before I could remind him that he was meant to be kissing my mouth, his fingers were impatiently sliding my underwear to the side so he could press his open mouth to my clit.

Oh, the wet feel of him, the vibration of the words he said over and over I couldn't quite make out. The sucking soft kisses and heat of his breath on me. Another jolt of disbelief ran through me and I had to reach down, and dig a hand into his hair to anchor me to this room and this floor and this thing that he was doing with his tongue and lips and—holy fuck—even his teeth.

The door to his apartment wasn't even closed, and I realized it only when he kicked at it, groaning loudly into my skin. His eyes were closed, though, fingers digging into my hips as he sucked at me and spoke into my skin, and I had to prop myself up on my elbows to watch. It would have been a crime not to. The only thing better than what he was doing was watching him do it, as if each flick of his tongue and quiet sound of relief unknotted something profound in him. I wanted to tell him, *this, right now, is how I know you're mine. You're not thinking about anything but this. I'm not even sure you're doing this for my pleasure.*

But I couldn't manage a single word let alone a coherent string of them; all of my sounds were gasps or the stilted words of begging for more and *like that*, and *yes, that*, and *there*, and

oh
shit
I'm
coming

His groan in reply shook me, and the way he murmured, "I dreamt of the taste," made me lose any semblance of control. I fell back, arms above my head, pressing my hips into him, rocking and circling until I went stiff and coiled, my orgasm pulling every muscle together until it consumed me, spreading out from where he kissed me and everywhere; to the tingling tips of my fingers, my flushed face, my curling toes.

I clawed at the back of the suit jacket he hadn't even bothered to take off, and tried to find the collar to pull him up and over me. I needed him naked and inside. I needed his weight on top, and the feel of his narrow hips between my thighs.

He sat up, not even bothering to wipe his face as he shrugged out of his jacket, loosened his tie, and removed it, followed by his shirt. From where I lay on the floor, I could see the rise and fall of my chest but it was all in my peripheral vision. I wouldn't be able to tear my eyes from his face until someone physically removed me from this apartment and this man.

I was spent. My skin was humming, muscles loose, brain a giant, blissful, thought-free zone. Niall reached to pull my underwear down my hips, and then my skirt, taking the time to undress me, kissing every bit of skin he revealed. I expected him to climb over me, be inside me immediately—I could feel how hard he was when he kissed my neck and pressed into my thigh. But he surprised me, curling one arm beneath my knees and the other around my shoulders so he could lift and carry me down the narrow hall.

"Where are we going?" I asked.

"I don't relish making love to you on the floor again."

Sucking at his neck, I said, "Is that what we're going to do?"

He nodded. "All night, and a good portion of to-morrow."

I hadn't really taken the time to examine his bed-room before, having woken up in the room and fleeing almost immediately. The windows were wide and tall, walls white and stark but for a few framed photographs of Ansel Adams prints. *Signed*. I felt my eyes go wide before looking around at the rest. His bed was enormous, neatly made with dark sheets and a dark blanket. A small bath-room came off at the far end of the room, and a single light was illuminated on a table near the bed. It was a masculine room, not overly decorated.

Niall came up behind me, his hands smoothing from my shoulders down to my naked hips before he pressed his bare chest against my naked back. "Get on the bed." His quiet command was softened by the kiss he pressed to my neck.

I climbed on the bed and watched him follow me in a predatory crawl, and he settled again between my thighs.

"Come kiss me," I quietly urged.

"Soon."

He bent, sliding his tongue between my legs again. It

was so different than before, his kisses were slow and gentle, more tender and expressive than directed.

"Either you really like doing this or you're feeling *deeply* apologetic."

"It feels a little wicked, still," he admitted, kissing the inside of my thigh. "Like it's naughty to stare at your tits, very naughty to watch you masturbate, exceedingly naughty to put my fingers inside you, but to actually put my tongue just here?" He licked me, humming, "This sweet place only I can see? Well, that feels sublimely naughty."

"I think you mean possessive."

"That as well. I admit I like the idea that this body belongs to me."

"Technically it belongs to me."

"Whatever you say, my love."

"Careful," I teased. "You don't want to veer into the L-word territory." Could he feel just then how much I needed him to say it?

"Don't I?" he asked, looking up the length of my body at me. "Did you not hear me say that I love you every time I spoke into your skin just now?"

I smiled, opening my mouth to crack a joke before I realized he wasn't teasing. And he had. He'd whispered *I love you* over and over on the floor, with reverence.

"Oh."

His smile was unreal: teasing and mischievous. "Did you need it spoken directly into your ear?"

I bit my lip, shrugging down at him. "I like where your mouth is right now, but I have to admit I wouldn't exactly mind hearing you say that a little closer . . ."

He kissed up my body, his lips wet from me, hands squeezing, teeth grazing. Every single touch echoed the words.

He was so long, enormous above, blocking out everything else and the safety I felt beneath Niall was unlike anything. He'd seen me at my craziest and my most grounded—both states had been caused by my feelings for him. In the months I loved him from afar and the four short weeks I loved him up close, he'd become more than lover; he was my new best friend.

"I always felt like the only person in my life who didn't know his own mind from the moment he was born. My siblings—they came out knowing exactly who they were. Not me. But I do with you. I want to trust that. *Need* to, rather. So yes, it only took a month after we officially met in the elevator"—he smiled down at me—"and I ruined it stupidly and you ran away from me perhaps even more stupidly . . . but here we are. And I love you."

I felt goose bumps spread along my arms.

"I love you," he repeated in a whisper and kissed my ear lobe. "I *adore* you."

I unfastened his belt, and he helped me push his pants down his hips far enough for him to kick them off the end of the bed. I didn't want to wait anymore; I had this flushed aching need to be with him, filled of him. Wherever it touched mine, his skin was warm and smooth, the soft hair on his legs brushed against my thighs, his chest pressed against my breasts as he climbed over me.

"You feel so good," I whispered.

"I know. This . . ." He shook his head. "I feel like I didn't pay enough attention the first time we were intimate like this," he admitted, kissing me. "I was too focused on not freaking out. I want to feel every second."

I reached between us, stroking him and watching his face. His mouth opened, eyes grew heavy.

"You're still on birth control?" he asked, bending to kiss my neck.

"Yes."

"And you haven't . . ." He paused, his breath catching as he met my eyes. "You haven't been with . . . ?"

My heart jerked to a stop. "I've barely left my apartment except for work. Is that a serious question?"

"No," he admitted. "I guess I just wanted to hear it. I've been a mess, Ruby. Thinking of you seeing someone else while we were apart . . . it was horribly painful."

He hovered above me, blocking out all of the light in the room so the only thing I could see or feel or smell was his skin.

"I thought you might make love to Portia that night," I told him. And why was this conversation so much easier when I could feel the warm, thick slide of him over me, just an inch from where he could slip inside? "I left your office and it was the only thing I could imagine, that you

would be with her that night. I don't think I've ever c̶
that hard."

"Ruby—"

"It just took me a while to be able to get it out of
my head. To not be mad, or feel betrayed. To not worry
that every time I was with you I would need you to reassure me."

He opened his mouth but I stopped his words with a
finger to his lips. "I don't need you to reassure me. You
had a *lot* of history with her, and practically no history
with me. I want to move on from that night."

His voice came out thin and tight: "I wish I'd never
gone there."

"Me, too."

He winced and bent to press his face to my neck.
"Ruby, fuck, sorry . . . I know we're talking . . . but I'm
going to come if you don't stop stroking my cock."

I let go of him immediately, barking out a laugh. "Oh
my God! Niall! I've been being all serious and expecting
you to listen while I'm giving you a hand job and rubbing
you all over my—"

He cut me off with a kiss that didn't even start sweet
at all. It was immediately deep, searching and the movement of his hips causing him to slide up and over my clit
told me that the conversation was done.

I moved my hands up his stomach, to his chest, feeling
the smooth, firm skin, the muscles tensing beneath as he
rubbed over me, faster, with more pressure, until I felt

on his chest, the telltale tightness of his

he whispered, squeezing his eyes closed.

down between us, feeding himself slowly into me and hissing out an "Oh, Christ. Oh, *fuck*," when his hips were fully pressed to my thighs.

I'd forgotten how it felt, and held my hands on his waist, silently asking him to give my body a second to get used to him.

"All right?" he whispered, arms shaking where they were braced beside my head.

"Yeah." I stretched to kiss his throat and then rolled my hips under him, feeling my heart take off in a sprint as he pulled back and then started to move. Slow at first, and then when he could tell I was okay, when he slid so easily out and back in, he sped up and his sounds . . . *oh*, the sounds. His quiet grunts and exhales, fragmented words that made me feel possessed and urgent.

His eyes moved over my face, and down to my chest to follow the movement of my breasts with every snap of his hips. "Ah, fuck, love."

He bent, kissing me, but it wasn't really a kiss. It was his mouth, soft and distracted, open and sliding over mine. It was his breath, warm across my lips, my tongue.

"I love you." I was in so deep with him. I felt like I'd been destined to love Niall Stella.

His hand covered my breast, squeezing gently as he

bent to suck before sliding his palm down my ribs to my hip, my ass, my thigh to pull my leg higher up his waist. He was impatient, clearly lost to sensation, with eyes open but so glazed over I felt high with the power of it.

I squeezed him and his eyes rolled closed as a deep groan fell from his lips.

"Tell me," he gasped. "Tell me what to do."

"Faster."

His hips pivoted with intent, hard snaps into me, his hand gripping the back of my knee so tightly I could feel the pressure of each fingertip.

"Let me see you."

Niall blinked, long dark lashes brushing against his cheeks before he looked up at me, pulling from me as soon as he understood. I felt every inch of him withdraw.

He was wet, so hard he was jutting straight out, and I reached between us to touch him, to bring the crown against my clit and use the thick edge of him to circle and circle and circle over me. I didn't want his fingers or mouth. I wanted the soft skin, the rigid flesh of him to get me there.

At the edge, when sensation seemed to pool between my legs, waiting to overflow and pull me under, I slid him back inside and felt his groan, felt the frenzy of it. As soon as his hips met mine he lost it, pulling back and giving me exactly what I'd wanted: to be fucked—*hard*—in his bed.

It was several seconds before I realized the screaming I heard was *me*, that the skin I felt pinched beneath my nails was *his* and that he was moving so hard his bed was roughly cracking into the wall.

His back was slick with sweat and his teeth were bared, pressed to my shoulder as pleasure filled me, pushed deep with his body. Just as I started to come down, he began to come, his fingers digging into my thighs as he made a hoarse sound of relief I'd never heard from him before, and which I knew I would spend every night for the rest of our lives trying to elicit again.

Slowly, he caught his breath, sliding lazily in and out, his lips pressed to my jaw.

"That was some bloody good fucking."

I made some unintelligible sound of agreement.

"It's yours, you know."

Blinking up to the ceiling, I asked, "What is?"

"My heart, of course, but also my body." He struggled to catch his breath. "My hands, my lips, my cock. I trust you with all of it more than I even trust myself."

My chest seemed to clench so tight I lost my breath. Even more intimate than the sound of his coming was the way he spoke so plainly, so crudely, after he'd already finished. "I liked when you used it to play with your body. The idea of you coming because you're rubbing me all over you?"

"Yeah?" I asked.

"Fuck. I love it. And how you wanted it harder, too. I want you to push me to be a little filthy."

"Only a little?" I asked playfully.

He looked directly into my eyes, and I caught the vulnerability there. I knew this conversation felt like a completely new language to him.

I stretched to kiss him, desperate to take the tone of teasing out of the moment. "What do you want to try?"

"Everything," he admitted in a whisper. "But I think mostly I'm . . . a bit wrapped up in what it's like to be intimate while being in love. I don't want to hide from it anymore. This is so new to me, and it's a bit mind-boggling how different it feels."

"You mean physically?"

"I mean all of it. To speak openly while we're making love. The way it *feels* to make love."

He was still over me, inside me, asking for what he needed and for a long moment, I couldn't really catch my breath. We were doing this. He was all in. We were in his bed, in his flat, and he'd said *yes*.

"What are you thinking?" he asked, kissing my neck.

"Just . . . so relieved that we're back together, I might explode."

"I rather like you in one piece, particularly beneath me, naked, and wet as a lake."

I wrapped my arms around his neck. "Then I'll just have to keep you on top of me all night."

He laughed, and then kissed me. "I love you, Ruby."

Number of Times Niall Stella Used My Name When He Said He Loved Me:

One, and counting.

Beautiful
BELOVED

In *Beautiful Stranger*, finance whiz Sara Dillon met the irresistibly sexy Brit, Max Stella, at a New York City club. Throughout the series we've watched them learn to balance commitment with their *less than* private brand of playfulness.

In *Beautiful Beloved*, Max and Sara take it to the next step. But the question is: Will they be able to find a balance between the wild sexcapades they aren't ready to retire, and the demands of parenthood that come along with their new Beautiful bundle of joy?

Parenthood: it's not for the weak of heart.
(And featuring a guest appearance by Niall Stella!!!)

Available for the first time in print!
Packaged with *Beautiful Secret* exclusively for Target

CHAPTER ONE

The dishes were done, the flat tidied, and Sara had begun to sing quietly to our little miss in the nursery. I said a simple prayer to the god of sleeping children, because on her way in there, Sara had given me the look.

The *don't fall asleep before I come to bed* look.

The *I'm still not over the sight of our baby sleeping on your naked chest* look.

The *you're getting very, extremely laid* look.

I fucking loved my life.

Across the room on the coffee table, my phone lit up with a call. Going over and seeing whose name flashed across the screen, I broke out in a massive smile.

"You've called the happiest bloke on the planet," I told my brother, in lieu of a proper greeting.

I was met with a heavy pause of silence, and then: "It's impossible for you to be smugger."

"True. But make it quick. I'm about to be ravaged by the natives." Sweet mother Mary it seemed like it'd been forever since we'd had anything more than a quick grope en route to passing out from exhaustion.

I was even considering doing some extensive stretching first.

My youngest brother, Niall, laughed. "In that case, I hope you survive the night because I'm coming to visit next week and I'd be terribly disappointed to miss the Max Stella tour you've promised all these years."

"Brilliant!" I smacked the table with my palm. This night kept getting better. The promise of sex two nights in a row with my gorgeous wife and a visit from my brother next week. "Absolutely, bloody brilliant." I hadn't seen Niall since the last time I went home, over a year ago, and he'd been too busy to visit much. "Work letting you out, then?"

"More or less." He paused. "Right. That's it, then, it's bloody late. Just letting you know. I'm coming to visit little Annabel, not you lot."

Laughing, I said, "Understood."

"I'll arrive on Tuesday. Leaving Sunday."

I noted the rest of the details and rang off before heading to find Sara to share the news.

The singing had stopped, and to my complete lack of surprise, I found my beautiful wife asleep in the rocking chair beside the crib, with the baby in her arms. I pulled the little Beloved away from her mum, swaddled her up, and placed her in the crib. Although until recently Annabel generally slept only two or three hours at a time, at least we could put her to bed beside a brass band and she wouldn't rouse.

I suspected we wouldn't be as lucky with the next one.

Next one?

I blinked, feeling slightly mad for having this thought. It was only in the past two weeks that we were getting any sort of decent sleep at all.

With the baby taken care of, I crossed the room to wake Sara. Her eyes drew open just as I reached her, and she inhaled deeply, blinking up at me. "Oh. I fell asleep."

I crouched in front of her, using my thumb to move a strand of hair off her face. "I don't think you were supposed to do that."

"No, I was going to get you naked."

"That's still an option."

Sara took my hand and stood, pulling me after her out of the nursery and down the hall. "What were you thinking, just standing there looking down at me?"

"Just feeling rather in love with my life, is all."

"Well, I fell asleep wondering whether our second will be as good a sleeper as our first."

She glanced over her shoulder at me with a grin, and I gaped at her, eyes wide and incredulous. How could she know the exact thought had crossed my mind only minutes before?

"You call Anna a *good sleeper*?" I asked.

"She has been lately," she clarified. "We just had to give her time to grow into it."

I watched Sara's hair slide over her shoulders as she turned back and shook her head. Her hair was longer now, thicker, and the way it slid across her skin made me want to gather it into a ball, hold it in my fist, and fuck her over the side of the bed.

Oh, but it had been forever since we'd done anything as rough as that.

I swallowed, closed my eyes, and attempted to steady my hunger when she sat on the edge of the mattress and slowly slid her thighs apart.

"You've lost your mind," I said with a grin.

"Probably true." Her sexy little shrug told me she was only half serious, and a naughty playfulness lingered beneath the surface.

Stepping between her legs, I helped her pull her tank top over her head and guided her onto her back so I could slide her thin cotton shorts down and off.

Slow, Max.

My mind frenzied with thoughts of pushing her thighs to her chest, biting my way down her torso, sucking and spanking the sweetness between her legs until she screamed so loud it shook the walls. Instead, I kissed her navel, her hip, moving my mouth to her ribs and then up higher to the firm swell of her breasts. They were already full, and growing tight the longer the baby slept. I bent, sucking at the pink flush of her nipples.

"Do you really love to look at them so much?" Her voice dropped slightly. "You like the taste?"

I *loved* her body like this, but I didn't know how to truly admit it. I loved her hips, her breasts. Loved to watch her feed our baby and come curl around me after. It felt like every fucking thing in the world had come together with the arrival of our daughter. But it still felt a bit shameful to want her body to stay this way after what had admittedly been a tough labor.

I shifted forward carefully, pressing my cock through my boxers into the warm skin between her legs.

Sara pulled me down over her and slid her mouth down my neck. "Is it weird that I want to stay like this?" she asked as I spread my hand over her hip. "To fill this home of ours with little ankle biters?"

I laughed into her shoulder. "Sleep deprivation is eating your brain."

"I know you want a big family," she said. "And I've never been more in love with you than when I've seen you be a daddy . . ." She noticed where my attention had gone, to the firm swell of her breast again, my mouth closing over her nipple. "They get full like this . . ."

I kissed my way up to her neck. "They provide me with a rather spiritual experience."

"So you *do* like my body right now?" she whispered.

There was a delicate edge to her voice, a vulnerability that shocked me. Sara knew I loved her body, every inch of her perfect, soft skin.

Didn't she?

I pulled back to look at her. "I fucking *love* your body. And I love how happy motherhood has made you. I like how you seem rather blissful lately." Bending, I spoke into the warm space between her breasts: "I also like how ripe your tits are."

She took a handful of my hair and pulled me back, laughing. "Finally, he admits it!"

"What does that mean?"

Her brow furrowed a little as she studied my face, warm brown eyes moving to take in every aspect of my expression. Sara often studied me like this: quietly, earnestly. She ran a fingertip across my chin, her eyes trained on my lips. "I want you to not worry so much," she whispered. "I want more babies—maybe not right away, but someday—and when I say that, I see terror in your eyes."

I swallowed around the heavy lump in my throat. "It's not as hard on my body."

"My body seems to be weathering it fine. I'm going back to work soon. Look at us. We *did* it."

I bent, tasting her skin again. Kissing her stomach.

She pulled me up, whispered in my ear, "Tell me you didn't love having your baby in here."

Laughing, I admitted, "She was certainly easier to take care of all tucked away in there."

She looked back up at my face as I shifted over her, spreading her thighs with my knee and settling there, growing tighter at the feel of her, soft and warm, beneath me. "All right, love?"

Her breaths were already coming faster, short bursts against my neck, her hands sliding lower over my back to push my boxers down my hips. "Yeah."

I slipped my finger into her mouth, wetting it against her tongue before bringing it between us to touch her. I hummed, rubbing myself on her thigh. "You sure? You're not sore?"

She stared up at me, expression shifting into one I couldn't quite read. "I'm *sure*."

"We made love last night, too. I don't want to hurt you," I explained.

She closed her eyes, pulling my head into her neck. "I know, baby."

I slid in, slow, and pressed my mouth to her jaw, groaning. Each time . . . each fucking time I was sure I would never get used to the feel of her. Her nails dug into my back as she let out a relieved moan.

"Christ, Petal. You're heaven beneath me." Cupping her breast in one hand, I squeezed, relishing the slide of milk on my palm. "Fuck," I managed. "*Fucking hell . . .*"

"This is a new thing," she whispered, scratching her nails down my back.

I clenched my jaw, fighting the admission that wanted to burst free. "I bloody love them like this. I'm sorry—I know they're mostly a drag for you—but fuck, Petal. I love your tits like this."

I felt her still beneath me and stopped moving so I could pull back and look at her face.

"What?" I asked. "What did I say?"

She didn't look upset, just a funny mix of disappointed and amused. Sliding her legs up my sides, she whispered, "Since when do you have to give me a disclaimer?"

Smiling, I bent and kissed her sweet, full lips. My heart was beating a little too fast; I still wasn't sure what I'd done wrong.

"You don't have to apologize for being turned on by that," she whispered into my mouth. "I miss seeing you lost in me, and unapologetic about it."

My immediate instinct was to *show* her how lost I really was: to lift her arms over her head, pound into her, and relish the sight of her breasts moving below me, relish their weight and the spike of lust I felt when they leaked onto my skin. But instead, I began to slowly move above her, making sure to ease her pleasure from her with every draw of my body inside hers.

She grabbed my ass, urged me faster and harder, and I tried to give her more but it was almost like something newly hardwired in me with every shift forward:

Take it easy.

Take it slow.

Take it easy.

Take it slow.

We'd had sex many times in the months since the baby was born, but it hadn't yet returned to the wild days of before, with fucking on the kitchen table or the floor, or sweaty and reckless play in the club. Those days we'd had spanking and bondage. Those days I'd taken her in every manner imaginable, sometimes with strangers watching, sometimes with only my video camera as witness. Once I'd bit her shoulder so hard she'd bled and it nearly made her savage with excitement.

Before—and during—her pregnancy, it never occurred to me how *fragile* she was.

And then she'd had my baby: nearly nine pounds and over twenty-four hours of hard labor. For two months after Annabel came, we'd stumbled our way through new parenting, fallen in love with our daughter, fallen in love all over again with each other, and found tiny winks of sleep whenever we could. Eventually, we'd also found ways to be carefully intimate with hands and mouths, playful with words and toys.

Then, nearly two months ago now, Sara said she was ready to make love again.

I'd been terrified at first, but one kiss led to another, and soon I'd been harder than I could remember being in weeks. The sound she made when I pushed into her would forever echo in my thoughts. It was a broken sound, the sharp, surprised cry of pain. I'd immediately stopped, and although she swore she felt no pain *now,* I couldn't help but feel I was handling her differently: being careful with a treasure I'd only recently discovered could be broken . . .

We had yet to return to the club.

We had yet to even pull out the camera for anything other than pictures of our daughter.

We had yet to have sex that did anything more than rustle the sheets, let alone break furniture.

But here, in our bed, with her beneath me, and making her hungry, gasping little noises, her words echoed in my head—*pounding*—each one like a mallet hitting a drum.

I miss seeing you lost in me, and unapologetic about it.

She was letting me be gentle. She was patiently waiting for it to sink in that she'd asked for more, for real sex, again and again.

She'd say, *Do you want to make a movie tonight?*

No, Petal, it's enough just to feel you.

Do you ever miss the club?

No, Petal, I love being right here where we are, with our baby asleep down the hall.

You really like to look at them like this? You like the taste?

I'd wanted to make things easy for her. I'd wanted her to feel safe and cherished. I closed my eyes, absorbed by the paradoxical sensations of relief when Sara began to quietly come beneath be, and heartache in the realization that somewhere along the line, I had forgotten what she needed.

———

At four in the morning, I sat on the floor of the nursery while Sara fed Annabel. The sky outside was deep blue-black, and even on the Upper East Side at this hour, the streets were relatively quiet.

"You didn't have to get up with us," she whispered.

She said the same thing every morning, worried about my lack of sleep and a long workday ahead. But this, right here, was my favorite part of the day.

"I'll bundle her up and go for a run when you're done."

Sara watched me in the darkness. "I love you."

I swallowed, nodding as I struggled to work past the lump in my throat so I could repeat the sentiment. I'd barely been able to sleep last night after realizing I'd been so focused on enjoying Sara the Mother that I'd barely let myself enjoy Sara the Woman.

"What's wrong?" she whispered, watching me struggle.

"I think we need to make a deal to return to us before we can get pregnant again."

" 'Us'?" she repeated.

"I think I heard what you were saying last night."

Her brows pulled together and I could tell she wasn't exactly sure what I was saying. "Oh?"

"I want to be the husband you need again. Photographs. Film. Knowing I'm giving you what you need."

"What I need?"

"What *we* need."

She licked her lips, blinking down to the baby. "You're so much more than I could have ever hoped for. You know that."

"I'd like to occasionally outdo myself," I said, and she giggled, putting her hand over her mouth when the baby pulled off her breast in surprise.

"Shh, shh," Sara murmured to her. "Come here."

"Maybe Mum can watch little Beloved and we can start with dinner out? Slowly work our way to something else?"

She looked up again, eyes wide. "Like the club?"

I watched her holding our child in her arms and felt a protectiveness so violent lash over me I wasn't sure how I would handle letting others see her so vulnerable, so *ripe*.

"If that's what you want," I managed.

She nodded, gently answering the question in my voice. "It is."

———

I folded up the stroller and stowed it in the foyer closet before stripping off my shirt. Although so far it had been a mild winter, it was still January and the long-sleeved running shirt I wore to keep me from freezing outside immediately felt claustrophobic upon entering the warm apartment.

Bending, I unzipped the carrier and pulled out the extremely bundled child inside.

"Was that good, baby girl?" I murmured, kissing her pink cheek. She was warm and drooly and her enormous brown eyes crinkled exactly like her mother's when she smiled. "Got a good run in, didn't we?"

I sat on the couch and laid Annabel on my chest while I caught my breath.

"You're sweaty and sitting on the couch, aren't you?" Sara called from the master suite.

I stuck my tongue out at Anna and she tried to grab it. "Very sweaty," I answered my wife. "Quite disgusting, actually."

Sara's heels clicked down the hallway and she froze when she saw us. "Max."

400

"I'll wipe it down, Pet—"

"I don't care about that," she said, walking closer. "You're shirtless with the world's sweetest baby cuddled on those muscles. Put a shirt on, you beast, or I can't be held responsible for my actions."

I fucking loved it when Sara looked at me like that. "Imagine how I feel when you're feeding her."

She gave me a bright smile as she bent, kissing Anna's chubby thigh. "She looks like a little peach on you."

I took in her outfit and immediately wondered if we'd be able to get the baby down for a nap this early in the day. I hadn't seen Sara in work clothes in months and didn't realize until just then how much I missed it. Her little black skirt hit just below her knees, giving a tiny flash of skin above her soft leather boots. Her tits looked fucking unreal in the gray sweater she'd put on.

Following my attention, she looked down at her chest. "I think I need to go shopping today. Everything is too small in the chest."

"Don't you dare get rid of that one."

She pulled her lip between her teeth, blinking over to me. "Yeah?"

"Yeah," I murmured, and the moment grew heavy. "You look bloody beautiful, Petal."

"Is it . . . inappropriate, though? I mean, the way you're looking at me makes me think this sweater is no longer very professional."

"I guess it depends on where you're headed."

She shrugged, sitting down next to us. "I thought I'd go into the office for a couple of hours, just so next week doesn't feel so disorienting. I'm meeting the girls for breakfast and then heading in."

I kissed the top of Anna's head. "Want me to take her with me?"

"Either way. I could, too."

What was it about her face in that moment, right there, that made me feel so many things at once it was overwhelming? With her dressed and headed out the door, it was like I was seeing this combination for the first time: my lover, my wife, and also a mother, a nurturer and . . . *fuck,* a bird with the best pair of tits I'd ever seen.

Standing, I motioned for her to follow me back down the hall. I grabbed Annabel's musical baby seat from the nursery and put it beside the dresser in our bedroom, facing the set of framed photographs of trees that she loved, and then guided Sara to the bed.

"Max . . ."

"Just a minute." I retrieved my camera from the shelf, stabilized it on the tripod, and set it to automatic shots every five seconds. Sara's breath was rapid and shallow when I bent low, kissed her neck, and told her, "I won't keep you long."

"Anna's fine," she said, pulling me closer. "Keep me as long as you can."

Laying her back, I pushed her skirt up her hips and began kissing my way up her stomach, feeling my cock tighten with each nostalgic click of the shutter, with the feel of her hands digging into my hair. I moved her sweater up her stomach, revealing smooth, bare skin. She tasted like rain, like fruit, and had the same sweet scent I'd always worshipped on her body. Reaching behind her, I unhooked her bra and pushed it up over her breasts.

I'd always loved Sara's breasts but I'd never particularly been a breast man until recently. The weight of them, the soft smell of her skin, and the odd spike I felt in my abdomen whenever she fed our child . . .it was an odd reflex to want to look at them, touch them like this, and one I realized I'd been fighting the last few months.

You don't have to apologize for being turned on by that.

My mouth closed over the peak, tongue pulling her deeper into my mouth, and I groaned at the feel of it. She was warm and firm, so full—

I did this . . .

I made her this way

—and when she reached for my track pants and pushed them down my hips to take me in her hand, the moment dissolved into frenzy.

I could imagine her looking through the pictures later, seeing how much I relished the feel of her in my mouth, the taste of her on my tongue. She would know, then, just by looking at my face, how I loved the slide of milk on my hand, the way her hips looked spread around mine. I worshipped her.

I bloody worshipped this woman.

I rocked into her fist, groaning at the feel of her mouth sucking at my neck, her desperate, sweet little cries into my skin. Shoving her panties aside, I licked my hand and used it to make her slick so I could push deep inside with one sharp stab of my hips.

She gasped, eyes wide with thrill and relieved—fuck, she was *relieved,* as if I'd been missing and maybe I had. I pulled out and shifted forward, fucking her so hard and fast that within the span of a minute I knew I was coming; coming before I had time to get her there, before I even had time to consider whether she wanted me to spill inside her before leaving for work. I just . . . *wanted* with such intensity, with a kind of jagged need I hadn't felt in so long that I couldn't seem to slow myself down.

The tenderness and protectiveness had been pushed aside, just for the moment, by something older and familiar: a heavy need to claim her.

I reached between us, playing with her with my fingertips until she was bucking into my hand, gasping and squeezing around my cock. She cried out, three sharp pleas to drag her through her pleasure, and then she fell quiet, pulling me fully on top of her and exhaling heavily into my neck.

She'd seen me every day; we'd cuddled, talked, laughed, fallen asleep at the dinner table together, and done all manner of intimate things. But the relief in this moment was profound. I knew exactly what she meant when she whispered, "I missed you."

And all I could say back was "I missed you, too."

———

Mum was already at her desk when I arrived at the office wearing Annabel in the carrier. She jumped up, ran around the desk, and reached for her granddaughter without even looking at my face.

"Mum," I hissed, laughing as I reached for her shoulders so she wouldn't jostle the baby. "She's asleep. Settle down, woman. You'll get her in a bit when I've got a meeting with Levinson."

My mother looked up at me and replaced her mild scowl with a sweet smile. "Mornin', love."

I'd never seen myself as a mum's boy growing up but having her with us at Stella & Sumner for the past several years was one of my favorite things about coming to work. Especially since we'd had Annabel, I appreciated the proximity of family and their ability to tell us when we were acting like neurotic idiots.

And although Mum had raised ten of us quite capably, I registered I was due for a sizable heap of shit when I asked her—for the first time—to watch the baby so we could go out. We'd always taken the baby with us, but this was . . . well, this was entirely different.

"Mum," I started as she walked back around her desk to sit down. "I was hoping to take Sara out this coming Friday. Would you mind heading over and watching Annabel?"

Her face fell. "Max, you forgot."

I groaned. *Fuck.* This was the second time a woman

had said this to me in less than twenty-four hours. "Forgot what?"

"I leave for Leeds tomorrow, dove. I'm going to stay with Karen for three weeks."

"Aw, bugger."

"I can watch her tonight?"

"No, you've got to pack and we don't have any sort of plan in place. I get the sense we'll both need this to be a military operation."

"You're mental. I've been telling you for weeks: just take the wife out and have some dinner, for crying out loud. By the time you and Niall and Rebecca came along, we were letting the dog watch you for a night out."

Laughing, I agreed, "I don't doubt it."

"The fuck are you wearing?"

I looked down at Annabel still asleep in the carrier and replied to Will, "It's called an Ergo."

He followed me into my office and sat on my couch. "It looks like you went tandem skydiving and forgot to unlatch."

Bennett walked up behind him. "You look like a marsupial."

"It's called baby wearing, you twats." I laughed, and then whispered to the baby, "Is that right? Are you my little joey?" I looked up at my mates and only then did I do the mental calculation. "Bennett, what the hell are you doing here?"

"Will and I had a meeting with Gross and Barrett at eight. Did you forget?"

"Bloody hell will you lot cut me some slack! I've not slept in four fucking months!"

They both stared at me, wide-eyed, for several silent seconds.

"Are your nipples sore?" Will asked.

I shook my head, laughing. "Tosser."

As carefully as I could, I unhooked the carrier behind my neck and let it fall so I could lay Anna down on the couch beside Will. She startled—both arms and both legs flying out in a spasm—but then immediately fell back asleep.

For his part, Will looked like I'd just put a giant hollow eggshell near him. His hands were clasped in his lap and his eyes were trained on the baby as if she might suddenly roll and explode. He'd been around Anna nearly every weekend since she'd been born and still looked at her like breathing too heavily near her might cause her to shatter.

"Since when are you an idiot around children?" I asked.

"I love kids," he said, looking up at me. "But she's just so *little*."

"She's not," I assured him. "She's enormous."

"You know what I mean."

"Look," I said, sitting down in a chair near my desk. "I need to ask a favor. I want to take Sare out for dinner this Friday—"

Bennett interrupted: "You're finally going to let someone watch Anna?"

Scowling, I explained, "It's a lot easier said than done, right? Anyway, Mum is leaving for Leeds tomorrow so she can't watch her this weekend. Can one of you . . . ?"

They both stared at me with terrified eyes.

"Aw come on, it's not that hard. We'd only go out for a few hours. You and your better half give her a couple of bottles, change a couple of diapers, she sleeps, we get home."

"We can't," Bennett said, wincing in apology. "Chloe and I are headed up to the Hudson Valley."

"This weekend?" Will asked, nodding several times in quick succession as if to talk himself into it. "I could probably do it."

"Brilliant," I said. "Thanks, mate."

"I've never changed a diaper. Or fed a baby. Hanna jokes that the only girl I've ever failed to charm is Liv's daughter, Aspen." Shrugging, he added, "But I'm sure it's instinct, right?" He ticked the rules off on his fingers: "Don't scald Anna in the bath, don't leave the milk in the microwave too long." He paused and seemed to continue to draft a mental list. "Oh, and don't drop her."

I imagined walking out of the office right now and leaving Annabel in Will's hands for even a minute; my stomach flipped over and I wanted to vomit. "Couldn't you bring Hanna?"

"She's got some visiting-faculty dinners this weekend."

Rubbing my hand across my chin, I asked, "You know . . . maybe you could come over and have dinner with us tonight to watch and learn?"

He nodded, but swallowed heavily. To be fair, I knew what I was asking was a big deal. It was one thing to hang out with us when we had Annabel, and quite another to imagine being alone with this tiny little girl.

"Can't you just take it to the restaurant with you?" Bennett asked.

"That sort of defeats the purpose. Also, Annabel isn't an 'it.'"

"I didn't call her an 'it.'"

Will and I replied in unison, "Yeah, you did."

Scrubbing my face, I muttered, "Fuck it. Just come over for dinner and we'll have some beers."

We'd figure something out. We had to.

Chapter Two

Sara

I turned down Fifty-Sixth and caught sight of the Parker Meridien near the end of the block.

The gray stone façade was as bleak as the morning sky; the clouds overhead fat with snow that was certain to start falling any minute. Winter in New York after Christmas was dreary: cold and wet, dirty slush, and days at a time without a hint of blue sky. But this year had been blessedly mild compared to others, and warm enough for Max to regularly push the bundled-up stroller alongside Will and Hanna as they ran through the park.

My phone buzzed in the front pocket of my coat. I didn't need to look to know it was Chloe, sending the third Where are you? You are not backing out on us Sara! message in the last hour. So maybe I'd missed a few lunches with the girls since Anna had been born, it wasn't easy getting out of the house with a newborn who would be permanently attached to my breast if given the chance.

I ignored my phone, my head still full of my morning with Max. Chloe could wait.

But of course only two steps later I was clutched with the fear that maybe the text hadn't been Chloe. Maybe it was Max with a message that Anna was sick or had hurt herself or—

I moved off the sidewalk to stand in the shelter of a nearby building, and pulled out my phone.

Will might come over for dinner, Max had written. You good with that?

I replied that it was fine and slid my phone back into my pocket. With each step, my favorite boots crunched through the salt that had been scattered along the sidewalk. Chloe wanted to take me shopping before I braved the office today, but I'd declined. I wanted the comfort of my favorite skirt and the heels that added just a little swing to my step, the sweater that rendered Max speechless and then *consumed* this morning. I needed to feel like myself.

I straightened my jacket and tightened the grip on the purse Max had bought me for my birthday. A Burberry clutch, not a diaper bag. I hadn't been out of the house without my baby, let alone diapers, bottles, wipes, and a change of clothes, since Anna was born, and the soft leather felt too light in my hand.

Just a few hours away from her today, I reminded myself. *Just see how it goes.*

⁂

I smiled at the doorman as I stepped inside the marble lobby. The floors were gleaming white and inlaid with glossy black squares, the walls made of polished stone. People gathered on benches and sat hunched over their phones. Conversations carried through the giant space and up, echoing off stone walls. I walked under a giant arch and turned left, climbing a set of stairs that led to Norma's. As usual, I could hear Chloe before I could see her.

"There she is," Chloe said, standing on skyscraper-tall boots, all long legs and cascading wavy hair and an expression that said there was no way I'd get out of being late without getting a little shit for it first. "Fucking finally."

"I know, I know," I said, crossing the wood floors to reach them. "Sorry. Just trust me that time warps when you have a kid, and you think you're getting out of the house on time and then suddenly you're half an hour late."

"Are you sure it wasn't because Max saw you in that outfit and got a little handsy?" Hanna asked from beside Chloe.

"Spoken like a woman who's with a boob man," I said, laughing. "And . . . maybe."

I adored Hanna, but Max in particular had grown especially fond of her in the past year, saying that anyone who could keep Will Sumner by the balls was aces in his book.

"Just ignore Attila the Hun over here," my assistant and good friend George said, motioning to Chloe. "The woman isn't happy unless she's bossing someone around."

"Hell yes," Chloe said.

I hugged them all and hung my coat on the back of my chair before taking my seat.

"How's the princess?" Chloe said, blowing over the top of her mug. "*Where's* the princess?"

"Perfect. She's with Daddy today." A proud smile spread across my face. "How's the Bennett?"

"A nightmare," she answered, equally proud.

"And what's new with you and Will?" I asked, turning to Hanna. "I feel like I hardly see you, even if Max has taken it upon himself to crash your runs lately. Sorry about that."

Hanna leaned an elbow on the table and smiled. "I love when he comes along. And judging by the goofy look Will gets on his face when he sees that running stroller heading down the path, I can assure you he doesn't mind, either."

"Good, because as bad as I feel, the extra hour of sleep I get makes me feel a *lot* better."

"Maybe I should join those runs," George offered. "Does Will run shirtless in the spring?"

"George," Hanna said, ignoring this, "are you going to tell Sara about the little dreamboat you've been seeing?"

"*Was* seeing," he corrected. "As in past tense. Ugh, it was a stage-one breakup. I don't want to talk about it."

"A stage what?" Chloe asked.

"*A stage one,*" he clarified. "I swear, do I always have

to be the gay urban dictionary for you people? Stage one is where you break up via text message trying to come off not looking like a total douche bag. Stage two is where you tell the person, 'Look, you're not ringing my bell and I'm clearly not ringing yours. Let's move this train along to grander stations.' Stage three is where it's not working and you sort of fade the person out over time. It's painful because by then the other person has become sort of a habit. They know how you take your coffee and what days you can have carbs and just . . . it can be sad."

"Of course it can," I said, stirring my coffee. "Bonding over dietary restrictions can be very romantic."

George gave me a playful jab to the shoulder. "You get a sarcasm pass because you're lactating and it's clearly eating your brain. Where was I? Oh, stage four. Well . . .stage four is where one person is totally invested and the other is just . . . over it. Awful, right? So, stage one doesn't sound so bad, but in my opinion it's the worst after stage four. If someone feels comfortable breaking up via text message, you clearly haven't gotten to a place where you can ask a lot of questions, and you definitely can't call them up and be all *Oh hi, it's me, the guy you wore the Lion Tamer outfit with? Can you tell me what happened?*"

We all nodded sympathetically, and George glared at the bowl of muffins in the center of the table before reaching for one. "Now I'm eating my feelings."

"Aww, George. Were you totally infatuated with him?" Hanna asked.

"Oh, girl, no," George said with a laugh. "I don't do infatuation unless his name is Sumner."

The waiter stopped by our table, filling my coffee before taking each of our orders. "I'll have the crispy waffle with berries and Devonshire cream," I told him.

"I have no idea how you look like this," Chloe said, motioning to my body, "and still eat like that. You don't run with Hanna, and I know I haven't seen you at the office gym in months."

"One of the joys of breastfeeding," I said. "I have to eat more calories to keep up my milk."

Which was true. I still worked out when I could, but pregnancy and motherhood had left me with this new body I was only now getting used to: a slightly wider waist, but curves that had never been so full. I'd always been a bit on the skinny side, but I felt softer now, with rounded hips and boobs that surprised even me. It didn't hurt that sometimes I'd turn around and see Max flat-out staring at my chest, completely unable to look away. I'd be lying if I didn't say those moments made me feel like a fucking queen.

"What's the plan when you go back to work?" Hanna asked, and taking in my outfit, added, "I'm assuming that's where you're headed now?"

I nodded as I took a sip of my coffee. "I don't officially

go back until next week, but thought it might be easier to ease myself into it."

"Are you actually going to walk into your office and sit at your desk today?" George asked.

George had been a godsend while I was on leave. I was out for sixteen weeks, but I'd never wanted to feel disconnected from my career at Ryan Media Group, so I'd stop in on a pretty regular basis even though anything I needed to look at could have easily been couriered over to the apartment. Without really talking about it, we'd built up a system: Anna and I would meet George at his desk in the outer office, he'd hand me the stack of files and any messages that required my attention, and I'd leave him whatever I'd been working on at home.

I never went inside my office and he never questioned why.

Which was ridiculous, when you thought about it. I was Sara Stella, capable of managing multimillion-dollar campaigns and overseeing an entire finance department.

But I hadn't quite figured out how to do all that and be mommy, too.

"You haven't gone into your office yet?" Hanna asked. "Is it going to be weird to go back?"

"I don't think so? I mean, I want to go back to work. I *need* to. It's such a part of who I am and I need that part of my life. But Anna . . . the idea of leaving her for eight hours a day still fills me with this guilt like I'm ruining her somehow or I'm missing some vital mommy muscle that makes me want to stay home. Plus, I know I want more at some point and how will we make all that work? Is it fair of me to want more children when I'm pretty sure I'll always need *that* side of me, too?"

"Bullshit," Chloe said. "You think men ever have this conversation with themselves? Of course they don't. You've killed yourself to get where you are. If you can have both, have both. It might take some adjustment but who cares? You figure it out as you go." She tilted her head and added, "You don't see Max wanting to stay home."

"Actually," I started, and it was enough to get Chloe's attention. She put down her mug and sat back in her chair, waiting. "I don't really know what's going on with him right now. I know he wants me every bit as much as he did before Anna, but I think it's been more of an adjustment for him than he thought it would be, the idea of my being a wife *and* a mother. He's so careful, like he's not sure how to treat me."

"Can you blame the man?" George said, and we all turned to him. "Have you seen what childbirth does to a vagina?" He did a full-body shudder.

"*George*," Chloe said, shaking her head.

"What!" he shouted.

"Shut up!" she shouted back.

"As horrible a flashback as that was," I said, "George has a point. I think Max is worried he'll do something to hurt me, and I'm not really sure how to show him I'm the same Sara I was before. That I *want* the same things I did before."

Chloe shrugged and picked up her coffee. "I don't know, Sara. He went from having you all to himself to watching you learn how to be a mama. Doesn't surprise me his brain is having to rewrite that code a little."

"I don't think it's about having to share me . . ." I hedged, but Chloe held up a hand.

"I mean it's about shifting how he sees you," she said, lifting an arched brow. "First you were the lust of his life, and now you're the mother of his daughter."

I chewed my lip, nodding. "He worries that I'm delicate now."

"Exactly," she said, a bit more gently. "Having Anna was traumatic. It wasn't as easy a birth as you both expected. You've already forgotten it, but maybe he hasn't and still needs to get over it."

Chloe was right. Sex this morning had been wild and hard, as if wanting me took over the part of Max's brain that told him to slow down. *That*'s what I wanted.

"When was the last time just the two of you went out?" George asked.

"Since Anna? We haven't."

It was his turn for a little eyebrow snark. "Well there's part of your problem right there, babycakes."

"Are we just talking wild sex here?" Chloe asked. "Because it's not like Annabel would have a clue what's going on."

"True," George said, "but it's probably a lot harder to fuck like wild animals with a baby asleep two doors down. You need a little space."

He had a point. "I love my baby more than anything in the world, but I want hours and hours. I want to bang my husband until he can't remember his name."

Silence bounced around the table for a few breaths.

"Too blunt?" I asked, laughing.

"Never," George said quickly. "I think we're all just working on that mental image."

"God, I sound desperate," I say, resting my chin on my fist. "Maybe we should just start with dinner out? I think Max is asking his mom if she can watch Anna this weekend."

"Otherwise next weekend Bennett and I can help," Chloe said.

"Whoa, whoa, whoa," George cut in. "What am I here for? My subtle charm? My pretty face? What about me?"

Chloe whipped her head around dramatically. "*You?*"

"I'll have you know that my mother ran a day care, and I taught preschool all through college. Hell, I worked in the infant room when I was in high school to pay for majorette class." Chloe went to respond but he held up a hand: "Shut it, Mills." He turned to me. "I'll watch Anna. I can even watch her tonight."

"You'd watch her?" I asked. "You could really do that?"

"With my eyes closed. Besides," he said, eyeing the

muffins again, "it's not like I have any kind of social life to speak of. My nights are wide open."

⌁⎯⎯⌁

The smell of home hit me before I'd even walked in the door. My talk with the girls and George had done wonders, and I'd successfully navigated the day with no freak-outs, no tears, and only one breast milk incident when a phone call went long and I couldn't get to my pump in time. Next time, I'd just do it while I was on the phone. Boom. My friends were right; I'd figure it out as I went.

Basically, I was feeling pretty unstoppable as I rounded the corner, ready to tell Max about our dinner that night. Then I found him shirtless—again—wrapped in nothing but a towel, with a tiny sleeping baby in his arms, and I was ready to forget about dinner entirely and let him get me pregnant again that very second.

Focus, Sara.

"I'm taking you to dinner," I said. "Surprise! Also, I can't believe I'm saying this, but I'm going to need you to put some clothes on for real this time or we'll never get out of the apartment."

Max looked up, confused. "Dinner? How did you—?" Sitting up, he said, "And no, I meant to ring you today. I wanted to take you to dinner this weekend but Mum is leaving for Leeds tomorrow. I completely forgot it was in my schedule."

"That's what I'm saying: *George* is watching Anna tonight."

"Tonight? Has George ever even seen a baby?"

I crossed the room and kissed him softly on the mouth. "Hi," I said, and kissed him again. "I know what you're thinking, but it's perfect." I took the sleeping baby from his arms and leaned in, pressing my face to her soft little head, breathing in as much of her as I could. She had Max's hair for sure, only a shade darker than mine but already with a bit of a wave to it. Her clean-baby smell hit me, and I felt my breasts grow heavy, my milk letting down almost immediately.

A chair Max brought me from England sat tucked beneath the window in the nursery. It was my favorite place in the apartment, where I was able to look out over the city while I nursed. I got Anna situated, and then looked up at him.

He clearly thought I'd lost my mind. "Are we talking about the same George?"

"I had breakfast with everyone this morning before I went in to work. Did you know that George's mom ran a day care while he was growing up? He worked there while he was in high school and all through college. He worked with *infants*."

He gave me his best skeptical face. "We're talking about the same twenty-something bloke who wore a Wisconsin cheese hat and some flowy Jesus robes for Halloween, calling himself 'Cheesus'?"

"The one and only," I said, laughing at the memory. "He's probably more qualified to take care of her than we are. Plus we'll stay close. Just around the corner. He can text or call with any questions and we can be back up here in less than three minutes."

"But . . ."

"No buts. This is exactly what we need. Now get dressed, he'll be here in fifteen minutes."

George showed up exactly fourteen minutes later.

From the bathroom, I could hear Max open the door and let him in, and begin grilling him as they went from room to room.

"And what about her bottle?" Max asked, clearly hoping to be proven right, and that George had absolutely no idea what he was doing.

"Sara's breastfeeding so I assume you have expressed milk in the freezer? Maybe even fresh in the refrigerator," George said, more to himself than to Max, I was sure. "What am I talking about? Honestly, I think I've seen more of Sara's boobs in the last four months than my own." There was the sound of the freezer door as it opened and closed, and I stepped out into the living room, watching as George answered Max's questions one by one. Max looked begrudgingly impressed.

"I assume she's getting about six ounces a feeding,"

George continued. "Probably every three hours or so? I'll heat the refrigerated milk first—only ever under warm water, never the microwave. It kills beneficial properties, you know—and I'll use the frozen if needed. Though you'll probably be back by then . . ." George trailed off.

"We have a bottle warmer," Max said, brow furrowed in what I was certain had to be confusion. George really did seem to be more knowledgeable about taking care of an infant than we were. "And nappies?"

"You mean diapers? Oh you Brits are so damn cute. And please, Maxwell. I could probably diaper you in your sleep and you'd never have any idea. I am a pro."

"Or so you've been told," I said, stepping out to kiss his cheek. "Sorry, Chloe's not here and I had to throw that in for her. Thank you so much for doing this."

He waved me off. "No problem. The little princess and I will probably just sit here and cry through *The Notebook*. For very, very different reasons, I'm sure."

Between kisses and cuddles and last-minute instructions, it took another fifteen minutes for George to shoo us out of the apartment.

But we didn't go to the restaurant around the corner. George had apparently made such an impression that Max made us last-minute reservations at a little Italian place a few miles away. I was nervous at the prospect of leaving Anna when I didn't have to, but I was also giddy. We were going on a *date,* just the two of us, and my pulse hadn't slowed down yet.

I watched his profile as he drove us both to the restaurant; as I studied the way the streetlights passed overhead to emphasize the fullness of his lips, the cut of his jaw, I thought back to our first real *date*—is that what that was?—when he'd taken me to Queen of Sheba and I hadn't been able to stop looking at his mouth. I *still* couldn't stop looking at his mouth.

The press didn't follow him like they did before we were together, but since Anna had been born, there was an uptick in Hot Daddy Max Stella photos in Page Six and on various Internet gossip sites. I couldn't say that I blamed them, no matter how much I still resented them for ever spooking me in the first place.

I closed my eyes, my heart squeezing tightly as I was pulled back in time to our first night together after the pictures in the papers, the ones that made me think he'd cheated. He'd thrown a party, and after not answering his calls for over a week, I'd shown up, finally ready to talk. But it hadn't been as simple as I expected—he'd been genuinely hurt—and I had some apologizing to do.

I remembered the small, grudging smile Max gave me when we woke up together the next morning; he had handed over the last tiny bit of himself with that.

I remembered how that look had squeezed my heart,

painfully. He'd been scared to let me back in, and in the stark white light of the morning, with both of us sweaty and spent, we couldn't hide with our faces pressed to the other's skin, or in the game of transparency through photos. He looked at me directly, baldly, and there was nothing else between us.

"Stay," he said, bending to suck at the skin just beneath my ear. "Stay with me. It's good, Petal. *Us*. It's so sodding good and if you spook again it will absolutely wreck me."

"I won't."

"I love you, yeah?"

I nodded, heart trapped somewhere between my throat and the sky. "I love you."

"That means we're settled. It means there's no question where my heart is. You'll stay here."

It had been that easy. It had always been that easy. And I had learned to trust it.

But now it was a different shape: bigger, yes, but unwieldy, and the ease of it all—Max and Sara, a rhythm ricocheting between us like a shared heartbeat—was now pounding too hard for me to bear.

Because now I felt *everything*. It was like a faucet had been turned on inside me, filling me with warmth and pride and thrill and terror and vulnerability and strength and powerlessness and lust and it never shut off. It filled and filled until I was sure I was bursting from it, but how could I ever complain that I felt too much? How could I explain that I was burning up with the constant awareness that if anyone ever tried to hurt my man or my baby I would rip them inside out with my rage?

How could I ever complain that it was often hard to find myself in the desire to be mother and lover in equal measure to the two people in my life who seemed to matter above even my own need for air?

Max held my hand as we drove, until a text from George pulled me out of my memories.

"Aww," I said, turning the screen to face him. It was a picture of Anna asleep on George's shoulder, her fat little fist pressed against her perfect mouth.

"Maybe we should send him flowers next week to thank him," Max said, and then I recognized the little twist in his smile that signaled he was up to no good. "And say they're from Will."

"Don't you dare," I told him, saving the picture before tucking my phone away. "If this works out we're going to use him again. Hell, I might just change his job position from assistant to nanny and offer him a raise."

"I might have to let you," he said, and brought the back of my hand to his mouth for a kiss. "Maybe then I can sneak you away for a weekend? Someplace we can lock ourselves in our room the entire time, not a stitch of clothing on either of us?"

"That sounds pretty close to perfect."

My phone buzzed in my clutch, and we stopped long

enough for me to reach for it, unsurprised to find another text from George.

Look how gorgeous she is!! it said, along with a photograph of Anna fast asleep in her crib and several heart-eyed emojis.

"This is way too easy," I told Max. "But instead of questioning it, I'm going to put this away and enjoy the hell out of this night. And maybe if you're lucky, I'll let you have your way with me on the way home."

"That, Petal, is the most amazing thing I've heard all day." Max curved his hand around the back of my neck and pulled me to him. I went willingly, my mind already spinning ahead to what could happen after dinner, where we might go and the delightfully filthy things he might do to me. This is what we'd been missing. Max and Sara. Tonight was absolutely perfect.

Max pulled up to the valet at Granduca's and an attendant reached for my door. "I've got it, mate," he said, rounding the car and offering a hand to help me out.

Mindful of the fact that I was in a dress, I carefully swung my feet out onto the ground and moved to stand. Max's hand felt warm and reassuring in my own and I took a step, intending to follow him into the restaurant. But I couldn't.

What the . . . I almost gasped when I realized that I was stuck. Or to be more accurate, that my *dress* was. The subtle beading on my skirt had snagged on the inside door latch of Max's BMW.

"I'm just . . ." I started, letting go of Max in an attempt to get a better look. "My dress seems to be caught."

Max kneeled next to me but I waved him off.

"No, just one second, let me."

By now the attendant with Max's keys had realized something was wrong, and so had a few of the others. "Maybe if you try and slip that piece right there through the latch," one of them said.

"No, that will make it worse. See those little beads? They'll get stuck. I've got some scissors. I can go grab them," said another.

"Man, it is really *in* there," said their supervisor. "How did you even do that?"

Four pairs of hands all tried to help me untangle myself, but I batted them away.

"No," I said. "Please. This skirt is vintage." There was a grimace in my voice as I pulled on a tiny thread, careful not to snag it further. Damn, it did not want to give and I was practically sweating. "A gift from my mom," I added. "Just let me—"

"Oh," they all said in unison, along with a "Fucking hell," from Max.

I'd ripped it, like, *really* ripped it. And now, instead of a small, easily concealable snag, there was a slit that began at the bottom of my skirt and moved up, stopping at the top of my thigh.

"No way that just happened," Max said.

"It happened," I told him.

"I'm sorry, Petal. We can go back and you can change into something else?"

"This is nothing," I said, and straightened, pushing up on the balls of my feet to press a kiss to his neck. "This is just karma's way of proving a point because I said this was too easy. *Of course* something would go wrong after that."

"I'd be lying if I said that I disliked this slight alteration," he said, eyes moving up and down my thigh.

"It's not too obscene?" I asked, a little thrill passing through my stomach at his wide eyes as he shook his head.

"Absolutely not." He ran his hand down over my hip, and touched the bare skin of my thigh, right in front of everyone outside the restaurant.

Warmth slid into my veins. Was he going to play a little tonight? Would he touch me beneath the table?

"Listen," he said, kissing my neck, "why don't I check us in and you can run to the ladies, fix anything that needs fixing and maybe check in on George?"

I wilted immediately. "Sounds perfect," I said, squeezing his hand.

I didn't call George, opting to text instead of running the risk of waking Anna.

I know I don't need to check in so just saying hi. Hi, I typed.

His reply came less than a minute later. If you two aren't naked yet I'm going to be so disappointed.

I laughed dryly as I typed back, Nope, definitely not naked. How's my baby?

Perfect. Just waking up so I'm heating her bottle. Then tummy time and a movie.

You're a lifesaver, I typed.

Tell me something I don't know.

I looked at the full-length mirror in the ladies' room and Max was right, it didn't look bad at all. Satisfied, I left to go find my husband, typing out a response on the way. How will I ever repay you, George?

Bring me back something shiny.

I smiled. Done.

By shiny, you know I mean chorus boys wrapped in sparkling swim trunks, right?

Obviously.

His response appeared only a second later. This is why we're friends.

⁘

We were led to our seats shortly after. With the way Max was looking at me from across the table—like nothing would please him more than to spread me out in front of all these people and have *me* for dinner—I hoped I'd be able to make it through the next two hours.

I opted for clam risotto with bacon and chives, and Max ordered a creamy fettuccine with asparagus. The waiter brought a bottle of pinot noir and held it out for

Max's inspection. Max smiled and then motioned for him to show it to me—which was ridiculous considering I barely drank—but my eyes widened in recognition. It was the same wine we'd had at the quiet dinner after our wedding at city hall. My husband was *so* getting laid tonight.

"Perfect," I told him.

The waiter smiled and began to remove the cork. "It's an amazing choice," he said, wedging the bottle between his knees to get a better grip. He laughed nervously and jostled the opener, but it didn't seem to want to budge. "Wow, it's really stuck in there."

"Maybe if I—" Max started to say, but the cork came out with a wet suction and both the waiter and Max eyed it dubiously. It was black with sludge.

"Oh," both the waiter and I said in unison. Max looked like someone had just popped his balloon.

"This is a pretty bleak metaphor," I joked, but Max's expression told me he didn't think it was remotely funny.

"I'm so sorry," the waiter said, and looked around as if someone would be standing there to help him. "This bottle is clearly off. I'll just go get you another." He paused, and I knew right away that it wasn't a good sign. "I just remembered, that was the last one."

"No worries, mate," Max said, glancing through the wine menu. "Happens to all of us. We'll just have a bottle of the MacRostie instead."

The wine had been poured, and I tore off a small piece of warm bread while we waited for our meal. "So how was Anna today?" I asked.

Max looked at me over the rim of his glass, mouth turned up in a teasing smirk. "I believe there was to be no baby discussion tonight, Mrs. Stella," he said. "But since I relish the chance to talk about our daughter, I'll tell you that she was perfect, as usual. Mum quite enjoys having her there. Not to mention Will, even if he does nothing more than sit and make ridiculous faces at her from across the table."

As if on cue, my phone vibrated next to my plate and I glanced over as the screen lit up.

Your daughter is not impressed with Ryan Gosling. This is clearly your husband's DNA. Attached was a photo of the two of them on the couch, Anna making a hilariously frowny face at the camera.

I showed Max and typed out a quick reply, before placing my phone—facedown—on the table.

Max reached for my hand and took it in his, rubbing his thumb over my wedding band. "It's okay to look at your phone, you know. This is our first night out without her. It's all right to feel a little anxious. *I'm* a little anxious."

"You don't look it," I told him. "You never do. I swear you have a poker face like nothing I've ever seen."

"I don't know about that. Seems I couldn't keep anything from you, now could I? Quite certain you knew I was ass over tits for you within a few days of meeting."

"You played the rogue part pretty well, though. Even I—" My phone vibrated again and I bit back a groan.

It was more movie commentary from George, and honestly, if the accompanying pics weren't so adorable and I didn't love him so much for doing this for me, I'd probably offer to buy him a car to lose my number for the next forty-five minutes.

Has Anna been fussier than usual? Or doing this thing where she pulls her body up into a little bit before kicking out and crying?

"Was Anna fussy today?" I asked Max, suddenly worried that I'd missed something being away.

"Maybe a tad more toward the end of the day, but nothing big. Was just ready to go home, that's all."

Not that we've noticed, I typed. Why? Is she ok?

I'm sure it's nothing, came George's reply. Her tummy feels a bit noisy to me, so I'm going to do a little baby massage on her. See if we can get all those gas bubbles gone.

"She's not feeling well," I told Max. "I mean, he thinks it's just gas but, I don't know."

"Would you feel better if we left, Petal?" he said, concern growing in his features.

"I don't know." I didn't, I wasn't sure if this was one of those moments where I needed to tell the overprotective side of myself to calm down, or give in to the worry pressing on my chest. A baby cried from somewhere near the back of the restaurant and I squeezed my eyes closed. Of course this would happen now. I could already feel the way my breasts felt heavier, tender. My milk was beginning to let down and I had no baby, no pump anywhere in sight. The night was going downhill, and fast.

Movement caught my eye, and I felt my shoulders sag with relief as I saw the waiter coming toward us with our dinners.

"Thank fuck," Max said. "Shall I get them to go?"

The phone buzzed on the table again, so close to my cutlery that it caused a shrill clanking as they vibrated against each other. As he set my plate down, the waiter gave me a look.

`So baby girl feels better now,` the text said. `Un-fortunately, she feels better because she threw up all over me. And your couch. It fought the good fight though.`

"She threw up, all over George's fancy Italian shirt. Maybe send chocolates *and* flowers," I said. "And let's definitely get it all to go."

There are moments when you definitely know life has a sense of humor, when you swear that someone is up there screwing with you. My phone went off again, sending my silverware clanging across the table. I reached for it as the waiter picked Max's plate back up, at the *exact same moment* the person next to us stood, pushing out their chair. I grabbed for my phone, the chair collided with the waiter, and Max's plate of white cream sauce went tumbling . . . into his lap.

Water was everywhere, across the tablecloth, inside my phone, and all over Max's pants, where a wet, creamy mixture now lay steaming. I scrambled back from the chaos, my eyes wide with horror. A child next to us burst into tears, and I looked over at Max and the enormous mess in his lap.

"It's fine," he assured me, grabbing a napkin and wiping his pants.

My phone buzzed on the table with another picture from George.

"It's okay, Petal. Just leave it."

I sat down, shaking. "This is a disaster. I just want to get home to my baby." I paused as Max dabbed at his pants again and looked down at my chest, my neck and cheeks flushing with humiliation, "Oh, *shit.*"

When Max looked up and realized my milk had let down and soaked through my red dress, creating two big, wet circles, I could tell he was *done.*

Tossing a few twenties onto the table, he stood and helped me up, wrapping me in his coat. "Let's go home."

I tucked into his side and strode beside him quickly, wordlessly, until we got outside, where I couldn't help but start laughing madly. "We could have had cereal for dinner in our pajamas!"

"Fucking too right," he growled, handing the valet the

ticket for our car. Protectiveness and frustration rolled off him in waves. "Giant bowl of Froot Loops and—"

"Sir," the valet interrupted, glancing at the number. His face was ashen. "Our deepest apologies, but I need to let you know there's been a slight accident . . ."

CHAPTER THREE

MAX

I could hear Anna crying from the elevator and immediately knew George hadn't been able to get her to take a bottle.

Sara took off, running to the door and fumbling with her keys before I was able to take them from her and let her in. Just inside, George handed her the baby and—correctly reading Sara's expression—insisted, "She's okay, she's okay, she just woke up and wouldn't take the bottle. She had one earlier."

It wouldn't matter to know that she'd eaten not long before. Sara thanked George in a panicked whisper and took the baby into the nursery to feed her.

"Did you have an accident?" George nodded to my pants.

I looked away from where Sara had disappeared down the hall. "A waiter did, just before Sara had one, just before the valet introduced my car to a concrete pillar."

"So dinner was awesome, then?"

"A brilliant night, really." Only when I looked up at him again did I register what he was wearing. "Is that my shirt?"

George ran his hands to his hips. "It's more of a dress

437

on me." He pulled the extra material into his fists. "I almost used one of Sara's scarves as a belt."

"So . . . a touch of vomit then?"

He nodded, releasing the shirt. "Exorcist baby."

"Sorry about that," I mumbled, suddenly hit with a debilitating wave of exhaustion. "I swear there are times she throws up more than I think she's eaten."

"Not a thing, I swear. It was so much better than that time my date threw up on me, because at least Anna cuddles afterward."

"Thanks, mate. Taking care of the baby tonight was bloody generous of you."

George patted my shoulder. "I'll leave you to it. Tell Sara I'll see her next week?"

"Will do."

After I closed the door behind him, I threw my trousers in the washing machine and went down the hall to the nursery, sitting in my usual spot on the soft carpet near the rocking chair. "How's my girl?"

Sara smiled down at Anna. "She's fine."

I licked my lips, studying her face. She'd relaxed almost as soon as she had our baby in her arms. "I meant my wife."

Her enormous brown eyes met mine and narrowed as she laughed. "I'm fine, too."

She looked back down at the baby and sang quietly, stroking Anna's cheek with her thumb. I watched Anna's small hand reach up blindly, finding and squeezing Sara's index finger. Reaching forward, I curled my hand around my wife's ankle and closed my eyes.

I couldn't hear anything but Sara's quiet humming and our daughter's little baby noises. Our world was infinitely better and we had to come to terms with the fact that, at least for the time being, it was so much smaller.

———

A hand on my shoulder startled me awake. The floor of the nursery, I'd fallen asleep on the floor of the nursery . . .

Looking up, I was greeted by the sight of Sara in a tiny lace bra that pushed her tits up and together until they nearly spilled from the cups. My gaze traveled south and snagged on her minuscule matching thong.

"New pajamas?" I asked, pushing up onto an elbow.

"A gift from Chloe."

"For me or you?"

"Both." She curled her finger to me as she backed out of the room, and I stood, trailing after her until she stopped halfway to the bedroom on a slim, soft hallway rug.

"Here?" I asked, stepping close and bending to kiss her neck. She'd put the smallest touch of perfume on— the familiar light scent that seemed half fruit, half floral, and which she knew made me wild. Seeing her like this, in lingerie, her hair grown long and thick, reaching halfway down her back and brushed smooth, reminded me that it had been forever since we'd put in this sort of effort. It used to be either frantic fucking or a luxurious game.

Now we'd only known exhausted or frantic, and I couldn't shake the feeling that I should take her to our room, be slow and gentle with her.

"Yeah, here," she whispered, standing on her toes to scrape her teeth over my jaw. "Remember that time we ate dinner in front of the TV, and I surprised you when the movie I put in was a video of us?" She dragged her teeth along my earlobe. "You got so turned on you fucked me against this wall. Bent at the waist, hands on the plaster and legs spread? Remember?"

I definitely remembered. We'd made love in the hall before—the frantic kind of pre-baby sex when we'd been unable to wait until we could reach the bed. Those times were fast and messy, a flurry of wild thrusts until we both collapsed sweaty and half dressed on the floor. On that particular occasion I'd just watched a video of me spanking her, and was so fucking turned on we re-created it, right here.

But tonight, when Annabel was fast asleep, why were we—

"I like this rug," she explained, sliding down my body to her knees and my brain stuttered when she looked up at me with wicked eyes. "It's soft and thick under my knees." She guided my boxers down past my hips and freed my cock, watching it grow long as her fist curled around the base. She drew a slow circle with her tongue around the tip. "I also like the way you taste," she continued, smiling knowingly up at me. "Is that weird?"

I opened my mouth, searching for sound, and finally grunted out a "No."

She bit her lip, watching her fist work me for a few strokes before sucking at the crown again. I groaned, tensing from the pleasure of her swirling tongue. "I like this sweetness," she whispered and stared up at me. "Relax. Tonight was a disaster, but a *funny* disaster. Give me more."

Sara squeezed me, coaxing liquid from the tip and sucking at it. "What's it like to watch me do that?"

My mouth opened and I tried to speak but only a garbled sound came out. Her tongue rubbed across the spot just beneath the head of my cock and my hand tightened on the back of her neck, breath tight and high in my throat.

Popping off with a wet kiss she asked, "When was the last time you came in my mouth?"

I knew the answer without having to think too long. It was two weeks after the baby was born and we couldn't have sex yet. We were delirious with sleep deprivation and on some sort of high over the perfection of our lives anyway. I came on her lips not because she played with me for so long, but because we hadn't touched intimately in several weeks and I'd felt spring-loaded.

"A while ago," I admitted.

She nodded, lips pouting before she smiled and bent to kiss a wet, sucking line up my cock.

I wanted her hands around me, gripping and pulling, frenzied in that way that we seemed to never have energy for anymore. Wanted that slick slide of tongue over my skin and the vibrating sounds of pleasure, the urgency. She bent, licking another wet line from the head to my balls, smiling with her eyes up at me as she pointed her tongue and ran it around and around and around in a wet circle at the very tip of my cock.

Fuck.

My fingers found their way into her hair, massaging, guiding her down and I was speaking nonsense; encouraging her and begging her and praising her fucking perfect, sweet little mouth.

"Love that mouth. Fucking *love* it." I ran a finger down from her temple to her lips, feeling her slide back and forth over me. "I bet you could take me all the way down, couldn't you?" I said, giving in to what I wanted so *so* much.

She took me farther and farther until her eyes watered and she pulled back, sucking in air and staring up at me. I was harder than I'd been in ages, practically shaking with the need for her.

I needed Sara's deep brown eyes and quiet, scratchy voice and hands that were both soft and strong. I wanted only the arch of Sara's spine and the taste of the wet between her legs and the clench of her when she came around me with a shocked cry. I'd been with her a hundred times and every one of those times she'd been a different woman—a new discovery—revealing something new of herself.

With my cock between her lips, she reached back and

unfastened her bra, letting it slide down her arms and land silently on the floor.

Her eyes twinkled as she looked up at me and when she reached forward and played with her nipple, I was fucking done.

Perfect suction, her hot little ass in perfect view . . . *holy fuck.* I closed my eyes and gave in to the clawing ache that built in my thighs and stretched upward, tightening . . .

A tiny thump sounded in the other room: Anna rolling into the side of the crib. She coughed a few times.

I started to step away but Sara planted her hands on my hips with quiet urgency. "She's fine. You're so close, baby, *stay.*"

And then the baby started to cry.

Sara slid her mouth down again, sucking hard and fast, begging with her eyes for me to relax, to come, to keep this moment alive somehow, but how the bloody hell was I supposed to fuck her mouth with our infant daughter crying in the other room?

The hungry cry, Sara once told me. *"Do you hear it?"* she'd asked. *"How different it sounds?"*

I knew without having to even ask that her breasts were growing heavy and uncomfortable.

This time, when I stepped back, she let me.

I ran the pad of my thumb from her temple down across her cheek to rest on her full, wet bottom lip. "Petal. Go on."

With an apologetic grimace she took my hand and stood. She looked so fucking beautiful in front of me: topless, wearing her tiny lace pants, legs toned and smooth. She stretched and kissed me once, soft and slow, trapping my cock between us.

"We'll finish this later?"

"Sure," I murmured, kissing her forehead.

Her ass, when she turned and stepped into the nursery, was sublime. And then she bent, picked up our baby, and walked to the rocking chair.

Instead of sitting at her feet like usual, I went down the hall into the bedroom to let my body come down.

Twenty minutes later I felt Sara crawl into bed behind me. Her hand was warm when it slid around my chest. Her mouth was soft and wet on the bare skin of my shoulder.

"You awake?" she whispered, letting her hand run down my stomach to where I was naked under the covers. My body began to respond when she gripped me, but I was so fucking close to sleep, so exhausted. I took her hand in mine and pulled it up to my chest, wordlessly telling her we'd find another time.

———

"Good morning, sunshine." Will was sitting in my chair, his feet perched on my desk.

I glanced at him and then shut my office door behind me. "Comfortable?"

"My office is better," he said in response. "How was the epic shagfest?"

"Mildly disappointing."

His playful expression dimmed at my probably-too-honest answer and he sat up, planting his elbows on his knees. "What happened?"

I dropped my laptop bag near my office closet and sat across from him. "George was good, it was just a lot of updates, a lot of mishaps at the restaurant, and then the sex that never quite happened after."

"What kind of mishaps?"

"Alfredo on the trousers, water dumped on the mix, Sara's breasts leaking through her dress, the valet scraped my car. You know, the usual date night."

Will held up a hand. "Her breasts and the dress and the *what* now?"

I sighed. "William. Sometimes you disappoint me with your predictability."

But he was already shaking his head. "I'm honestly curious. They . . . *leak*?"

I felt my brows pull together. "Well . . . yeah. 'Course they do. You do realize where milk comes from, right? What they're actually for? That they weren't created simply for you to enjoy."

"Do *not* blaspheme, Max," he said, holding out a single finger in warning. He looked a little dazed. "And they leak like, *constantly*?"

"Not constantly, you bleeding idiot. Just when she hasn't fed Anna in a few hours or if she hears her cry . . ." I winced, meeting his eyes. "Or another baby cry, apparently. I didn't really anticipate that one, to be honest."

I didn't know what to say. It wasn't that I felt like I was betraying Sara's privacy in talking about this; it was more that I felt I had access to a secret room in the man tavern and I really shouldn't hand over the password to Will until it was his time. Let him suffer a bit.

I gave him my most condescending smile. "Lots of things happen with the female body that even you haven't seen."

He rolled his eyes. "Don't patronize me."

"Why?" I clucked my tongue sympathetically. "It brings me such joy."

Will tilted his head, and seemed to consider whether or not to tell me something. His blue eyes narrowed and a little smile took over one half of his mouth.

I waited it out until I knew he couldn't stand it anymore. The staring contest continued for at least ten seconds longer.

"Fine," he said on a bursting exhale. "I've been with a pregnant woman before."

I regarded him with mild disgust. "Okay, given that I know you've never impregnated anyone yourself, I'm just going to say it: that's slightly fucking weird."

"Yeah . . . I did a lot of shit then that I wouldn't do now. But I've never been with a woman who . . ." He glanced down to his chest and looked back up at me, brows raised.

"Right," I said, rubbing the back of my neck. Will was such a notorious breast man, it occurred to me that it was strange that he hadn't seemed to think about this perk of motherhood before now.

"What does it taste like?" he said, like a crack in the air.

I groaned, rubbing my eyes. "William."

"*Maximillian*. Don't even try to pretend like you haven't tasted it."

I remembered the conversation Sara and I had about it the first week we were home. We were in the newborn haze, with dishes piled in the sink and in the same clothes we'd worn the day before. Sara was in pain, and I did what I could to help relieve it: with my hands, my mouth. She'd watched, eyes wide and grateful, her nails gently scratching my scalp and asked me how it tasted.

I blinked back over to Will. "It's . . . sweet," I admitted.

He whimpered, closing his eyes. "I feel like I need to meet Hanna at the apartment for a lunchtime—"

"Christ, you're pathetic."

He opened his eyes and studied me, eyes narrowing. "You dig it."

"Her tits are glorious. Of *course* I dig them."

"Not just that. *It*." He leaned forward, forcing me to hold his gaze. "You do! Holy shit! You dig that they leak and think it's weird. Are you feeling shame, Gentle Giant?"

I pulled back, shaking my head at him. "Absolutely not."

"And by 'absolutely not' you mean, 'I am absolutely horrified that I dig the—' "

"I'm close to kicking you out of my office."

He laughed, rocking the chair back on two legs. "Which means I'm close to unearthing the truth."

"The *truth,* you sodding wanker, is it's just a weird balance right now." I hesitated for a moment, trying to organize my thoughts. "Yes, of course there are things about it that are surprisingly hot. But before, it was just *us*. Max and Sara, living together, still getting to know each other. It's like you and Hanna now: you can stay out as late as you want, fuck as loud and often as you want, go on a weekend holiday without notice. We were deep in the throes of that, and now there is a little girl in my life who is more important than anything. And . . ." I pulled at the back of my neck. "I didn't expect it. I didn't expect to feel so many things at once. I feel like I'm walking around with my heart outside my body, and I know it's even more true for Sara. I didn't know how hard it would be to see her energy split. So yeah, the fact that I basically want to fuck her all the time but worry that I'll . . ."

He sat quietly, listening. But when I couldn't figure how else to explain the strange tension in me, he guessed: "You feel guilty."

"A bit." I slid my palm across my mouth. "I mean, look. There's only so much I'm needed for right now. Sara feeds her, holds her. Anna wants her mum, you know? I can change her and sing to her and take her running, but she doesn't need *me* yet." I grimaced, hating how it sounded to admit: "But I still need a lot. It feels selfish to want the 'epic shagfest'—as you so delicately put it—to be just as wild as it ever was. It isn't just about me anymore."

"Funny that you haven't mentioned what *Sara* wants it to be like."

I groaned. "She wants me to be a bit rougher again, I think."

He stilled across the desk. "What the fuck is the problem? You two are on the same page, you asshat." Will leaned in, expression deliberately neutral. "You still doing . . . the club thing? At Johnny's?"

I'd always wondered how much Will really knew. Apparently, he knew quite a lot.

"We haven't in a long time," I admitted quietly, "not since she was pregnant. She wants to go."

"But you don't?" he asked, surprised.

"You fancy the idea of people watching you with Hanna?"

He started to nod, and then paused. "Yes, and no. I like the idea of people watching me unravel her, but I don't really want men fantasizing about her like that."

"See, and I don't mind that aspect. But take your feelings, and now imagine when Hanna's had your baby," I said. "When she's a nursing mum, and tired all the time and tiny the way Sara is. Yes, I fucking love her body right now but it all feels private and like if the world pushed her too hard I would break it in half with my bare hands. That it might break *her*. It didn't occur to me to feel like this when she was pregnant because there was nothing vulnerable about her, even when she was ready to pop. She carried herself like she knew she looked amazing. Now, if someone didn't appreciate how sexy she is, I would put my boot up their arse and kick out their teeth."

Will regarded me blandly and pretended to yawn.

"So you think this is me being over-fucking-protective."

"Like a *dick*," he said. "Like you said, this is your kink. It may not be mine, but if Sara likes it, why do you think it has to be different just because you have a baby at home?"

I leaned back in my chair, shook my head at him. "This is a pretty intense heart-to-heart we're having. Breast milk, kink, marriage, and sex with children in the mix. Can you handle it? When did you become a man, William?"

"Ha. This is nothing compared to some of the shit Hanna wants to talk about," he said and then laughed. "I mean, look. Anna is four months old. You know when you go to a matinee and come out and it's still light out and you're blinded and disoriented for about five seconds until your photoreceptors—"

"*Will.* Fucking focus."

"What I'm saying is, you're still stuck in those first five seconds. You've walked out of the building and have no idea what it looks like outside yet."

"Right. Good metaphor."

"You want to see some of your life you recognize. You want barely-inside-the-door sex. You want breaking-furniture sex. You want club sex. *And* you want to do it with those amazing tits."

I gnawed my lip and then admitted, "Right."

"Let us watch the kiddo. We're her godparents, right?" He held up a hand, keeping me from answering. "I mean, I know you haven't decided yet, but we'd be way better than Chloe and Bennett because let's be real: they're assholes."

I burst out laughing. "Bennett knows kids, though. He has a niece."

"He's terrified of newborns. Henry says he held Sophia at arm's length until she could walk and then he never let her out of his sight. He's sure he'll break Anna with a stern glance. Which I don't doubt, if I'm being honest. He is scary as hell sometimes. Hanna and I . . . we'll figure it out." Leaning forward, he winked. "We're *scientists*."

Chapter Four

For all the ways that Max, Bennett, and Will were alike, there were even more ways they were different. Bennett's first instinct was *always* to take charge, to work out the quickest way to get the upper hand and never let go. Max was the charmer—still one hell of a businessman, but a bowl of sugar—the guy who knew you caught more flies with honey than vinegar. But Will was the thinker, the one who would puzzle out a situation and figure out exactly what the problem was so he could fix it. Which was why when Max suggested that Will and Hanna watch Anna while we attempted Dinner Disaster number two, I agreed. Will and Hanna were two of the smartest people I knew; if anyone could figure out how to crack the baby code, it was them.

We were both ready to go when they showed up at the apartment the next Friday night.

Will was wearing a T-shirt from some show I'd never heard of, and a wary expression on his face. Hanna—as usual—seemed to be getting a kick out of his nerves.

"You're not scared of a tiny little baby now, are you?" she asked as they stepped inside.

"Of course I'm not," Will said, unwrapping a blue scarf from around his neck. "But between eight and forty percent of babies get colic, Hanna. Eight and *forty* percent. That's almost half on the high end, and if you factor that into the number of babies born every year, then the chances that Annabel has—"

"She isn't colicky, you twat," Max said, pulling him in far enough that he could close the door. "Hanna, I hope he's at least brilliant with your taxes or at the very least one hell of a shag."

"Both, actually," she said, and handed Max her jacket. "And don't worry, I babysat a ton growing up. Probably watched every kid in the neighborhood at some point. I'm really great with babies."

Will stepped up to her side, leaned in to wrap his arms around her and press a small kiss to her nose. "How is that even possible when you were so busy pining for me?" he asked, grinning.

Hanna shook her head and patted Will's face gently. "It's so cute how you think everything's about you," she said, and Max barked out a laugh. Will was our notorious womanizer, and to see that he had finally met the woman who knocked him on his ass was amazing.

"Thank you, again, you guys," I said, pushing Will away so I could hug Hanna. "I'm not even sure optimism is the way to go, so I guess I'll just wish you luck."

"Don't be silly," Will said. "We—and by 'we' of course I mean Hanna—will take care of everything. I'm just here to open jars, kill spiders, and change lightbulbs if needed."

Hanna nodded.

Still, I made sure they knew where everything was, went over a list of emergency numbers, and then thanked them for what had to be the tenth time. "She's just eaten and been changed. I'm sure she'll be good for . . . in fact, this is about the time she'd go down for the night, so she shouldn't wake up to feed until long after we're home. But just in case, we'll be around the corner."

Hanna nodded, and picked up one of Anna's little onesies from a stack on the couch. "Don't worry," she said, straightening the pile again. "Even if she does wake up, I'm sure the biggest problem will be getting this one"—she pointed to Will—"to stop making googly faces at her."

Max put on his coat and helped me with mine. "No boys in the house, kids," he said. "No rated-R movies and we've left pizza money on the counter."

Will rolled his eyes and pushed us out the door. "I told you, it'll be fine," he said, waving to us from the doorway. "I outweigh her thirteen-to-one. Thirteen-to-one! What could possibly go wrong?"

There would be no fancy restaurant or sentimental bottles of wine. Instead, we stopped at a little diner a few doors down and sat at the first open table we found.

There was a sense of urgency in the air, a sense that a clock was ticking somewhere and there was zero way we'd make it through this night, maybe not even this dinner, without Will or Hanna calling with some sort of real or imagined emergency.

"You think they're going to be okay?" I asked Max, folding and refolding the paper napkin in front of me.

His eyes met mine from behind a laminated menu and he shrugged. "Of course they will. Annabel's disposition is matched only by her mother's. I can't imagine her giving anyone a problem."

I laughed. "It's possible you might be wrong on both counts, Mr. Stella."

The waiter stopped at our table and we each ordered, although I wasn't really sure why. We were at a restaurant as a formality, as a normal date-type thing before I ripped off his pants.

Which I wanted to do right now.

Our food arrived, and it took only fifteen minutes more before Max's phone buzzed on the table and he picked it up, smiling before turning the screen toward me.

"Look at him," he said. It was a photo of Will holding Anna, his expression so proud you'd think he'd just split the atom, not changed a diaper. He was giving the camera a thumbs-up.

A very white thumbs-up, to be more accurate.

He did it! Hanna had typed.

"Is that . . ." I started to ask, squinting as I leaned in, trying to get a better look. "Is that baby powder?"

"I believe it is," Max said, looking for himself. Will looked like a powdered donut had exploded all over him. It was in his hair and eyebrows, smeared across his cheeks and covering both hands, the one supporting the baby and the one he held in front of the camera.

"He's going to have a good time cleaning that up," I said, shaking my head before finishing off my burger.

"It's good for him," Max said, replying to Hanna before setting his phone down.

"You think Will and Hanna are ready for babies?"

"I think Will would be ready for just about anything Hanna wanted. Christ, she could suggest he join a knitting group and he'd ask her what color yarn was best suited for his skin tone. Bloody brilliant watching that one so whipped. Something tells me tonight is just what they needed."

"So it's possible we might actually get a few more hours?"

Max wiped his mouth and tossed his napkin to his plate. "Don't want to jinx us, but yeah."

It had been ten minutes since Will's last text—far longer than with George—and I got an idea. Everything was fine at home and I was *not* about to waste a golden opportunity like this one.

"What exactly is it you're doing over there, Petal?" Max said, motioning to my phone.

"Oh, just looking for something."

"Something?"

"Mm-hmm."

"Care to elaborate?"

Instead I flipped my phone so he could see the screen, and knew the exact moment he understood. "Things are going so well at home, and we'd be idiots to waste it so . . . I'm booking us a room where you can be as loud as you want and not have to keep one ear focused on a baby monitor. If you're interested, that is," I added, giving him a cheeky grin.

"Interested? I will pay everyone's bill in this bloody diner if it gets us out of here more quickly," he said, and made a hand signal at the waiter for our check. "Have I mentioned that I love you?"

"Once or twice," I said, smiling widely as the waiter set the bill on our table. I continued scrolling through the listings, and stopped when I found what I was looking for.

"So we're people who check in to hotels by the hour now?" Max joked, standing to take our bill to the register. He scratched his jaw. "I am surprisingly comfortable with this."

It was impossible not to feel like we were up to something as we checked in to a swank little hotel down the block. We had no luggage, had made the reservation less than fifteen minutes ago, and I'm sure the way I kept looking at Max—like I might throw him down on the counter at any minute—might have suggested we were up to something a bit less wholesome than a nap.

Not to mention that the New York State driver's license Max showed as proof of ID had a mailing address located less than ten minutes away. Whatever. I was going to fuck my husband; they could think whatever they want.

"If possible we'd like a room in the most empty part of the hotel," Max said. "We plan on being loud."

The clerk looked down at Max's ID and blinked back up at him again, bored, before rolling his eyes and moving to swipe our card.

Inside the elevator, Max pressed me against the far wall, pushing his hand into my hair. "Tell me what you want, sweet Sara," he said, running his nose along my jaw. "This is your night, and I want to do every filthy thing in that devious little mind of yours."

"I want you," I said. "Over me, behind me."

He hummed against my skin, and I felt every bit of anxiety melt away. He wasn't overthinking. He wasn't treating me like something he had to handle with kid gloves.

"And?" he said.

I tilted my head, looked up to see our reflections in

the mirrored ceiling of the elevator. The sight of our bodies together—even clothed—sent a shiver down my spine.

"I want your face between my legs," I told him. "I want you wild."

He exhaled, and made the tiniest, neediest sound. "You know I love how you taste. Would I lick you, Petal?" *Jesus.* "Yes."

"Would I be greedy and suck, get my face covered in you? Or do you want me to take my time?"

"All of it. Rough at first and then again, slower. Savoring," I said, though who knew how much time we would actually get. I watched as Max pushed open the collar of my shirt to reveal the top swell of my breasts. I could easily imagine what we would look like from that angle: me naked on my back, legs spread shamelessly open with Max between them. I would see the flex of muscle as he devoured me, my fingers in his beautiful hair as I pulled and held him where I wanted. The flex of my toes as my orgasm moved up my body and out. As I screamed.

The elevator stopped and Max reached for my hand, practically tugging me down the hall and toward our room. "All of it," he said, slotting the key into the door. "I'll give you fucking all of it." The light glowed green as the lock clicked, and he pushed it open. Inside, it was my turn to push Max against the wall. I stood on my toes to reach his mouth, pressing my lips to his and not wasting any time as I opened his belt and began pulling his shirt from the waist of his pants. "I want to take pictures of you," I said, and he pulled away just long enough to meet my eyes.

"Of me?"

I nodded and leaned in to suck on his bottom lip. "Of what you look like while you lick my . . . pussy."

Max groaned and let his head fall back against the door. "You have no idea what it does to hear you talk like that." I wondered if maybe this would help. If what Chloe had said was true, maybe it would be easier for him to let go if I used *him* first.

I trailed a hand over his navel and down to where he was hard and straining against the material of his pants. I gripped the shape of him, rubbing my thumb where I felt the head of his cock. "Oh, I think I have an idea of what it does to you."

Max began walking us backward, stopping just at the side of the bed. He pulled his phone from his pocket and pressed it into my hand. "Let's pray that this stays quiet, and that it's because Will has found his maternal instinct, and not because our child has suddenly learned that everyone will do precisely what she wants, and has enslaved them both."

I laughed, and set it on the bedside table.

"So what will you do with those pictures, sweet Petal?" he said, opening the buttons on my shirt one by one, and letting it slip from my shoulders.

"Look at them. Remember."

"When? At work?" he asked, and unfastened my bra,

pulling the straps down my arms, and absently tossing it into a chair against the wall. "Maybe you'll be in a meeting, everyone talking around you while you look down at your phone. They'll think you're looking at your calendar, maybe reading through an email. They'd never guess you're looking at photos of me with my face between your legs. Of your clit pressed against my tongue."

"Oh God," I said, his words mirroring *exactly* what I imagined doing. Max's eyes moved over my face, down my neck and lower. My breasts tingled, my nipples hardening with the weight of his gaze on me. My skin felt too hot, the rest of my clothes constricting.

"Would that get you wet, Petal?"

I nodded, stripping Max of his shirt first, and then his pants, finding the head of his cock visible just above the waistband of his boxers. He was so hard, the tip already wet in the setting sunlight. I licked my lips, almost able to feel the weight of him in my mouth, hard and smooth against my tongue.

"Take the rest off," Max instructed, before he reached for the bedding, pulling it down the mattress to reveal crisp, white sheets. The pile of carefully stacked pillows fell to the side and he reached for one, setting it in the middle of the bed.

I slipped out of my skirt and panties just in time for him to turn back to me and nod his approval. "Right here," he said then, motioning to the pillow. "Want that pretty little cunt up where I can get to it."

Even now, after the club and marriage and a baby and all we'd done together, I felt my cheeks heat as I did what he asked and climbed on the bed, careful to keep the pillow directly under my hips. It propped me up and I felt open and exposed, my thighs spread and the air cool against my skin. I knew that if I touched myself I'd be slick and swollen, my clit sensitive to even the smallest touch.

I kept my eyes trained on him as he stepped out of his boxers and climbed up on the bed, on his slow advance toward me. I reached out for him, wanting to feel him inside me and—

His phone vibrated on the table. *Fuck.*

I reached for it blindly, unable to look away from him and his perfect cock, the way it jutted out between us. I knocked over the alarm clock and what I assumed to be the room service menu, before I finally found what I was looking for, and held it out to him.

"Sara," Max said, and I had to tear my attention away from his body.

"Yeah?"

"The phone? You read it, yeah?" he said, and placed a hand on my knee, letting his palm smooth down my skin until it rested between my legs. "I'm a bit busy here, and unless the apartment is on fire or there's something wrong with our baby, I don't want to see a text from *anyone* right now. Just reply."

"Reply while you . . . ?" I trailed off, and he nodded.

My throat felt dry and I had to focus on what I was doing, rather than the way Max ground the heel of his hand against my clit.

"It's Will," I said, blinking down to the message. It was a close-up of Anna's face, her nose scrunched up, and her lower lip turned down into a pout. The edge of a yellow polka-dot blanket curled up near her cheek, so I assumed she was still in her crib, asleep.

What is this face? the text said.

Has she been crying? I asked, momentarily distracted from Max's fingers slipping over me.

No. Just noises. Like a puppy or something? She's ok, was just curious.

Sometimes she fusses a little while she sleeps, I typed, and had to stop and regroup when I felt Max's fingers replaced by puffs of warm breath. She usually settles herself back down! I think you're good!

That might have been a bit more enthusiastic than the situation warranted.

I waited, but when it didn't look like Will was going to respond again, I dropped the phone to the bed and groaned, throwing my head back. "Oh my God," I said, tucking my hands into Max's hair.

"Yeah?" he murmured, and licked along me in long, slow strokes.

"Fuck yes."

"Taste so fucking good, Petal," he said, circling his

463

tongue around my clit and murmuring the words right against me.

I opened my legs wider and held him there, rocking my hips up to meet his mouth until I was practically fucking his face. "More, Max," I said, looking down at him. "And fingers?"

Max did as I asked, and I felt as he slipped first one finger inside of me, and then a second. "The camera, Petal," he said, and I remembered the phone sitting on the mattress next to me. Max pressed his mouth to me again, lips wrapped around my clit as he sucked and sucked, even humming. My hands shook as I aimed the camera at him, touching the screen with trembling fingers as I took photo after photo.

Max made a little noise each time the camera clicked, and the thought that this was what was getting him off— that I would look at these later and think of him and this and his sounds—made it hard not to flip him over and fuck him right then.

With two fingers pumping in and out of me, he turned his head, sucking and pressing kisses into the pale skin of my thigh, and me nearly screaming as the single day's growth of beard brushed against my clit. It was so much. He looked up at me, eyes meeting mine as his tongue peeked out, and I moved to focus the camera again, to capture that moment, when another text flashed across the screen.

How do you heat the milk? it read. Hanna says

we do it under water but I told her we can do it in the microwave provided we use a digital thermometer and warm it to body temperature or 98.7 degrees. WHO'S RIGHT SARA

It took me three attempts to finally type out a simple LISTEN TO HANNA before I threw the phone down and had to bite my forearm to keep from screaming.

Max had pulled away a bit, concerned that something might be wrong, but I waved him off.

"It's fine it's fine," I said, embarrassingly breathless. "Don'tstopohgodplease. Keep," I started, but had to lick my lips, and suck in another desperate lungful of air. "Keepgoingplease please please. I'm so close."

Max redoubled his efforts, licking and sucking my clit, and somewhere, through the fog of what was happening, I heard him groan, heard the sound of his hand working over his cock.

"Oh God . . . are you?" I started, attempting to push myself up and look, but the phone went off again.

I groaned in defeat, so close I could cry.

She's not taking it, it said. Are we sure she needs to eat this much? There's no way an actual human could eat this much. When you figure in her size in comparison to how many ounces of fluid she consumes . . .

"What the fuck does he want now?" Max said, and pushed himself up on his hands.

"Anna won't eat for him," I started, and Max let his

cheek fall to my hip. "Max, I'm beginning to think this isn't going to work. I'm never going to have an orgasm and you're going to have to adjust to a life of blue balls."

"Fuck that," he said. "Give me five more minutes, I can do it, I swear."

But it was no use. I wanted him—*God, did I want him*—but now all I could think about was my tiny baby crying at home, hungry.

We both lay there for a moment, trying to calm our breaths and . . . other things, before we got up.

"We'll get the hang of this, Petal," Max said, climbing up my body so he could kiss my forehead. "We've got all the time in the world."

I went to reply to Will, to tell him we were on our way home, but instead stared in horror at my screen. Somehow, while juggling the camera and texts . . . *holy shit, I texted Will a picture of Max's head between my legs.*

"Oh . . . oh, my God," I groaned, handing Max my phone so he could see what I'd done. "I should not be in charge of the camera anymore."

I rolled into the pillow with another groan as Max read Will's reply and burst out laughing: Okay . . . that was unexpected but message received. Take your time. We'll figure out the milk thing.

Chapter Five

I'd seen photos of Niall Stella, so of course I was prepared for the resemblance between my brother-in-law and my husband—same lighter brown hair, same warm brown eyes, *way* too pretty to be fair—but what I wasn't prepared for was the impact of having not one, but two Stella men standing in the doorway of our apartment.

Niall let a black leather laptop bag slip from his shoulder, and straightened to his full height, before smiling widely at his brother.

He was just as tall as Max, but a bit more on the slender side. Years of rugby had left Max with broader shoulders and arms and legs defined by ropes of thick muscle. Niall was definitely built, but leaner, the type of build with wide shoulders and narrow hips. A body designed to wear a suit.

From the way he walked into the apartment, it was clear he was comfortable in his own skin, but he was quieter, missing that boisterous quality that seemed to seep into a room whenever Max entered it. In its place was a gentle confidence and a touch of vulnerability that

467

made me want to push Max out of the way and hug Niall myself.

Niall had been unable to come to the States for our small, last-minute wedding ceremony—he'd been in the middle of a divorce, a new job—but had promised to come as soon as he was able. I knew he and Max, being only ten months apart, were the closest of the siblings, and Max had been more excited for this visit than he'd wanted to let on.

Max loved Will and Bennett—and there wasn't a situation in which I could imagine him not doing whatever it took to help out his boys—but it had nothing on the embrace he gave his younger brother. The two men wrapped their arms around each other in an all-encompassing hug, and maybe it was the hormones talking but it's possible the closed eyes and small smile on each of their faces might have left me a bit teary. Maybe.

Max whispered something in Niall's ear I couldn't make out, before he clapped him on the back and pulled him inside. It was clear that Max had been even more worried about his brother than he realized.

"It's been too long," Max said, reaching for Niall's bag before closing the door.

"Absolutely," Niall said, and oh. *Two* British men under my roof. I didn't stand a chance.

I stepped out of the hallway and into the living room, and offered Niall a small wave when I caught his eye.

"And you must be the lovely Sara," he said, crossing

the room to place a kiss on my cheek. "So lovely to finally meet you."

Niall was a great hugger, bending at the knees and wrapping his arms completely around me. When he pulled back to meet my eyes, I almost swooned.

"I can see what has him so smitten," Niall said.

"Truer words were never spoken," Max said.

"I may need the two of you to cut down on the cute for a bit," I said. "I'm not sure I can handle it."

"We'll do our best, Petal," Max said with a wink, and led Niall to the living room. "You look bloody fantastic. Divorce suits you."

Max had explained the circumstances behind Niall and Portia's divorce, that they'd married when they were fresh out of high school, and been with only each other up until the previous summer, when they both decided it wasn't working anymore. Max also told me that "not working anymore" was code for *Portia was a beast.*

If Max's comment bothered Niall at all, he didn't show it. Instead, he sank back against the sofa and exhaled in what looked like his first real breath in a very long time.

"You know I would never speak poorly of Portia," Niall said, shaking his head with a smile, "but yes. I feel better than I have in years."

A small sound emanated from the baby monitor on the end table, and I stood, explaining that I'd go get the baby up from her nap.

I could hear the men talking while I changed Anna's

diaper, hear the clink of their beer bottles and laughter, and I smiled down at my daughter.

"Ready to go meet your uncle?" I whispered, and she cooed, smiling up at me and kicking her little sock-covered feet. I gathered her up and we made our way into the living room, and both men stopped. Max looked like the proudest daddy in the world, but Niall looked completely in awe.

"She's breathtaking," Niall said, setting his bottle on the table and standing to meet me. "She's absolutely bloody gorgeous, Sara. Well done."

"She's a beauty, yeah?" Max crossed the room to take her from me, kissing me on the forehead before sitting next to his brother.

"Mum must be over the moon," Niall said, running a finger along the edge of the blanket.

"You've no idea," Max said. "I'll be at her flat not five minutes before she's nicked her from me."

My heart swelled as I watched them together, and I took a few steps back and into the kitchen, leaving them alone while they caught up.

———

Tired from a long day of travel, Niall excused himself for the night around the same time I tucked Annabel in her crib.

With the apartment blissfully silent, I shut off lights and made a final check of the front door before finding

Max in our room, folding tiny pink onesies and socks, and placing them in a basket on the bed. I lay down next to him and watched.

"You're pretty sexy when you're domestic," I told him, running a hand up the back of his thigh.

"If you think this is hot, you should see me change a diaper."

"I have, actually; why do you think I married you? That and your accent. Oh and your giant penis."

"Too right," he said, and bent to kiss me. "And I married you because you're lovely and smart and sexy as hell. Not to mention the fact that you can take on the world."

"Taking on the world," I said, folding a pair of socks. "Guess I'll be going back to that soon enough."

Max set the basket aside and kneeled on the floor in front of me. "Are you not ready, Petal?"

I picked up one of Anna's little T-shirts, one that fit her only weeks ago and was now ready to be packed away. I barely remembered her in that shirt, and she had *just* outgrown it. What in the world would I miss when I was gone all day? And yet . . .

"I am," I said honestly. "I'm just having a hard time shutting out that guilty voice over *wanting* to go back to work."

"Why on earth would you want to silence it? Let yourself feel all the things, Sara. Then take a step back and realize that you can do whatever you bloody want. You can take over the world *and* still be the world's greatest mother and wife. Annabel will grow up seeing you do all the things and know that she can do all things, too, if she chooses."

Max got up and sat next to me on the bed.

"And I've been thinking. I know you want to go back to the club, and I want you to know that I want that, too. I was thinking over something we talked about the other day, how there was a time when it felt like Annabel never slept. But slowly, we got through it?"

I nodded.

"Maybe that will be our new rule. We figure it out as we go."

"You know, I was thinking the same thing. I've been so set on proving that I'm the same—that we are—but we're not, are we? And we don't have to be. I love this new life and I love the new you, just as much as the old one. Maybe even more."

Max leaned in and tilted my chin up to meet him before pressing a slow, lingering kiss to my lips. "I like the sound of that," he said. "So you'll go back to work, and we continue to do this." He kissed each of my cheeks and then motioned between us. "Doing what works best for *us*. I'm actually looking forward to having her with me more at the office, and Mum—not to mention Will—will be thrilled."

I pulled Max to lie next to me, and fit my leg between his thighs. "You know, everyone's asleep."

"You think you could be quiet with what I'd do to you? I'm insulted," he said, smiling against my mouth.

"I don't know. But I'd certainly be willing to try. Maybe you could gag me?"

Max's eyes widened before he started unbuttoning the top of my dress. "I think we can work something out. In fact—"

As if on cue, Annabel picked that exact moment to start wailing.

"Let's give her a minute. She might just fall back to sleep." I told him, tucking my face into his neck. He smelled so good, like the Max I had always known, but a little like Anna, too. He was getting *so* laid.

Two minutes of crying went by, and I had just extricated myself from Max's arms to go pick her up, when the apartment fell silent.

We looked at each other, before both of us turned our attention down the hall. "What is that?" Max asked.

I listened, unable to make out the soft humming I could hear from the living room. We both stood and quickly dressed, before we began tiptoeing down the hall.

We turned the corner and Max stopped, quickly enough that I ran into his back. "What is it?" I whispered.

Max moved over the tiniest bit, and there was Niall: tie off and top of his shirt unbuttoned, shoeless and walking back and forth, talking softly to a bright-eyed Annabel.

"Well I'll be damned," Max said. "Didn't take long

for her to fall in love with him. Not that I'm surprised, mind you."

"That's it, baby girl," he murmured, kissing her softly on one of her puffy cheeks.

Anna continued to look up at him in awe, and Max and I turned to look at each other.

"Niall's a natural," I whispered to Max.

He looked back at his brother, before turning back to me. "Are you thinking what I'm thinking?"

Chapter Six

I stared at my brother the next morning as he took a bite of toast and scanned the business section, oblivious to my inspection. It had been too long since our last visit—longer than we'd ever been apart. Marriages beginning and ending, careers growing, babies born, family obligations, and a myriad of other obstacles had kept me from England and him from the States. Though I was only ten months older than him, seeing him here brought back the older-brother protectiveness his calm stoicism had always triggered in me.

Because he rarely said otherwise, I needed to make sure he really was doing all right.

He looked thinner, but fitter, too. I meant it when I said divorce suited him. Instead of seeming beat down by the taxing drag of the proceedings, it seemed as if a literal weight had been removed from his shoulders. His face was less shadowed, mouth less drawn. He smiled easily again.

Of all my siblings, Niall and I were the most similar physically but dissimilar mentally. We were both tall, had tended toward athletic builds, and had our father's lighter brown hair. But whereas it had taken me years to get my head on

475

straight about school and birds and the bleeding enormous what-to-do-with-my-life decisions, Niall was born thinking like a little engineer: logical, calm, meticulous. I'd worked my way through most of Manhattan's single women; he'd married the first girl he kissed. I had barely found a single job I loved until I met Will and we started the firm together; Niall had excelled in civil engineering so early he'd been the second in command at the London Underground when he was only twenty-eight before being wooed away to a private firm. I spoke freely, shared too readily, loved perhaps too openly. Niall considered every word before he let it out, held his private truths close to his chest, and had never been with a woman who let him love openly at all.

"How's the ex-monster?" I asked.

"Portia's mostly off doing whatever it is she does," he told me, letting out a quiet laugh. "I get the occasional note about needing to fix this or that at the flat."

I felt the familiar protective heat rise in my chest. "She can hire out for that. Lord knows she has enough of her own money, as well as yours."

"She can, indeed," he agreed with the genuine smile of a man finally liberated.

I hated what Portia had done to him. She'd started with a shy, sweet, and devoted teenage Niall and left us with a deeply emotionally reserved version of the same man. I didn't mind his reserve; I didn't even mind his new emotional discipline. I missed the lad with the easy dimpled smile and enormous, curious eyes.

But fuck it. He was here in my flat, finally coming back to life.

"You should have fucked Teena Smith at Robbie's party when I told you to," I said to him.

He barely missed a beat: "*Oi*, this again. I was already with—"

"Oh, fuck Portia. Teena would have bounced on your knob for days."

He laughed, scratching his jaw. "A bit too eager, though, yeah?"

"Eager with a cocksucking mouth and great tits."

"Great tits," he agreed ruefully. "Bloody great tits."

"Who had great tits?" Sara asked, walking into the kitchen to grab her coffee.

"Teena," Niall and I answered in unison.

"The one I should have shagged," Niall explained further.

"And it's unfortunate he didn't," I explained. "Portia would have married that insufferable arse Richard, and Niall would have been a sex god in uni instead of saddled with a wife and mortgage."

He hummed, blowing over the surface of his hot tea as his eyes returned to the paper. "Maybe."

Sara looked at us with a sweetly quizzical grin before leaving again.

"So." I brought my coffee to my lips.

He smiled without looking up. "Hmm?"

"Good to have you visit."

My brother nodded, sipping his tea. "Been too long."

"Everything good across the pond?"

Shrugging, he said, "Same, I suppose? There's a chance I'll be back in a few weeks' time for a summit here."

"Yeah?" I said, a little more eagerly than I'd intended.

He nodded. "I'll be around a bit more, you see. So you might as well just bring up whatever it is you're working up to."

"Oh, you mean the thing about how you're watching the child tonight while I take my woman out for some fun?"

He brought his toast to his mouth and smiled around it, "Yes, that thing."

"We'll be out late," I warned.

"I certainly hope so." He maintained eye contact, eyes wry and knowing as he chewed, swallowed.

"I'm not going to tell you what we're doing, if that's what you think."

He laughed, shaking his head as he poured some more tea. "Well, until you said that, I assumed it was just dinner. Now I think maybe I'd rather not know."

Sara brought Anna out into the kitchen, making her way over to me, but Niall wiped his mouth and his hands with a napkin before he reached for the baby. "Come here, love. Guess who gets to watch you tonight?"

Sara folded the baby in his arms and turned to the fridge, pulling out a bottle of milk. "Are you sure?"

He nodded. "Might kick you out myself."

She smiled at him gratefully. "Well, I'm leaving around six, but there's plenty of bottles in here for the rest of the night," she said, looking at him over her shoulder. "We use this bottle warmer. See?" She put the bottle in, pushed the button, and we all watched as it began to steam, and then beeped when it was done. "Easy."

"We'll manage fine," he said, taking the bottle and expertly shaking it to warm the milk evenly as he looked down at Anna again. "Won't we, princess?"

Watching him like this, I realized how much more experience he had with babies than I did: between our eight siblings there were seventeen nieces and nephews, and Niall was the favorite uncle to them all.

Sara put her hand on his shoulder. "Thanks for doing this."

He waved her off, making one of his stiff, dismissive grunts.

"That's awkward Brit for 'you're welcome,'" I said, laughing as I waited for Anna to push the bottle away and cry for Sara.

Niall gazed down at her as he offered her the milk. "That's a girl. Who's a good baby?" He bent and kissed her forehead. "Ah, but she's a hungry one, isn't she?"

I gaped at him, at her tiny hand clutching his thumb as she drank happily.

Bloody hell.

If my daughter had one superpower it would be the ability to locate her mum from several rooms away. If Sara were anywhere in the house, Anna wouldn't dare take a bottle from me.

I scowled at Niall. "You must smell like a woman."

"Piss off," he said to me, still using his baby-soothing voice. "Why is your daddy such a wanker, hmm? I've got a hundred nieces and nephews and he expects I can't give this tiny miss a bottle?"

Laughing, I stood and cleared our dishes.

"Baby girl knows which uncle's gonna spoil her rotten," Niall whispered just loud enough for me to hear. "Who wants a pony? Is it you? You do? I'll make sure you get a pony."

I groaned, smacking the back of his head as I walked past him to go find Sara.

"You're welcome, wanker," he sang sweetly.

———

I found Sara in the bathroom, putting on the pair of diamond earrings her father sent after Anna was born.

Bending to kiss her neck, I said, "I'll have Scott come for us here at eight—"

"No." She turned to face me, running her hands up my dress shirt and straightening my collar. "Don't."

I blinked, tilting my head as my stomach dropped. Had she changed her mind? "You don't want to go?"

Her smile was a sweet reassurance. "Of course I do. But I want to meet there. Scott can bring me. You come separately."

She wanted to leave for the club separately? "But we've always gone together."

"I don't want to drag anything behind us when we leave. If he picks us both up here, we'll fuss over the details of leaving Anna, we'll talk about her in the car. I think I'm going to take her out and do some back-to-work shopping then head to your mom's. I'll coordinate with Niall. Scott can get me there and I'll see you at Johnny's. We can just be *us* tonight."

"You sure?"

She pulled her lip between her teeth and smiled around it before whispering, "Yeah, I'm sure."

Innocence, anticipation, lust, and something sweeter than pure sugar. It was everything I loved about Sara distilled into a single expression.

"Right then. I'll meet you there at nine."

———

I left for work, expecting to see Sara at lunch, or even get a call from her as I usually did during the day, but knowing I might not. I suspected Sara might want a little distance today to help put her in the right mind-set, and I was right. A text came just as the office was clearing out, to let me know Niall was picking Annabel up at Mum's flat and she would meet me at the club, as planned.

The distance was odd, but also thrilling.

I went home, showered and dressed, and walked through the rooms of my empty flat. Niall had rung to say he'd be back with the baby shortly, and I had to admit that I agreed with Sara, it would be better if I left before they got here. Annabel was in excellent hands, and Max and Sara as parents could be put on hold for a few hours.

There was nothing left to do; it was time to meet my wife.

My phone buzzed on my way out, a text from Johnny: Use the front door.

We always came in through the back hallway and directly into Room Six. Having performed dozens of times at the club, Sara and I were recognizable to nearly everyone who would be there on a Wednesday night. Johnny wanted her to walk in, right in the middle of all of that?

My protective instinct flared.

Did Sara request this? I replied.

Shut up. In a fucking meeting.

This was as good as a yes; if it was for any other reason he would have said so.

Laughing, I replied in eight separate messages:

It's

A

Shame

About

Your

Tiny

Shriveled

Dick

Once I confirmed with our driver Scott that he was picking Sara up at my mother's flat, I called for a cab to get me over to the club, Red Moon. I'd put on something simple, not knowing how Johnny would have the room set up for our return to the club. I wore black trousers and a simple pressed gray check button-down shirt. It had been so long since we came in through the secretive front entrance that I was actually nervous—wanting to make sure I remembered how to get down there: with a key, down several flights to the receptionist. Except standing at the desk waiting my arrival wasn't Lisbeth, but a stunning redhead who circled the desk, hand outstretched.

"I'm Trin," she said, smiling in welcome. "You must be Mr. Stella."

I fucked my wife for everyone to see in this club. It seemed a little odd to be so formal. "Max, please."

"Lovely to meet you." She gestured to the heavy steel door that would lead into the club itself. "Mr. French is very much looking forward to having you and Mrs. Stella back in the rotation."

I smiled, arching a brow. "The pony play and multiple ménage scenarios are growing a little tired?"

She laughed, shaking her head. "I think the regulars like your story," she said. "It's sweet. It's different from everything else we get in here."

And of course it was. What other married couple would let their most intimate moments play out in such stark display for complete strangers? Who else would invite the world into their sex life?

But being back here, even in this unfamiliar anteroom to the main event, felt deliciously surreal. I could smell the mix of wood polish and leather emanating from the other room. I could hear the faint beat of music pounding through the enormous door. It was a sensory trigger for me, being here, knowing how Sara would get off on being watched, and how I would get off on watching her bloom. It never ceased to amaze me that her greatest turn-on was exhibition, given that in our everyday life she was beautiful but unassuming, brilliant but endlessly humble.

"How's the baby?" Trin asked, pulling my attention away from the door and back to her face.

"She's brilliant, yeah," I said, feeling my grin split my face. "Home with my brother."

Her eyebrows rose wickedly. "You have a brother?"

"I do," I said through a laugh. "He's tall, a genius, and has enough repressed sexual energy to power this club. I should give you his number."

Trin tilted her head before finding a card in the top drawer of her desk with her name and phone number. "Give him this." She turned and gestured that I lead us to the door. "Mrs. Stella is inside. I don't want to keep you."

Through the door, the club opened into a large main room, dimly lit with wall sconces and lined with a lavish, intricate wallpaper of subtle stripes and swirls. Velvet curtains hung beside a number of small alcoves surrounding low tables, making the entire room feel both lavish and faintly medieval. A small bar stood in the corner, where I remembered, but the design of the room had been modified so that the stage was directly in the center, rather than jutting into the floor from one far end of the expansive space.

Sara was tucked into an alcove in the middle of one long wall, sipping a cocktail and looking surprisingly comfortable all on her own here. She watched the show—a woman stripping to a slow beat while a man behind her was tied naked to a chair.

It was surreal how quickly my brain switched from the daily reality of diapers and investors, bottles and contracts, to the present reality of a private—and rather illegal—space where only the most well-connected and wealthy clients came to indulge their darkest voyeuristic fantasies. It didn't seem odd that the woman performing was stripped down to a long string of pearls hanging heavily between her small breasts, or that the man had begun quietly begging for pleasure. All around us, people sipped drinks and talked in low voices or simply sat and watched the main show, waiting for the individual rooms to open for the audience.

There were six other rooms in this club, connected to the main room by a long hallway. The setup was simple: each room had a different scene to watch, with tables outside a window looking in. Clients could have drinks while enjoying a perfect view of some of the darkest, sweetest, and filthiest fantasies come to life.

Some of the performers in the club were regulars—expe-

rienced Doms, Broadway performers with exhibitionist lean-
ings earning some good money on the side, or dancers who
were willing to try anything—and some were vague acquain-
tances of Johnny who had begged him for the opportunity
to perform at the prestigious club. Sara and I were the only
friends of his granted a consistent time slot: Wednesday
nights were ours in Room Six for as long as we wanted.

Though we never took money—unlike a few others who
"performed" at the club—Wednesday night in Room Six
grew to be one of the most popular acts in the place, and
quite a profitable show for Johnny. The only reason Sara
and I knew this, however, was that he told us. We never saw
a single face in our audience; other than our first night and
until tonight, we'd only ever come into the club through the
back entrance.

And just on my short walk from the front door to the table, I could feel the rustle of movement, the way people sat
up straight in realization. I could feel the subtle gestures,
the quiet whisper of *They're back.*

Had Sara felt it, too?

Had she liked it? I felt a shiver climb up my spine, felt my
heart begin to thunder at the idea that she was sitting here,
thinking of how many times these people had watched me
fuck her. Thinking of her growing wet at just the *idea* of it all.

Sara looked up when Trin led me over to her, and stood,
making my blood come to a thudding stop in my veins.

She wore a short black dress, simple but with a beading
detail that gave just a hint of sparkle. It would look amazing

under the lights, I realized, then smiled when I noted that it would look even better *off,* lying in a pool on the floor. Her eyes were lined with a soft brown, her lips an edible red. There was nothing particularly special about how she had put herself together tonight, but the heat in her eyes—the devilish fire, the flirtatious tilt of her mouth, the way she looked at my face for only a beat before ogling my body—set my skin into a heated flush.

Bending, I kissed her jaw. "Hello, Petal." I inhaled the sweetness of her skin, dragging my lips to her ear. "You look fucking *beautiful.*"

"Hey, Stranger." She sat, glancing at the space on the bench beside her as if to say that I was meant to be immediately beside her, and not across the table. There were strict rules at the club: two-drink maximum, no touching between clients, everyone is there by choice and any evidence to the contrary results in the fist of God—aka Johnny—coming down.

I knew I wasn't supposed to touch Sara out here on the main floor, but did the rules really apply to us, when it was clear that we were part of the show? More people were watching us at our tiny table than were watching the naked woman deep-throating the man bound to the chair in the middle of the room.

Sitting beside, her, I leaned close, sucking at her neck.

"Max," she warned.

"They're watching," I told her. "You think they want to see me come in here and follow the rules?" I kissed my way to her mouth, parting her lips with mine and sucking deeply on her tongue before whispering, "I haven't seen you all day. I'm going to greet you the way I bloody well feel I should. Fuck Johnny and his rules."

And proving that I was right, no one appeared at the side of our table asking us to leave.

No one signaled a warning to me across the room.

Instead, it felt like the entire room held its breath, watching.

"How long have you been here?" I asked.

She shrugged, tucking her long hair behind her ear. That was another thing that had changed over the past year. Her hair had grown out, curves had bloomed. "About ten minutes before you."

I studied her face—the pink flush to her cheeks, the quick intake of breaths, the way her gaze could barely stray from my mouth. "Did you feel them watching you?"

She nodded.

"Was it weird?"

She shook her head slowly before whispering, "No."

I slid my hand under the table, up her bare thighs to the soft lace of her underwear beneath. I could feel the heat through, warming my fingers. "Did it make you wet?"

She watched my mouth. "Yeah."

"What do you think they remember the most?" I rubbed my fingers over her clit beneath the lace, kissed her cheek, and then moved to her lips, kissing her once at the fullest part of her perfect fucking mouth.

"Maybe the time I tied you up," she said, taking my face in her hands so she could tilt my head and scrape her teeth over my jaw. "Or maybe the first time we . . ." She trailed off, smiling knowingly.

I nodded. The first time we'd had anal sex, we'd had it here. Somehow it felt safer, slower. Her hunger, her surprise, her pleasure had been so raw. I was sure as soon as she said it that if anyone here tonight had seen it, they would never forget the soft curved shape of her mouth when she felt me fully inside her, and when she came harder than I think she ever had before.

The attention in the room ebbed and returned, ricocheting between the main act and us. We were the quieter option; we had *always* been the quiet act. What we offered wasn't hard kink, it was simply *us*—a relationship that deepened, trust that intensified, sexual exploration that matured. What we received in return was a safe place to try it all. Their focus was a paradoxical sort of respect: they watched nearly every move we made but they loved it. They were invested.

We didn't normally drink much before a show, but since this particular occasion seemed to be about breaking all the rules—arriving separately, entering through the front door, and touching each other on the main floor—I waved the waitress over with a subtle lift of my hand. She brought me a vodka gimlet, and Sara ordered a club soda with lime.

I was so excited for what would follow that my hand nearly trembled as I lifted the glass to my mouth, which was all the more reason to do this. I needed to be calm, to settle into the atmosphere before we walked back to our room. We sipped our drinks as we watched the others around us, and wordlessly agreed to save the real show for Room Six.

A tall woman in a flowing pink negligee, nothing but glittering pink pasties visible beneath, stepped to our table, signaling that it was time.

I followed Sara as she stood, and sensed the way the room grew still. As we headed toward the hallway, I could hear the quiet shuffle of chairs pushed back from tables, of footsteps following at a respectable distance.

"You ready for this?" I asked her.

I could hear her smile: "Yeah."

My heart seemed intent on hammering its way up my throat. We passed the scenes in the other rooms to our left.

An orgy of men.

An older woman masturbating a man who had such a young face, he may have turned legal only today.

I watched Sara walk confidently past clientele who looked up as she passed as if they knew her. I felt their eyes on my face.

To our left, a woman behind the glass was tied up and being prepared for anal penetration.

I could see the door to our room just around the slight bend and my body seemed to come to life.

I never knew what to expect as far as room décor went; some nights Johnny kept Room Six simple, with a bed and nothing more. Other nights it looked like my living room, a lavish hotel room, or, once, even a tropical bungalow.

Tonight Mr. French had gone with simple: a gleaming silver rolling cart with a decanter of scotch and some chocolates, a plush rug covering most of the smooth wood floor, and an enormous bed in the middle of the room. Soft plum-colored sheets covered the mattress but it was otherwise bare.

I walked to the rolling cart, looking over my shoulder at Sara. Already the thrill of being here overwhelmed me; I needed to distract myself with an activity other than throwing her onto the mattress and defiling her.

"Do you want a drink?" I asked. I poured myself a small bit of scotch and looked up at her.

"Sure. A little of that." She nodded to the bottle in my hand. Sara rarely drank hard alcohol, but, again: breaking all the rules. She looked so in her element right now, so fucking thrilled. I could tell by the flush of her neck how much the walk down that hall had turned her on.

I poured her a small glass of whisky and she took it from me before dipping a finger in it and painting a wet line across her neck.

An invitation.

"We're starting, then?"

Her laugh was a quiet, husky thing. "We started an hour ago."

I downed my shot, took a step closer, and bent to suck her neck.

"The last time we were here, I was pregnant," she whispered, and I wondered how firm the pressure of attention through the mirrored glass felt against her back.

"You were glorious," I corrected her.

"Tell me what we did that night."

"We were lying down," I said, looking over to the far side of the room where the bed had been that time, right up against the mirrored window that let others see in where we couldn't see out. "I was curled behind you, taking you like that."

"Gently," she interjected, laughing.

I smiled into her shoulder, nipping it. "Despite your efforts, yes, gently. But I watched you come with a scream, in the mirror just as clearly as they did."

Her fingers moved up my chest and touched the bare skin beneath the collar of my shirt. "And then what happened?"

Inhaling deeply, I closed my eyes as the memory caused my heart to pound harder, squeeze faster. "Your water broke in the car on the way home."

"And then what?"

And then what.

And then we turned around, drove to the hospital in a heady fog of terror and glee, and I burst into the ER, carrying Sara in my arms and yelling for help like she'd been shot instead of simply gone into labor.

"And then Annabel Dillon Stella was born thirty hours later."

"We had a *baby*, Max." Her chin was tilted up in her bad-ass, proud smile.

I smiled down at her, feeling my chest expand until it consumed the entire world. "Yeah we fucking did."

She ran her hand down my torso and cupped the swollen tip of my cock in her palm, pushing and slowly stroking it through my trousers. Just like that. There was no transition topic. No need to distance herself from remembering having our baby to touching me like that. No space between Sara the mum and Sara my lover.

"And here we are again," she said, stretching to kiss my throat. "Just being in this room makes me feel wild. I love it so much."

I closed my eyes and groaned. "I love *you*."

"And I love you." I felt her stretch, graze her teeth over my neck. "What do you think it's like for them to watch us tonight?"

I blinked over her shoulder and gazed at the giant mirror. "I think it's a milder version of how it feels for us to *be* here tonight."

"Like they're on this journey with us, kind of."

"Yeah," I agreed. "Did you feel them following down the hall?"

"All of them." She tilted her head back, running her hands into my hair as I bent and kissed lower, to her breastbone through her silk top. "I always knew people were watching. I just didn't know it was nearly *everyone*."

I unzipped her dress and slipped it down her shoulders

inch by inch, feeling like I was seeing her new body through their eyes. Knowing they could see what I did—the fuller breasts, the return of her narrow waist. They would see her tonight without the benefit of transition—from lush and pregnant to her body now: slim, ripe, fucking wicked. She was a siren half naked in her delicate dress, her nails a soft pink, lips full and wet. Soft. Everything about her was so fucking *soft*.

I blinked away but not before glancing quickly to where I knew people were watching, knowing each and every one of them could see my sharp possessiveness and pride.

Look at her, I thought, reaching to unhook her bra. *Look at this beautiful fucking woman.*

Her breasts were firm when I cupped one, and a flush of warmth pulsed through me when I registered she hadn't pumped before she came here.

"*Jesus,* Sare."

"Own it, Stella." She tugged my shirt from my pants with a devious little smirk. "If we're going to play tonight, we're going to *play*." Sara unbuttoned my jeans and slid her hand into my boxers. "In here you don't get to pretend it doesn't make you crazy to suck on them or get your palms all wet. You don't get to pretend my body like this is for her. It's for you, too. You did it. *Own* it."

She pressed the heel of her palm into me and let out a quiet groan. I was so rigid it skirted the line of pleasure and true discomfort. *This* is what she did to me. Scooped out every thought and sensation so she could fill me up with nothing but this searing ache for her.

"They're going to watch you and wonder how it feels," she said, "whether you like it." Her voice dropped to a whisper as she ran the nail of her index finger along my collarbone: "They're going to wonder how often you fuck them."

I could barely look at her like this—rapt and sexy and self-possessed—without feeling a heavy swell of emotion in my chest. I swallowed, hands shaking as I pushed her dress down her hips. Her need was a tangible thing, growing and filling the room, and it started to consume me, too, knowing what it would feel like in the tiny slide of skin between her legs. How slick and wet she would feel on my fingers.

The fabric pooled on the floor—looking every bit as good as I anticipated—and I didn't bother to lower her lacy pants before I slid my hand down in them, fingers searching and finding her soaked.

"*Fuck.*"

"They're wondering why your mouth isn't on my breast," she whispered, pulling my head down until I licked at the tight pink swell, until I felt the sweetness draw across my tongue. I groaned, squeezing her with a hand that had started to feel a little greedy, more than a little wild. She slid her hands down my back. "They're wondering what it's like to play with them like this."

I sucked, groaning and turning her until she faced the mirror and could watch what they watched: me, bent at the waist to reach her breasts, licking them into a wet shine, making them grow fuller and tighter.

"I'll fuck them," I whispered.

"Yeah," she gasped.

"I'll come all over that pretty neck and then lick your pussy so deep they'll see in my face how sweet you taste."

She pushed me until I reached the mattress and sat and then straddled me, bending to seal her mouth to mine. I let out a sound between a groan and a plea for more when her tongue pushed into my mouth, tiny and sweet but commanding, hungry to feel and dominate. I loved my Sara like this, in charge and powerful, fists in my hair so she could pull my head back and get me at whatever angle she wanted. She fucking owned every cell in my body, every breath, every reflex.

I could barely move my hands from her breasts, working and kneading, loving the feel of the tightness in my hands and the wet on my palms. I swiveled her so her back faced the mirror and they could see the slide of my hands around her ribs, over her back, down to her ass.

She ground down over my cock, and then pushed me until I was lying on my back so she could peel my trousers and boxers off in a fierce, determined tug.

"Socks," I commanded quietly, and she giggled as she finished undressing me completely.

My wife gave me a look that communicated some pretty wicked intentions before she licked her way up my legs and pushed them apart to draw her tongue across my balls.

"Filthy fucking girl," I said through a laugh, closing my eyes as she drew her slick tongue up my cock. I pulled her hair into my fist and guided her as she was sloppy and wild all over me. Pushing onto an elbow, I reached to spank her tight ass with my other hand and groaned when she pushed herself deep onto my cock in response, swallowing the tip deep into her throat.

It was *too* good—too much wet and suction and pull along my length if I was going to last at all—and I pulled out and flipped Sara to her back, smiling at her surprised giggle and climbed over her ribs, pushing her tits around my cock. I was still slick from her mouth and I rocked over her, fucking with a sort of savage abandon I hadn't let myself feel in so long. I might bruise her and I could tell neither of us cared. I could come all over her neck, defile her, feel the tip of my cock hit the delicate skin of her throat and it was the kind of rough and possessive behavior, I could see from her expression, that she needed.

She'd missed seeing me like this, I knew. She'd missed seeing me obsessed and hungry to claim, seeing me overcome and wild. Did she really need to be reminded? I told her every day she was beautiful. Every night she felt my desire for her when she curled against me. But of course, here it was different: here we were more bare somehow than we were even in our bedroom, as if constantly raising the stakes of what we were willing to share with the people on the other side of the window.

We gave them a show but it was never false. It was as if

it was a game where we could unveil every dark or wicked thought we had, every needy impulse, every vulnerability that needed to be given attention.

See? she said with her eyes. *You forgot how much I love to see you wild for me. You forgot this is where we play with fetish and boundaries.*

But I remembered.

And it was the *best* game. I could see the moment she felt it, too, because her lips parted in this elated smile and she laughed, sliding her fingers over me and arching her spine to press my cock harder into her skin.

I was close, could feel the ache behind my naval build and spin downward until I was wild—one hand braced beside her head while I fucked earnestly, hips pivoting faster and harder over her until the growling sound I heard was my own voice, warning her, begging her, telling her how hard I was going to come and where.

Her neck.

Her tits.

Her chin and bottom lip when she bent, wide-eyed, watching me spill out onto her.

Still gasping, I slid down her body, smearing my hand down her wet skin and resting my palm on her belly as I settled between her legs, kissing her hip, her thigh, and finally the sweetness just between her legs. Her hands found their way into my hair and pulled, hips lifting from the mattress, circling as I sucked and licked at her, knowing how to make it fast and easy, knowing how to make the hoarse cries tear from her throat when she came, and then slowed, smiling up at her eyes closed in relief, her upper lip glistening with sweat.

I rose to my knees and slid my fingers into her, watching from above as I pumped them, fucking her. I'd seen her naked in every conceivable way—spread wide beneath me like this, or showering alone, begging for more pleasure or less pain, absorbed in my touch and oblivious to my proximity—and there was something so intimate, so *safe,* about sharing this sight of her but being the only one who could ever touch her, who would ever know each of those quieter moments. No one else would ever see her give birth to our child or bend and shave her legs in the bath. No one else would ever see her sleeping, curled around a pillow in our bed or nursing our daughter at four in the morning. So the owners of each set of eyes out there watching her come apart under my touch would never, not in a million years, be able to give her what I gave her. For Sara, nothing turned her on more profoundly than my total, obliterating adoration.

Every second that I loved her—a love story for the ages condensed into not even two years—coalesced into this single fucking touch. My hand slowed, fingers carefully pulling from her as I bent and covered her body with mine, covered her lips with mine. I was nearly hard enough again, and pushed into her, wanting to be inside when she completely shattered.

Her legs wound around my hips, hands slid down my back and she pressed her perfect, soft sounds right into my ear, telling me she was close, to move faster, to suck her, harder, and harder.

She was sticky with my orgasm and her milk, with sweat and scotch. Pleasure built brick by brick until it tripped that feeling that was too intense to simply be called pleasure anymore and was nearly painful with how good it was. I kissed her one more time, a gentle growl and the tiny press of teeth before my restraint crumpled and I turned wild, fucking her in a flurry of thrusts, messy and wet.

I ground against her, the tension in me building until it snapped and jerked above, coming with a sharp groan. Beneath me, Sara let out hoarse, moaning cries that broke with very rhythmic clenching around me.

"Max," she whispered and pulled me close, the movement grating me against her sensitive skin so she shuddered at the friction. I began to pull back but she stopped me with her hands sliding down my sweaty back. "Stay in me."

I caught my breath in the soft space beside her neck, halfheartedly working to keep my weight off her. Her nails scratched lightly up and down my back, legs still curled around my hips.

"All right?"

Beside me, she nodded.

"That was fun," I whispered playfully, and felt her smile when she kissed my cheek.

"Welcome back, Mr. and Mrs. Stella," she said.

———

We rode together in the back of the car, with Scott up front, navigating us through the streets of Manhattan. I felt uncorked, able to release pressure for the first time in months, and it occurred to me only now that I'd been rather terrified: I hadn't known whether Sara and I would ever find our way back directly to each other, or if from now on there would forever be something else—children, careers, the gradual bricklaying of life itself—bridging us.

I would have been all right if it had gone that way, if the secret we had and shared had faded away and we had to learn to find our intimacy in other ways. But knowing how easily we could go back to that, and anytime, relieved something a bit guilty and dark inside.

"What are you thinking?" she asked, as she always did, right when I wanted to admit my thoughts the least.

"Something rather dickish."

"Ooh, then you *have* to tell me."

I turned to her, took her hand in both of mine. "I was thinking that I'm relieved we still have this. That if it had gone away, I would have been okay, but I think I would have been a bit devastated at first, too. I can share you with any number of kids, as long as there is a piece there that remains only mine."

"There's more than one piece that is only yours," she said, looking mildly surprised. "That's what our marriage is. It's the thing between us that we take care of, knowing that someday it will only be us in that enormous apartment again."

"If you want more kids, you know we can't stay in Manhattan forever," I told her.

She put her fingers over my lips, saying, "Shh. Let's enjoy this new baseline for a bit."

We both straightened, seeming to realize in unison that we hadn't heard our phones go off the entire time we'd been at the club.

"Shit," she whispered, digging in her purse. "Did I turn it off?"

"I know I didn't," I said, pulling mine from my pocket. It was just that there were no texts, no missed calls, nothing.

I quickly typed a message to Niall: All good? We're headed home.

His reply came almost immediately. Everything is fine. Anna is asleep. See you soon.

————

Niall was stretched out on the leather couch in the living room, watching John Oliver on the telly. Anna was asleep on his long legs, one fist in her mouth and the other curled around her lion blanket.

"Good night out then?" he asked quietly, watching as we hung our coats up in the closet.

"The best," I told him, taking in the scene in front of me.

"Are you sure you don't want to move in across the hall? There's a flat for sale. This would be very convenient for us."

He laughed. "It's tempting. Your building is rather posh, and this little one is brilliant, yeah?"

"Cheers, mate," I said quietly. "You let us forget to be worried."

He smiled up at me, giving me that look that told me he thought I was a sentimental wanker, and then rested his hand on Anna's belly. "It was really nice. Perhaps you can return the favor someday." His smile straightened for the span of a heartbeat, and in that tiny flicker in his expression, I felt the full weight of his disappointment in his marriage.

"Without a doubt," I reassured him.

Sara went to change out of her dress and I reached for Anna, picking her up with the confidence of a father who expects the child to remain sleeping. Except she didn't; for once she woke when jostled, and her sweet little face screwed up in frustration as she began to cry.

"Ah, sorry, sorry," I whispered, bouncing her gently. "Just a minute, little miss, your mum's almost done."

Anna didn't want to be held and rocked, she wanted Sara, and the sound of her angry cry pushed an ache into my chest. But it didn't bother me the way it would have only days ago. I felt recharged like a battery, full of patience and calm and the quiet that comes from genuine contentment.

Sara came into the hall, taking the baby from me, and I

followed them both into the nursery, watching them settle into the rocking chair.

"You're a lovely sight, my two girls."

"She's probably the cutest baby on the planet," Sara said, grinning up at me. So relaxed, so fucking giddy. It was as if she knew all along we would end up right here, in this night.

I bent down, kissed Annabel's soft cheek as she calmed down and began to nurse. "You got your sensitive side from your daddy," I whispered. "Sorry about that, baby girl. But you also got your mum's steel, so you'll be okay."

Acknowledgments

Some books roll off our fingers easily, while others seem to require some combination of the following: (1) rocking in a corner, (2) cake, (3) chaining self to computer, (4) tears, (5) bloodletting, (6) hard liquor, (7) starfishing on the floor, (8) Ryan Gosling and/or, (9) virgin sacrifice.

We're not saying *Beautiful Secret* required most of these strategies, but we're not *not* saying it, either.

So, thank you first and foremost to our editor, Adam Wilson, and our agent, Holly Root, for helping us whip this one into shape. Without the two of you, there would be no CLo, and not a day passes where we don't feel it. This book happened only with the best kind of team effort.

To Kristin, our Precious, our rock, our rogue. Thank you for listening to it all, keeping our crazy at bay with Honest Trailers, and helping get all of these books in the right hands. You are *so good* to us.

Thank you, Erin, for always, always, always making sure we get it right. Thank you, Tonya, for your honest reads, necessary feedback, and porny gifs on demand. Thank you, Sarah J. Maas, for the enthusiasm that let us exhale and the final pointers that put the polish on the pages. Thank you to our Captain Hookers—Alice Clayton and Nina Bocci—for keeping us insane, ugly selfies, and the text box that gets us through even the most stressful times. Thank you, Drew, for staying on top of Team CLo duties every day; Jen, for the best promo hookups two gals could ever ask for; Helen, for help with our British dialogue and London geography; and Heather Dawn, for being the Goddess of Graphics.

To our Gallery family: Thank you to Jen Bergstrom, Louise Burke, and Carolyn Reidy for being the Greatest Champions Ever for Ladies Writin' Smart Sexy Books. Thank you, Jen Robinson, Liz Psaltis, Diana Velasquez, Trey WASSUP Bidinger, John Vairos, Lisa Litwack, Ed Schlesinger, Abby Zidle, Jean Anne Rose, Lauren McKenna, Stephanie DeLuca, and—even though you've left us—Jules Horbachevsky and Mary McCue: we hope you feel our adoration. Truthfully, it takes a lot of effort to be this creepy, but you're all worth it.

Bloggers, reviewers, readers, and fellow authors: you make the greater writing community into the best sandbox. Thanks for letting us play.

Finally, thank you to our ever-patient husbands, the cutest three kiddos who know not to repeat the titles of our books at school, and this Partnership in Bestiedom that makes writing these books the best job in the world. We used to be only a couple's massage away from marriage, but we can't even say that anymore.

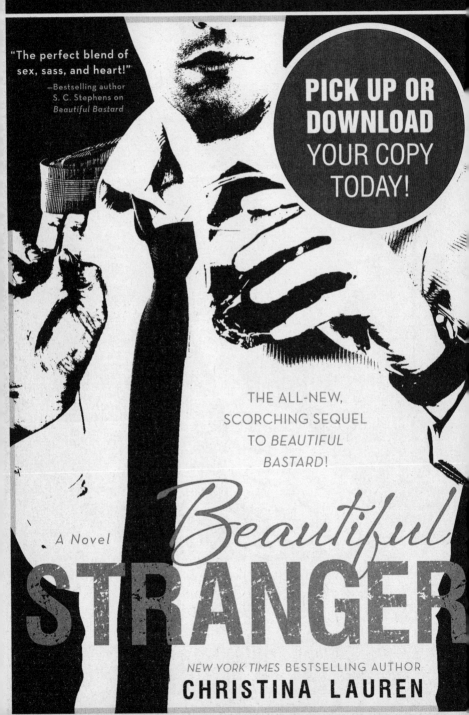